**Virginia Macgregor** was brought up in Germany, France and England by a mother ~~who read her many stories~~. From the moment she was old enough to hold a pen, Virginia set about writing her own, often late into the night. She was named after two great women, Virginia Wade and Virginia Woolf, in the hope she would be a writer and a tennis star. She never did make it to Wimbledon but her dream of becoming a writer has come true. Virginia divides her time between England and New Hampshire, where she lives with her husband and their little girl.

Keep in touch with Virginia on Twitter (@virginiawrites), or via her website www.virginiamacgregor.com.

*Praise for Virginia Macgregor*

'Insightful and compelling'
*Woman & Home*

'One to watch ... a touching look at the
meaning of motherhood'
*Good Housekeeping*

'An emotional and powerful family drama'
*Heat*

*Also by Virginia Macgregor*

What Milo Saw
The Return of Norah Wells

*For Young Adults*
Wishbones

# Before *I was* Yours

VIRGINIA MACGREGOR

sphere

SPHERE

First published in Great Britain in 2017 by Sphere
This paperback edition published in 2017 by Sphere

1 3 5 7 9 10 8 6 4 2

A CIP catalogue record for this book
is available from the British Library.

ISBN 978-0-7515-6522-5

Typeset in Granjon by M Rules
Printed and bound in Great Britain by
Clays Ltd, St Ives plc

Papers used by Sphere are from well-managed forests
and other responsible sources.

Sphere
An imprint of
Little, Brown Book Group
Carmelite House
50 Victoria Embankment
London EC4Y 0DZ

An Hachette UK Company
www.hachette.co.uk

www.littlebrown.co.uk

For Anne Jaquet Holtz, whose love
for her adopted children is an inspiration.

We are such stuff as dreams are made on.

*The Tempest,* WILLIAM SHAKESPEARE

# 25th of December

In the middle of the night, at Jomo Kenyatta International Airport, a seven-year-old boy kisses his mama goodbye.

And then he slips his fingers into the hand of the man who's going to fly him across the sky to his new home.

In London, in a small flat above a laundrette, a flat with low ceilings and thin walls and windows that rattle when the wind blows, a social worker sleeps, her head heavy against her pillow. She's been working hard: so many children and so many families and so few hours in the day to bring them together.

But today is Christmas. Today, she will sleep all day if she wants.

A little further on from the laundrette, in a grey office block, a Detective Inspector sits at his desk and sips from a mug of cold black coffee. His computer screen casts blue shadows over his face. The office is empty now; no one will be in today.

He puts his arms behind his head and looks at the coloured lights blinking through the window. Soon, they'll take them down and the year will begin again.

He sits up and clicks his computer back to life.

In Bridgeford, a town cut in half by a railway line, a man sits in his garage working at a piece of driftwood – the nape of a horse's neck coming to life between his fingers. He doesn't sleep. And so he sits there through the night, sanding pieces of wood to life until the birds sing the world awake again.

Inside the railway cottage, the man's wife stands in their bedroom, putting on her midwife uniform. She checks her phone again: *The baby's coming . . .*

Her first Christmas baby, she thinks.

Before she gets up, packs her bag, makes her flask of tea and heads to work, she sits for a moment on the edge of her bed. She strokes the small hill of her stomach and imagines what it must be like to feel a life stirring inside her.

In a hotel in Nairobi, the young mother picks up an envelope full of money, which the man left for her on the bed, and checks out of her room. Then she goes and stands by the pay phone in the lobby. She wants to hear her little boy's voice, and to know that he made it safely. He isn't going to land for a few hours yet, but she'll wait here all the same.

Up in the sky, the little boy grips his arm rests and looks out of the plane window. He looks past the slits of sideways rain that fall against the glass, at the grey sky and at the grey clouds, and wonders what the world will be like when he lands.

He reaches into his backpack for the photograph of his mama: she's standing on the beach in Lamu, wearing a yellow dress, the sun bouncing off her dark hair and water lapping over her feet.

She leans forward and whispers to him: *One day, Jonah, you'll come home. I promise.*

# Jonah

Seven-year-old Jonah looks at the people holding cardboard signs and bunches of flowers: old people and mamas and papas and children. His heart jumps, like the dolphins that shoot up out of the sea back home.

'I made it, Mama,' he whispers.

He scans the smiling, wide-eyed faces at the arrival gate and wonders whether maybe they've all come out to see him, like back home when everyone runs out onto the beach singing and waving to greet visitors stepping off the boats.

*Welcome to England, Jonah,* the people's faces say.

Or maybe they're Mister Sir's family, come to greet them after their long journey through the sky. Only, once Jonah and Mister Sir are standing on the other side of the metal gates, in amongst the people with their flowers and cardboard signs, no one's looking at them any more.

Jonah's head starts to hurt, like there are elephants stomping around in it. There are too many lights and too many screens. And the stomping in his head clashes with the Christmas music booming out of the walls.

It's the same music that was playing last night, when he sat in the corridor of the hotel waiting for Mama and Mister Sir to finish having their chat.

A whoosh of cold air sweeps past his legs and goosebumps rise on his arms.

Mama told Jonah there would be snow in England. White, sparkling and beautiful. 'Much more beautiful than sand,' she promised.

Jonah looks through the big swishing glass doors at the end of the arrivals room: he can't see any snow, only the lights of cars, buses and vans rushing past under a night sky. Thin rain spits against the glass doors. Maybe there'll be snow at Mister Sir's house, Jonah thinks.

He closes his eyes and remembers what it's like to feel the sun on his face. In Kenya, even when it's raining, everyone knows that the sun's just playing hide and seek – that any moment, it will pop out again and the world will come back to life.

'People in England like to talk about the weather, Jonah,' Mama told him. She said it was because the weather in England changed its mind every two seconds. So Mama taught him to say things like:

'It is positively tropical today.'

'It is a bit chilly out there.'

'It is raining cats and dogs.'

'Hopefully, it will be sunny tomorrow.'

Jonah can't wait to try the words out on Mister Sir's family.

Opening his eyes, he puts his hand in front of his mouth and yawns. He couldn't sleep on the plane: Mister Sir was snoring too loudly. And even when Mister Sir stopped snoring, Jonah couldn't get rid of the blinking from all the screens – the pictures played behind his eyelids and stopped his brain from resting. At home, when Jonah can't sleep, he listens to the sea or looks at the pictures in the book Mister Sir brought him from England. Or he sits outside his and Mama's hut and counts the stars flashing across the dark sky.

Mister Sir stops by a Christmas tree covered in coloured balls, silver string and twinkling lights. Sometimes, they have Christmas trees at Kizingo bar, where Mama likes to have drinks with her Mister Sirs, but Jonah's never seen one as big or

4

bright as this one. Christmas is Mama's favourite time of year: she spends more time praying and singing to Jesus at Christmas than at any other time, and that's saying something, because Mama prays and sings to Jesus *all* the time. 'We have to tell him how much we love him,' Mama says. Judging from all the people who go to Mama's church, Jonah thinks that Jesus must feel pretty loved already.

Mister Sir puts Jonah's bag down and clicks closed the handle of his suitcase. Then he gets out his phone. He jabs his fat fingers at the numbers on the screen and then holds the phone to his ear and says, 'It's me, love. I've just landed.'

Jonah looks up at Mister Sir. He seems taller and further away than he did in Kenya.

'Is it Mama?' Jonah asks him.

Mister Sir called Mama 'my love', so it *must* be her. Jonah's been waiting for ages to talk to Mama on the phone.

'Shush,' Mister Sir flutters his fingers in front of Jonah's face like he's swatting away a fly.

Mama said she'd call when the plane landed so that Jonah could tell her all the details about England. But maybe she got tired and had a nap and lost track of time. Mama's been napping lots lately. Only Mama *did* promise they would talk – and Mama never breaks her promises.

'I've been held up . . .' Mister Sir continues. 'No . . . nothing to worry about . . . I'll see you soon.'

*Soon?* Jonah's tummy does a flip. It would take another plane journey across the whole sky before they could see Mama. And Jonah knows that neither he nor Mister Sir is going to see Mama for a long, long time.

So, who *is* Mister Sir talking to?

Mister Sir ends the call and looks around the room. Jonah

5

does the same. He thinks of the anthills on the beaches back home. Millions of arms and legs and bodies scrabbling around, passing each other crumbs, twigs, leaves, shells: more insect than sand.

Jonah catches a glimpse of himself in a mirror that runs along a tall pillar. The day before they left, Mister Sir took him to a shop in Nairobi. Jonah had hoped that maybe Mister Sir would buy him a suit like all the Mister Sirs from England wear: trousers, a jacket, a waistcoat, a tie, a white shirt, cufflinks, shiny black shoes and maybe even a hat. But the shop did not have any of those things.

When the shopkeeper came back with a pile of clothes, Mister Sir said *perfect*, though Jonah didn't think there was anything perfect about the woolly green jumper that itched where it touched Jonah's skin or the brown corduroy trousers that were too long or the pair of shoes with thick rubber soles that pinched his feet.

The shopkeeper also gave Jonah a red woolly scarf that's longer than his whole body and a red woolly hat. Jonah couldn't ever imagine it being cold enough to wear all those clothes.

When he tried them on, he couldn't breathe. And when he looked at his reflection in the changing room mirror, he thought: *I don't look anything like an English Gentleman.*

Jonah told Mama this when they got back to the hotel but she said to stop being so ungrateful and that he should go to Mister Sir and say, *thank you very much for the lovely clothes.* So he did.

Maybe, now that they are in England, Mister Sir will take him to an English shop and buy him proper English clothes.

After taking him to the clothes shop, Mister Sir bought him a backpack from a market stall. Jonah chose a yellow one because it's Mama's favourite colour. Then Mister Sir took Jonah to the barbershop and a man cut off all of Jonah's curly hair, which had made Mama cry when she saw it. Now his hair is short and tight on his scalp. Here in England, without the sun, his head feels like an ice cube.

He takes out the red woolly hat from his backpack and pulls it down on his head.

*I look tiny in this big anthill,* Jonah thinks.

'May I ask a question, Mister Sir?' Jonah asks.

Mister Sir nods but does not look at Jonah.

*Do not be a nuisance, Jonah, Mister Sir is very busy and has very important work to do,* Mama had warned him. *Mister Sir will look after you, that is all you need to know.*

Not being a nuisance means not asking too many questions. But Mama doesn't understand that sometimes Jonah's brain hurts it's so full of questions, buzzing and crashing into each other.

Maybe if he asks the question politely, with one of his special phrases, Mister Sir will not mind.

'Please excuse my ignorance, but what are we waiting for, Mister Sir?'

Mister Sir stares at Jonah. He has bluey-black smudges under his eyes and there are lots of red veins on his eyeballs. He looks like a different Mister Sir from the one who danced on the beach with Mama.

'You'll see,' Mister Sir snaps.

Mister Sir has been snappy ever since they left Mama at the airport in Nairobi.

Before, when Mama and Mister Sir were together on the beach and then in the hotel in Nairobi, and all the other times Mister Sir has visited Mama, Mister Sir would make jokes and let Jonah wear his Arsenal football shirt. He and Mama would swing Jonah round on the edge of the water until he was dizzy and then they'd throw him into the waves and Jonah would drag them in with him and the three of them would end up wet and sandy and laughing.

Sometimes, Jonah even pretended Mister Sir was his papa.

Mama knew many Mister Sirs but she called this one, 'My special Mister Sir'.

Jonah's legs are tired; he wishes he could sit down, but Mama has taught him to wait for the grown-ups to sit first. Just as Jonah is about to point out to Mister Sir that there are two spare seats next to the shop with all the books and newspapers, Mister Sir's face lights up.

'Here we go.' Mister Sir says, his voice bouncy.

He picks up Jonah's bag, clicks up the handle of his suitcase and walks off really fast.

Jonah struggles to keep up and is grateful when, at last, Mister Sir stops in front of a woman who is holding a baby in a sling. They both have black faces, which makes Jonah think that maybe they come from Kenya too.

Mister Sir holds out his hand to the woman.

'Aunt Igwe – pleased to meet you.'

Jonah heard Mama and Mister Sir talking about Aunt Igwe last night at the hotel. But he doesn't know whose aunt she is.

Aunt Igwe looks at Mister Sir and blinks.

'I think you've got the wrong person,' she says.

'Oh . . . I'm sorry,' Mister Sir mumbles. And then he scans the room again and shakes his head.

The woman, who is not Aunt Igwe, looks at Jonah with the same eyes Mama uses when he's gone off on one of his walks without telling anyone beforehand. Jonah wants to tell the woman that it's OK, that he's with Mister Sir and that he's come to England to learn to read and to be A True English Gentleman.

8

'Come on,' Mister Sir says to Jonah and starts walking away from the woman who is not Aunt Igwe. 'Shit,' says Mister Sir as he walks. 'Shit, shit, shit.'

Jonah has never heard Mister Sir use that word before. Mama would not like it. She says that the words you use on the outside show people who you are on the inside.

At last, Mister Sir drops the bags and slumps into a chair. Jonah's happy to finally sit down. He slips his feet out of his shoes, which have been squeezing his feet ever since Mama told him to put them on before they left for the airport, then pulls off his socks. On Lamu, he always went around in bare feet. He wriggles his toes and, for a moment, everything feels better.

But once they're sitting, they keep sitting. They sit for hours and hours and hours.

More people come out of the gate that Jonah and Mister Sir walked through. Hundreds and hundreds of people. Jonah cranes his neck and looks over to the doors, which lead to the outside world, hoping he might spot the sea, but there's nothing but rain and cars and more rain. Along with snow, Mama promised Jonah that, no matter where he was in England, he would be able to see the sea, because England was an island, like Lamu, and islands have sea all the way around.

Jonah looks at Mister Sir and considers asking him whether he can go outside to check. Maybe if he stands on a bench or climbs a tree he'll be able to see it. Only Mama's words fill his head again: *England is not like Kenya, Jonah. No wandering off and getting lost.*

As the hours go by, more people arrive with cardboard signs, flowers and smiles and then leave together through the glass doors. The jingly Christmas music plays on a loop. An old man in a red suit with a big belly and a beard, a beard that is longer and woollier and whiter than Mister Sir's, walks past them saying, 'Ho! Ho! Ho!'

Jonah tries to sleep, but every time he closes his eyes and slumps in his chair, his stomach growls. He didn't eat any of the food on the plane because his stomach felt all choppy. Then he starts singing a lullaby that Mama used to sing to him when he was a baby: *Kabanyola- Barua ya Mlomo* … Mama's lullabies are the only thing guaranteed to get Jonah to sleep but now she is too far away to sing to him.

Mister Sir sucks his teeth and jiggles his leg up and down. He scans the room and then checks his fat gold watch. Back in Kenya Mister Sir sometimes let Jonah wear his watch. When Jonah has a job and is a Gentleman, a gold watch is the first thing he's going to buy. And he'll buy one for Mama too.

When he stops looking at his watch, Mister Sir takes his phone out of his jacket pocket and jabs at it again. Maybe he's writing a message to Mama to say that they've arrived safely. Only Mama doesn't have a mobile phone, she was going to wait by the pay phone at the hotel.

Jonah wishes he could talk to Mama.

'Pardon me, Mister Sir, but when are we going home?'

Mister Sir does not answer.

'Mister Sir?' Jonah asks again.

But Mister Sir isn't listening.

Jonah tugs on his sleeve. 'Will we be going to your house soon?'

Mama told Jonah about the houses in England. *An Englishman's house is his castle*, she said. And unlike the huts on Lamu, even the biggest winds and the biggest waves could never sweep the castles away. *In England, people's homes stay forever, Jonah.*

Jonah looks forward to living in a forever house.

'I would very much like to see your house …' Jonah goes on.

Mister Sir drops his phone.

*Always be helpful, Jonah . . .*

So Jonah bends over and picks it up. Before he hands it back, he stops to look at the screen: a woman and a little girl. Freckles. Orange hair, like the sunsets back home.

Mister Sir snatches the phone away. He doesn't answer Jonah's question about seeing his house.

Then Mister Sir sits up, his back and neck as straight as an arrow. He looks across the room and his eyes go wide like he's spotted a fire.

Jonah follows his gaze. A man in navy uniform, with a navy hat and shiny black shoes, is walking towards them.

Mister Sir bites the nails on his right hand, then he jumps up quickly.

'You hungry, Jonah?'

Jonah thought Mister Sir would never ask.

'Yes, please.'

'I'll get you a sandwich and some juice.'

All of a sudden Mister Sir is being nice again, like he was when Mama was with them.

Jonah looks around at all the people and worries that maybe Mister Sir will get lost on the way back to him or that he won't be able to find Jonah because Jonah's small.

'Would you allow me to come with you?' Jonah asks, standing up.

Mister Sir puts his hands on Jonah's shoulders and pushes him back into his seat.

'No, you'd better wait here and keep an eye out.'

'An eye out for what?'

Mister Sir looks back over at the man in the uniform. He's speaking into his phone.

'I won't be long.'

Mister Sir clicks up the handle of his suitcase and walks towards the row of shops at the far end of the room.

Jonah's used to being on his own. And he's used to waiting. But back home, waiting meant sitting on a chair outside Mama's hut or diving for shells while Mama had important talks with her Mister Sirs. It doesn't feel the same here.

*Be brave ... A gentleman is always brave ...*

But when Jonah looks at the man in the uniform, he wants to bite his nails too. Whenever men in uniform came snooping around their hut, Mama packed up their things and said it was time to move on to a new place. Mama said that men in uniform were trouble.

'Mister Sir!'

Jonah's words get swallowed up by the music and the squeak of trolleys and people's voices on their phones and the 'Ohs' and 'Ahs' at the arrivals gate.

'Mister Sir!'

Jonah has lost track of where Mister Sir is; he stands on tiptoes, his feet still bare, and cranes his neck.

And just then, he notices Mister Sir's head bobbing up and down. Mister Sir is not going *into* a shop, he's going *past* the shops – past all of the shops.

The man in uniform is so close now that Jonah can see the guns slotted into his belt. Men with guns sometimes came onto the beach and that always meant trouble too.

Even though it's cold, sweat runs down Jonah's back.

For a second, there's a clearing between all the people in front of Jonah, and that's when he sees Mister Sir dragging his wheelie suitcase through the big sliding doors and out into the whooshing world.

*

Jonah's head spins. The screens and lights blink at him, so bright they make his eyes blur. He can't hear himself think from the music and shouting and the grinding of coffee machines and the *ho-ho-ho* of the Father Christmas.

He stands up. His legs feel like they're going to buckle but he forces them to move.

The man in the uniform walks towards him. He's so big that Jonah can't think of a way to get round him.

But big means slow.

Jonah darts forward and veers to the left.

'Watch out, young man.' The man with the white beard and the red suit holds out his palms.

'Sorry,' Jonah says.

Jonah notices that the man in the blue uniform has turned on his heels.

Jonah takes off again, zigzagging between the crowds of people in the terminal.

When he gets to the doors, Jonah steps out.

The cold concrete shoots up through his bare feet.

'Mister Sir!' Jonah cries out at the grey sky.

Raindrops fall on his cheeks.

People with their trolleys rush past him.

A bus crashes through a puddle.

People call after taxis.

'Mister Sir!' Jonah scans up and down the road.

He must be here somewhere.

Maybe he went out for a cigarette.

Maybe he went out to find them a car to get home.

Maybe he went back into the terminal while Jonah wasn't looking and can't find him.

'Mister Sir!' Jonah calls again.

And then, out of the corner of his eye, Jonah sees the blue uniform again.

He bends his legs, ready to dart forward again, but before he has the chance to move, a heavy hand lands on his shoulder.

# FIVE MONTHS LATER

## *May*

# Rosie

'Maybe this wasn't such a good idea.' Rosie slips her hand into Sam's. 'I think we should go home.'

Sam gives her hand a squeeze. 'We've just got here, my love. And remember what Cathy said, this is our golden ticket.'

Cathy is their social worker. She's become such a part of their lives that sometimes it feels like there are three people in their marriage.

'Don't say that, Sam.'

Rosie hates this way of talking about the adoption process, like it's filling out a scratchcard. But Sam's right. Over sixty couples applied to come today, sixty whittled down to thirty that were deemed good matches for the children. And after that, it *was* a lottery – literally: Cathy explained how their names had been pulled out of a hat.

'I'm just saying we're lucky to be here,' Sam says.

Rosie scans the room. She spots a girl with the name *Lucy* printed on a sticker stuck to her back. Cathy had explained that they put stickers on the children's backs because they were more likely to stay on. *Children like to pick at things*, she said.

There's no number next to Lucy's name – the children who have numbers on their stickers are part of sibling groups. Rosie's heart sinks. She likes the idea of adopting more than one child. If she'd been able to have babies naturally, she'd have a people-carrier full of them by now. Before the miscarriages and the failed IVF, she'd imagined herself as Maria from *The Sound of Music*: dancing through the streets followed by a tribe of singing, dancing children. Even though Sam and Rosie's tiny railway cottage can barely hold the two of them, and even though they can't afford to have a big family, given half a chance, Rosie would take home every child here today.

Sam adjusts Rosie's lion headband and smiles. 'Your ears are crooked.'

Rosie keeps her eyes focused on Lucy.

'Maybe we should have come as monkeys,' she says. 'Monkeys are fun.' She spots the two gay guys they met as they walked in: they're dressed as monkeys. 'Children like monkeys . . . '

It turned out that adoption parties always have a theme. *Toy Story*. Disney. Under The Sea. Or Jungle, like this one.

For the last month, Rosie and Sam have watched every animal-themed film they could get their hands on. Rosie took notes in her special adoption notebook. Because they have to be ready for all eventualities. Which includes talking to children about fictional animals whilst trying to remember whether Baloo was the bear and Bagheera the panther, or the other way round, and the difference between Marlin, Dory and Nemo or whether Scrat is the sloth and Sid the squirrel, or Sid the sloth and Scrat the squirrel.

And then Rosie got worried that the films they'd watched were out of date.

And then she'd fretted about which costume to go for. What would the children like best? Or rather, which ones would give the best impression to the children's social workers and foster parents who, Cathy warned them, *have a lot of power*?

If there's anything Rosie's learnt about the adoption process, it's that everything is a test.

*You can't go wrong with lions, Rosie*, Sam's mum, Flick, had said when they asked. *Think of* The Lion King. *It's about a cub working out his place in the world – isn't that what adoption is about?*

Flick always says the right thing. And she understands kids. And so, although Rosie had worried that *The Lion King* was even more passé than the other films they'd watched, she decided to go with it: a mane for Sam; soft ears for Rosie; and lion onesies, rented from the fancy dress shop in Bridgeford.

'You look beautiful,' Sam says. 'Elegant and warm and strong.' He kisses her cheek. 'The perfect mother.'

Sometimes, it makes Rosie nervous, how much hope Sam invests in her. What if there's a reason she can't have children? What if it's not just about biology, about her ovaries failing to release eggs as they should? What if someone, somewhere, has weighed her up and decided that she isn't cut out to be a mother? What if they know that she'll muck it up?

Maybe the world is divided up between people who should and shouldn't be allowed to have children and Rosie just hasn't woken up to the fact that she's on the *shouldn't* pile.

She blinks away the thought and takes a breath. 'Let's go and play with one of the children.'

'That's more like it,' Sam says.

Rosie spots a little girl sitting on the carpet, playing with jungle puppets. Her blonde hair is gathered into wispy pigtails.

Rosie's chest tightens. Cathy has told them over and over to avoid imagining an ideal child. And Rosie has tried to follow her advice, to shake off thoughts about age or gender or ethnicity. But she can't help it. And she can't help remembering how, when they started trying for a baby, Sam would stroke her stomach and say, *A girl ... a little Rosie, that would be just perfect ...*

Perfect. Again.

The little girl's T-shirt is covered in pink and white sequins and she has wings on her back: she's a beautiful, shimmering butterfly.

They should have come as a more delicate animal, Rosie thinks, a hummingbird perhaps – do hummingbirds live in jungles? Something a little girl would like, anyway.

Rosie guesses Lucy must be about five. At the briefing, the organiser of the adoption activity day said that they kept the ages off the children's profiles to help the adopters remain open-minded. 'You might think you want a child under the age of five,' the organiser said, 'but once you meet a real, in the flesh nine-year-old, trust me, you'll be won over.'

Rosie doesn't need a label to tell her how old a child is. Over the last ten years, children have become her specialism: her friend's children, the children who pour out of Bridgeford Primary, the children she sees in the supermarket, at the hairdressers, in coffee shops, on the bus, on the train, at the park near their house. And she's read hundreds of books on child development – she's determined to be prepared for the day when they have a child of their own to care for. So she can tell a child's age within a few seconds of meeting them. Lucy is definitely about five. Which means she's still young enough to become theirs.

There's another adopter looking at Lucy, a single woman. Rosie noticed her at the briefing: leopard-print tights, a leopard-print shirt, gold eye shadow and gold glittery heels.

Rosie glances around the room and then whispers to Sam, 'Is it me or is everyone looking at Lucy?'

'Lucy?'

Rosie nudges her head towards the little girl dressed as a butterfly.

'Oh . . . ' Sam shrugs. 'Maybe . . . I don't know. '

But Rosie knows. If being here is their golden ticket, Lucy is the golden child. And every adopter here has worked that out.

*Don't be deceived by appearances. All the children will have significant issues*, Cathy had told Rosie and Sam in their meeting last week. *That's why they're coming to the adoption party. This is their last chance.*

And it feels like Rosie and Sam's last chance too. They've been trying to adopt for two years and they still haven't found a match.

But Lucy doesn't look like a child who's on her last chance. She looks like a happy little girl with rosy skin, a delicate mouth and eyes that sparkle as she makes her giraffe puppet fly through the air. The kind of child that anyone in their right mind would love to call theirs.

Sam puts his hand on the small of Rosie's back and guides her to where Lucy is sitting. They crouch down beside her.

'I didn't know giraffes could fly,' Sam says to Lucy.

Lucy looks up at them and smiles. Rosie's heart swells. Sam's right: it's good that they're here. This is what they've been waiting for. Their golden ticket.

## Jonah

'They always go for the girls,' says the boy next to Jonah.

They're sitting at the craft table making animals out of Play-Doh. The boy's in a wheelchair.

Jonah follows the boy's gaze over to the little girl dressed as a butterfly; she's sitting on the lap of a woman in a lion costume. A man in a lion costume makes a zebra puppet dance in front of her. The little girl laughs. There are lots of other grown-ups with green badges standing around the little girl too. Jonah's social worker, Trudi, explained that green badges meant the grown-up was an adopter.

*Your Forever Family might be here today*, Trudi said to him earlier as she squeezed his hand.

Trudi still hasn't understood that Jonah doesn't want a Forever Family – or any family at all for that matter.

'They always focus on cute kids first,' the boy in the wheelchair says.

Jonah thinks the boy must be quite a lot older than he is: he seems to know about everything and he keeps using words Jonah hasn't heard before.

'They'll get bored of her soon.' The boy picks up a red feather that's dropped onto his lap and smacks it back onto his chest. He's covered with feathers – reds and yellows and greens, all Sellotaped onto his black T-shirt. 'Stupid costume,' he mumbles.

'At least there are parrots in the jungle,' Jonah says, helping the boy stick one of the feathers back onto his T-shirt.

The boy looks Jonah up and down and laughs. 'Yeah, you'd have to be a pretty magical starfish to survive in the Amazon.'

Jonah nods. 'Julie, my foster carer, thought the theme was Under The Sea – like the last one she went to.'

Jonah doesn't really mind about having the wrong costume: maybe it'll put the adopters off and then Trudi will stop trying to find him a new family.

'This your first activity day, then?' the boy asks.

Jonah nods. It's something else Mama left out when she told him stories about England: that there were parties for people without children and children without parents.

He looks over at Trudi talking to Julie, his foster carer, by the buffet table. Julie's holding two-year-old Mimi in her arms. Mimi's straining forward, trying to reach one of the fairy cakes. Mimi isn't fostered or adopted: she's Julie's real little girl. Apparently, Mimi's papa went away when she was born and then Julie wanted to have more children, but she didn't want to get married again, which is why she looks after other people's children instead.

Jonah's glad that he's met Mimi. She's the only one he really ever talks to. And because she can't say many words yet, it's not like she's going to tell anyone his secrets.

Jonah is quite happy living with Mimi and Julie, which is another reason why he doesn't want to be adopted.

Julie and Trudi keep looking over at Jonah, which means they're talking about him. They're always talking about him, their faces frowning like he's a knot they're trying to undo.

Jonah pulls his red woolly hat further down on his head and then shapes the wodge of blue Play-Doh into a dolphin. He misses watching the dolphins shooting in and out of the water off the coast of Lamu. He misses lots of things. He's started a list. Jonah misses:

Swimming to his special rock, with Mama.

Holding his breath under water until his head goes light and dizzy.

Feeling the warm sand under his feet.

Going for walks on his own without anyone telling him off.

Snuggling up in Mama's bed and making up stories from the pictures in the book Mister Sir gave him.

Feeling warm, and not just on his skin but right down to his bones.

And he misses all these things even more because of how things have turned out in England. If he were living with Mister Sir in his castle, like he was meant to, then he's sure everything would feel better.

He still can't believe what Trudi said: that Mister Sir never wanted him to begin with.

Jonah looks out at all the men and women milling around trying to find a child.

'Have you seen any adopters you like?' Jonah asks the boy.

'It doesn't work like that.' The boy pounds his fist into a bit of orange Play-Doh.

'How does it work then?'

'Did they tell you that you get to choose your family?'

Jonah nods.

'Well, it's not true.' The boy makes a pyramid shape with the bit of Play-Doh and pushes his thumb in the middle to make it look like a volcano. 'The adopters have to be interested first. They pick you.' He pauses. 'And adopters don't really want children like me.'

'Why not?' Jonah asks.

'Seriously?' The boy leans over and taps the wheels on his chair. 'I come with too much equipment.'

Jonah looks at the boy's legs. They end, suddenly, at his knees; there's a knot on each side of his tie-dye trousers.

'They'll even go for a black kid like you over a kid in a wheelchair like me.'

Jonah cheeks burn.

'We're the difficult cases,' the boy adds. 'And adopters don't want difficult cases.'

Jonah had decided that he didn't want to be adopted. But he hadn't thought that maybe no one would want to adopt *him*.

'How do you know all these things?' Jonah asks.

'I've been to loads of these days.' The boy scans the room. 'This is my last one.' He punches the air like he's just won something.

'Why is it your last one?'

'I'm getting too old.'

Jonah's eyes widen: 'Too old?'

24

'Depends how long you've been in the system. For me, they're going to cap it at nine.' He pauses. 'It's my birthday in two weeks.'

Jonah will be eight on the 15th of August, in three months' time. Which means it's ages away until Trudi and Julie give up on finding him new parents.

He wonders how old he'll be before he gets to see Mama again. She said that he couldn't come back until he'd learnt to read and to become a True English Gentleman – and until she'd had a good rest. Jonah worries that might take a long, long time. He'd hoped that maybe he could persuade Mister Sir to sneak him back for a visit when he goes to Kenya on one of his holidays. But that was before he found out about Mister Sir.

'I'm Max,' the boy says, holding out a hand. His fingers are crooked and Jonah doesn't know whether he should shake his hand in case it hurts him, but then he probably wouldn't be holding it out if that were a problem, so Jonah takes it.

'I'm Jonah.' Jonah smiles. 'I am very glad to meet you.'

'Jonah? That's a cool name.'

'It's from a story.'

Jonah thinks about the small red bible and the page Mama asked the minister from her church to fold over so that they could find the story of *Jonah and the Whale*. Sometimes, Mama would ask Mister Sir to read the bible story out loud to both of them.

Jonah's never liked the idea of being swallowed by a big fish and having to live in its dark, smelly belly for three days and three nights – and then being spat out again. But he's never said that to Mama because she chose his name and it's her favourite story.

'*Jonah and the Whale*, now that's real magic.' The magician who's been setting up a stage at the front of the room is suddenly sitting beside them. He balances Jonah's Play-Doh dolphin on his

25

hand and then covers it with a red silk handkerchief. When he lifts the handkerchief away, the dolphin has disappeared.

'How did you do that?' Jonah blurts out. Every bone in his body tingles. The magician just made something disappear in thin air: Jonah would love to be able to do that. Sometimes, he wishes he could make himself disappear too. Maybe then everyone would stop fussing over him and trying to get him to have a new mama and papa.

'Here.' The magician pulls something out from behind Jonah's ear. It's the dolphin.

'Wow!' Jonah says.

He wishes Mimi had seen the trick, she would love it.

'Seen it all before.' Max rolls his eyes.

The magician ruffles Max's hair. 'Good to see you again, Max.'

'Haven't you been adopted yet, Danny?' Max grins.

'Afraid not.' The magician gives Max a wink and then walks on to a little boy in a zebra outfit lying on the floor looking up at the ceiling with wide eyes.

'You know him?' Jonah asks.

'Yep. Danny does magic shows at all the activity days.'

Jonah looks over to Danny. The zebra boy is sitting up now and he's asking him to pick a card from a pack. Maybe Danny could help Jonah to magic back Mister Sir. And maybe he could ask him to magic away Mama's headaches and tiredness, because even though Mama is on the other side of the world, if Danny is a true magician, he should be able to do that, shouldn't he?

The grown-ups in blue bibs have been talking to the grown-ups standing around the little girl and now they're all moving away from her. The man in the lion outfit walks towards Jonah and Max, smiling. The woman with the lion ears hangs behind him.

'Here they come ...' Max says under his breath.

The lion woman looks from Jonah to Max. She's got frizzy hair and a chubby face with pink skin and freckles on her nose and cheeks. Mama used to make jokes about tourist women like her, the ones who get burnt easily in the sun and who don't have any shape to their bodies. *African women are the most beautiful women in the world,* Mama would say. Jonah remembers thinking that if African women are the most beautiful women in the world then Mama must be the most beautiful woman in the universe.

Only Max is wrong, the lion couple don't come over. Instead, two men in monkey outfits jump in front of them before they have the chance. The lion man's face drops and he turns round to the woman who must be his wife and they walk off to the buffet table.

Jonah can't get used to all the grown-ups dressed like children. He didn't think that English people would do that. But then he's found out that there are many, many things that English people do that he hadn't expected. Sometimes, he wonders whether, if Mama had known what it was really like in England, she might not have sent him here in the first place.

Jonah looks at the two men: one of them is very tall and one of them is really small, which is kind of funny.

*Would you mind having two dads?* Trudi asked him the other day.

*That's an interesting question*, Jonah had answered.

Mister Sir had taught Jonah to say that if someone asked him a question he didn't know the answer to.

'Hi,' the taller man says. 'I'm Will.'

'Hi,' Max says and smiles back.

'It is good to meet you,' Jonah says, holding out his hand.

Will takes his hand and gives it a shake.

'That's quite the handshake for a little guy,' Will says, blowing on his hand like it hurts.

*A gentleman always gives a firm handshake*, Mister Sir had

27

taught Jonah. They had practiced until he could squash Mister Sir's fingers so hard that he had to pull them away and blow on them.

'And this is Simon.' Will points to the shorter guy.

'I hear there's a sensory dance room,' Simon says. 'Want to check it out?'

Then Simon looks at Max's legs and goes as red as the lobsters the fishermen pull out of the sea on Lamu.

'Oh Christ!' Simon smacks his hand over his mouth. 'I mean – I'm sorry.'

'It's a cool room,' Max says. 'I'd like to see it.'

'You sure?' asks Will.

'Sure,' says Max. 'If you don't mind giving me a push.' He looks over to his foster carer again. 'And you'll have tell her where we're going.'

Jonah follows Max's gaze to a corner of the room and sees a woman with similar tie-dye trousers to Max's. She has long, straggly hair and a million bracelets on her arms and every few minutes, she laughs really loud.

Will and Simon walk over to her.

'Your foster carer looks nice,' Jonah says.

'Amber got an award for being Best Foster Carer of The Year,' Max says. 'She specialises in taking on difficult cases. There are five of us at home: wheelchair, autism, ADHD, Attachment Issues and Violent Tendencies. You should come round for tea one day, it's pretty entertaining.'

Amber winks at Max from across the room and then blows him a kiss.

Jonah looks over to Julie and Trudi again. They're facing away from him. It wouldn't take a second to get to the door of the conference room and to disappear into the London crowds. Maybe if he runs away and Trudi and Julie get worried, they'll understand about him not wanting to be adopted.

But before he has the chance to move, Will and Simon are back.

'We've got the all clear. Let's go,' Will says, pushing Max's wheelchair down the corridor. And then he stops and looks at Jonah. 'Where are your shoes?'

Jonah looks at his bare feet.

'They're in my backpack,' he says, tugging on the straps at his shoulders.

'Aren't you cold?' Simon asks.

Jonah shakes his head. 'I'm OK.'

He's cold. He's always cold. That's why he wears his red woolly scarf and his red woolly hat all the time, even inside. But he's not going to put his shoes back on.

Will smiles. 'Right then, let's go.'

As Jonah follows Will, Simon and Max, he looks over at Trudi and Julie. They're talking to the lion couple now. He decides not to tell them where he's going in case they try to force him to find a Forever Family.

The sensory room is a room with the main lights switched off, a CD player in the corner and coloured beams projected onto the ceiling.

Simon spins Max in his wheelchair and for the first time, Jonah sees Max smile. Will starts dancing on his own. And then he holds out his hand to Jonah. Jonah used to dance with Mama, jumping around the hut or swaying in her arms to the slow songs they sometimes played at the bars in Shela. Jonah takes Will's hand and then closes his eyes and lets himself get swept up in the music. He imagines that he's with Mama, that she's holding him in her arms, like when he was little, and that she's singing to him under the big Kenyan moon.

# Sam

Sam stands outside the ladies' toilets, waiting for Rosie. She's been in there for half an hour.

He looks back out at the conference room. On a chair, in the corner, a foster parent cradles a sleeping toddler in her arms.

Sam hadn't prepared himself to see the affection these kids have for their foster parents. And he wasn't prepared for how it made him feel: like a villain, waiting to scoop up some poor child and steal him away from everything that was safe and familiar.

*Children have the most astonishing capacity to adapt, much more so than we do as adults*, Cathy told him when he'd asked her how a child goes from being a stranger one minute to your son or daughter the next.

Maybe she's right. Maybe children do just adapt. But still, these kids *love* their foster parents. That can't just be switched off.

Sam gets out his phone and sends Rosie a text.

*You ok?*

He's been trying to hold her together all day, but he's barely coping himself. It's not just seeing the kids with their foster parents. It's registering the sheer number of people involved in this whole process: kids, adopters, the kids' social workers, the adopters' social workers, foster parents, the foster parents' other kids, the adopters' kids, volunteers – and the magician – all of them dressed up like jungle animals, navigating the green streamers and the life-sized toy tigers and baboons.

So many people. And more or less every one of them will have a say in whether Sam and Rosie get to be parents.

A picture flashes in front of him: a row of people with clipboards stand at the foot of their bed in the railway cottage. Sam and Rosie are lying in their pyjamas, propped up against the pillows, as the clipboard people fire questions at them and make notes.

Not for the first time, he wonders how normal people would cope if they had to pass a million tests before they were allowed to make a baby.

A dull thumping sets in behind his forehead.

Cathy walks down the corridor towards him. She's in her fifties and always looks weary with something more than tiredness. Sam wonders how many hundreds of families she's stitched together over the years – and how many of them have worked out.

'Everything OK?' Cathy asks.

Sam nods. 'Fine.'

Rosie would hate for her to know that she was upset: she'd see it as a black mark against her name. *We mustn't give her any ammunition*, Rosie told him, as they sat at the kitchen table filling out the first round of adoption forms.

He remembers how that word had hit him right in the sternum. *Ammunition for what?* he'd asked her.

*Not to pick us*, she'd said: simple and clear and pragmatic.

So it was war, of sorts. An offensive. Or rather an election campaign in which keeping skeletons well buried in closets was part of ensuring that their adopter profile sparkled.

Rosie's low spells had started when the IVF failed. They'd been through so much already and she'd pinned all her hopes on the miracles of science. Everyone they knew who'd tried IVF had been successful. There were two sets of IVF twins at the bottom of their road: several times a day, the mothers pushed their double buggies past the window of the cottage, bursting with joy at their good fortune.

After a third round of IVF, Sam and Rosie ran out of money.

And when a baby still didn't come, Rosie retreated even further into herself.

She's better now, but the lows come back whenever she hits a speed bump: when a colleague goes on maternity leave; when another schoolfriend replaces her Facebook profile picture with the beaming face of her newborn; when a checkout assistant praises Rosie for leaving the kids at home.

Or worse – when there's a problem at work. When one of the home births don't go to plan. Rosie sees not being able to have children as some kind of failure. And being a midwife, bringing other people's babies safely into the world, is her way of redeeming herself.

What makes it all worse is that Sam *can* have children. There's nothing wrong with his fertility. Sometimes, he wishes that he were the one with the problem – at least carrying the burden of that would make him feel like he was doing something to help; at least then she could have someone to blame other than herself.

*Just think about it, Sam*, Rosie said in one of her more self-destructive moments. *You could just walk out onto the street and sleep with just about any random stranger and have a baby.*

Only Sam didn't want to have a baby with any random stranger. If he wanted a baby at all – and he'd never been as desperate to have children as Rosie had – it was with her: his darling Rosie. The Rosie who was made for him. The Rosie who, until only a few years ago, had been filled with more light than anyone he'd ever met. The Rosie he fell in love with when they were kids.

And that's why Sam is willing to go along with all this adoption business: because he's convinced that, once they have the family she dreams of, he'll get his old Rosie back.

'I meant you,' Cathy says. 'How you are bearing up, Sam?'

'Oh . . . right . . . fine, yes, fine . . . '

Cathy tilts her head to one side and frowns. 'You look pale. And tired.'

He taps his forehead and smiles. 'Oh, just a bit of a headache.'

They hadn't told Cathy about his insomnia either. There wasn't a box for it on her form. And anyway, he'd lived with it for so long that it didn't matter, not really.

'Here, have some food, it'll help.' Cathy holds out a paper plate filled with crisps and sausage rolls. 'I've had too much already.'

Sam's not hungry but he takes a sausage roll anyway.

Both of them look back at the conference room and Sam's sure that Cathy is looking at Lucy too, the little girl Sam and Rosie played with until the other adopters made them feel like they'd had their turn and that they should step aside.

Lucy's with the leopard-print, glittery heels woman. They're dancing to a song from *Frozen*. Sam's glad Rosie isn't here. She'd had a premonition about *Frozen*: *It'll come up,* she'd said, like it was a question on a test they were swatting up on. *Children love it. We should learn the words to all the songs.* She'd found the sing-along versions on YouTube. But this was the point at which Sam had drawn a line. Surely, he argued, there wouldn't be music from an animation set in eternal winter at a jungle-themed party.

But of course Rosie had been right.

Like she'd always been right about the questions that came up in the exams they studied for together at school. And if Rosie was here now, she'd be standing beside him, dead quiet and biting her lip, feeling that, once again, they'd fallen short.

The magician holds his microphone to Lucy's mouth. Her small voice floats through the room: 'Let it go . . . Let it go . . . ' The leopard-print woman claps her hands and then spins Lucy around the room. Sam feels sick. What if Lucy decides she wants

33

a cool, glittery eye-shadowed mum rather than his practical, forward-thinking Rosie with her tomboy clothes and her lists and her insistence that everything can be tackled if only you have a plan?

He knows Rosie would want him to do something. For a second, he imagines himself charging across the room and rugby-tackling the woman out of the way.

Does anyone ever get violent at these events? Sam wonders.

'It's sometimes the children who look perfect that you need to be most careful of.' Cathy says.

Sam gulps down his sausage roll and wipes his mouth.

'Lucy has attachment issues,' Cathy goes on. 'When I saw you and Rosie playing with her, I spoke to Lucy's social worker to get some background.'

Sam has lost count of the number of times he's heard the phrase *attachment issues*. He and Rosie had learnt that children who'd been in care would struggle to form a bond with their adoptive parents, in the first instance at least. They understood that there would be challenges to work through. They'd gone on the courses. They'd read the books (Rosie had read the books and given him summaries). All these years of jumping through hoops has made them experts.

'She's got a complex background,' Cathy adds.

Complex. Another word that's become part of their adoption vocabulary.

'I understand.'

What Sam understands is that Cathy is warning him off. But Rosie has her heart set on the little girl. Which means it's Sam's job to do everything in his power to make adopting Lucy a real possibility.

'Have you spoken to any of the other children?' Cathy asks.

'Sure,' Sam lies.

'If you cast your net a little wider,' Cathy goes on, 'you might be surprised. Children who you wouldn't see as a good match – on paper, I mean – might turn out to be just right for you. Maybe you can sit next to a child you don't know yet at the magic show?'

Sam feels like he's back in school, being told to mingle with other boys and girls, when all he wants is to sit alone in the corner and chisel at bits of wood he's found on the beach.

'Will do,' Sam says.

Though Sam's plan is to do the exact opposite. He's going to get this one right. He's going to make sure that their expression of interest for Lucy is the strongest – and that means Lucy remembering them too.

'Time for the little kids and the big kids to do some magic,' Danny the magician's voice booms over the microphone. 'Come and join us down here on the mats.'

'I'd better go and find Rosie.' Sam looks at the door to the ladies. 'Think anyone will mind me going in?'

'I thought you said she was fine,' Cathy says.

'She is ... she is. Just a bit tired. You know, all that nervous energy gearing up for today.'

Cathy nods. 'Sure.'

'We'll be there in a minute.'

He waits for Cathy to leave and then pushes open the loo door. Rosie stands by the sink.

'Come here,' he says and holds out his arms.

She walks to him and buries her head in his chest.

'Ready to go out again?'

He feels a faint nod.

'It's the magic show. You'll love it.'

When they were kids growing up in Wales she was always the

one to drag him to a visiting circus and fairs and touring musicals. She loves the magic of performance.

Rosie looks up at him. He takes the pads of his fingers and wipes at the smudged lion-whiskers on her cheeks. 'I love you,' he whispers.

He kisses her lightly on the lips.

'Do you think . . . ' she whispers, her breath warm on his face. 'Do you think it will work this time?'

It's a phrase that always makes his heart sink. A phrase she'd used when they were first trying for a baby. When they started taking fertility drugs. When they had IVF. Ever since they were children, Rosie has wanted him to promise the impossible. And it's always made him feel completely helpless.

But, still, he gives her the answer she needs to hear. Because he loves her. And because he doesn't have the courage to say anything else.

'Yes, it will work this time.'

The corners of her mouth lift. 'You like Lucy too?'

He nods.

'Really?'

'Really.'

She sniffs, glances in the mirror and smooths down her hair.

'Ready for the magic show?' Sam asks.

She smiles, a proper, big smile this time. He takes her hand, kisses her palm and guides her to the door.

A group of children and adopters spill out of the sensory dance room. Rosie and Sam file in behind Will and Simon, the gay couple they met at the briefing. They're with the boy in the wheelchair (yellow sticker: Max) and a little black boy with short woolly hair and big eyes and a wide mouth (yellow sticker: Jonah). For some reason, Jonah's dressed as a starfish – a starfish with a red scarf and a red hat. And he's not wearing any shoes.

As they move forward into the room, Sam catches the boy's eye.

'Rosie . . . ' Sam puts a hand on her arm and tries to draw her attention to Jonah.

But Rosie is already charging towards Lucy.

Then he notices Jonah looking around him and a second later, he's walking towards the front door of the conference room. Sam blinks and Jonah's outside and heading across the courtyard and towards the gates.

What's he doing?

Sam looks round the conference room for someone to alert, but everyone's too busy finding seats for the magic show to notice that Jonah's slipped out.

'I'll join you in a minute,' Sam says to Rosie.

She doesn't hear him; she just keeps walking towards Lucy.

'Jonah!' Sam calls out as he steps into the courtyard outside the conference centre.

Jonah spins round.

Sam catches up with him. 'Don't you want to see the magic show?'

Jonah looks from Sam to the main road beyond the gates of the courtyard. He drops his head and stares at his bare feet.

'Did you lose your shoes?' Sam asks.

Jonah shakes his head.

'It's all a bit mad in there, isn't it?' Sam nods his head back to the conference room.

Jonah doesn't answer.

'I don't like crowds either,' Sam goes on.

Finally, Jonah looks up. 'I want to see London.'

'You do?'

Jonah nods.

Rosie and Sam moved to Bridgeford, a small town on the out-skirts of London, so that they'd be close to the city art galleries. It was Rosie's idea. She understood, better than he did at the time, that if his work as a sculptor was to gain any attention, they had to be near London.

But he misses home. The music in people's voices. The air. The sea. His mum.

'Why don't you come back in?' Sam asks.

He's worried that Jonah's going to make a run for it – and Sam's not sure he'd be fit enough to catch him. And then he'd really be in the doghouse with Rosie. And Cathy. An adopter who lets a kid escape in London. That would ruin their chances of ever getting a kid. But then he's the only one who noticed Jonah leaving the room – that should count for something, shouldn't it?

'The magic show is about to start.' Sam stretches out his hand. 'And they've put out chocolate doughnuts for after.'

Jonah looks up at Sam. 'I like chocolate.'

'So do I.' Sam stretches out his hand. 'So, you'll come back in?'

'You won't tell anyone?' Jonah asks. 'That I came out here?'

Sam had planned do to exactly that: take Jonah back in and hand him straight back to his social worker or foster carer. Because that was the responsible thing to do.

'As long as you promise not to run away again without telling someone,' Sam says.

Jonah looks back at the road, hesitates for a moment, and then slots his palm into Sam's hand.

When they get back into the conference room, Jonah goes over to sit next to the boy in the wheelchair. Sam looks across the room and spots Rosie, who's managed to get really close to the stage where the magician is setting up for the show. Lucy's in touching distance. But just as Rosie reaches Lucy, leopard-print woman steps in front of her and sits down next to the little girl.

Rosie freezes.

Sam walks up to her and puts his hand on the small of her back.

'Why don't we sit down here?' Sam points to a space near Jonah and guides her to sit down next to him.

A little girl totters over to Jonah. She sits on his lap and Jonah puts his arms around her and holds her tight.

'This is Mimi,' Sam hears Jonah say to Will, Simon and the boy in the wheelchair.

'Me – Mimi!' The little girl shouts out, her eyes shining.

'Now, I'm going to need a very brave volunteer,' Danny the magician says.

Lots of small hands dart into the air.

Danny scans the room. Then he smiles and points at a podgy little boy dressed as a zebra.

Although the zebra boy had put his hand in the air, it was probably more because he was imitating the other children rather than because he understood he was volunteering for something. His foster dad has to guide him up to the stage. And then the boy starts crying.

Danny kneels down in front of him, takes a coin out of his pocket and says, 'See this?'

The boy looks at the coin and nods, sniffling.

'The Queen of England has one of these. And if you're a brave boy and you help me with my magic trick, you'll get one too.'

'Will we get one?' A boy in a bear outfit shouts out.

Danny gets to his feet and holds up the coin for the children to see.

'Yes – every one of you can take a coin home. You can keep it in your pocket or put it under your pillow and every time you rub it, you can make a wish.'

The spotlights above the stage bounce off Danny's white-toothed smile.

'It doesn't matter what your wish is, whether it's a little wish or a big wish or a crazy old wish: if you believe in it, it will come true.'

As Sam looks around at the children's beaming faces, their eyes fixed on the coin in Danny's hand, he feels a pang of sadness. Promising these kids that their wishes will come true doesn't feel right.

Danny closes his fist, blows on it and then opens his palm. The coin has gone.

Sam hears Jonah gasp; the little boy's eyes are as wide and shiny as Danny's gold coins.

He knows he's meant to be focusing on Lucy, but his attention keeps being drawn back to Jonah.

'You like magic?' Sam whispers over to him.

Jonah nods quickly.

Through the rest of the magic show, Jonah doesn't take his eyes away from the stage once. His eyes shine and his mouth is set in a massive grin. He believes it's real, all of it.

'Hey, Rosie, look . . . ' Sam says, nudging her.

Rosie doesn't move.

'That kid, his face, it's priceless.'

Rosie still doesn't react.

'Rosie . . .'

But she doesn't hear him. Her eyes are fixed on the front row of children where Lucy is nestled in leopard-print woman's lap.

# FIVE MONTHS EARLIER

## 25th December

# Trudi

Trudi takes out her mouth guard, removes her eye mask and pulls out her earplugs: her armour against Blessing who snores through the night and then switches on all the lights when she gets up at the crack of dawn.

Blessing is Trudi's aunt. When Trudi's parents died in a car accident on a mountain road in Uganda, she was sent to England to live with Aunt Blessing and Uncle Albert, in their small flat above the laundrette they ran together. They raised Trudi as their own.

Trudi's mobile keeps buzzing.

She dangles her head over the side of her bed and scans the room. She spots her mobile vibrating along the floorboard next to a pile of yesterday's clothes.

What if she doesn't answer it? What if, just for one day, she lets it ring and ring?

The phone keeps ringing and buzzing and vibrating. *An instrument of the devil,* Blessing calls it. Trudi thinks she might have a point.

Another shrill ring. She grabs the phone and leans back against her pillows.

'Trudi?'

It's her boss at Hounslow Adoption Services.

'Hi . . .' Trudi says, her voice thick with sleep.

'I've been calling you for hours. What were you doing?'

Trudi glances at the clock on her radio-alarm. 7.34am.

'I was sleeping.' Trudi says. 'It's Christmas Day.'

There's a silence. It's *because* it's Christmas Day that her boss called Trudi. Every other adoption social worker in the borough will be spending the day with their family. Whether it's a Sunday, a bank holiday, Christmas, Easter, Diwali, Ramadan or Yom Kippur, Trudi is her boss's go-to girl. In fact, Trudi is her boss's go-to girl full stop.

'I've got a sensitive case for you.'

That's another reason her boss called: sensitive cases are Trudi's speciality.

Trudi rubs her eyes.

'Fire away.'


'Damn it.'

Only one of the windscreen wipers is working and it's pissing it down.

Blessing stands, arms akimbo, in the doorway of the laundrette shaking her head. Sometimes Trudi wonders whether, as a prize for her devotion, God has given Blessing supersonic hearing. If mobile phones are the devil, swear words are the devil's tongue.

Trudi puts her old rust bucket of a Peugeot into gear. If her car decides to give up the ghost, she doesn't know what she'll do. Her clients live all over London and she can't rely on the vagaries of the British public transport system to get her to places on time.

'Immigration found a kid at the arrivals gate,' her boss said on the phone. 'No passport. No sign of Mum and Dad. Guessing he's around seven years old.'

The security guys are checking the CCTV cameras now.

Trudi's seen it before. Kids shipped to England and left standing alone at the airport when something goes wrong. She understands that the world is screwed up. The world being screwed up is why she has a job. But still, this takes the biscuit. Seven years old? Christ.

'The child won't speak to any of the officials,' her boss said. 'We're hoping you'll work your magic.'

And sometimes that's what Trudi felt her job called for: magic powers.

Fifteen minutes later, Trudi pulls up into the staff space in the Heathrow Terminal 3 car park. She grabs a piece of gum from her handbag, pulls her security lanyard over her head and glances at her face in the rearview mirror. She hasn't had time to put make-up on and her braids needed re-plaiting weeks ago.

*You'll frighten the cats going out like that*, Blessing has told her more than once.

*I don't like cats*, is Trudi's usual reply.

But Trudi knows that Blessing's not really talking about cats: she means that Trudi's going to frighten away potential suitors. Blessing actually calls them that: *suitors*, like the guy Trudi's been waiting for her whole life is just going to step out of one of Blessing's Jane Austen novels, take one look at Trudi, scream and run right back in again.

There's a smudge of yesterday's mascara under one of her eyes. She spits on her finger and rubs hard.

'Right. Into battle.' Trudi smiles.

Trudi's smile is the one thing everyone comments on. A big, white-toothed smile that takes over her face. Even when she's feeling miserable, she can't help it from creeping into her mouth. Trudi knows it's an asset, that it wins kids round – that and her being as short as them. But sometimes she envies those scowly, moody, clever-looking people. No one would ever mistake Trudi for looking moody or clever.

*

45

He's tiny, that's the first thing Trudi thinks. Tiny both ways: short compared to the seven-year-olds she's worked with and so skinny you can see the bones of his skull pressing up against his forehead. Two banana skins, an empty packet of Hobnobs and a small carton of orange juice sit in front of him. And even though the heating's cranked up to max, the boy's wearing a red woolly hat and scarf. He makes her think of a little version of Wally from *Where's Wally?*

His legs dangle off the chair, nowhere close to reaching the floor. And his feet are bare.

'Lost his shoes in Arrivals,' Bruno, the immigration officer whispers.

They're in the bowels of Terminal 3, the shabby staff offices, kept well hidden behind the bright lights of duty free.

Kneeling in front of the little boy, Trudi asks, 'What happened to your shoes?'

He furrows his brow. 'I lost them.'

'Where?'

'In the airport.'

'You took them off?'

He nods. 'When I was sitting down.' He pauses. 'They hurt.'

Trudi winks at him. 'I don't like wearing shoes either.' She holds up one of her scuffed boots.

The corners of the boy's mouth edge upwards.

Trudi must have been this boy's age when she was sent from Uganda to England. And she'd struggled, too, to understand why people in England wore shoes all the time. In Uganda everyone went around in bare feet, especially children. But then she'd felt the grittiness of the English pavements and the dirt that stuck to the soles of her feet, dirt that wasn't anything like the red, Ugandan earth. And the cold, that was the worst. A cold which crept through her toes and into every bone of her body. So, much to Blessing's relief, she'd given in to wearing shoes.

But Trudi understands the boy: whenever it's warm enough, she still loves to kick off her shoes and socks and enjoy the lightness of walking around in bare feet.

'It's cold here. *Really* cold. You need to keep your feet warm.'

Trudi picks up a packet of red BA socks from Bruno's desk, rips open the plastic and eases them over Jonah's feet. She feels a pressure on the top of her head as he puts his small hand there for balance. And when she's done with putting his socks on, he doesn't take his hand away. He holds one of her plaits between his fingers.

'You like these?' she asks.

He nods. 'They are extremely lovely.'

The boy doesn't just belong to another country: he belongs to another century.

'Now, you ready to talk, mate?' Bruno says, too loud.

Jonah's drops his head back down.

Trudi glares at Bruno. Like a bull in a bloody china shop, she thinks.

'Why don't you go and get us both hot chocolate from the machine,' Trudi asks Bruno.

'DI Taylor will be here in a moment and I said I'd be here to meet him. Plus, the boy shouldn't be hungry: he's eaten all my biscuits.'

The boy looks down at his feet.

'I'll deal with DI Taylor,' Trudi says. 'And hot chocolate isn't about being hungry.' She turns to the boy. 'You want a hot chocolate, don't you?'

The boy looks up at her and nods. There are dark circles under his eyes. 'That would be very nice, thank you,' the boy says.

He might just be the politest seven-year-old she has ever come across.

'There, Bruno. You have your orders: two hot chocolates.'

What Trudi really wants is time alone with the boy. They have no name for him yet, no exact age, no papers to indicate which plane he's just walked off – and no clue as to why he was found sitting alone on Christmas morning at the arrivals gate. Once the security guys get a move on, they should have more info, but even then, she's going to need to find out what really happened, and that means the kid's going to have to trust her. And if there's one thing she's learnt in her ten years of social work, it's that kids don't trust you if they're scared of you.

She waits for Bruno to leave and then comes to sit on the chair next to the boy.

'My name's Trudi,' she says, holding out her hand. 'What's yours?'

The boy looks at the door and then back at Trudi and then holds out his hand, his palm.

'I'm Jonah,' he says. 'Like Jonah and The Whale from the Bible. I'm delighted to meet you.'

'Great to meet you too, Jonah.'

*Jonah, a nice, Old Testament name,* Blessing would say. She'd love this kid.

'Sounds like you've had quite the morning, Jonah.'

Jonah looks at the mobile phone on Trudi's lap.

'You like this?' Trudi holds it up. 'Here, try this game, I'm addicted.' She taps on the Dolphin Bubble Game she downloaded for moments like this.

The Dolphin Bubble Game is another reason kids like her.

Jonah reaches out for the phone and then just stares at it, frowns.

'Here.' She opens the game. 'You need to get the bubbles in the dolphin's mouth . . . '

He swipes his little finger across the screen.

'Does it do phone calls?' he asks.

'You want to call someone, Jonah?'

He shakes his head quickly. 'I was just wondering.' He hands the phone back.

'Did you lose your mum in the airport?' Trudi asks.

They'd released a series of tannoy announcements to locate Jonah's family but no one showed up at the information desk.

Jonah doesn't reply. His eyes are still fixed on the mobile phone.

'How about your dad? Did you lose your dad?'

Jonah shakes his head again.

Then he looks up, his brown eyes enormous in his tiny face. 'I don't have a mama or a papa.'

Trudi's stomach contracts.

'You mean you don't have a mum or dad here, at the airport?'

Jonah tightens his woolly scarf around his neck.

'I don't have a mama or a papa anywhere. I should be with Mister Sir.'

'Who's Mister Sir?'

'Mister Sir is the man I'm meant to be living with in England.' Jonah's eyes sparkle. 'He's a gentleman and he has a big house and he's going to teach me to read my book.'

'Your book?'

Jonah opens his backpack and hands her one of those ancient, cloth bound hardbacks you find in charity shops: yellow pages, pen and ink illustrations, a font so small you have to squint to make it out.

She brushes her fingers across the title page: *The Tempest*.

'You read Shakespeare?'

The boy holds her gaze for a moment and then looks back at the book. 'A bit.'

'Well, that's very impressive, Jonah. What's it about?'

Jonah looks back up and smiles. 'It's about magic.'

'That sounds like a good story.'

He nods again. 'Ariel's my favourite character. He can fly. And take any shape. And disappear. And make storms.'

'Wow, I wish I had some of those powers.'

Jonah smiles. 'Me too.'

'So, Jonah, tell me more about Mister Sir. Does he have a name?'

Jonah tugs his scarf again and then shakes his head.

'You sure?'

He nods.

'And do you know where he lives?'

'In London.' Jonah holds her gaze. 'I think he might be looking for me, but the security man who brought me here said I couldn't go back to the airport.' The sparkle goes out of his eyes.

Trudi takes his tiny hands in hers and squeezes them tight.

'Don't you worry, Jonah, we'll look after you.'

Trudi sits back in her chair. This is going to be a long old Christmas.

# FIVE MONTHS LATER

## *May*

# Rosie

Rosie stands by the window watching the 10.46 pulling out of Bridgeford Station. The walls of their house shudder. Catching a reflection of herself in the mirror, Rosie smooths down the creases of her blue NHS uniform. Then she threads her fingers through her frizzy curls. She came back from a home birth two hours ago.

Usually, after so many hours awake, Rosie would try and get some sleep, but Cathy's coming this morning, so she's been standing at the window instead.

When she gets too nervous, standing there, waiting, Rosie does another tour of the cottage. She tries to look at it through Cathy's eyes.

It's like all the bits of the cottage have got together to conspire against her: the dust and the sharp edges to the kitchen cabinets and the clunks in the plumbing and the tufts of cat hair stuck in the door of the cat flap.

*Don't let them adopt a child!* They hiss.

Rosie goes to the door at the end of the kitchen, which leads into the garage, and listens to the radio humming alongside the *whoosh, whooshing* of Sam's sanding. She thinks of going in, but Sam's working hard on his Ascot bid. Five British horse sculptors have been challenged to create a feature, which will be put up outside the Royal enclosure. The four other sculptors are famous already; they have exhibitions in big art galleries around the world and at Glyndebourne and Marble Arch. So Sam knows that his chances are slim. But making the longlist means that someone, somewhere, has noticed his driftwood horses – and that must count for something. The sculpture needs to be done by December, seven months from now.

She swallows hard. Maybe they'll have a child by then.

Maybe it's like when bad things cluster together, only this time, everything will go right. Sam's work will take off. And they'll be a family.

She closes her eyes and feels the weight of a child's body in her arms. The little girl's head, heavy in the crook of her neck, her small arms tucked into Rosie's chest, her breath warm and sleepy. Rosie draws the child in closer, strokes her hair and kisses her warm forehead.

*My darling little girl . . .*

Rosie is jolted out of her daydream by the thud of hammer against wood. She opens her eyes and looks back at the garage door.

There's another reason Rosie decides not to go into Sam's workshop: she wants some one to one time with Cathy. Sam's already charmed her. Rosie still feels she needs to win Cathy over, to show her that she'll be a good mother.

Rosie turns away from the garage door, walks back through the kitchen and comes to stand on the porch. Hop, their cat, slips out of the front door and weaves his small body between her feet, his spine arched, his tail brushing her legs.

Rosie found Hop five years ago. He was wandering along the railway tracks. Six weeks old. A kink in his tail. A nick in his ear. Patches of his white fur missing, like they'd been pulled out in tufts. Odd eyes – one blue, one brown, like David Bowie – and only three legs. It was a miracle he survived.

*Noah,* Sam calls Rosie sometimes. Or *Frankie,* short for Francis of Assisi, the animal-loving saint – because she's forever finding animals and calling out the RSPCA. A broken-winged pigeon. A limping fox that collided with a car. A mangy dog sniffing by dustbins.

Only Rosie doesn't feel in the least bit saintly. And she's honest enough not to pretend that dealing with these strays has anything to do with her being good: she needs to scoop them up and fix them, much more than they ever need her.

Rosie watches Cathy walking up from the station.

'You'd better put on a good show,' Rosie says to Hop.

'Hi!' Cathy calls from the garden gate.

Rosie's heart lifts. This is where it all begins. The moment they've been waiting for since the activity day, two weeks ago.

She opens and closes her fists to shake out her nerves.

'Cathy – come in!' She kisses Cathy on both cheeks.

Hop looks up at Cathy and chirrups.

'What a greeting!' Cathy says, reaching down to stroke Hop behind the ears.

Cathy likes animals. And Rosie has to remember that she likes Rosie and Sam too. 'I'm on your side': wasn't that what she was always saying?

'Sorry I'm late,' Cathy says, following Rosie to the kitchen. 'An issue came up.'

Rosie doesn't like being reminded that she and Sam are just one on a long list of adopters Cathy works with. She needs to think that Cathy's working night and day just to get them a child.

'Sam working?' Cathy asks, following Rosie through the hall and into the kitchen.

'Yes – but he'll be out in a minute.'

When Sam and Rosie first showed Cathy the house, they made a big thing of Sam's workshop in the garage. *You see*, Rosie had stressed, *Sam works from home, he'll be here all the time.*

She liked to boast that Sam would be a modern, stay at home dad. And an artist with a sensitive soul too.

But the truth is, they hadn't had a choice but to put Sam forward as the primary carer. Rosie is the one with the stable income.

Not being the one to stay at home feels like another blow to Rosie's dreams of motherhood, but they have to be practical. Having a child is all that matters.

And Sam would be an amazing dad, you'd have to be blind not to see that. He has a light touch with children. He strikes up conversations with them more easily than he does with adults. At bus stops. On trains. In coffee shops. Rosie loves children, in a motherly way – she wants to brush their hair and kiss their doughy cheeks and put plasters on their grazed knees and rock them to sleep. Sam's different. He understands them. Makes them laugh. Taps into their worlds.

Rosie remembers a day when they were eighteen and out shopping in a big out-of-town supermarket near Criccieth, the small Welsh town where they'd grown up together. Sam found a four-year-old bawling by a tower of baked beans. He'd lost his mum.

The boy was dressed as a cowboy, so Sam lifted him onto his back, neighed, and rode the four-year-old around the supermarket until they found her.

By the time they got to the boy's mum, he'd forgotten that he'd ever been lost. And he wanted Sam to stay, preferably for ever. *Giddiup! Again!* the boy had cried out, his face beaming.

Most of the eighteen-year-old boys Rosie knew at the time were too self-centred to notice kids. Not Sam. It was one of the things that made her certain that he was right for her. And that one day they'd have a big family and that he'd ride their children around the house on his back and that they'd love him as much as she did.

It was what convinced her, too, that pushing to have a child was the right thing to do: Sam was made to have kids.

'I imagine his work as a sculptor must be very absorbing,' Cathy says.

'His mum sent him a piece of driftwood,' Rosie tells Cathy. 'He hasn't left the garage since.' Rosie bites her lip. 'But he'll have plenty of time to look after a child . . . he says that having a child around will inspire him.'

Cathy smiles but doesn't say anything.

Rosie watches Cathy looking around the kitchen and the second-guessing starts again: the cramped, cluttered surfaces, the draught coming through the single-glazed window, the scuff marks along the skirting boards.

Rosie imagines Cathy filling in a chart with a long column of black marks.

She shakes off the thought. Today's a good day. Today, they'll get good news.

Cathy walks to the door at the back of the kitchen and looks out through the glass panel. 'I've never noticed the swings before.'

'They're new,' Rosie says.

There's barely room to turn round in the tiny plot of grass next to the cottage, but Rosie's squeezed in a double swing, one for a child, the other with a special bucket seat for a toddler.

'I wanted to do *something*, you know?' Rosie adds.

'It's a nice idea,' Cathy says.

Rosie's face brightens. 'You think so? The swings are child-proof.' She laughs nervously. 'Obviously. What I mean is that I chose the company carefully – and they guaranteed that the swings passed all the health and safety tests. They said it was ideal for a child of five . . . ' Rosie holds her hand to her chest. 'I'm talking too much, aren't I?'

Cathy smiles and puts a hand on Rosie's arm. 'You're doing just fine.'

For a second, Rosie allows herself one of those crazy thoughts she gets whenever Cathy visits: that maybe it's this one thing – this red and blue swing – that will clinch it. That Cathy will leap in the air and clap her hands and exclaim: *Why, of course, you MUST have a child – in fact, I've got one waiting for you just outside the front door* . . .

Rosie stares at the file in Cathy's arms. She knows it's all in there, the papers that will pave the way for her and Sam having a child. Cathy places the file on the kitchen table. The cardboard edges are curled; the label with SAM & ROSIE KEEP has been smudged by raindrops.

Rosie's eyes sting. She blinks and lifts her gaze from the file.

'Tea?' she asks. 'And cake?' She claps her hands.

Rosie runs over to the counter next to the fridge, lifts a Victoria sponge cake out of a tin and places it on a stand. Earlier this morning, she roughed up the edges and gave it an extra dusting of icing to disguise the fact that it had been made by a machine in a Tesco warehouse rather than right here, in her kitchen. Rosie is terrified of Cathy finding out that she's a hopeless cook. She's sure it'll lead to an extra big black mark in her file. Being able to feed your family was a basic requirement for a mum, wasn't it?

'This is a treat,' Cathy says. 'I'm used to digestives – or bourbons, at best.' She smiles. 'Sam's a lucky man, Rosie.'

Rosie's cheeks burn. 'Thanks.'

'Ah, cake – I see I've arrived just in time.' Sam walks into the kitchen, comes over to Rosie and kisses her forehead.

Rosie hopes that Sam doesn't make a joke about her baking. And then she realises how stupid she was to accept Cathy's compliment. It's one thing being a mum who can't bake; it's worse being found out as a fraud.

'Good to see you, Cathy,' Sam says.

She notices him steal a glance at the file too; he knows as well as she does that their future lies between those cardboard covers.

The three of them sit down at the kitchen table.

'So, the activity day,' Cathy says. 'It was quite something, wasn't it?'

Rosie nods.

'Must have stirred some emotions,' Cathy adds.

Rosie nods again. Sam takes Rosie's hand under the table.

'Yes – yes, it did,' Rosie says.

'That magician guy is a genius.' Sam smiles and shakes his head. 'I still don't know how he got that boy off the table.'

'I saw Lucy's face – she loved it, didn't she, Sam?' Rosie says.

Sam nods and smiles at her. They've replayed every word and gesture associated with Lucy a million times.

'About Lucy . . .' Cathy starts.

Lucy has been the subject of every single one of Rosie's emails to Cathy in the past two weeks. Rosie feels it in her gut: Lucy's the child for them.

'Yes, we were wondering whether there was any news?' Sam asks. 'We know these things take time . . . but, you know, it's hard not to get excited.'

'Actually, things can happen quite fast after an activity day.'

Rosie's heart jumps. A new child for the summer; might that be possible?

'We thought she warmed to us – didn't we, Sam?' Rosie looks at him and waits for him to expand. When he doesn't, she goes on. 'She said she liked horses. She said she had a collection of My

Little Ponies, didn't she, Sam?' This time Rosie doesn't wait for him to answer. 'Sam's started making some small models ... a miniature stable ...' Rosie clears her throat. 'We were thinking that maybe we could see her again ... maybe if we got to know each other better ...'

Hop leaps onto Cathy's lap.

Rosie suddenly panics: 'Lucy isn't allergic to cats, is she?'

'Allergic? No ... not that I'm aware of ...'

The three of them sit in silence for what feels like ages.

Cathy pushes Hop gently off her lap, laces her fingers together on the table and leans towards Sam and Rosie.

'The matching process might not always make sense, looking at it from the outside, but a great deal of thought goes into bringing together a child with her family.'

Rosie feels a thud in her chest.

'And, as you can imagine, there were lots of expressions of interest for Lucy.'

Rosie nods. 'We know, we understand, it's just—'

'Let Cathy finish, love,' Sam says gently.

'And as I said on the day, Lucy's needs might not have been as visible as those of the other children. But she has a tricky background.'

Rosie sits up. 'We've been volunteering at the homeless centre in town. We've been befriending ...'

'Befriending?' Cathy asks.

'People with drug problems,' Rosie says.

'Oh ... I see.'

'We thought it would help us understand the background of some of the children. You said that Lucy's mother was a user.' Rosie turns to Sam. 'We've learnt so much, haven't we, Sam?'

Cathy said once that Rosie and Sam should treat the adoption process like getting a qualification – the most important qualification of their lives. That learning everything they could about the kinds of children they might be asked to care for would maximise their chances of finding a good match.

'That's very admirable,' Cathy says as she opens her file.

Sweat gathers along Rosie's hairline. She pulls her hand out of Sam's.

'It was the glittery heels woman, wasn't it?' Rosie blurts out. 'The leopard-print woman with the gold eye shadow.'

Cathy stares down at the page in front of her and says, 'I'm afraid that's confidential information.'

Rosie shakes her head. 'I knew it.'

She tries to catch Sam's eye but just as she does, he lowers his gaze. She can't work out whether he's embarrassed by her or whether he feels the same disappointment she does about Lucy. Sam had fallen in love with her too, hadn't he?

Hop jumps onto Rosie's lap and nestles his head against her stomach.

Sam looks up at Cathy and says, 'We realise it was a long shot.'

Rosie's head snaps up.

'Did we?' she asks him. 'I thought you agreed that we'd be a good match, Sam. That Lucy was right for us.'

Before they'd even happened, she'd formed the memories that they were going to share:

Sam taking Lucy with him for early morning swims at the Bridgeford pool. How they'd coming home together, hand in hand, laughing, their hair dripping, bursting to tell Rosie all about it.

Sam giving Lucy piggy-backs around the garden.

Sam pushing Lucy on the new swing-set.

Sam showing Lucy how to make his special eggy-bread breakfast.

Sam and Lucy sitting next to each other at Sam's workbench in the garage, Sam chiselling out the shape of a pony for her.

In Rosie's head, Sam and Lucy looked perfect together. Lucy wasn't just a good match: she was the perfect match. Rosie had been so sure of it.

'I know it's disappointing, love,' Sam says. 'But there's always a bigger picture, right, Cathy?' Sam looks at Cathy as though he wants her to stand up for him or something.

Disappointing? That's all he's got to say?

Sometimes, Rosie wonders whose side Sam is on.

She grabs a hankie from the box on the table and blows her nose hard. Then she takes a breath and looks straight at Cathy.

'How are these things decided? I mean, who decides that she's a better fit that we are?'

'Like I said, I can't go into specifics of the case. But generally speaking, a child expresses interest in an adopter and an adopter expresses an interest in a child and, if they're a good match, we move forward.'

'Could you maybe help us understand why we weren't a good match?'

Sam's voice is steady and calm and Rosie recognises the look in his eyes: he's instructing Cathy to reassure Rosie, to tell her something that will make all of this bearable. But nothing Cathy can say right now will make things better. Lucy didn't pick them. Simple as that. And instead, she went for the woman who wears glittery heels to a children's jungle party.

Cathy takes a breath. 'I know it's disheartening ...'

Rosie sits back in her chair and drops her hands into her lap. A small diamond glints on her ring finger. She thinks of eighteen-year-old Sam kneeling on the cliffs outside his mum's cottage in Criccieth. Dusk. The white moon rising over the sea.

'Do you mind if Rosie and I go for a walk?' Sam asked his mum.

Flick looked from Sam to Rosie and then threw her arms around them both.

'Just don't go messing things up, Sammy,' Flick said, giving them a final squeeze before stepping away.

Rosie looked at Sam. 'What aren't you meant to mess up?'

Sam blushed, looked down at his feet and didn't answer.

'And don't stay out too long – the rain's coming in,' Flick threw over her shoulder as she walked back to the house.

It was the anniversary of Alwyn's death, Sam's dad. Rosie spent the day helping Flick paint the front of the house, a job Alwyn always used to do. Sam locked himself away in his dad's workshop and polished off the driftwood horse he'd been working on for months, the one he wanted to leave on his dad's grave. Then, in the late afternoon, the sun already sinking into the sea, the three of them walked over to the churchyard.

Although it had been a year, the three of them were still in shock. Rosie kept expecting Alwyn to crash into the kitchen, thump his tool kit down on the table and hold out his arms to her. *My girl*, he'd always call her. The daughter he never had. She would run to him and bury her head in his chest and breathe in the smell of wood shavings and salt from his walk home along the sea front.

When Rosie and Sam got to the top of the cliffs, Sam stopped walking. He took her hands and looked her right in the eye:

'I love you, Rosie,' he said.

'Even like this?' Rosie asked.

Sam laughed. 'Even like what?'

Rosie made a show of looking down at the old, faded dungarees she was wearing: frayed hems, holes at the knees. Flick lent them to her for painting.

It was a relief, the first time Flick gave Rosie a pair of Sam's old shorts to wear. She was nine and had got her dress so muddy playing outside with Sam that she needed something clean to go home in. Her mother never let her wear anything but dresses.

Rosie remembers being amazed at how Flick didn't mind looking like a boy. How she didn't make a distinction between her side of the wardrobe and Alwyn's. How she wore his socks and his corduroy trousers and his shoes. Since Alwyn died, she'd taken to only wearing his clothes. Which made Rosie realise that the dungarees she was wearing were probably his.

'Sorry, I should have got changed,' she said.

Sam shook his head. 'You're perfect as you are.'

He leant forward, took a strand of her hair and smiled. She looked up through his fingers and noticed a thick strip of white paint tangled into one of her curls.

'I think there's more paint on you than on the front of the house.' Sam laughed. He found another curl and wound it round his finger.

'Hey, at least I was painting!'

Sam had never been good at practical things, not in the DIY sense. Although he and his dad shared their love of working with wood, they lived in different worlds: Alwyn was a carpenter, Sam was an artist.

Sam brushed the pad of his thumb across the tip of her nose. 'There's another bit here.'

Rosie rubbed her nose. She hadn't looked in a mirror all day. She hadn't *really* looked in a mirror for months. There weren't many in Sam's house, not compared to the millions of reflective surfaces in her parents' B&B. Rosie found it liberating not to have to worry about how she looked on the outside.

'And here.' He kissed a bit of skin just by her ear, his lips warm. Her body shivered.

Sam trailed his lips along her face, kissed her cheek, the side of her mouth, her lips. His warm breath filled her body.

Then he pulled away, shook his head and said, 'That was meant to happen after.'

'After what?'

'I'm getting the order all wrong.'

'The *order*?'

He grabbed something out of his pocket and knelt in front of her.

'Oh!' She clamped her hand over her mouth.

'Close your eyes,' he said.

She closed her eyes and listened to the sea crashing on the shore below. A raindrop fell on her cheek. And a ring slipped onto her finger.

Her eyes flew open.

'Sam?'

He knelt there, looking up at her, his eyes glassy in the dark.

'You will, won't you?'

She nodded quickly.

'*Say it*, Rosie.'

'Yes.'

'Yes what?'

She took a big breath. 'Yes, I'll marry you.'

He kept kneeling for a moment, his head low between his shoulder blades, as though something in his body had snapped free. Then, slowly, he stood up and took her by the waist and kissed her again.

'Thank you,' he said, his words warm in her mouth.

'Thank you?' she asked, their lips still touching.

He pulled away.

'For you.'

And she knew that he meant it. That he loved her. That she was his family now.

The rain fell harder. He took her hand and they ran back along the cliff path to his mum's house.

'I knew that ring would look good on you,' Flick said, holding Rosie's hand under the kitchen light.

Rosie and Sam sat at the kitchen table, smiling goofily. Their rain-sodden clothes dripped onto the tiles.

'Are you sure it's OK?' Rosie asked. It was Flick's engagement ring, the one that she'd worn every day since Alywn proposed, forty-three years ago.

Flick gave a sharp nod. 'Surer than sure.'

Flick put down Rosie's hand and went to pick up the saucepan of milk from the stove. She came back and poured the milk into the mugs and stirred each of them until the hot chocolate dissolved. She'd made hot chocolate for Sam and Rosie at this kitchen table ever since they were kids. The first time was on Rosie's tenth birthday when she ran away from home and announced that she was moving in with them.

It took another five years for her to move in properly, in the days following Alywn's death. But long before that day, the Keeps' home was Rosie's home, much more than any house she'd lived in with her parents.

Flick sat down and looked around the kitchen. 'At least the house will get used now.' She paused. 'Alwyn would be pleased to see that.'

Rosie had heard these words a thousand times. How Alwyn had built this house from scratch, how the neighbours mocked him for making it so big: *the white molar*, they called it, a huge square building rooted into the shore, dwarfing all the other small cottages along the sea front.

Flick and Alwyn were going to have lots of children. Of course they were. Ten at least. And when Sam came along quickly, just as planned, they knew that their dream would soon come true. But then years of nothing. It was as though, Flick said one day, her body had forgotten how to have a child. Eventually, Flick and Alwyn had to accept that Sam would be their only child, Sam with his quiet, artist's soul which struggled to fill even one room.

Rosie often thought that their grief at not having more children of their own was the reason the Keeps welcomed her so unquestioningly into their family. Unlike Sam, she was a loud child. She skipped and laughed and sang through the rooms of their house. She swallowed the space.

And she filled their rooms with rescued animals too, turning the house into her very own veterinary surgery: seagulls with broken wings; stray cats and dogs; oil-slicked crabs and starfish.

'I'll spoil my grandchildren all rotten, just you try and stop me!' Flick said, beaming.

'Mum!' Sam said, an expression of mock horror on his face. 'We're not even married.'

But Rosie's heart swelled. She imagined the clatter of footsteps down the stairs, games of tag in the garden, a line of wellington boots by the front door, babies on high chairs at Flick's kitchen table. And she knew that Flick would be true to her word: she'd love those children just as much as she loved her Sam and her Rosie, the little girl from next door who'd been forgotten by her parents.

And this is what Rosie wanted too: a house full of children, *her* children. A real family, at last.

Rosie pushes her palms into her eyes, trying to block out the memory of that day.

What if she'd know then that, fifteen years later, she'd be sitting with Sam in this ramshackle cottage, hundreds of miles from home, fighting to have a child that wasn't even theirs?

A tear drops down her cheek and into her palm. She doesn't bother to brush it away.

'Oh, my love.' Sam puts his arm around Rosie's shoulders.

She shakes him off. 'Just give me a minute.'

Rosie cradles Hop in her arms, gets up, and runs out of the kitchen.

For a minute, Rosie stands in the hallway outside the kitchen, her spine pressed into the wall. She holds Hop tight against her chest and buries her nose in his fur.

'She'll be OK,' she hears Sam say to Cathy. 'She'd just got her hopes up.' A pause. 'She wanted to paint the walls pink ... she picked out the curtains ... in the room that would have been Lucy's.'

Rosie's stomach clenches into a fist. It wasn't just her. He'd got his hopes up too. Hadn't he?

'I warned you not to get carried away ...' Cathy's voice from the kitchen.

*Don't get carried away.* Rosie has heard those words come from Cathy's lips more times than she can remember. But doesn't Cathy understand that getting carried away is part and parcel of longing for a child? That if Rosie were pregnant, she'd be *expected* to get carried away – that people would think there was something wrong with her if she didn't?

Rosie walks down the hall, opens the front door and sits down on the top step.

The 11.05 shuttles past. She looks at the passengers walking from the station past the cottage, their clothes already lighter than a few weeks ago. No more coats and scarves.

A child for the summer; had that hope been so very greedy?

Rosie takes a breath, stands up and goes back inside.

'You both need to open your minds to other possibilities,' Rosie hears Cathy say as she walks back into the kitchen.

Sam and Cathy look up at her.

'Sorry,' Rosie says. 'I'm fine now.'

She sits down on the chair next to Sam, places her palms on the table, looks straight at Cathy and says, 'The children have to express interest in adopters. That's how the process works, right?'

Cathy nods. 'Yes . . . '

'So.' Rosie looks over at the file. 'Which of the children liked *us*?'

Sam sucks in his breath. He knows as well as she does that they didn't give any of the other children their attention. But she has to keep the process moving. If it's not Lucy, there has to be another child.

Cathy blinks. 'Sorry?'

'Taking Lucy out of the equation, which of the children told their social workers and their foster parents that they'd like to have us as parents?'

Cathy doesn't answer.

'It's OK, Cathy . . . ' Sam says.

And then something flickers across Cathy's eyes.

'There is a child . . . '

'There is?' Sam asks.

Cathy nods. 'He's got a tricky background . . . but yes, I think he might make a good match. We have to take it one step at a time, of course . . . '

69

Sam sits forward, his eyes wide.

Electricity rushes through Rosie's fingers.

'*He*?' Rosie asks.

Cathy nods, opens her file, takes out a plastic wallet and places it in front of Rosie and Sam on the table.

'He told his social worker that he liked you.'

'He liked us?' Rosie turns to Sam. 'Did you talk to any of the boys at the adoption day?'

Sam looks at Rosie for a second and shifts in his seat. Then, very slowly, he shakes his head. 'I don't think so.'

Rosie picks up on the hesitation. But if he'd talked to Jonah, she'd have noticed, wouldn't she?

Cathy shrugs. 'Well, I guess he noticed you. Anyway, he's a very special little boy.' She pauses. 'His name's Jonah.'

# FIVE MONTHS EARLIER

## 25th December

# Jonah

Jonah's pretending to sleep.

When the other policeman called DI Taylor came into the room saying that he needed to ask some questions, Jonah told Trudi he wasn't feeling well and that he wanted to sleep. So Trudi took him to the sofa and put a blanket over him.

Jonah had hoped that if he lay here long enough with his eyes closed, DI Taylor would get bored and go away.

But it looks like he's staying.

Jonah hears him talking to Trudi:

'I need some more answers.'

'The kid's just been through a traumatic experience,' Trudi says. 'Give him some time.'

'We don't have time,' DI Taylor says. 'What we do have is a tiny window to get to the bottom of this. After that, all this gets a hell of a lot more complicated.' He pauses. 'I need you to wake him up for me.'

Jonah hears the door open.

'Found them!' Bruno's voice.

Jonah opens his eyes, just a slit. Bruno's holding up Jonah's shoes and socks.

Jonah looks at Bruno's big belly and the sweaty patches under his white shirt. He's definitely not a True English Gentleman. The non-uniform policeman looks a bit more like Mister Sir but much taller and skinnier, and his trousers are too short on his long legs: Jonah can see hairy strips of skin poking between where his socks end and the hem of his trousers begin.

Bruno drops the shoes and socks on the floor by the sofa.

73

Trudi turns to DI Taylor:

'We know that he's called Jonah and that he's seven years old—'

'That's what he *told* you,' DI Taylor says. 'They're not facts.'

DI Taylor and Trudi lock eyes for a moment. Then DI Taylor breaks the silence:

'We need to take a look at the boy's backpack.'

Jonah hugs his backpack closer to his chest.

When Bruno picked Jonah up at the arrivals gate, he tried to get it off him too. But they're his special things, the things he brought over from Kenya.

'It might give us a clue about who he was travelling with, and why he's here,' DI Taylor goes on.

Jonah gulps hard. He wishes that they'd all go away and leave him alone. They're wasting time: if only they'd let him go and look for Mister Sir, he's sure he could find him.

'I've asked the guys in Nairobi to have a look at their CCTV for the past twenty-four hours,' Bruno says.

'Good job,' DI Taylor says.

Jonah forces open his eyes and sits up.

'May I please go to the bathroom?' he asks.

Three faces turn to look at him. Bruno with his double chins and his big belly. Trudi with the wormy plaits sticking out of her head. And DI Taylor with his Adam's apple that looks like he's got a stone wedged in his throat.

English people are definitely not as beautiful as people from Kenya, Jonah thinks.

'Of course,' Trudi says to Jonah. 'I'll take you.'

As Trudi helps Jonah put his shoes and socks back on, DI Taylor says, 'Watch he doesn't do a runner.'

Trudi rolls her eyes and takes Jonah's hand.

*

As they walk down the corridor she says:

'I know it's hard, Jonah, but you're going to have to trust us. We're here to help.'

'Thank you,' Jonah says. But the only help he needs is to find Mister Sir.

And no one seems interested in doing that, so he's not going to say anything more than he needs to.

Trudi guides him to the toilet door.

'Want me to hold that for you?' Trudi asks, nodding at Jonah's backpack.

Jonah shakes his head. 'I can manage very well.'

'You're a funny one.' Trudi laughs. 'OK, I'll wait for you out here.'

'Thank you,' Jonah says and goes into the loo.

He sits on the loo, waits a bit and then he flushes it several times to make it sound like he's going. As he does, he quickly zips open his backpack. He pulls out the pinky-white shell from the beach on Lamu, puts it to his ear and listens for the sea, but all he can hear is the flushing of the loo.

Then Jonah takes out the other things from his backpack: Mama's red pocket Bible with a page folded over by the story of his name and the special book that Mister Sir gave him about a magician who lives on an island with his daughter.

He flushes the loo again, and pulls out a photograph of Mama in a yellow dress. She's standing on the edge of the water: the sun's bouncing off her black hair and she's smiling and her face still looks soft because the photo is from before she got so thin. Jonah takes off one of his shoes, folds the photo and places it under the insole. If they're going to take his bag away from him, at least they won't find Mama's photo.

Then Jonah zips closed the backpack.

Just as he's about to open the loo door, he notices a window. It's small but Jonah is small too, and he's good at slipping through narrow spaces.

Maybe he could climb out and go and look for Mister Sir by himself.

Jonah puts his things away in his bag and climbs up onto the toilet seat. He pushes open the window and the icy December air stings his face. He tightens his red scarf around his neck.

'Jonah . . . everything OK in there?' Trudi's voice through the door.

He thinks of Trudi's big smile and how she's been kind to him when Bruno and DI Taylor asked all those questions.

Jonah steps off the toilet lid. 'I'm coming.'


'Your English is very good,' DI Taylor says. 'Why is that, Jonah?'

He makes it sound like Jonah's done something wrong. *Everything* DI Taylor says makes him sound like he's done something wrong.

'I only know English,' Jonah says. 'It's the most wonderful language in the world.'

Trudi laughs.

'You don't speak African then?' Bruno asks.

'African isn't a language,' Trudi says.

Bruno's big cheeks go pink.

'I mean your own language. Swahili? Is that right?' Bruno says.

Some of Mama's friends, like Miss Mary with the healing hands, tut-tutted about Jonah not being able to speak the language of where Mama was born. But Mama said they were just jealous and that, unlike Jonah, they would never see England and that Jonah should hold his head up high. And that

English was the language of True English Gentlemen. And of Shakespeare.

DI Taylor writes something down on his pad.

A short woman with spiky blonde hair pokes her head round the door and hands DI Taylor a piece of paper. He traces a long, bony finger down the page and mumbles:

'As I thought – BA064 … red eye from Jomo Kenyatta International … landed at 4.56am … ' DI Taylor turns to Jonah. 'So you're from Kenya?'

Jonah looks at him blankly.

DI Taylor shifts his eyes back to the piece of paper.

'Accompanied by a white male … '

Bruno lets out a whistling sound through his lips. 'No one questioned a black kid travelling with a white bloke? They must be getting lax down at passport control.'

'I spoke to immigration. They remember him – and they did challenge him, but I gather it was all above board: he produced Jonah's birth certificate and a letter explaining that he was accompanying Jonah to England where he would be met by his family.' DI Taylor keeps reading: 'Robin Morse, that's our guy.' He keeps reading. 'Here we go: Jonah Baako.' He looks up from his paper at Jonah.

*Accompany him to meet his family?* Jonah doesn't understand.

'I was meant to live with Mister Sir,' Jonah says.

'Don't worry, Jonah,' Trudi says quietly. 'We're just untangling a few things.'

DI Taylor keeps reading:

'Mr Morse was last seen exiting the airport at 8.52am. Then we lost him.'

'You *lost* him?' Trudi asks. 'Isn't the place crawling with CCTV?'

'We're looking into that,' DI Taylor says.

'You will you find him, though?' Jonah asks.

DI Taylor looks straight at him.

'Don't you worry, lad, we'll nail him.'

But Jonah doesn't want to nail Mister Sir. He wants to find him and go home with him. That's what Mama wanted.

'So, Jonah, are you going to tell us why you left Kenya?'

'I'm going to live with Mister Sir.'

'Bloody perv— ' Bruno says.

'Bruno, keep it zipped,' Trudi says.

Jonah doesn't know what the word *perv* means, but it doesn't sound nice. Mama wouldn't like a bad word being used about Mister Sir.

'What about your mum and dad?' DI Taylor says.

'I do not have a mama or papa.'

That's what Mama told him to say. *All anyone needs to know is that you're staying with Mister Sir.*

'Come on . . . ' DI Taylor says.

Jonah can't breathe: it's like the air has been sucked out of the room. And there aren't any windows. And the strip light is giving him a headache.

'I think we've done enough questioning for today,' Trudi says.

DI Taylor unfolds his tall, thin body and stands up. He comes and stands in front of Jonah and, for the first time, he smiles at Jonah. 'Why don't you tell me about your mama . . . then we can find her for you and bring you back together.'

But DI Taylor's smile doesn't make a difference. Mama wouldn't want anyone looking for her – especially a policeman.

'OK,' Trudi says. 'Let's get out of here, Jonah. Find you some hot food. A proper bed. A good night's sleep.'

Jonah's heart skips a beat. Maybe, at last, she's going to help him find Mister Sir.

'We're not done with the questioning . . .' DI Taylor says.

Trudi's eyes go dark and she puts her hands on her hips. She and DI Taylor definitely don't get on.

'We can pick up the questioning when you and your team have got further in your Robin Morse investigation,' Trudi says. 'Right now, my priority is Jonah.'

Trudi takes Jonah by the hand. He grabs his backpack from the floor and, together, they go out of the windowless room and down the corridor and out through the airport with the jingly Christmas music and the big green tree with the shiny balls and the brightly coloured lights. The man with the red coat and the white beard and the big belly waves at them as they go past.

Then they approach the doors through which Mister Sir disappeared, and Jonah feels a fizz of excitement. At last he's going to see England.

When they get to Trudi's car, Jonah says, 'May I ask a question?'

'Fire away.'

'Am I going to stay with Mister Sir?'

'I'm afraid we haven't found Mister Sir yet.'

'Mister Sir lives in a castle.'

Maybe that will be enough to help them in their search.

Trudi smiles. 'A castle, eh?'

Jonah nods enthusiastically.

Trudi tilts her head to one side. 'Is that what he told you?'

'It's what Ma—' Jonah takes a breath. 'Yes, it is what he told me.'

'I'm afraid that there are many big houses in England, Jonah. And quite a few castles too. It will take us a while to find him.'

'Am I coming back home with you, then?'

Jonah doesn't want to meet any more strangers. And he likes Trudi. She has a big smile and kind eyes.

Trudi shakes her head. 'I'd like that very much, Jonah, but I'm afraid that's not possible.' Her voice wobbles.

Jonah's whole body feels cold and this place with its long stretches of concrete and its rows and rows of cars doesn't look like the England that Mama told him about.

Trudi strokes Jonah's cheek. 'But don't you worry, Jonah. We're going to look after you.' She pauses. 'Everything's going to be OK.'

Jonah nods and smiles but there's a hollow feeling in his chest, which tells him that nothing's even close to OK.

# THREE WEEKS LATER

## January

# Trudi

'Met any nice boys at the office?' Blessing asks.

It's Sunday evening. Blessing, Trudi's aunt, stands in their small bathroom, plaiting Trudi's hair.

'Ow,' Trudi says.

Blessing plaits Trudi's hair much like she does anything else in her life: with an evangelical zeal.

'*Il faut souffrir pour être belle,*' Blessing says.

She'd taken French lessons a while back, one of the many projects she'd embarked on when her husband, Albert, died. But when she realised that all the French lessons and cake decorating and flower arranging courses in the world wouldn't fill the space he left behind, she gave them up and extended the opening hours of the laundrette instead.

'When this is done, we could invite someone over,' Blessing says, smoothing some coconut oil along a strand of Trudi's hair.

'Invite who over?'

'A nice young man from the office.'

Trudi sighs. Blessing's doing her usual trick of trying to wish something into existence. This particular wish (that her only niece – her only child – should meet the man of her dreams and ride off into the sunset) has been burning bright for the last ten years.

'There are no men at the office,' Trudi says. 'It's all women. So unless you'd like me to enter a same-sex civil partnership ...'

Blessing's bosom heaves under her nylon housedress. 'You're courting the devil, girl.'

'I'm not courting anyone – I thought that was the point. And I'm just taking your thought to its logical conclusion: you want me to fall in love with someone at work and the only people at work are women . . . '

'I want him to see you in all your glory.'

'There is no him – and what glory?'

'Your hair, child, your hair.'

No matter how many years go by, no matter how many exams she passes or promotions she secures, it's always the same: when Trudi talks to Blessing, she's seven years old again, having her hair yanked and being squeezed into a white, frilly dress for Sunday school. Even before Trudi's parents died, Blessing took charge of Trudi's spiritual education.

The thought of leaving Blessing on her own had made it feel impossible to move out, but Trudi knows she has to find a place of her own or she'll go mad.

In the mirror, Trudi watches Blessing pulling at her hair in a way that reminds her of a gardener pulling at weeds.

Trudi's mobile rings.

Blessing sucks her teeth.

DI Peter Taylor's name flashes up on her screen.

'I've got to take this,' Trudi says, standing up.

'I haven't finished your hair!'

As she answers the phone, Trudi glances in the mirror again. One side of her head is plaited, the other side a frizzy cloud of candyfloss.

Trudi accepts the call and presses the phone to her ear.

'It's important,' DI Peter Taylor says.

Trudi walks through the lounge and into her bedroom and closes the door.

'There's been some progress,' he goes on.

Trudi sits down slowly on the bed.

'We've arrested Robin Morse,' he says.

It's been three weeks. She'd all but given up hope that they'd find the man who'd brought Jonah to England; from her experience, child smugglers are adept at vanishing acts.

'Can I come round?' he asks.

Trudi reaches for the frizzy side of her head and tries to smooth it down.

'When?'

'Now.'

Playing the *it's Sunday* card crosses Trudi's mind, but she senses that DI Peter Taylor is like her boss: a workaholic who goes through his week without a clue as to which day of the week it is or how one day differs from the next.

'OK, come over.'

There's a knock on Trudi's bedroom door. 'Trudi!' Another knock.

Trudi puts her hand over the receiver. 'I'm on the phone!'

Blessing strides in. 'There's a police car parked outside the shop.'


DI Peter Taylor is the first man they've had in the flat since Albert, Trudi's uncle, passed away last Christmas.

The moment he walks through the front door, Blessing goes into a tailspin of excitement.

'Please sit down,' Blessing says, clearing a pile of ironing off the sofa. 'Cup of tea?'

'No thank you, I won't be staying long,' Peter Taylor says.

*Thank God.*

As Trudi watches him sit down, she's reminded of those long-limbed pop-up toys, the ones that collapse into themselves when you press their base before shooting back up again the moment you let go. Peter Taylor is as freakishly tall as Trudi is tiny.

'Could you give us a minute, Blessing . . . ?'

'Of course.' Blessing disappears into the kitchen and starts to empty the dishwasher. A clatter of plates and mugs, which Trudi knows won't prevent her from hearing every word of their conversation.

Trudi smooths down the frizzy side of her hair. 'Sorry about this . . . ' She says, hoping that her vagueness will cover all the apologies she's making right now: her aunt who has no sense of personal boundaries; the state of the flat; her hair.

Peter Taylor tilts his head to one side and examines her for a moment. 'I like the natural look.'

Which totally takes Trudi aback. Not in a million years did she think that DI Peter Taylor would comment on a woman's hair.

He leans back against the cushions.

'So, it turns out that our man's the CEO of a major chain of hotels along the African coast.'

Trudi feels her jaw go slack. 'Really?'

'Yep. And he's married with two kids. House in Chelsea. Weekend house in Surrey . . . '

'Not a castle, then?'

'Sorry?'

'Oh, just something Jonah said.'

'Anyway, he's clean as a whistle. Except, of course, for his extra-curricular activities in Kenya and the fact that he smuggled Jonah into the country.'

'And abandoned him – in my field of work that's considered neglect. And neglect equates to child abuse.'

DI Peter Taylor folds his hands over his knees. 'Maybe.'

He's being far too casual, thinks Trudi. Robin Morse should be locked up for life. Anything could have happened to Jonah.

'Did you question him, personally I mean?' she asks.

'He's lawyered up to the hilt but yes, we managed to secure a short interview.'

'And?'

'He's not talking much. He's probably been told to keep quiet until the trial, so he doesn't incriminate himself further.' He pauses. 'He just kept saying that it wasn't his fault.'

Trudi clenches her jaw and she feels her back teeth grind together. The dentist said she should start wearing her mouth guard in the day. She'd really attract Prince Charming then, wouldn't she? Anyway, what else is your jaw meant to do when you hear crap like this?

'How can it not be his fault?'

Peter shrugs. 'I guess we'll find out.'

'What about Jonah?' Trudi asks.

Peter looks at her blankly.

She managed to find Jonah a foster mum. He seems to like her but every time they meet up, Jonah still bangs on about Mister Sir, like they were best friends or something.

'Didn't he show any guilt for abandoning Jonah like that?'

'Like I said, he's being guarded. But he did ask if Jonah was OK.'

'Wow, that takes some nerve.' She tries to relax her jaw. 'What did you tell him?'

'I said that he was as well as could be expected.'

Trudi smiles. 'Nice and evasive.'

Peter smiles back, a crooked smile that softens his face.

'Did he say anything about Jonah's parents?' Trudi asks.

'He didn't mention there being a dad . . .'

'Which is what we expected.'

'Yeah, I guess so.'

'So he *did* say something about Jonah's mum?'

Peter nods. 'Claims he only met her recently, in Nairobi.' He pauses. 'A work connection.'

'You don't buy *that*, do you?'

'No, I don't buy that. You don't take someone's kid halfway across the world for a woman you've just met, not unless you're being paid a shedload of money. And we've checked his bank statements. No unusual activity in the last two years. And anyway, he couldn't have got Jonah's passport sorted that fast – most Kenyans never leave the country. So he must have known Jonah's mother for a while.'

'They had a relationship, that's what you're saying?'

'Well, let's put it this way: he's been to Kenya six times in the last three years, more than double the number of times he's visited any of the other countries where he manages hotels. And there was CCTV footage of them at Jomo Kenyatta. They were holding hands. They hugged before he and Jonah went through security.'

'Didn't you see that CCTV footage months ago?'

He blushes. 'We missed this. It was earlier in the tape.'

Trudi bites her tongue. Peter Taylor has come all this way to talk to her, on a Sunday – she has to be civil.

'So, Robin Morse was one of her regulars?' she asks.

Something had made her suspect this might be the case. A rich white man. A poor black African girl.

'Looks like it, which is probably why he's protecting her.'

Peter Taylor puts his hands on his long, skinny thighs. His legs are longer than my entire body, thinks Trudi.

'There's just one anomaly,' Peter Taylor goes on. 'We found the hotel where they were staying, near the airport—'

'One of his hotels?'

'No. I doubt he would have taken them somewhere he was known. Anyway, they had separate rooms. An adjoining door but separate all the same. And one room was under his name, Robin Morse, and the other under the name Miss Baako.'

'Maybe it was a room for Jonah,' Trudi says.

'Maybe. Just strikes me as odd.' He pauses. 'And the receptionist said they arrived separately. Which all confirms his assertion that they're just friends,'

'Or that he's good at covering his tracks.'

'Maybe.'

'Did you ask him whether he had a contact number for her – or an address?' Trudi asks.

'He says that he doesn't know where she is and that he can't get in touch with her.'

'That's convenient.'

'Yes, it is.'

But Trudi's glad. The less chance they have to find her, the better. Jonah has been through enough.

The clink of a plate from the kitchen.

'What's going to happen to him?'

'Well, the good news is that he's not being let out on bail. With all his travelling and his connections to Africa, the judge considers him a flight risk.'

'And the bad news?'

'He's got good lawyers.'

'So, you're saying he might get off? Christ . . .'

'I doubt he'll get off but there might be a reduced sentence.'

'But he's guilty.'

Peter's eyes cloud over. He hesitates and then says, 'I know.'

Trudi thinks of Jonah sitting alone in Terminal 3 and every

nerve in her body feels raw with anger. Isn't clamping down on men like Robin Morse what the British legal system is for?

'So when's the trial?'

'As he's being held in custody, we won't need to wait long – probably April, after the preliminary hearings.'

Blessing comes in carrying a tray of tea and biscuits.

'English Breakfast OK?' she asks in her la-di-da voice.

By which she means builders: Tesco Economy.

As though Blessing's arrival has released the pressure button on the push-up toy, Peter Taylor stands up, unfolding his long limbs, and brushes down his trousers.

Trudi stands up too and looks up at him.

He turns to Blessing. 'Thanks for the offer of tea but I'd better be going.'

When he reaches the door, he turns back round. 'The best thing now is for us to keep pressing Jonah,' he tells Trudi. 'He's our key to finding his mother.'

Trudi nods, but only because she knows she has to. Because her training has told her that what matters more than anything is keeping a child with his biological mother – or at least maintaining contact. As her boss is always telling her: 'research shows that maintaining contact with the birth family creates better outcomes from the child.'

But what about Trudi's research? What about all the wonderful adopters she'd seen, their lives disrupted by the unreasonable demands – the threats even – of birth families that, only a few months ago, had neglected their children?

No, right now, the only thought Trudi has is one that she would never articulate to her boss or any of her other social worker colleagues: she hopes that Jonah never breathes a word about his mother. Better still, she hopes that he forgets ever having known her. She sent her seven-year-old son off to a foreign country, thousands of miles away, under the fiction of relatives waiting for him on the other side. It was a huge risk: one that didn't pay off. She doesn't deserve to have them all looking for her.

*Don't judge* is another mantra that had been drummed into Trudi, but she doesn't care: that woman doesn't deserve to be Jonah's mum. This beautiful, sensitive, scared little boy needs parents who will love him and nurture him and give him a chance at life. And she's going to make damn sure that happens.

# FIVE MONTHS LATER

## *June*

# Sam

On Sunday morning, Sam and Rosie stand on the doorstep of No. 27 Faircross Avenue in Barking. A terraced house with hanging baskets on either side of the door and a neat front garden.

Sam watches Rosie look up at the house, taking it all in. She bites her lip.

'Excited?' he squeezes her shoulders.

Rosie gives him a quick nod. And then she looks down at the cake tin she's holding. She spent last night making brownies and ended up leaving them in the oven for so long that they came out looking like small lumps of coal and, although Sam's palate had hardened to Rosie's cooking over the years, even he'd agreed that they should go in the bin.

In the end, Rosie had got up early and bought two packets of chocolate chip cookies from the Tesco Express down the road.

'Maybe I shouldn't have brought these,' Rosie says now, still staring at the tin. 'Maybe Julie will have prepared something already – and then she'll get offended. I bet she's a really good cook. I bet Jonah's been having amazing home cooked meals . . .'

Sam lifts her chin and makes Rosie look into his eyes:

'Jonah's going to love you.'

She bites her lip. 'You think?'

Ever since Cathy gave them a date for meeting Jonah, Sam's watched Rosie pacing the cottage, her brain whirring, running through hundreds of scenarios. He's the one who suffers from insomnia but these past few weeks, Rosie hasn't slept well either. Two nights ago, when he'd come up late from the garage, he'd found Rosie sitting at the kitchen table, staring at the photograph of Jonah that Cathy had given them. It was as though she was trying to learn his face by heart.

Please God, may Jonah like the cookies, thinks Sam.

'He likes chocolate,' Sam suddenly remembers and then he realises what he's done.

Rosie frowns. 'Really? How do you know?'

Damn. He knew he'd slip up. He'd kidded himself that maybe Jonah won't recognise him – but of course he will. And then Rosie would be even more upset. *What an idiot*, he thinks.

'How do you know he likes chocolate, Sam?'

Lying to Rosie never turns out well. He takes a breath.

'He told me.'

'He *told* you? When?'

Oh God. Why did he have to go and bring this up now?

'Why don't we go in, Rosie, they'll be waiting for us. We can talk about this later.'

Rosie steps away from the front door and holds the cake tin to her chest like it's a shield.

'*When* did you speak to Jonah?' she says again.

'At the adoption activity day.'

The blood drains out of Rosie's face.

Sam had thought it was best not to say anything. That she'd be upset to know that he'd had some contact with Jonah before she had, that it somehow gave him a head start.

'We only had a quick chat.'

'When? We were together the whole time.'

'At the end of the day. Before the magic show. You were—'

'I was what?' She's clutching the tin of cookies so hard that her knuckles have gone white. 'I was what, Sam?'

'Concentrating on Lucy.'

96

The front door flies open. A woman, who must be Julie, Jonah's foster carer, stands at the door looking from Sam to Rosie.

'Do come in,' Julie says.

Grey roots grow out of her dark hair. Lines mark her forehead.

Rosie puts on a smile, steps forward and holds out a hand to Julie. 'It's so good to meet you.'

Julie stares at her and, after a pause, takes her hand.

Trudi had said there might be resistance. She'd explained that some foster parents – even some social workers – felt nervous about white adopters taking on a black child. Sam and Rosie had heard the words 'transracial adoption' over and over in the last few weeks. A loud, clunky, roadblock of a term.

The little girl he recognises from the adoption fair grips Julie's leg. Julie lifts her onto her hip.

'You are being a little barnacle today, aren't you, Mimi?' Julie says.

She kisses Mimi's cheek and the little girl smiles and echoes: 'Barn-a-cle.' Her small, pink tongue flicks out when she gets to the last syllable.

Sam watches Rosie's gaze flicker over Julie and Mimi, as it does whenever she observes a child and a mother. A longing and a sadness and a hope that, one day, it might be her.

And then it hits him: if all this works out, if the social workers decide that he and Rosie are up to adopting Jonah, Rosie won't be looking at other parents holding other children anymore – she'll be looking at Sam.

At Sam lifting their child into his arms.

At Sam playing with him in the park.

At Sam teaching him how to swim or sand down a piece of wood.

At Sam putting him to bed.

He's going to have to do all that stuff. He's going to have to be a parent. And, right now, as he watches Mimi clinging to Julie, that complete dependence, he's not sure he can do it.

He closes his eyes and takes a breath. *Get a grip,* he tells himself. He takes Rosie's hand and, as they follow Julie into the hall, Sam leans in and whispers, 'Sorry for not telling you about Jonah.'

She doesn't respond.

'Jonah knows you're coming,' Julie throws over her shoulder. 'He'll be down in a minute.'

'Jonah! Jonah! Jonah!' Mimi echoes.

Sam feels a tightening across his rib cage. Mimi must have got used to having Jonah around. She'll miss him.

They follow Julie and Mimi through the narrow hall. Sam lets go of Rosie's hand so that she can go first. He looks around the house: the walls are marked by crayons and grubby fingerprints and toys lie scattered across the hall, spilling out from the lounge. A wodge of dried-out Play-Doh sits on the window ledge. This is Jonah's home, Sam thinks. And we're about to take him away from it all.

Out of the corner of his eye, Sam notices a change in the light at the top of the stairs. A shadow moves across the wall. He looks up and sees huge brown eyes peering down at him through the banisters. He recognises Jonah immediately. Not just from the photos and the DVD, but from the activity day, how those eyes had pleaded with Sam not to tell anyone about him trying to run away. He wonders what he's pleading for now.

He raises his hand and gives Jonah a small wave.

Jonah retreats from the banisters.

'Jonah!' Julie calls out. 'Get down here.'

Rosie turns round and looks up the stairs. They're all looking now: Julie, little Mimi, Rosie and Sam, waiting for Jonah.

There's a pause. Sam thinks he can hear Jonah's breathing. And then a tentative step forward. He comes down the stairs, taking each step slowly and deliberately. His feet are bare again.

The doorbell goes.

'That'll be Trudi,' Julie says.

'Trudi!' Mimi cries, toddling forward, her body light and bouncy and expectant.

Sam feels Rosie retreating behind him. They both know that Trudi is the one they have to impress.

Julie opens the door and Trudi boulders in, kicking off her shoes and putting down her Mary-Poppins-sized bag. Her hair looks different, like a sharp wind has pinned her plaits down on her scalp.

Mimi runs up to her and gives her a hug.

'Hey there,' Trudi says, swinging her round.

Sam looks around: there are so many people in Jonah's life, Sam thinks. And next to them all, he and Rosie are strangers.

'Why don't you get yourself and Mimi a snack?' Julie asks Jonah.

She whispers to Sam and Rosie: 'Eats like a horse. Don't know where it all goes!'

'Mimi Jonah snack! Mimi Jonah snack!' Mimi chants as she climbs down from Trudi's arms.

'That sounds like a great idea,' Trudi says. 'Maybe you can bring me a snack too.'

Jonah smiles and sweeps Mimi up off the floor. Sam can see the strain in Jonah's back from holding the little girl, but it's clear he's determined to carry her.

'Goodness, what a strong boy,' says Rosie.

Jonah doesn't seem to hear. He carries Mimi to the kitchen.

Sam wishes he could follow Jonah and Mimi. He wants to be

with Jonah as much as he can. Because, Sam thinks, maybe if he learns everything he can about Jonah over the next few weeks, by the time he moves in with them, by the time he's their son, it'll be OK, Sam will know what to do. And it won't feel like they've taken a stranger into their home.

'This is just a quick hello, a chance for you to see Jonah in his environment,' Cathy had said.

This was the first of a series of timetabled visits. Each one would be a little longer and more involved. On Wednesday they'd stay for supper. On Thursday they'd do bedtime. Then he'd come for a sleepover at the cottage and, the week after, Rosie and Sam would take Jonah to school.

Rosie had taken some time off work and Sam had warned his agent that there might be a delay on completing his Ascot bid.

Barring any unforeseen obstacles, by the end of the next week, they'd be taking Jonah home. And a few months after that, if all went well at the adoption hearing, he'd be theirs. For ever.

For ever. Christ.

'Let's go into the lounge,' Julie says.

Rosie and Sam sink into a soft, brown sofa. Trudi sits on the floor next to the farm Sam recognises from the DVD of Jonah.

'We've brought the scrapbook Cathy asked us to make,' Rosie says, digging the booklet made of sugar paper from her bag. 'We hope it's OK.'

Julie takes it and puts it down on the coffee table without opening it.

Rosie spent hours over it. She trawled through thousands of photos on their PC, went to Snappy Snaps and printed three times the number they needed for the album, bought jungle-themed stickers and labels to put between the photos, wrote small inscriptions in her neat, tight writing.

The photos chart their lives. Rosie and Sam's wedding day on a beach in Criccieth, Wales; Sam carrying Rosie into the sea, wearing dungarees and wellies in the place of a dress; Hop when he arrived as a kitten, so small and thin that he could fit inside a toilet roll; another one of Rosie feeding Hop milk through a pipette; their lounge; the kitchen; Sam's garage studio; the railway station with the blur of a train passing by; Rosie standing in front of the cottage in her blue nurse's uniform; Sam hunched over a piece of driftwood at his work bench, the side-lamp casting a thick, yellow glow over his face; the front gates of Bridgeford Primary, the school Jonah would go to. And then a picture of Sam's mum, a label under it spelling out: *Grandma Flick*. She's wearing a pair of his dad's old corduroy trousers and pulling out some carrots from the patch she kept next to the small white house in Criccieth. Her head is lifted to the camera and the sea and the sky reflects her grey-blue eyes.

'I'm sure he'll love it,' Trudi says, nodding at the scrapbook.

Sam feels Rosie relax. A tick from Jonah's social worker.

'Jonah's still getting used to the thought of being adopted,' Julie says. 'But he'll come round.'

Sam feels Rosie tense up again.

'He doesn't want to be adopted?' Rosie asks.

'Change is hard for all children,' Julie says. 'Even good change.'

In one of their long interviews with Cathy they'd asked why Julie didn't want to adopt Jonah. They'd heard stories of foster parents falling in love with the children they cared for and being fast-tracked as adopters. Cathy had said that Julie wasn't ready to take on a child long-term. That although she loved fostering, her priority was Mimi.

Jonah comes back in, holding Mimi's hand. She dangles a pink sippy cup in her hand and is gnawing on a fruit and oat bar. They

101

sit on the orange carpet next to Trudi and Jonah hands Trudi a bar too. He hadn't forgotten her request for a snack. Then Jonah picks up a handful of plastic farm animals and puts them in front of Mimi.

'Jonah's a kind boy,' Julie says. 'He likes to take care of people.'

Rosie nods. 'I can see that.'

'Why don't the two of us go and make some tea?' Julie says to Rosie.

Rosie looks at Sam, her eyes wide. He tries to give her a reassuring look and says: 'That sounds like a good idea.'

If Rosie wins Julie over, things will go better. Trudi had told them how influential foster parents could be. How even at this stage, after all the assessments, the adoption process could grind to a halt if a foster parent expressed concerns. There was still a series of panel meetings to come and Julie was bound to have her say.

Before she leaves the room, Rosie picks up the tin of cookies. 'I've brought some treats,' she says, 'maybe we could put them on a plate?'

'Sure,' Julie says.

They both disappear into the hall.

Sam reaches into his pocket and pulls out a package wrapped in tissue paper. He goes to kneel beside Jonah.

'Here,' he says. 'I thought you might like this.'

Jonah stares at the package and then looks up at Sam.

'It's only a small thing,' Sam says. 'Nothing at all, really . . .'

He feels himself blush. And then he looks up at Trudi to check her reaction. He hadn't thought that giving a child a gift might be against protocol. But Trudi smiles and Mimi's already tearing at the tissue paper.

'Horsey! Horsey!' Mimi cries.

Jonah lifts the tiny driftwood horse out of Mimi's palm and turns it round between his fingers. It's the smallest horse Sam has made. He wanted Jonah to have something he could slip in his pocket, something he could carry with him, always.

'I made it,' Sam says.

Jonah's eyes go wide. 'Really?'

Sam nods. 'It's my job.'

'It's your job to make horses?'

'Yes, I'm an artist – a sculptor. Usually the horses are a bit bigger. When you come to visit us, I can show you.'

'Who do you make the horses for?'

Good question.

'Lots of people.' Or that was the idea. 'People who ride horses, or just like horses. They like to put them in their homes and their gardens.'

Sam realises that if this were a sales pitch, he'd have failed.

And anyway, it's all a fiction, isn't it? Sam hasn't made a sale in months. Which is why the Ascot bid is so important. A life-sized horse right outside The Royal Box. A sculpture that would be seen by thousands of people.

'I like horses,' Jonah says.

Sam feels the muscles in his jaw relax. Thank God he's got something right.

'I'm making my biggest horse yet,' Sam goes on. 'A proper life-sized one.'

Jonah doesn't answer.

Mimi yanks at the horse. 'Mine horsey, mine horsey.'

Jonah looks at the horse and then, slowly, places it in Mimi's hand.

'If Mimi wants this one, I can bring you another one on Wednesday,' Sam says.

He'd made this one especially, had taken longer over it than any of the larger sculptures, had polished the grey driftwood until it was so smooth you couldn't feel a single nick in the wood. But he'd make another one. He'd make a thousand horses, if that's what it took. And maybe all those horses would keep Jonah from noticing all the other bits that were missing – the dad bits that he was supposed to get right.

'We could make one together,' Sam says.

Jonah's eyes light up. He nods.

'I didn't know you brought Jonah a gift.'

Sam turns round and sees Rosie standing at the door, holding her plate of cookies.

'Oh, it's nothing really ...'

He should have told her. *Of course* he should have told her.

'Everything OK?' Julie comes in behind Rosie.

Sam feels Trudi's gaze shift from him to Rosie. Every exchange is giving her clues about their life as a couple, their potential as parents.

Sam notices Julie looking at the tissue paper and the horse. Maybe he should have asked someone permission about bringing gifts. Why was everything so complicated?

Jonah steps forward and takes Sam's hand. 'Do you want to see my room?'

He can feel Rosie shifting in the doorway. Is he inviting her too?

'I'd love to,' Sam says. 'If that's OK with Julie?'

Julie nods.

Jonah stands up, still holding Sam's hand. He drags him to the door. Rosie steps aside.

'I'll stay here and play with Mimi,' Rosie mumbles.

Sam looks over his shoulder at Rosie, her back to him now. He

104

notices the stoop in her shoulders. And he knows why: Jonah's barely acknowledged her.

'Don't be surprised if, at first, he warms more to one of you than the other,' Trudi had told them when she visited last week. 'It's a natural part of the process.'

Sam remembers thinking, without a second's hesitation, that, of course, he'd be the one left out in the cold. That their child would see, straight away, that he was totally underqualified to be a dad. Sam had prepared himself for that. What he hadn't prepared himself for was watching Rosie, the one who'd wanted a child ever since he can remember, the one who'd pinned all her hopes on this adoption, who's *made* to be a mum, being sidelined like this.

Sam promises himself that he'll find a way to get Jonah to see how amazing Rosie is. Along with making horses, that's something he can do.

## Sam

Jonah and Mimi's names are stuck in coloured wooden letters on their bedroom door. Inside, there's a cot and a little boy's bed. Mimi's side of the room is littered with soft toys, dolls, books and clothes. Jonah's side is spotless: his bed is made, his pyjamas folded up next to the pillow, a small, bulging backpack by his bedside table.

'You're very tidy,' Sam says.

Jonah nods. 'It's easier.'

'Easier for what?'

'For when we have to move.'

'We?'

Jonah blinks. 'When I have to move.'

Compared to other children, Jonah's file was thin, vague and incomplete. In some ways it felt like a blessing. Rosie and Sam had read hundreds of profiles outlining the troubled backgrounds of the children they might one day adopt: the neglect, the developmental difficulties, the attachment disorders. By comparison, Jonah felt like a clean slate.

But of course, that was nonsense. He'd been neglected too – what else would you call sending a child halfway across the world without a home or family to take care of him when he got there? And the guy who brought him over and just left him there – Sam felt a burning in his chest whenever he thought of that – what kind of man would do that to a child?

The fact that Jonah refuses to acknowledge having a mum or dad, that's an alarm bell too.

Maybe it's this absence of information that scared other families off. All Rosie and Sam had to go on were bits of pieced-together stories from Jonah's words and notes from the police investigation. Despite Jonah's denials, they know that, back in Kenya, he lived with his mother. That, as Jonah had just hinted, he moved around a lot. But the rest was a mystery. A mystery full of trap doors for them to fall through.

'You kept it,' Sam asks, picking up the gold coin from the adoption activity day.

He remembers the promise the magician had made to the children: that wishing on the coin would make all their dreams come true.

Has Jonah been making wishes? And do those wishes look anything like Rosie and Sam?

'I like magic,' Jonah says.

'You do?'

Jonah nods and gives him a wide, tooth-filled grin.

'Julie says maybe I can be a magician one day.'

'That sounds like a fun job,' Sam says. 'I like magic too.'

'Like your wooden horses?'

Sam looks at Jonah and smiles. 'Yes, exactly like my wooden horses.'

Jonah goes over to the desk and picks up an old battered book, the kind that Rosie brings back from the second-hand bookshop she loves in Bridgeford. The title is written in gold letters across the front: *The Tempest* by William Shakespeare.

Jonah sits down on his bed, opens the front cover and asks Sam: 'Can you read?'

Sam rubs his forehead.

'I'm better with pictures than words, but yes, I can read.' He looks at the book. 'Though Shakespeare's a tall order.'

Jonah's brow furrows. 'You're better with pictures?'

Sam nods. 'I'm dyslexic. It means my brain mixes letters up.'

Jonah's shoulders drop.

A lump forms in Sam's throat: they've known each other for less than an hour and already he's managed to disappoint Jonah.

'But I do like stories,' Sam says quickly. 'It just takes me a little longer to read them than most people, that's all.'

Sam flips through the thin pages. He can't remember the last time he picked up a book.

'I must learn how to read,' Jonah says.

Trudi had explained that Jonah couldn't read even the simplest words like *cat* or *dog* or *house*.

A memory flashes across Sam's brain. He's sitting in Criccieth Primary School, being asked to read a verse from the poem *The Tiger* by William Blake. If he'd got advanced warning, he could have learnt it by heart. The teacher's waiting. So are all the other children. And he knows that he's going to make a mess of it.

Sam feels sick. How's he meant to protect Jonah from all that stuff?

'Mister Sir was meant to teach me,' Jonah clarifies.

Trudi had explained that Mister Sir was the name Jonah used for the man who abandoned him at the airport. And that Jonah still spoke fondly of him – and expected him to show up and take him to his home.

Sam brushes off the thought and turns back to Jonah.

'Rosie's very good at reading – she's the clever one,' Sam says.

Funnily enough, it was reading that brought Sam and Rosie together.

'I don't know what kind of rules you've been used to at your old school in England, Rosie, but in Criccieth Primary, we pay attention in class.'

Miss Hudson said *England* like it was a swear word.

Slowly, Rosie lifted her head from the book she'd propped up on her desk. It had a picture of a big tree on the front with stars and animals and children hanging off its branches.

Miss Hudson placed her hands on her hips like she was preparing for battle.

'Rosie – are you going to explain yourself?'

All the year five pupils at Criccieth Primary looked at Rosie. Her shoes were muddy, her hair was a mass of corkscrew curls and her school shirt hung out, un-tucked, a tear at the hem.

Rosie's parents had just opened a new B&B next to the castle. Sam's dad had helped with the carpentry.

'Why shouldn't I read?' Rosie's eyes sparkled.

The class sucked in its breath. No one ever answered back to Miss Hudson.

The network of veins on Miss Hudson's cheeks burst into a bright pink, her eyes bulged and her eyebrows shot up her brow. She opened her mouth but before she had the time to say anything, Sam blurted out: 'It's my fault.'

He didn't know why he said it. Only that he reckoned that it would be easier for him to get the blame – because he always got the blame for everything in Miss Hudson's English classes – than for the new girl, who was probably feeling nervous about her first day and starting in a new school and having an English accent. Having an English accent which was just about the biggest sin you could commit in North Wales.

Miss Hudson spun round on her heels, jutted out her chin and fixed her eyes on Sam.

'How is your fault, exactly, Samuel?'

Sam cleared his throat. 'I told her it was OK to read. That you always encourage us to get stuck into new books.'

'Well . . .' Miss Hudson rubbed her forehead. 'That may well be the case, but there's a time and a place for everything, and that includes reading. Especially reading material that hasn't been provided by the school.'

'Well, I told her she could.'

Miss Hudson pinched shut her mouth. He could tell she wanted to say something back but couldn't think of the right words. Which never happened to Miss Hudson who basically knew the whole dictionary off by heart.

'It wasn't his fault. I was reading because we weren't doing anything,' Rosie said.

The class gasped.

'Excuse me?' Miss Hudson asked.

'You set us a writing task. I've finished it. It was easy.' She held up her exercise book. 'So I started reading.'

Sam couldn't understand why Rosie didn't take a way out of Miss Hudson's firing line when she had the chance.

Miss Hudson went over to Rosie, snatched the book she was reading off her desk and walked back to the front of the class. '*I'll* decide when a task is over,' Miss Hudson said, shoving the book into the top drawer of her desk and slamming it shut.

Later, at playtime, Sam noticed Rosie sitting under a tree on her own. She was reading a book again, a different one. She must have had a whole library in her school bag. And she was reading again at the end of the day when she was standing at the school gate, waiting to be picked up. Sam and Rosie were the only ones left to be picked up.

Rosie sat by the school gate, her back pressed into a pillar, her nose buried in the book she had at break time. You could hardly see her face under all those curls. Sam wanted to go over and pull at one of them to see whether they felt as springy as he imagined.

Rosie turned the pages of the book she was reading so fast he didn't understand how she could be taking it all in. Sam didn't like reading, especially not on his own. Even when his mum helped him, he found it hard to un-jumble the letters – words just swam in front of his eyes.

After a few minutes of kicking stones on the playground and snatching glances at Rosie, Sam plucked up the courage to go up to her.

He stood over her, expecting her to say something, but she kept reading.

He cleared his throat.

'So your mum's late too?'

She still didn't look up from her book.

'My mum's always late.' Sam's mum lost track of time like other people lost gloves and umbrellas. She'd go out in the garden and start planting something and hours later, she'd look up and it would be dark.

'Have I done something wrong?' Sam asks.

Rosie shrugged.

'I'm sorry you got in trouble in English.'

'I don't need you to lie for me.' She still didn't look up from her book. 'I can look after myself.'

He thought about how Miss Hudson and the other people from the village who were always saying that the English were stuck up. Maybe they were right.

He turned to walk away.

'Sorry,' she called after him.

He turned round.

'I know you were trying to be kind,' she added.

Sam walked back to her slowly.

She patted the bit of concrete next to her and he sat down.

'Do you read a lot?' Sam asked her.

She nodded.

'How can you read so fast?'

She shrugged. 'I don't really know.'

'You don't find it hard?'

She looked at him. 'Hard? No, of course not.'

'Can I touch your hair?' Sam clamped his hand over his mouth. What an idiot. Now she'd think he was totally weird. 'I mean ... it just looks so springy ...' *Shut up, shut up, shut up* screamed a voice in his head. But his brain wasn't listening. 'It looks really nice.' He gulped down all the saliva that had gathered in his mouth. 'I'm sorry ...'

Rosie furrowed her brow for a moment and then tilted her head to one side and leant towards him.

'Go on, then,' she said.

All the blood in Sam's body rushed to his fingertips. He closed his hands into fists and stretched his fingers out again to calm the shaking. Then he reached out and took a strand of Rosie's hair between his fingers. Very slowly he pulled until the ringlet was straight – and then he let go. It bounced back and then bobbed around a bit by her head and then settled in with all the other curls.

'Your hair's cool,' he said.

Rosie blushed under her freckles, which made her eyes go an even brighter blue.

'Sam!' His mum's voice bounded across the playground. He looked up and saw her standing on the pavement outside the school gates. 'Sorry I'm late, my darling!' she called over, out of breath.

Now it was his turn to go red. His mum wasn't like the other mums. She preferred wearing boys' clothes and she didn't fuss about her hair or her eyebrows or make-up.

As Sam's mum walked up to them, he watched Rosie look her up and down and prepared himself for that sneering look that the other girls in his class got whenever they saw his mum. But Rosie's eyes went wide and bright and her face opened into a smile – the first proper smile he'd ever seen on her.

Sam's mum looked at Rosie and smiled back. They were acting like they'd known each other for ever.

'Your mum must be busy with the B&B,' Sam's mum said to Rosie. 'Why don't we walk you home? You're right around the corner from us.'

Rosie looked from Sam to Flick and then stood up, brushed

the dust off her black polyester trousers, put her book away in her school bag and skipped along the pavement beside them.

'Rosie would love to help you with your reading,' Sam says.

Jonah goes silent and looks down at the book in Sam's hands. Then he raises his head and says: 'I'd like you to teach me. I'd like you to read this one with me.'

'Maybe Rosie and I could both teach you, how about that?'

Sam holds the book out to Jonah.

Jonah takes it and, for a while, he sits there, on the side of his bed, dangling his legs and hugging the book to his chest. Then, he looks up at Sam and says: 'Do I have to come and live with you?'

Sam looks at Jonah and realises that he hasn't got a clue what to say. Then he makes his face go as bright and cheerful as he can manage and says: 'Why don't you give us a go? See how you like us? If we're not your cup of tea, you can always give us back. Deal?'

Jonah smiles. 'Really?'

Sam gulps. Rosie would kill him for having just said that. 'Yes, really.'

# JULY

# Rosie

'You must be starving.' Rosie puts a plate in front of Jonah.

It's so full of food that the runny mashed potato spills off the edge. The sausages are split and burnt and the baked beans have gone dry.

She should have binned the whole thing and ordered takeaway.

Jonah pushes his plate away.

Rosie wipes her brow.

The Marks and Spencer chocolate caterpillar cake Rosie bought sits uneaten on the kitchen counter; Julie had told them that if there's one thing Jonah would never turn down it was chocolate cake.

Rosie swallows a sigh and looks around the kitchen.

Helium balloons drift up from the chairs. Cards from their neighbours, from some of Rosie's patients and colleagues, sit on the windowsill. Some say 'congratulations' in that vague, cover-all kind of way. Others have animals on the front or boy pictures like a space rocket and cars. It seems there's no 'welcome to your adoptive family' section in Clintons. But still, it was nice of people to think of them.

'Maybe you'd like something else?' She goes to the fridge and scans the shelves stacked with food.

Two hours in Tesco last night to prepare for Jonah's big arrival. Julie had warned them that he ate like a horse.

'I'm not hungry,' Jonah says.

Today is Jonah's first day living with them. *He's our child now,* she keeps telling herself. She wonders whether one day, it will sink in.

Their child who hasn't eaten a thing.

Not the picnic lunch they took out to the park.

Not the afternoon tea and cake at the café on the high street.

Not the snacks Rosie packed in the rucksack Sam lugged around town.

Maybe it's my food, she thinks. Maybe he's worked out that I'm a rubbish cook and it's made him suspicious.

Sam tilts his head to one side and tries to give Rosie an *it's going to be fine* look.

She looks away.

There's a clatter of footsteps outside and then a voice tumbles in through the open kitchen window.

'Daddy, there's a boy in there!'

A moment later, a little girl with white blonde hair peers in. She grins at Jonah.

Jonah looks up. 'Who's that?'

'That's Alice Anderson,' Sam says. 'She lives on the other side of the railway bridge with her dad.'

Rosie remembers the day she delivered little Alice, a home birth in the Swedish couple's beautiful home across the railway tracks. Everything about their lives had seemed perfect.

Lying there, nestled against her mother's chest, Alice had looked so new, she glowed. All newborns had that look, of course, but Alice was special, like she'd come to them from the moon.

Rosie had wondered whether she'd feel like that about her own child one day – that sense of wonder, that sense that a gift from the heavens had just landed in her arms.

Alice's dad appears at the window; he gives Sam and Rosie an apologetic nod and pulls her away.

Half of Bridgeford usually walks past the railway cottage.

Rosie imagines them shaking their heads and whispering behind cupped hands: *That poor, childless couple . . .*

Rosie takes a breath and straightens her spine. Well, all that's going to change now. They have a little boy, sitting right here at their kitchen table. And he's theirs to keep.

## Jonah

Later that night, Jonah sits in the bathtub looking at his wrinkly fingers and wrinkly toes. He's been in the water for an hour. At least here he doesn't have to answer their questions or eat their food or listen to them talking like he's going to be theirs for ever.

He lowers his head in the water and swallows some water by mistake. He gulps and coughs. For the last week, ever since Trudi and Julie sat him down and said he was definitely going to move in with Rosie and Sam, he's found it hard to swallow, like something's really pressing against his throat.

Sometimes, the pressing gets so bad that Jonah feels like he can't breathe.

It reminds him of when he was a little and he got malaria. If it hadn't been for Miss Mary and her healing hands, he would never have got better. Even years later, when he wasn't ill at all any more, Miss Mary would put her hands on his chest and whisper to Mama: *Jonah's got a weakness, don't ever forget that.*

He puts his hands over his ears and tries to block out Sam and Rosie's voices, which float in through the door.

'He must be starving . . . '

'Give him time, love . . .'

'Don't you think I should go in, help him wash his hair . . . ?'

'I think he can manage . . .'

'But I'm meant to help . . . I'm his new mum . . .'

And that makes the pressing in his throat even worse. *Mum?* Jonah doesn't understand what makes Rosie think she can just call herself his mum when they hardly know each other.

Rosie will never be Jonah's mum. She won't even be his pretend mum or his until-he-finds-Mister-Sir-mum.

Jonah takes a big breath and slips under the water.

*Mama*, he calls out. *Mama . . .*

But all he can hear is the clunking of the pipes and the squeak of his body on the side of the tub and the meowing of that silly cat.

He tries to hold his breath a little longer, in case Mama answers this time, but he knows that it's hopeless: she hasn't spoken to him for months. His head goes light and dizzy. But she still doesn't say anything.

*Please, Mama . . .*

There's a pressure on his lungs and his throat's closing up. Stars dance in front of his eyes.

*Mama . . .*

Jonah shoots back up out of the water and gasps at the air. His chest contracts and his head pounds and his throat burns. Water runs down his forehead into his eyes. The water is cold now. His teeth begin to chatter. He brings his legs up and rests his eye sockets on his knees.

Sometimes, Jonah wonders whether Mama's forgotten about him altogether. Or whether maybe Miss Mary, who can heal anyone with her hands and her prayers, hasn't been able to make her better and she's got even more tired and that Mister Sir was right in what he said that last night in the hotel: that she should have gone to one of the hospitals in Nairobi. And that Jonah should have stayed to look after her.

He wonders whether maybe, even if he does learn to read and even if he does learn to be A True English Gentleman, he'll never see her again.

## Rosie

Jonah stands in the doorway of the kitchen, staring at Hop, who's curled up on top of the washing machine.

Wrinkling his nose, Jonah asks: 'Why doesn't Hop sleep outside?'

'He likes to be inside with us, don't you, Hop?' Rosie says.

Hop twitches his ear.

Jonah's brown eyes shine under the kitchen light. His feet are bare; Rosie bought slippers and placed them at the foot of his bed, but he hasn't touched them.

For the past hour, Rosie and Sam have been sitting at the kitchen table, waiting for Jonah to have his bath, brush his teeth and get into his pyjamas. He didn't want their help.

It's his second day and it feels like he's been with them a thousand years – and like he's still a total stranger. He's spent most of the last two days in his room.

'Come on, let's say night night to Hop and then it's time to go to bed.'

Rosie goes over to the door and takes Jonah's hand. She holds on, even though his fingers don't fold into hers.

Trudi said they had to go through the motions of being a family, to act out their roles, even if it felt stilted and hard. *With time, it will all slot into place,* she'd said.

Rosie guides Jonah to the washing machine. 'You can stroke him,' she says. 'He likes to be rubbed on his belly.'

Jonah doesn't seem to hear her. He looks down at Hop and asks: 'Can he run with only one leg?'

'In his own way.'

'Where did you find him?'

Sam comes and puts his arm around Rosie.

'You found him down by the tracks, didn't you Rosie? Christmas, five years ago. He was in a very bad way, Jonah. Rosie nursed him back to life.' Sam leans over and rubs Hop behind the ears. 'But you were destined to be with us, weren't you, Hop?'

Hop purrs, then stands up and head-butts Jonah's hand, angling for a stroke.

Jonah steps back.

Then he looks up at Sam and Rosie and asks, 'What does *destined* mean?'

'It means that someone or something planned for Hop to be with us all along,' Rosie says.

Jonah shifts from foot to foot.

'If Hop was so sick when you found him, why didn't you let him die?'

Rosie stares at Jonah and blinks. Sam's arm tightens around her shoulders.

'Because if you love someone, you help them get better,' Sam says.

'But how did you know you loved Hop?' Jonah asks.

Rosie gulps. 'Sam and I love all animals.'

'*All* of them?'

Rosie looks at a cobweb in a corner of the kitchen. 'I'm not a great fan of spiders but I dare say they deserve to live as much as any other creature.'

Jonah stares at Hop.

'What if an animal doesn't want to live?' Jonah asks.

A train rushes past outside. When it's gone, the three of them stand there in silence.

'What did you say, Jonah?' Rosie asks, hoping she didn't hear right.

'What if an animal wants to die?'

'What do you mean?' Sam asks.

'Maybe Hop isn't happy living with only three legs.'

Rosie thinks of all those babies she's delivered: pink and wrinkly and yelling and gasping at the air.

'In my experience, all animals want to live, Jonah. Even those that are sick or have been badly hurt. And Hop's happy enough.'

Hop settles back onto the towels on the washing machine and closes his eyes.

'Come on, time for bed.' Rosie kisses the top of Jonah's head. He flinches but doesn't pull away.

Jonah tilts his head to one side and looks at Hop. 'I thought cats didn't sleep at night. Isn't night time when they go hunting?'

Rosie and Sam look at each other and laugh.

'Hop wouldn't hurt a fly,' Sam says. 'He's our resident Buddhist, isn't he, Rosie?'

Rosie smiles.

'What's a Buddhist?' asks Jonah.

'Oh, it's just an expression ... ' Sam says. 'Buddhists don't believe in hurting any form of life. Even bugs and spiders.' Sam comes over and puts his arms around Jonah's shoulders. She notices that Jonah leans in a little.

'Goodnight, Hop,' Jonah says in a small, quiet voice.

Rosie's heart skips a beat. She knows she mustn't get carried away by these small victories, that one step forward might be followed by ten steps back. But still, a moment ago Jonah was saying that animals should live outside – and implying that, if they were sick, they should be left to die. Something small has shifted in him. And that's a start.

'It's getting late, Jonah. I think it's time to say night night to Mum and Dad too,' Sam says.

Silence settles over the kitchen. Nothing but the drip, drip, drip of the tap Sam's been meaning to fix for years, and the sound of Hop's rough tongue licking his fur.

Jonah moves out from under Sam's arm and looks down at his bare feet.

'Can I go to my room now, please?'

'Mum was hoping to read you a story,' Sam says. 'Maybe she could read to you from your special book ...'

Jonah keeps staring at his feet. 'I can read my story without Rosie.'

Ten steps back, thinks Rosie.

'It's OK to say *Mum*, Jonah. Remember – like Trudi explained?'

Jonah still doesn't look up.

Sam walks over to him, kneels in front of him and takes his hands. 'And it's OK to call me Dad, too.' He pauses and tries to hold Jonah's gaze, but Jonah's head is hung so low that it's impossible. Sam keeps going anyway. 'We are both so, so happy that you are part of our family.'

'I didn't have to call Julie Mum,' Jonah mumbles.

'Julie wasn't your mum,' Sam explains. 'She was just looking after you for a while until you came to us.'

'I would very much like to go to my room now,' Jonah says.

'OK.' Sam stands up. 'Why don't we both come and read to you, then?'

Jonah doesn't answer but he starts walking up the stairs, so Rosie and Sam follow.

Sam takes Rosie's hand and whispers into her hair. 'He'll come round ...'

Rosie nods, but a sick feeling pushes up her throat. Trudi had said that if they didn't insist on it straight away, he'd fall into a pattern of calling them by their first names and then it would be nearly impossible to go back. Maybe they'd missed the boat already.

When they get to Jonah's door, Jonah says:

'Only Sam.'

'Only Sam what?' Rosie asks.

'Only Sam read with me.' He pauses. 'Please.'

'Oh – OK ...'

Sam brushes his fingers through Jonah's hair and laughs. 'I'm a terrible, terrible reader, remember? Trust me, Rosie's the one you want.'

Jonah shakes his head.

'It's all right,' Rosie says, forcing a smile. 'Maybe I can read to you another night.'

Sam gives her an apologetic look.

She watches Sam following Jonah into his bedroom and then goes to sit at the top of the stairs. Leaning her head against the wall, she listens to the murmur of their voices and then to Sam stumbling over the words in Jonah's copy of *The Tempest*.

*Why, that's my dainty Ariel! I shall miss thee;*
*But yet thou shalt have freedom.*

She still remembers the story from school. Recognises,

immediately, the words of the magician, Prospero, talking to his spirit, Ariel.

Rosie wonders what it is she keeps doing wrong. And that old, nagging thought comes back to her: maybe she just isn't cut out to be a mum.

# FIVE MONTHS EARLIER

## *February*

# Jonah

'Will I see him?' Jonah asks.

Trudi comes and sits beside Jonah on the sofa in the police station waiting room. They've been here for ages.

'See who?' Trudi asks.

'Mister Sir.'

Trudi closes her eyes for a minute and takes a breath. Then she puts on a smile (which doesn't look like a real smile) and says: 'It's not like that, Jonah. It'll just be you and the policeman asking you questions.'

'Just me and Detective Inspector Peter Taylor?'

'Yes, that's right.'

Jonah isn't sure he wants to speak to Detective Inspector Peter Taylor: he wasn't much help at the airport on the day Jonah lost Mister Sir.

'And there will be a camera too?' Jonah asks.

'Yes, and a camera. So that the police have a record of your answers.'

'Why do they need a record of my answers?'

'For evidence.'

'Evidence for what?'

Trudi pauses and looks up at Julie, who's been pacing up and down, jiggling Mimi on her hip. Jonah heard Julie telling Trudi that she doesn't want Jonah to do the interview. *It'll unsettle him*, she said. But if there's a chance that Jonah might see Mister Sir, then he doesn't mind being unsettled. Not one bit.

'Evidence for the trial,' Trudi says.

'So that Mister Sir doesn't get in trouble?'

Trudi sighs.

Julie comes over and says to Trudi: 'I told you this was a bad idea. All Jonah's evidence is going to do is to help the defence.'

Jonah doesn't understand what *The Defence* means but if it'll help Mister Sir then it has to be a good thing. And if he helps Mister Sir get out of trouble, maybe he'll forgive him for getting lost and take him home.

Detective Peter Taylor comes into the waiting room. It's the first time Jonah's seen him since that day at the airport. Jonah had forgotten about how long his legs and arms were and how shiny his bald head was.

'You ready for our little chat, Jonah?' the policeman asks.

Jonah nods. He stayed up late last night thinking about all the things he wanted to tell the policeman and the camera.

'You're sure he's properly trained?' Julie whispers to Trudi.

Peter Taylor steps forward and holds out his hand to Julie. 'You must be Jonah's foster mother. I'm DI Peter Taylor and I'll be conducting the interview. Delighted to meet you.'

Julie shifts Mimi to her other hip and shakes his hand.

'I can assure you that I'll take good care of Jonah. Working with children formed part of my training.'

Jonah thinks that's a pretty strange thing to be trained in.

Julie goes red and says. 'Of course, of course.'

Then DI Peter Taylor turns to Jonah and says: 'You'll be back with Trudi and Julie before you know it.'

'And Mimi?'

The policeman looks at Mimi sitting on Julie's arm and his face softens. He tickles her under the chin and Mimi giggles and buries her face in Julie's armpit.

Jonah didn't expect the policeman to like babies. And from how Trudi's frowning, she didn't expect it either.

*Maybe he's OK after all*, thinks Jonah.

'So we wait for him here?' asks Trudi.

'Yes please. Like I said, we won't be long.'

Trudi goes over to the policeman and whispers: 'Go easy on him, Peter.' Only Trudi isn't very good at whispering and everyone can hear her. And then she keeps not-whispering, saying: 'And for goodness sake make sure you nail the guy.'

Jonah likes Trudi very much but he doesn't like how angry her face goes every time she talks about Mister Sir. And he definitely doesn't like the thought of Mister Sir being nailed.

The policeman doesn't say anything back to Trudi, so maybe he agrees with Jonah about not wanting Mister Sir nailed. Instead, he goes to the door of the waiting room and holds it open for Jonah.


The interview room isn't like any of the other rooms Jonah saw as they walked through the police station. It's got sofas with teddy bears on it and the walls are yellow like the sun is shining on them, even though it's raining outside. And the carpet feels soft under Jonah's bare feet – much softer than Julie's carpet. And there's a bowl of sweets that look like coloured beans on the coffee table. Jonah would like to eat some of them but he knows that he has to wait to be offered them first.

The only thing that's a bit strange is the camera set up on big steel legs in the corner.

'Make yourself comfortable, Jonah,' the policeman says, as he fiddles with the camera.

Jonah sits down on the edge of the sofa.

Once he's got the red light beaming out of the camera, the

policeman takes a clipboard with lots of typed paper on it from his briefcase, and comes to sit on the armchair in front of Jonah. He folds his legs over each other, puts a pair of glasses on the end of his nose and looks at Jonah.

'Ready?'

Jonah nods.

'Good. So, let's go back to the beginning. When did you first meet Mister Sir?'

'When I was very little.'

'How little?'

Jonah looks at his fingers and counts them off. Then he holds up five of them.

'You were five years old?' the policeman asks.

Jonah nods. He remembers because the first time Mister Sir came it was in August for Jonah's fifth birthday.

'So you knew him well?'

Jonah nods.

'He was a friend of your mother's?'

Jonah shakes his head.

'He *wasn't* a friend of your mother's?'

'I don't have a mama. I only know Mister Sir.'

The policeman glances at the camera and then makes a note on his clipboard.

'So how did you meet Mister Sir?'

'He came to the beach.'

'Which beach?'

Jonah shrugs. 'Where I lived.'

'Does the beach have a name?'

'I don't remember.' Jonah's not going to tell them about Lamu, otherwise they might go looking for Mama. He's already got Mister Sir in trouble, he's not going to get Mama in trouble too.

'And this man you call Mister Sir, when did he decide that you were going to go to England?'

'The last time he came.'

'The last time?'

'He comes on holiday to the beach. The time before the time when we came over to England, he said that everything was ready for me to come home with him.'

'And did he say what you would do once you got to England?'

Jonah's eyes brighten. 'Yes. I was going to learn to read and to be A True English Gentleman.'

'And where were you going to learn how to do those things?'

'At Mister Sir's house.'

'Did Mister Sir actually say that?'

Jonah thinks back to all the conversations he's had with Mister Sir about England. He can't remember what Mister Sir said exactly but he's sure that was always the plan.

'Mister Sir never said that I *wasn't* going to live with him,' Jonah says, hoping that will help.

The policeman makes another note on his clipboard.

Jonah stares at the sweetie bowl on the table and hopes that the policeman will notice and offer him some, but he's too busy writing.

'Will I be living with Mister Sir soon?' Jonah asks.

The policeman looks up from his clipboard. 'I'm not sure that's going to be possible, Jonah.'

Jonah feels a thud in his chest. 'Why not?'

'It's a bit complicated. Trudi will explain it to you, I'm sure.'

Jonah realises that he has to try even harder to give the right answers: maybe then the policeman will let him go to Mister Sir.

'When Mister Sir was in Kenya, what did you do together?' the policeman asks.

133

Jonah smiles. 'We had fun. We went swimming. And we had Coca-Colas. And he bought me clothes for England.' He tugs on his red woolly scarf. 'And he got my hair cut because he said that people in England do not like boys to have long hair.'

'If you had to describe what your relationship was like to Mister Sir, Jonah, what words would you use?'

Jonah looks out of the window at the rain. After a while he turns back to the policeman. 'He was like a friend . . .' He pauses. 'And a papa.'

The policeman tilts his head to one side and looks at Jonah with sad eyes. Maybe he is sad that Jonah isn't with Mister Sir too.

'If you had to describe Mister Sir, what would you say?'

'He has a funny red beard . . . and a gold watch . . . and he always wears gentlemen's clothing, even when it's really hot . . .'

'What about the things he did and said, Jonah, how did they make you feel?'

'Oh, that's easy. When Mister Sir came on holiday to the beach, everything was always better.' Jonah pauses. His smile goes even wider. 'Mister Sir is kind.'

That's what Mama had always said: *Mister Sir is Kind*. That's why he agreed to take him back to England with him.

A big Adam's apple slides up and down the policeman's throat.

'He was kind?'

Jonah nods. 'Very, very kind.'

For example, if Mister Sir were here now, he'd definitely have offered Jonah some sweeties already.

'Let's turn to the day you arrived in England, Jonah. When you got to the airport. What happened after you walked through the arrivals gate?'

'The gate with all the people with signs and flowers?'

'Yes, exactly.'

Jonah's heart speeds up. This is the bit he got wrong. This is the bit he wants to get right now.

'I got lost.'

'You got lost?'

'Mister Sir went to get me some food and some drink and then I walked outside when I was meant to stay in my seat and then the man called Bruno found me and took me away to a room and then Trudi came and then you came.' He pauses. 'Mister Sir was looking for me and couldn't find me.'

The policeman scratches his head. 'Why did you go outside?'

Jonah bites his lip. 'Because I was looking for Mister Sir.'

'I thought he was buying you food?'

Jonah nods. 'He was. But I like to go for walks and I'd been sitting for a while ... ' Which was a bit true. He did like to go for walks.

'It must have been quite frightening, Jonah, being in such a big place all by yourself?'

'It was very loud. But I wasn't scared. I had Mister Sir.'

And it's true. Jonah hadn't been scared – or not *really* scared. Because he knew Mister Sir would come back.

'Jonah, there's one last question I'd like to ask you. Did you want to come to England?'

Jonah waits a really long time before answering. Because, at first, when Mama told him, he was sad about having to leave her and so he didn't really want to go to England. But if he says that then maybe they'll send him back.

'I knew I would be with Mister Sir,' Jonah says. 'So yes, I wanted to come to England.'

'You wanted to come to England?' the policeman says again.

Jonah nods. 'Yes.'

And then Jonah leans forward and picks up a yellow sweetie bean and pops it in his mouth.

# FIVE MONTHS LATER

## July

# Jonah

On Sunday morning, Jonah looks up at the grey tiles of Bridgeford pool. There's a faded sun painted on the far wall. There are so many people that there's no room to swim, not properly.

The only two things which look even a bit interesting are the slides and the special pool with a sign that says: RESERVED FOR SWIM TEAM. They're doing butterfly stroke at the moment – one girl who's really tiny is going much faster than any of the others.

'Maybe you could try out for one of the teams?' Sam says. 'When you're settled in, I mean.'

'Maybe.'

Jonah wonders whether there's a free diving team here. He'd seen free divers on Lamu and it's been his ambition since forever to be able to hold his breath under water just like them. It's the best kind of magic he's ever seen. But you'd have to have a pool that goes down for metres and metres, like the sea does, and that doesn't look likely. Not in Bridgeford, anyway.

Sam stands with his hands on his hips, his flabby belly sticking out.

'They built the Bridgeford Aquatic Centre about five years ago. People come from all over. We're lucky to have it on our doorstep.'

Jonah wonders whether Sam's ever seen the sea.

'Why don't we go in,' Sam says. 'Rosie won't mind.'

Rosie's still getting changed.

Jonah nods and follows him into the main swim area. While Sam is still easing his body into the pool, Jonah ducks under the water and swims hard. The chemicals make his eyes hurt and there's nothing interesting to look at, not like in the sea, but he's swimming, and for the first time since he got to England his body feels like it's in the right place.

When he gets to the far end of the pool, he pushes his body up out of the water and holds onto the side. His hands and feet tingle and his lungs are wide open.

The most water he's been in since he's arrived was Julie's bathtub and then Sam and Rosie's bathtub, which is even smaller than Julie's.

'Hey – wait up!' Sam calls over.

When Sam gets to him he's red in the face and out of breath.

'Wow, you're fast, Jonah!'

Jonah doesn't think he was fast. Not nearly as fast as he used to be, anyway.

Sam starts waving frantically towards the changing rooms.

'Rosie!' he yells.

Jonah rubs the water out of his eyes, blinks, and looks at Rosie. She stands at the shallow end of the pool in her goggles and her swim hat and her big, chunky, one-piece swimsuit. Her legs and arms are pink and blotchy and there are red marks around her ankles from where her socks have dug in.

'Let's go over,' Sam says to Jonah.

'I like it better here,' Jonah says. He doesn't want to go back to the shallow end where you can't dip under the water properly.

Sam scratches his head. 'Rosie isn't a very confident swimmer, Jonah. I think it would be kind to go over to her.'

'Why not?' Jonah asks.

'Why not what?'

'Why can't she swim?'

'She can swim – just about. It's just that she learnt late—'

'Her mama and papa didn't teach her?'

Sam scratches his head again. 'They were very busy with their business. My mum – your Grandma Flick – taught her a bit.'

'Oh.'

He can't imagine what it must be like not to be able to swim. And then he wonders who Grandma Flick is and when he'll get to meet her and whether he'll have to call her Grandma.

'So, you'll come over with me?' Sam asks.

'OK,' Jonah says and ducks under the water.

He swims the whole length of the pool. Sounds from around the pool echo around him; water rushes over his body and the thoughts that crash around in his head drift away like the bubbles that escape from his mouth. It's not the sea, not even close, but it's the best he's felt since he's come to England. If there weren't those silly walls around the pool, Jonah feels like he could keep swimming forever.

When Jonah gets to the shallow end, he sits, cross-legged, on the bottom of the pool, his head only just covered by the water.

He hears voices above him.

'He's been down there for a long time . . .'

Rosie's voice.

'Oh, he's a real little fish. You should have seen him at the deep end.'

Sam's voice.

Jonah's head starts going light and fuzzy from holding his breath.

A moment later, Rosie's face appears in front of him underwater: it's big and pale and too close. She's trying hard to smile. Then she runs out of breath and pushes herself back up out of the water.

Jonah stays down for a bit longer. It's only when his lungs start burning from holding his breath for so long that he floats back up to the surface.

141

Rosie's gasping at the air, her face red. She can't have been down for more than thirty seconds. That's nothing. Mama could stay down for at least two minutes.

'I'm going to the loo,' Sam says. 'I'll come back and find you.'

Sam's always finding excuses to leave them alone together: going to his studio in the garage; going out to get milk at the shops even though there's lots of milk left in the fridge; going off to talk on the phone to his agent about the Ascot horse he's making. Jonah knows that it's because Sam wants Jonah to spend time with Rosie. And he knows it's because he wants Jonah to see her as his mama.

But Jonah prefers spending time with Sam.

And having a new mama was never part of the plan.

## Rosie

Rosie watches Sam heading back into the changing rooms and wishes he'd come back. At first she'd been grateful for Sam's attempts to leave her alone with Jonah but for a while now, every time he stages an exit, it's like he's setting her up for a massive fall. The subtext is clear: *Get him to love you . . .*

'Can we go on the big slide?' Jonah asks Rosie.

Rosie pokes a strand of curly hair back under her swim hat.

'Maybe we should wait for Sam to come back,' Rosie says.

'I would like to go now, please,' Jonah says.

Rosie bites her lip. *'Now?'*

She'd hoped that maybe they'd spend a bit of time splashing

together in the shallow end. And if he decides to swim rather than walk over to the diving board, she won't be able to follow.

'Yes please,' Jonah says.

Rosie looks over at children and grown-ups whizzing down, screaming, and sinking into the big, deep pool at the foot of the slide. Her heart sinks.

'I can go on my own,' Jonah says.

Rosie looks over at the long queue snaking round the foot of the slide. There are several children, younger than Jonah, who seem to be standing there without parents. Maybe he'll be OK.

'*Please*,' Jonah says.

'OK, I'll stay here so Sam knows where to find me and then we'll come over and wait for you at the bottom of the slide.'

Jonah gives her a huge grin and her heart melts. She wishes she could do more things to make him happy.

For a moment, Jonah doesn't move. He looks at Rosie and then he looks up and down the pool and then turns to face her again and says:

'You need to pretend that you're a dolphin.'

'A dolphin?'

'If you want to learn how to swim, you've got to pretend that you're a dolphin. Then you won't be scared of the water.'

The back of Rosie's eyes sting. 'Is that so?'

'Yes.'

She touches his arm lightly. He doesn't pull away.

'Well, I'll bear that in mind. Thank you, Jonah.'

Jonah smiles again. 'Maybe you can practise while I'm on the slide.'

Rosie sniffs back the tears, glad that her face is already wet from the pool.

'OK,' Rosie says.

Before she has the chance to say anything else, Jonah dips under the water and a moment later he's at the far end of the pool, climbing over the side.

Sam was right to suggest they come swimming; Jonah looks at home in the water.

As Jonah walks off, Rosie's gaze is diverted to the baby pool. A group of mothers sit bobbing their babies up and down into the water. One of the mums places her hands under her baby girl's back and swirls her across the surface of the water. The baby looks up at her mum like no one else in the whole world exists.

The mum and the baby, they know each other, Rosie thinks. *Really* know each other.

Before her friends had stopped tippexing baby stories out of their conversations when Rosie was around, she remembers how a school friend admitted to feeling like her baby was a stranger. *It surprised me, you know,* she'd said. *After having carried him around for nine months. I thought I'd know everything about him – that I'd be able to read every frown and blink and gurgle.*

Then she'd leant in and whispered like she was divulging a government secret: *But you know what? They're strangers. They really are. You have to get to know them, just like you would any other person.*

The difference was that Rosie's friend had carried her baby for nine months. She'd looked into his eyes within a few seconds of him being born. She'd seen his first smile. She'd comforted him when he cut his first tooth. And she'd held his hand when he took his first step.

Seven years. Rosie had missed out on *seven years* of Jonah's life.

Her friend didn't have a clue what it meant for your child to be a stranger.

'Where's Jonah?' Sam swims up behind her, startling her.

Rosie looks away from the baby pool. 'Jonah? Oh, he wanted to have a go on the slide.' She points to the queue of children snaking around the foot of the slide.

Sam squints. 'I can't see him.'

'He probably just got caught behind one of the bigger kids. I said we'd go over and watch him come down.'

Sam nods, turns to her. 'So did you have a bit of a swim together?'

'Sort of.' She pokes another stray curl back under her swim hat. 'He said I should pretend to be dolphin. That I'd feel less scared.' She smiles.

Sam grins. 'That was nice of him.'

She nods.

He leans forward and kisses her. She closes her eyes and is transported back to Criccieth, to their first kiss. They were twelve years old, sitting on the edge of the water, their toes buried in the wet sand. She remembers the saltiness of his lips and the warmth of his arms and how she'd wanted that kiss to go on for ever.

Maybe, now that they've got Jonah, things will be better between them. Maybe they can recapture that time when they believed that life was going to be good.

Sam pulls away.

'Let's go and watch Jonah come down the slide,' he says.

Rosie nods. 'Sure.'

They trudge through the shallow end of the pool, climb up the ladder and walk over to the slide.

Rosie scans the queue. Sam's right, Jonah isn't there.

'Maybe he came down while we weren't looking,' Sam says.

Rosie shakes her head. 'I would have seen him.'

But she's got a hollow feeling in the pit of her stomach. They should have waited for Sam. She shouldn't have let him go on his own.

'Why don't you stay here and I'll have a little scoot round. He's probably just gone to try out another pool.'

'He wouldn't just go off,' Rosie says. 'I told him that we would wait for him.'

'So, when you were Jonah's age, you always told your parents where you were going?'

Rosie didn't need to tell her parents where she went. First, because she only ever went to one place: Sam's house. And second, because they didn't really care.

'Just go and look for him, Sam.'

Rosie realises she's raised her voice. People are staring. She imagines how she must look to them: a dripping, panicked mess who can't even keep track of her child.

Sam had always assumed that Rosie would be a great mother. That it would come naturally. Because if you want something that badly, you're meant to be good at it, aren't you?

But it looks like she can't even get the basics right.

Without saying a word, Sam turns and walks off.


## Jonah


Jonah pushes through the plastic slats, which lead to the heated outdoor pool.

It feels even better out here, with the air on his skin and his body in the water. He can pretend that it's the sea, that it goes on for ever.

He swims to the far end of the pool and sinks under the water.

He stays there until his lungs feel like they're going to explode and then he pushes back up to the surface. For a while he floats on his back and looks at the sky, at the clouds racing across the sky.

He flips over onto his tummy, ready to do another lap around the pool, but his legs start to tingle and then they go numb and his arms won't work properly either. Goosebumps flare across his skin. The bits of his body that are outside the water feel frozen. And his throat feels tight and it aches every time he breathes and swallows.

He treads water and rubs his eyes. The edge of the pool blurs in and out of focus.

Taking a big breath, Jonah tries to propel himself through the water, but nothing in his body seems to work. His heart speeds up and his head goes light and dizzy.

*I have to make it to the edge,* he says. *I have to.*

A face appears in front of him. Skin as pale as paper and short, scruffy, white-blonde hair.

A moment later, the little girl's arm lock around his chest and he feels himself being dragged across the pool.

When he's sitting on the edge again, his breathing fast, his head pounding, he feels a small hand on his back.

'Do you have asthma?' the girl asks. 'I have asthma,' she says. 'You could borrow my inhaler.' She chews on her lips and looks across the pool like she's trying to work things out. 'Or maybe you had a panic attack. I've never had one of those but I've read about them.' She touches his forehead. 'Ouch – you're hot. Maybe you're coming down with a fever.'

The girl's words spin around in Jonah's head. He doesn't know why he's not feeling well. Or what asthma is or a panic attack.

Jonah looks into the little girl's blue eyes. He feels like he's seen her before but he can't quite place her.

'Thank you for getting me out of the water,' Jonah says.

'That's OK. I've done a life-saving course. And when I'm older, I'm going to be a doctor. I'm going to save lots and lots of people's lives.'

Jonah's never heard anyone cram so many words into a sentence.

'Shall I get your mum and dad?' the girl asks.

He shakes his head. 'I'll be fine.'

But his hands are trembling and his head feels like it's going to split in two and despite what the girl said about his forehead being hot, he can't stop shivering. And his legs feel so wobbly that he wouldn't be able to get up and walk away, even if he wanted to.

'You don't look fine.'

Jonah notices that the girl is wearing a full wet suit, like the divers sometimes do back on Lamu.

'It's for the chemicals,' the girl says, looking down at her suit. 'I've got sensitive skin.'

She grins and then he remembers. Her face at the window of Sam and Rosie's cottage. How she'd stared at him like she knew him. Just like she's doing now.


## Sam


'What are you doing here, Jonah?'

Jonah sits on the bench of the changing room, fully dressed, his hair dripping. He's wound his red scarf tight around his neck. And he's shivering.

Sam comes to sit beside him, puts one arm around Jonah's shoulders and rubs his back with the other.

Jonah leans his head into Sam's chest.

Relief washes over Sam: they found him. And he's safe.

He draws Jonah in tighter. But then, as Sam closes his eyes, a new dread settles in. They found him *this* time. He's OK – *this* time.

It's Sam's job to look after Jonah, but as he sits here, holding onto this shivering little boy, he realises that he hasn't got a clue how to do that.

'What happened, Jonah?' Sam asks. 'We were looking for you everywhere.' He pauses to calm his tone. 'We were worried.'

The only reason they found him was because Alice Anderson, the little girl Rosie delivered all those years ago, came up to them and explained that she'd found Jonah in the boys' changing rooms.

'Jonah?' Sam prompts.

Jonah looks at his feet. Sam follows his gaze and notices that, for once, he's put his shoes on.

'Didn't you hear the announcements?' Sam asks. 'The pool manager has been calling out your name for ages.'

Jonah looks up at him. 'Could we go now?'

'Go home?'

Jonah nods.

'You don't like the pool?'

Jonah looks back down at his shoes and mumbles:

'I did . . . at first . . . '

'At first?'

'But then . . . ' Jonah takes a breath. 'When I was swimming outside . . . '

'Outside?'

'The outside pool, I got tired . . .' Jonah's voice chokes up. He squeezes his eyes tight and shakes his head.

'You can tell me, Jonah. What is it?'

Jonah slumps his shoulders.

'I couldn't swim any more,' he says. 'I didn't think I'd be able to make it back.'

'Oh, Jonah . . .'

Of course he's tired, thinks Sam. Every night this week, when Sam's woken up in the middle of the night to do some work in the garage, he's seen the light on under Jonah's door.

'Everything's rather new for you lately, and you haven't been sleeping that well, have you?'

Jonah doesn't say anything.

'And you don't get much energy into that tummy of yours, do you?'

Jonah shakes his head.

'Well, then it's normal that you ran out of steam.'

'But I'm good at swimming.'

'Yes, yes you are. Very good.'

'I never used to get tired.'

'Before you came to England?'

He nods.

'Swimming's something I can do.'

Sam knows how that feels. To have one thing in your life that doesn't feel like a struggle and how horrible it is when even that doesn't come through for you. During those years of fertility treatments and IVF, he barely picked up a piece of driftwood.

'Why don't we go and find Rosie to let her know you're OK and then we can go home and warm up. We'll come back another day and take it a little slower. You'll see, you'll soon build up your strength again.'

Jonah nods but doesn't look up.

'It's going to be OK, Jonah.'

Sam walks to the door of the changing rooms, which leads out the pool. Then he turns round and calls over.

'You'll stay here, won't you, Jonah? You'll wait?'

Jonah nods.

Sam finds Rosie talking to one of the lifeguards.

'He's in the changing room,' Sam says when he reaches her. 'He's fine.'

Rosie folds her arms across her chest. 'He went back to the changing room all by himself?'

The lifeguard excuses himself and goes off to deal with a group of teenagers trying to get into the baby pool.

'He said he was tired,' Sam says. 'It was probably all a bit too much for him.'

He puts his arm around Rosie's shoulders, draws her in and kisses her head. 'It's all OK now,' he whispers into her tangle of wet curls.

But things don't feel OK. As he stands there, holding Rosie, he realises that it's not just Jonah he has to look after, it's Rosie too. And he's even more scared of getting that wrong.

'If he was feeling tired, why didn't he come and find us?'

'It'll take a while for Jonah to trust us,' Sam says. 'We'll work on it, love.'

But as they stand there, surrounded by the noise of kids shouting and splashing, Sam wonders whether Jonah will ever see them as his parents. And whether he'll ever feel anything close to a dad.

# THREE MONTHS EARLIER

## April

# Trudi

Trudi runs out into the streaming rain and throws herself into the front seat of her Peugeot. She grips the steering wheel to calm her shaking hands.

As she thinks about how she's about to see Robin Morse for the first time, she realises that ever since she met Jonah on Christmas Day at Heathrow Terminal 3, she's been angry – no, scrap that: she's been bloody furious. Trudi's seen too many grown-ups mess up the lives of children. Robin Morse with his big house and his happy family and his well-paid job doesn't get to do this to Jonah and get away with it.

The offences are clear, Peter explained it to her: child cruelty through wilful abandonment of Jonah at the airport and aiding illegal immigration to the UK. All the evidence shouts loud and clear that he's guilty. And, come the trial, Jonah's video interview is bound to move the judge and jury towards a guilty verdict.

Yes, it's all going to turn out fine. And then she can focus on finding Jonah a new family.

Trudi turns out of Faircross Avenue, presses on the accelerator and speeds through an orange light.

'Please take a seat over there,' a court official says, nodding at the long rows of plastic seats in the waiting area of Isleworth Crown Court.

'I've been sitting *over there* for the last hour. The hearing was meant to start at 11am.'

The official looks up from her computer screen. 'There's been a delay.'

'What kind of delay?'

'The lawyers will be out soon.'

'What do you mean, the lawyers will be out soon – from where?'

'I'm afraid I'm not at liberty to give you more information at this time.'

She sounds like a robot.

'If the court proceedings have started, I should be allowed into the public gallery.'

She needs to see Robin Morse facing justice.

'I'm afraid you'll have to wait,' the court official says.

'Fine.'

Trudi goes back to the waiting area, slumps down on a chair and gets out her phone. She sends Peter a text:

*What's going on?*

He was meant to be here too. He interviewed Jonah. He was the first DI on the scene.

She waits for an answer but her messages stay empty.

When all this is over, she's planning to go and speak to Jonah. She has to put his fantasy about Mister Sir to rest, once and for all so that they can focus on finding him a family. A family who loves him and gives him the chance of a real future, a million miles away from Islesworth Crown Court.

Damn it, someone has to tell her what's going on. She picks up her phone again and selects DI Peter Taylor's number.

Trudi watches a bunch of men in robes and wigs walking out of the court room where Robin Morse's trial was due to take place.

She jumps to her feet. 'What's happening?' She grabs at the arm of one of the barristers. He looks up at her.

'Why's everyone walking out?' she asks.

The man drops his shoulders. 'Last minute plea bargain.'

Blood shoots up to the surface of Trudi's skin. 'A plea bargain? What the hell?' She tries to steady her breath. 'Wasn't the trial date meant to be set today?'

'He's been sentenced.'

Trudi's heart jolts. 'He has? When?'

'Just now.'

'And?'

'Ten months in Wormwood Scrubs. Might get out earlier on good behaviour.'

'*Ten* months – that's nothing.'

'Look, I'd better go,' the barrister says and before she has the chance to stop him, he disappears down the corridor.


## Trudi


'You're soaking,' Peter Taylor says, smiling at Trudi from behind his desk.

A pool of water forms around her feet. She had to park miles away from Hounslow police station. And she didn't have an umbrella.

'Why weren't you at court this morning?' she asks him.

He leans back in his chair and folds his arms behind his head. 'I was told not to bother coming in.'

Trudi feels water dripping from her plaits, down her neck and into her shirt. She'd made an effort to look smart for court.

'Told by whom?'

'The prosecution.'

'And you didn't think to contact me?'

'I'm sorry, it's been a busy morning.' He pauses. 'Look, I didn't know you were going to be there.'

'You think I'd miss seeing Robin Morse sentenced?'

'I'm sorry.'

Trudi sneezes. Then gets a packet of tissues out of her dripping handbag and blows her nose hard.

'Do you want a towel?' Peter asks.

She glares at him.

'Or a coffee . . . ?'

She still doesn't answer.

'Or maybe something else?'

'What I want,' Trudi says, throwing the balled-up tissue into DI Peter Taylor's bin, 'is for someone to explain to me how Robin Morse got away with this.'

'He hasn't – not really.'

'Anything could have happened to Jonah. *Anything!*'

'Would you like to sit down?' Peter stretches out his arm towards the chair in front of his desk.

Trudi looks at the chair. She's exhausted. And her feet are killing her from wearing those stupid, stupid heels. But she's not going to sit down. Sitting down means that everything's OK – and it's not OK. Not even close.

'No, thank you.'

'You knew that a plea bargain was a possibility.' Peter tilts his head to one side in that patronising, *there-there* way policemen and teachers and nurses do. And social workers too. But she doesn't. Trudi never makes people feel pitied.

She shakes her head. Water flicks around her. 'A *theoretical* possibility, maybe. But you said he plead guilty – at the pre-trial preparatory hearing.'

'So he changed his mind.'

158

'He's allowed to do that?'

'He was in shock. He was terrified of going to prison. Of all this coming out in the press – of course he pled not guilty.'

'And, what happened?'

'He got some good legal advice.'

'"Good"?'

'Good for him. His legal team worked out a strategy for lowering the sentence and for minimising the damage to his reputation.'

'So he admitted that it was his fault, then? That's what a plea bargain is, right?'

'Sort of. He plead guilty to child cruelty and was let off for aiding the entry of an illegal immigrant.'

'But ten months – that's *nothing*, Peter, and you know it. This should have gone to trial.'

Peter stands up, lifts his jacket from the back of his chair, and walks over to her.

'You're going to catch cold,' he says. 'If you don't want a towel, at least take this.' He adjusts his jacket on her shoulders; it's so big it makes her feel like a little girl again, wearing her father's coat on cold nights in Uganda.

All the strength seeps out of Trudi. She takes off her heels, places them on the floor, and stumbles to the chair.

'Explain it to me, then,' she says. 'How something like this happens?'

Peter goes back to sit behind his desk.

He leans forward and looks Trudi in the eye.

'He was worried about the publicity of a trial.'

'Of course he was.'

'Robin Morse is a well-respected businessman. He gives generously to charities carrying out aid work in the countries where he has hotels. And he's a family man, he wanted to spare his wife and kids from the media attention. You know how it is,

159

Trudi – *White Male Smuggles Small African Boy into England:* the tabloids would have had a field day.'

'And he didn't want his wife to know about his relationship to Jonah's mother either, right?'

'Right.'

'And that would have come out, at trial?'

'Probably, yes.'

Trudi shakes her head. 'So why does Robin Morse get what he wants while Jonah's left on his own, in a country he doesn't know, without a single friend or relative . . . ?'

'I know it doesn't seem fair.'

'For Christ's sake, Peter, he's a criminal.'

Peter runs his fingers through his thinning hair.

'He said he agreed to take the boy to England as a favour to Jonah's mum. That Jonah was meant to be picked up by his aunt – only the aunt never showed up.' He pauses.

'You buy that?'

'It's not uncommon for African children to be sent to live with their relatives. Though Robin Morse claims it was a set-up. That there never was an aunt.'

'So why did he just leave? Why didn't he take Jonah home with him?'

'Seriously, Trudi? He panicked. He was terrified that he'd get in trouble for bringing Jonah over here, that he'd be accused of being a child trafficker or something. And he couldn't very well take Jonah back to his wife and kids, could he?'

Trudi laughs coldly and shakes her head. 'You want me to feel sorry for him?'

'Of course not. But I want you to see the whole picture. He's got a clean record. The guy's never even had a speeding fine. Like I said, he's given away millions to charity. And it's the first time he's done anything like this. And he's unlikely to do it again – he has no reason to. He wasn't gaining anything from taking Jonah over to the UK. In fact, he was risking a hell of a lot in doing Jonah's mum a favour.'

'But he abandoned a seven-year-old child. What kind of a man does that?'

'Like I said, he got scared.'

Trudi jumps back onto her feet. Her shoes squelch and she notices a big, bum-sized wet patch on the chair.

'*He* got scared?' she yells. '*He* got scared? What about Jonah?'

'It was stupid of him to run – to think that he could get away with it. But he didn't know what else to do.' He pauses. 'And, up to that point, he'd treated Jonah well.'

'How do you even know that?'

Peter doesn't answer.

'Peter – how do you know that?' Then it hits her. Jonah's video interview.

She wants him to say it: that his stupid video idea has helped to get Robin Morse off the hook.

'It was Jonah, wasn't it? What he said on the video?'

Peter nods.

Trudi shakes her head. 'So his words helped the defence.'

'He idolises the guy, Trudi.'

'That's a classic symptom of abuse.'

'I don't think there was any abuse here.'

Trudi leans forward and eyeballs Peter. 'Whose side are you on?'

He blushes. 'Trudi . . . '

'Seriously, Peter? Whose side are you on? Because from where I'm standing, you're sounding very much like one of Robin Morse's overpaid defence lawyers.'

Peter stands up, walks round his desk and puts a hand on her shoulder. 'You must be exhausted . . . let's go and grab a coffee.'

Trudi shakes him off, picks up her bag and heads to the door. Before she goes she turns to look at him one last time. 'What about Jonah? Has anyone thought about him in all this? The trial was meant to bring closure for him, too.' She pauses. Her hands are shaking. 'Jonah's the one you should be defending, Peter.' Trudi opens the door.

'You forgot your shoes!' Peter calls after her.

But she's already slammed the door on him.


## Jonah


'We'll leave you to it,' Julie says.

Jonah watches Julie swing Mimi up onto her hip. Then she closes the lounge door behind her.

He doesn't know why Trudi is here. Or why she looks so upset. Or why she's so wet either. Her straggly plaits are dripping and so are her clothes.

'I need to talk to you about something important, Jonah.'

Jonah's chest goes tight. When grown-ups want to talk about something important, it's usually something bad.

Trudi comes and sits next to him on the sofa.

He turns one of Mimi's plastic Peppa Pigs round and round in his fingers. One of Peppa's arms has been pushed in so far that it's disappeared into the armhole and Mimi begged him to fix it.

'You know that we found Robin Morse – Mister Sir – a few weeks after you arrived in England?'

He nods.

'And you did that video interview with Detective Taylor?'

He nods again.

'And we told you there was going to be a trial? So that we could find out what happened when you came over to England?'

Jonah's told them already. A million times. He doesn't understand why there had to be a trial.

'Well,' Trudi goes on. 'Today was meant to be Robin Morse's trial.'

Jonah wishes she wouldn't call him that. Robin Morse makes him sound like a stranger. Mister Sir is his proper name. That's what he and Mama always called him.

Jonah shakes the Peppa Pig harder and then squints and looks into the small hole where the arm is meant to be.

'Jonah?'

He looks up at Trudi. Her plaits have gone frizzy and her clothes are all wet. And she doesn't have any shoes on.

'I'm not going to live with him, am I?' Jonah asks.

He's been thinking it for weeks now. How, if Mister Sir really wanted him to come and stay, he would have found a way to get him, especially as he knows that he isn't lost any more.

'No, no you're not, Jonah.'

'Because I got him in trouble?'

'In trouble? Oh, Jonah. No, you didn't get him in trouble. Quite the opposite.'

'The opposite?'

'What you said to DI Taylor means that Robin Morse won't be in prison for so long.'

Jonah's eyes go wide and his heart speeds up. 'Mister Sir is in *prison*? But he didn't do anything wrong!'

'He did, Jonah.' Trudi's voice is hard and cold and not at all like her usual voice. 'He did many things wrong. I know it's hard to understand . . .'

'But we have to get him out. And then I can go and live with him . . .' Jonah's voice is frantic.

He looks down at the Peppa Pig and shakes it hard. That stupid arm.

Trudi takes the figure out of Jonah's hand and places it on the arm rest of the sofa. Then she wraps his hand in hers.

'Listen to me, Jonah. You were never meant to live with Robin Morse.'

'Yes, I was.'

Trudi shakes her head. Her eyes have gone watery. 'I know you think you were but he has his own family to look after. His own wife and his own children.' She gulps. 'I know it's hard to hear, but he never planned for you to come home with him.'

'I don't believe you!' Jonah's voice cracks.

Jonah stares at a stain on Julie's carpet and replays all the conversations he had with Mister Sir and Mama in Kenya –and then with Mister Sir on the plane and at the airport. He's sure they'd talked about it, how Jonah was going to live with him in his big castle – but he can't hear Mister Sir's voice in his head.

Trudi gets out a soggy tissue from her pocket and blows her nose.

'I could kill him,' she says under her breath.

Jonah notices a thick tear rolling down Trudi's cheek. She doesn't bother to brush it away. He's used to her booming voice and her strong opinions and her clumpy way of walking. Seeing her crying like this doesn't feel right. And it makes his eyes sting too.

He blinks his eyes to try and make the tears go back in. Then he asks her: 'So what happens to me now?'

Trudi puts her arms around Jonah and draws him in tight.

'We'll work it out, Jonah. We'll work it out.'

# THREE MONTHS LATER

*July*

# Rosie

'Jonah?' Rosie knocks on Jonah's door. 'Can I come in?'

No answer.

It's Jonah's first day at school and she doesn't want them to be late. They'd debated whether it was worth starting him at Bridgeford Primary when there were only three weeks left of term but Trudi thought it would be good for him to make friends in the community. And teachers said that the work shouldn't be too hard at this time of year, that they were winding down, so he could ease his way in.

But still, Rosie hadn't been able to stop worrying. It would be the first time that he was without either her or Sam.

After tossing and turning for most of the night, she finally fell asleep in the early hours and then woke with a start as the 7.05am rattled past on its way to Paddington.

'Jonah?'

She pushes open the door. It's empty, his bed made so neatly it looks like he hasn't slept in it.

Rosie feels a stab of panic.

'Jonah!' she calls through the cottage.

She runs back to her and Sam's bedroom, in case, by some incredible feat of logic, he snuck in without her seeing him. It's empty too. She dashes to the kitchen.

'Jonah!'

But he's not there.

And he's not in the lounge either.

Or in the bathroom.

She tears out through the kitchen to the garage. The radio hums through the wooden door.

Rosie bursts through the door:

'Sam – I can't find—'

And then she stops. Sam and Jonah are sitting at the workbench, their heads bowed towards each other, a long piece of driftwood in Jonah's hands. A shaft of morning sunlight falls through the tiny window Sam knocked into the back wall of the garage. The light bounces off their hair, both dark, both curly.

Rosie remembers walking in on Sam and his dad like this. In the months before Sam's dad died, he spent hours in the workshop with his little boy, desperate to teach him everything he knew. And, long after his dad had gone to bed, Sam stayed on in the workshop, practising everything he'd learnt. Rosie suspected that Sam thought that, maybe if he picked up all the skills, maybe if got everything right, it would somehow keep his dad alive.

Jonah and Sam look just as much like father and son as Sam and his dad. It feels like a miracle. That they've got a child at last.

And then she feels a pinch. No one would ever mistake her for being Jonah's mum, not in a million years.

Hop sits on the workbench too, lying on a pile of Sam's drawings. It seems that everyone is here except Rosie.

'Jonah – I didn't know where you'd got to,' Rosie says.

Jonah looks up at her blankly.

'He's been helping me,' Sam beams. 'I've been teaching him about the different types of driftwood I'm using for the Ascot horse.'

'This one comes from Africa.' Jonah holds up a piece of driftwood in the shape of an archer's bow.

Rosie looks Jonah up and down. Except for his bare feet, which are blue with cold, he's already dressed: he's put on the uniform she placed on his chair for him last night. He looks so smart. She feels a swelling in her chest: seeing him like this, in his school uniform with its Bridgeford badge, makes her feel that Jonah's a little more theirs.

Rosie goes up to Jonah and smooths down his collar. 'It fits.' She smiles.

Jonah nods.

'I've made pancakes – to celebrate your first day at school,' she says.

Mix from a packet but still, it's more trouble than she's ever gone to for breakfast. Pray to God she doesn't burn them. 'With fresh mango,' she adds.

She'd racked her brain trying to think of types of food that would taste familiar to Jonah and coax him out of his refusal to eat.

'We've had some toast already,' Sam says. He nods to a plate of crumbs next to Hop.

*Did Jonah have any toast?* Rosie wants to blurt out. *Did you even notice?*

'You look tired,' Rosie says to Jonah. Then she turns to Sam. 'How long has he been awake?'

Dark shadows sit like bruises under Jonah's eyes. Trudi had prepared them for this too. That along with a loss of appetite, he might struggle to sleep. That all these were common symptoms of a child making a transition to his new family. Only, after Julie's description of Jonah's appetite and how hard she found it to get him out of bed in the morning, how he slept like a teenager, Rosie can't help but feel that she must be getting something wrong.

'He needed to be fresh for school,' Rosie adds under her breath.

'Oh, he'll be fine, won't you, Jonah?' Sam tussles Jonah's hair.

Jonah gives Sam a sideways smile.

Why doesn't Sam worry? Rosie worries *all* the time. She worries that a misplaced word or gesture could undo days of trying to get Jonah to trust them. She worries that if he doesn't eat he's going to get sick and it will be her fault and Trudi will find out and take him away from them.

Hop gets up, chirrups, wobbles for a second on his three legs, then walks over to her and rubs his face against her hand.

Rosie straightens her spine. *He's my son,* she reminds herself. *And this is his first day of school. Pull yourself together.*

'I thought I'd take Jonah to school on my way to the clinic,' Rosie says.

'That sounds like a great idea,' Sam says. 'Doesn't it, J?'

Since when had Jonah become 'J'?

Jonah bows his head. 'Can't I go with you?' he asks Sam – so quietly that Rosie barely catches it.

Rosie senses Sam hesitating. But they'd talked about this: the need to show a firm, united front, to give Jonah the security of knowing that they made decisions together. To show him that they were good parents.

Rosie catches Sam's eye and holds it.

'I'll pick you up, Jonah,' Sam says. 'How about that?'

Jonah doesn't answer.

'Shall we go and pack your bag?' Rosie asks.

'I've got it here.' Jonah nods in the direction of the backpack that he hasn't let out of his sight ever since he moved in. It's bulging at the sides.

'What have you put in here, Jonah?'

Jonah shrugs. 'Stuff.'

He must have packed everything he owns.

'You don't need much on your first day,' Rosie says. 'They'll give you books and things.'

Jonah's eyes cloud over.

'It can't hurt to be prepared, can it, J?' Sam says.

Jonah smiles at Sam and his body relaxes.

Rosie takes a breath. 'OK then, let's get your packed lunch and then we can go.' She pauses. 'And you'll have to wear shoes.'

Jonah shakes his head.

'You'll get told off by your teachers,' Rosie says.

Though what she's really worried about is what the teachers will think of *her*: a mother who lets her seven-year-old walk through the streets of Bridgeford in bare feet.

Jonah's eyes go wide with panic. 'The teachers will tell me off?'

Rosie feels a pang of guilt. 'I'm sure they'll be understanding on your first day, Jonah, but we don't want to give them a reason to be cross, do we?'

He shakes his head.

'So where are they?'

'In my bag.'

Of course they are. Much as he refuses to wear his shoes, he won't let them out of his sight. It's the same with everything he brought over with him from Kenya.

'Well, let's put them on for now.'

She lifts him onto Sam's workbench and reaches for the bag.

'Don't,' Jonah says, grabbing it off her. 'I'll do it.'

Using his arm to shield her from the contents of the bag, he pulls out his shoes and, very slowly, puts them on.

She feels Sam staring at her. She knows he'd have let Jonah do what he wants. *We've got to pick our battles*, he'd told her. And he wouldn't see wearing shoes as an important battle. But Rosie disagrees: the small things do matter; the small things are what make a family.

*

171

Rosie and Jonah walk down past the station. Hop follows them, weaving his body through Jonah's legs. Jonah steps away from him. She'd thought that having a cat would help them to win Jonah round, but he doesn't seem to want to go near him.

Hop follows them all the way to the park and then gets distracted by a leaf and disappears through a hedge.

Although it's July, and although the sun is breaking through the clouds, it's still freezing.

Jonah looks up, squinting.

'You must miss the sun,' Rosie says.

Jonah keeps looking up and says: 'The sun is like magic.'

'Is that so?'

He nods. 'It vanishes and then reappears brighter than before.'

'That's a nice way to look at it.'

He hitches his backpack up higher on his shoulders. Rosie can tell he's feeling the weight of it.

'Why don't you let me carry that?' She reaches for the shoulder strap.

Jonah moves away. 'It's fine.'

They walk on a little further, no sound other than the trains rumbling past and the slapping of their shoes against the paving stones.

'Do you always wear those shoes?' Jonah asks, staring at Rosie's feet.

Rosie looks down at her white plimsolls. It's true that she's got into the habit of wearing them with everything: her jeans, her comfy joggers at home, with her work uniform. She must have five pairs of these exact same shoes lying around the house.

'I suppose I do,' Rosie says.

'You don't wear heels?' he asks.

Rosie laughs, 'I'd trip and twist my ankle.'

She has a brief picture of herself tottering around at a home birth in a pair of three inch, glittery heels. And then she thinks about leopard-print woman from the adoption fair. And about Lucy.

She can't help but think that things would have been easier with Lucy, the little butterfly girl.

Rosie shakes off the thought and looks back at her shoes, the rubber scuffed, a worn patch above her right big toe.

If there was one thing she hadn't prepared herself for, it was criticism of her footwear.

A bearded man in a business suit rushes past them, his face set hard as he yells into his mobile phone.

Jonah follows him with his gaze and then asks Rosie: 'Did they tell you about Mister Sir?'

Rosie gulps. She knows that Jonah can't just forget about the man who brought him over but every time she thinks about him, her heart jolts. He's the only bridge to Jonah's old life.

'Yes, Trudi told me,' Rosie says.

Trudi had explained how the man who'd abandoned Jonah at Heathrow Airport on Christmas Day, six months ago, was in prison on a short sentence. That it was likely he might get out early on good behaviour. And that they were still pressing him for information about Jonah's background.

It was one of the darkest shadows that hung over this adoption. In all the uncertainty of the previous years, Rosie had assumed that the child they adopted would be theirs to keep. She feels the sting of unfairness that, even now, there's an exception clause to them having a child. That Robin Morse might say something. Or that the DI in charge of the case might find Jonah's parents. Or that they might just show up out of the blue and ask for him back.

She'd tried to draw some information out of Trudi but she'd remained vague.

*We're still looking for her ... Jonah's dad doesn't seem to be in the picture ... Kenya is a big place ...* was all Trudi had said. *It's nothing for you to worry about.*

But what bigger thing could there be for them to worry about? If they came back into the picture, Rosie and Sam wouldn't have a single claim to Jonah. In a few months, Jonah was meant to be legally theirs, but even then, should Jonah's parents appeal, a court could overturn that ruling. And then they'd lose him. She was sure of it.

Jonah goes quiet and they start walking again through the park, past the swings and the slides.

One thing Rosie can't get her head around is why Jonah refuses to acknowledge he has a mum at all. Rosie doesn't know whether this should comfort her (they weren't close, otherwise he'd want to talk about her) or terrify her (Jonah loves his mum so much that he doesn't want anyone to know about her).

Or maybe there's another reason altogether for why Jonah wants to keep his mum a secret.

They walk side by side for a while, in silence.

Then Rosie says: 'You know that Sam lost his faher when he was young?'

Jonah slows his step. 'He did?'

'Yes. From when he was fifteen, it was just the two of them. And me.' Rosie smiles. 'Grandma Flick more or less adopted me.' It's the first time she's used the word *adopted* out loud. But it's true. She became Flick's daughter, much more than she'd ever been her parents' daughter.

'What happened to Sam's papa?' Jonah asks.

Rosie loves the softness of the words *papa* and *mama* and wonders whether one day Jonah might use those for her and Sam. But then she thinks of last night and how Jonah had clammed

174

up when Sam suggested again that he call them Mum and Dad. He wasn't anywhere close to seeing them as his parents.

'He got very sick,' Rosie says. 'No one expected it.'

Rosie remembers how the white house by the sea, where she spent her childhood, went quiet. How Sam refused to leave his dad's bedside: how he'd sit there, polishing bits of driftwood hour after hour, just like his dad had taught him to do. And how, on the day he died, a light went out in Flick's eyes.

It was Melanoma. Within a few months of diagnosis, he was gone.

They turn out of the park and onto the road where Jonah's primary school is.

'Does Sam remember him?' Jonah asks Rosie. 'His papa?'

'Yes, I'm sure he does. So do I.' Her eyes sting. 'He was a wonderful man.'

It was witnessing how much Sam's parents loved each other that convinced Rosie that, one day, she'd marry Sam. Her own parents were business partners. She wanted more from love.

'Did Sam's papa look like him?' Jonah asks.

'Sam's the mirror image of his dad,' Rosie says.

Dark, salt-thick hair. Transparent blue eyes. A smile to break your heart. And his way of being in the world was the same too. *He's just like his dad,* Flick said, whenever they both stood watching them working together on bits of wood. *A quiet way of shaping the world,* Flick called it. *It runs in the male line.*

Flick, too, had assumed that Sam and Rosie would have a child. Someone for her to love, someone to remind her of the man she loved.

'Does Sam still see his mama?' Jonah asks.

'Yes. She lives by the sea too, in Wales. It's where Sam and I grew up. We'll take you to see her sometime.'

Jonah's eyes go wide. 'The sea – really?'

'Yes, the sea.'

'What about your mama and papa?'

Jonah might not have accepted Rosie as his mum but at least he feels able to ask her questions. That should count for something.

'Oh, they used to live there too. They've retired now. They live in Spain.'

Jonah wrinkles his nose. 'Where's Spain?'

'It's a hot country. You'd like it.'

'Why aren't they here, with you?' Jonah asks.

'Oh, they like being on holiday.'

They'd gone straight from being workaholics to spending their days sitting by the pool drinking sangria. Neither lifestyle had space for children, let alone grandchildren.

'They must be happy,' Jonah says. 'Being on holiday.'

'Yes, they're happy.'

Rosie's parents hadn't understood her drive to adopt a child. Or the hell that she and Sam been through for the past ten years. *There's so much you can do without children, just think of the freedom,* her mother had said once, forgetting, as she so often did, that it was her daughter she was talking to.

At times, Rosie feels furious that her parents had her so carelessly. They didn't want a child, not really.

Rosie and Jonah's footsteps fall into sync again and they don't talk much for the rest of the way to school.

The school playground is swarming with children. A jumble of knees and elbows and lunchboxes.

Jonah freezes.

Rosie puts her hand on the small of his back, like Sam does to her when she's nervous.

'You're going to have a wonderful day,' she says.

She wants to hug him but every time she's tried so far, he's gone rigid.

'And if you need anything, you can talk to your teacher and they'll get in touch with me or Sam and we'll be right there. You're never on your own, Jonah.'

Mrs Boon, Jonah's form teacher who Sam and Rosie have met up with several times over the past few weeks, strides across the playground. Her skirt swishes at her ankles, beads swing around her neck, and her grey hair sits in a thick plait over her shoulder.

Alice Anderson skips behind Mrs Boon, her feet so light they barely touch the ground.

'Ah, Jonah, welcome!' Mrs Boon gives Jonah's hand a firm shake. 'Let's go in and meet your new friends.'

Alice steps forward, takes Jonah's hand and shakes it hard.

'I'm Alice,' she chimes. 'Remember?'

Jonah stares at her and blinks.

Alice looks at Rosie and smiles. 'Your mum was there when I was born.'

Jonah keeps staring at her.

Rosie crouches down to Jonah's level. 'Have a wonderful day, Jonah.'

Jonah looks from Rosie to the playground to the schoolhouse, back to Rosie; she can almost hear his heart hammering under his school jumper.

She wants to throw her arms around him so badly it hurts, but she's worried he'll pull away. She leans forward to kiss his cheek but before her lips make contact Alice yanks him away.

'Don't you worry, Mrs Keep, we'll look after him,' she says.

Before Rosie has the time to stand up, Mrs Boon and Jonah

are walking across the playground, Alice skipping behind them, her feather-white hair catching in the wind.

Rosie notices Jonah getting stares from the other children. Games stop. Whispers are mumbled behind cupped hands.

It's normal, Rosie thinks. He's new. And he's starting at a strange time in the academic year. But she knows it's more than that: Jonah's one of the only black children here.

Rosie keeps watching Jonah until he reaches the steps of the schoolhouse. And then it hits her that Jonah's not carrying his lunchbox. He must have forgotten it at home.

'Jonah!' she calls out to him.

A few mothers turn round and stare at her.

By the time she looks back, Jonah has disappeared through the door with Mrs Boon.

Rosie feels like a vital part of herself has been torn out. It's all moving too fast. She's only known Jonah for a few weeks and already she's having to send him out into the world alone. Once those school doors close behind him, she won't be able to do anything to help him. She won't be able to explain the meaning of a difficult word or to give him tricks for learning the times table or tell him that it's OK if he messes up a piece of artwork; she won't be able to tell the other boys in the class to grow up when they whisper about him just because he's new; and she won't be able to sit next to him in the playground at break time, when he's on his own, and to explain that it's normal, that he will make friends soon.

She presses her palms into her eyes.

*He's going to be fine ... he's going to be fine ...* Rosie repeats on the wave of each outbreath.

And then, unable to keep looking, she turns away and walks as fast as she can to the bus stop on the High Street.

An old man sits in the bus shelter, reading his newspaper. He's wearing a yellow corduroy cap, pulled down low to block out the sun.

Rosie sits next to him and sobs.

## Jonah

'It's a real privilege to have Jonah in the class,' Mrs Boon says to the boys and girls sitting around Jonah. Her earrings jangle as she turns her head.

Jonah likes that even though Mrs Boon is old and wrinkly, she wears colourful skirts and jangly jewellery and that she has long hair (even if it is grey), and that she wears make-up, even if her pencilled-on eyebrows make her look surprised all the time.

He thinks back to Rosie with her frizzy hair and her dirty shoes and how she wears trousers all the time. He knows that he mustn't think bad things about people but he's sure Mama would not approve of her: she doesn't seem to make an effort at all.

'Jonah comes from a wonderful, faraway place.' Mrs Boon goes on.

Jonah's stomach flips. He hasn't told anyone where he comes from. That was something else Mama made him promise. Because if they found that out, then they could find her and send him home.

Maybe Mrs Boon doesn't know. Maybe she's just guessing because he doesn't look like the other children.

'He has so much to teach us,' Mrs Boon says, 'I know that you will all make him feel very welcome.'

Out of the corner of his eye, Jonah notices a boy's hand shoot up. He's sitting next to a woman with pink strands in her hair and earrings that make her earlobes go so huge you can see all the way through. The woman's legs don't fit under the desk.

'Yes, Billy?' Mrs Boon asks.

'If the place Jonah came from is so wonderful, why didn't he stay there?'

Mrs Boon blinks.

'I'm just saying . . .' Billy adds.

Billy is not a True English Gentleman. He's not even a True English Gentleman in training.

'Shush,' says the woman with the big earlobes who's sitting next to Billy.

'Because he's an *imitant*, silly.' Alice, the girl with white-blonde hair and see-through skin grins at Jonah. 'Aren't you?'

Alice is sitting on the front row at the desk next to Jonah's. Jonah notices a rash in the crook of her arms. He hopes she doesn't tell everyone about how she saved him at the swimming pool.

Turning to face Mrs Boon, Alice says: 'And there's no food or money in Africa, and everyone's sick – that's why they become imitants and come to England.'

Jonah closes his eyes and swallows. His throat hurts.

He rubs the coin the magician gave him. When it's not in his backpack, he carries it around in his pocket.

*Please make this day go fast,* Jonah wishes.

And then he feels guilty because going to school was the main reason for him coming to England.

'I think you mean IMM-I-GRANTS, Alice,' says Mrs Boon.

She rubs her brow. 'And as I'm always saying, things aren't quite as simple as we first think they are.'

One of the boys sitting behind Billy makes a farting noise through his cupped hands.

The class erupts into laughter.

Mrs Boon blushes and looks at big earlobe woman who pretends not to notice what's going on.

*Why don't you just tell them off?* he thinks.

Although he'd only been to school a handful of times back in Kenya, (Mama's work and the fact that they had to move around so much meant that he never got to stay in any one school for very long), the teachers would never, ever have let the pupils behave like this.

Mrs Boon claps her hands. 'Let's get into our groups for our reading. Jonah, why don't you come with me and I'll show you to your place?'

For the next ten minutes, the classroom feels like the arrivals gate at Heathrow airport: everyone rushing around and crashing into each other.

Mrs Boon gives Jonah a book that only has five pages in it and sits him down at the table with the pink sticker. Billy and the woman with the big earlobes and Billy's farty-mouthed friend and two other boys join them.

Jonah looks across the room and notices that the girl called Alice is sitting at a table on the other side of the room with a gold sticker stuck to the middle of it. Their books are really thick.

She catches his eye and smiles at him. He gets the same feeling from her as he does from Hop: that her .eyes can see right into him. And he doesn't like it.

As Jonah flips through the pages of the book Mrs Boon gave him he notices that there are hardly any words in it at all and that the words there are, are written really big. Maybe the children sitting on this table can't see very well, he thinks. He pulls out his copy of *The Tempest*, hoping that Mrs Boon will take it as a hint that she put him on the wrong table, but she doesn't notice. The only person who does notice is Alice who cranes her neck and reads the cover and then gives him a thumbs up and mouths 'cool'.

After lots more shushing and clapping and Mrs Boon's voice going high-pitched and screechy, the class quietens down and the groups start reading their books.

At Jonah's table, they're taking it in turns to read aloud. When they get to Jonah, earlobe woman interrupts and reads for him.

'Why's Jonah not reading?' Billy says, loud enough for the whole class to hear.

'None of your business,' snaps earlobe woman.

'He doesn't need to practise his reading, Billy. He's helping Miss Gater, isn't he, Mrs Boon?' Alice calls over from across the room.

Miss Gater must be earlobe woman.

Mrs Boon coughs. 'That's right, Alice. Now get back to your own group. And no interrupting, Billy, you'll spoil the flow of the story.'

Jonah looks up at Alice and she gives him an even bigger smile than before. He doesn't smile back. She just made everything a whole lot worse for him.

He's got to do something to show the class that he's not completely stupid.

Jonah turns to Miss Gater. 'Could I read, please?'

Billy laughs, along with the other boys sitting at the table.

Miss Gater's eyes go big and her skin goes so red that even her earlobes glow.

'It's OK, Jonah, I'm enjoying reading this part,' Miss Gater says.

'But I would like to,' Jonah repeats.

Jonah doesn't know how to read, not properly, but he does know how to tell stories, and Mama said that's just as good. And anyway, he's caught the gist of the story from the pictures and from what the boys have read so far.

Back in Kenya, he and Mama used to play this game. When the Mister Sirs and Miss Mary and the priest from church weren't around to read to him, Jonah and Mama sat in bed together and made up stories from the pictures. Jonah thinks that the children in Year Two might like their game.

He sits up straight, swallows hard and puts on his big voice, like Mama taught him:

*'The man was feeling so full of magic that one day, when the sun did not come out, he stretched his finger to the sky and punished the clouds...'*

He decided to blend a bit from *The Tempest* into the story to make it more interesting.

As he looks back to his group he realises that they've all gone really quiet. And that the rest of the class has too. And that they're all staring at Jonah.

'I don't think he has the same book as us, Miss,' Billy says.

Billy's friends snigger.

'Shush, shush,' says Mrs Boon. 'Now Jonah's just doing what I asked you to do the other day in our creative writing class: he's using his imagination.'

'But making things up isn't reading,' Billy says. 'And he said he was going to read. So he lied.'

'Billy, that's enough!' Mrs Boon says.

Jonah doesn't understand why they didn't like his story. He pushes away the silly book.

'That was a lovely contribution, thank you, Jonah,' Mrs Boon says. 'Why don't we ask Matthew to pick up the story?'

'Where am I meant to pick up?' Matthew says. 'Jonah didn't read anything from the book.'

Miss Gater glares at Matthew. And then Matthew glares at Jonah like Jonah's got him in trouble.

Jonah slumps in his chair. School hasn't turned out anything like he'd hoped. Nothing in England has.

## Sam

Sam slips out of bed and walks across the dark landing. He rubs his eyes and checks his watch again. 3am. In the day, he can't stop the minutes from slipping between his fingers; at night, the clock stands still.

Sam's not sure exactly why the insomnia took root, but he does know that his dad always loved to work at night, that he liked the stillness of the world being asleep around him, and that it's the time Sam likes to work too. Even when his dad got sick and had to stay in bed all the time, Sam would sit next to him through the night, talking to him about his day while he chiselled at bits of wood.

Now, when Sam sits alone in his garage, working on a piece of driftwood, he sometimes feels his father leaning over him, a gentle hand on his shoulder, his breath on his neck – close, like he used to be.

Sam looks under Jonah's door. The light's on – again.

'Jonah . . .' He pushes open the door.

Jonah's sitting up in bed, holding a shell to his ear. The moment he notices Sam, he stuffs the shell under the duvet.

Sam comes and sits beside him on the bed.

'How long have you been awake, J?'

Jonah shrugs.

'I find it hard to sleep, too,' Sam says.

'I don't find it hard to sleep, I just want to look at my book.' His gaze shifts to the copy of *The Tempest* lying on his lap.

Two days ago, Mrs Boon called Sam to say that Jonah had fallen asleep in a Maths class. She said she was concerned about how his tiredness was impacting his work.

Sam is concerned, too: some days, the shadows under Jonah's eyes are so deep that he wonders whether Jonah has slept at all. But he's not going to make a big thing of it, especially in front of Rosie. She's anxious enough as it is.

It's like Trudi's always telling them: Jonah needs time to settle in. Once he's got used to everything, his sleep will fall into place.

Sam shifts along the edge of the bed and looks down at Jonah's book.

'Where have you got to?'

Jonah points to a picture near the beginning of the play: an old man in a blue cloak with wispy grey hair and a long beard stands on a beach holding out his hands. His fingers are spread out to the sky and the sea.

'That's Prospero,' Jonah says.

'It is?'

Jonah nods. 'Rosie told me.'

'She did?'

Sam has vague recollections of having to study *The Tempest* at school, but nothing stuck. He suspects that nothing went in to begin with. Rosie would sit next to him in class, whispering what was going on, and she'd write plot summaries for him to help him with his homework. They'd go on long walks along the cliffs and she'd get him to memorise whole chapters of their class reader so that he wasn't embarrassed when he was asked to read out loud. She even kicked a football around with him in the back garden of his mum's house, to build his confidence when they had PE and the boys waited for him to trip over his feet.

He didn't do much for her. Rosie never really needed help. But he did take her for swims. Not proper, far out swims, but small paddles by the edge of the water until her fear of the sea began to recede. And he made her wooden sculptures, hundreds of them: birds and lizards and fish and shells and horses, of course. He would make a whole world for her if he could.

'Rosie's good at explaining things,' Sam says.

Jonah nods. 'She said Prospero is a magician, like Danny from the adoption day.'

Sam feels a swelling in his chest. *At last, Rosie's getting through to him.* He looks at the picture. 'He does look rather like a magician.'

'He made the storm,' Jonah says. 'Do you think Danny can make storms?'

'Maybe . . . ' Sam says. He hasn't yet learnt to navigate the real and the magical in children's lives. Does Jonah still believe in Father Christmas? At least they've got a few months before they have to deal with that one. 'Maybe we could buy a magic set, for a special occasion?'

Jonah's eyes light up. 'Really?'

'I can't guarantee that it will teach us to magic up a storm, but it might be fun.'

Jonah's smile spreads across his face. Sam draws him in to give him a hug, but then he feels a damp patch on his back. It's the third time Jonah's sweated through his pyjamas.

'Oh, J . . . why didn't you tell me?'

Jonah hangs his head.

'We won't be cross, J, you just need to tell us—'

Jonah looks up at him, his eyes wide. 'Rosie gets upset.'

'About what?'

Jonah shrugs. 'About everything.'

'Rosie's never upset *at* you, Jonah, she just worries a bit, that's all.'

Jonah shakes his head again. 'Promise you won't tell her?'

The thing is that Jonah doesn't need to ask: Sam has no intention of telling Rosie. Keeping her happy means keeping her feeling positive about Jonah. The last thing she needs is to be worrying about his night sweats and lack of sleeping. And it'll pass soon.

'Why don't we get you into some clean, dry PJs and I'll pop these in the wash.'

Jonah nods.

'Good, good. Arms up then,' Sam says and pulls Jonah's pyjama top over his head.

Sam stares at Jonah's little body. His belly caves in, his ribs stick out of his chest, his collarbone is as sharp as a clothes hanger. He's sure Jonah didn't look this thin when he first met him at the adoption party.

Sam helps Jonah out of his pyjama trousers and then pulls a new set out from the chest of drawers. It has cowboys and horses galloping across the front.

'Cool PJs,' Sam says, brushing his fingers across the fabric.

'Have you always liked horses?' Jonah asks Sam.

Sam nods. 'I had one when I was back in Wales, after my dad passed away.'

'Do you miss him?'

'My horse?'

Jonah blinks. 'Your papa.'

'Oh . . . ' Sam looks into Jonah's eyes. 'Yes. Every day.'

On the day he got his horse, Sam was meant to be with his dad.

'Come on, we need to get you out of the house,' Rosie said, shoving her feet into a pair of his old trainers. She grabbed his hand. 'Your dad will be OK for a few hours.'

They were all dealing with Alwyn's cancer in different ways. Sam's mum spent longer and longer days in the garden, frantically planting and weeding and trimming and watering. Rosie read millions of books on Melanoma research and wrote letters to cancer specialists around the world asking them if they'd put Sam's dad into one of their trials. And Sam sat beside his dad's bed, day and night. He placed pieces of driftwood and sandpaper on the bed and made his dad feel like nothing had changed – like they were still sitting side by side in his workshop, thinking up new projects.

Sam shook his head. 'Dad's tired today, I'd better stay back.'

Rosie took his hand. 'I've got a surprise.'

Her eyes shone. She loved to think up surprises. And Sam went along with them, because he never quite had the heart to tell her that he preferred to know what was coming.

Rosie leant forward and kissed his cheek. His stomach flipped over.

After that first walk home from Criccieth Primary, Rosie and Sam became inseparable. They grew so close that sometimes it was like they were blurring into one person.

And Sam knew everything about Rosie.

He knew that she wouldn't go further than knee level in the sea, and that she'd want to hold his hand even that far.

He knew that her favourite flavour of ice-cream from Cadwaladers was mint chocolate chip – in a tub rather than a cone.

He knew that her throat got itchy when she ate kiwi.

He knew that she loved Flick more than she loved her own mum.

(He also knew that that she hoped that, one day, her parents might notice that she was never at home.)

He knew that she hated wearing skirts and make-up and heels.

He knew that she burnt every piece of toast she ever made.

He knew that she could read a whole book in the time it took him to read a page.

He knew that she'd always want to stop and look into the prams that mums pushed along the sea front and that her dream was to deliver babies one day.

And he knew her body too.

As children, they'd spent long summers running around under the sprinklers in the back garden. They shared toys and clothes. Most nights, they slept next to each other – Rosie in Sam's bed, Sam on a mattress on the floor. Sometimes both of them on the floor together in a tangle of sheets and pillows.

And so Sam knew how it felt to pull at the soft spring of her curls. He knew how his hand fitted perfectly in the dip at the base of her back, when they hugged. He knew the curve of her cheek, when she bent her head over her homework. He knew how, as soon as the sun came out, a scattering of freckles would appear on her shoulders. He knew that she had a small, dark mole next to the big toe of her right foot.

And he watched her body change too, until, one day, as she stepped out of her school uniform and pulled on a T-shirt and shorts, he realised that it was no longer familiarity that he was feeling, but desire.

'Come on, Sam, it won't take long,' she said, dragging him out of the bedroom.

'OK . . .'

She guided him down the stairs and out of the house. It was late afternoon and the sun was dropping fast into the sea.

'It'll be quicker if we take these.' Rosie pointed at their bikes propped up against the front wall of the house.

Sam's mum looked up, a bunch of freshly picked peonies in her arms. She smiled at them and waved.

'Don't be late back for supper,' she called over.

These days, they had supper in Sam's dad's bedroom. Sam's mum bought a big wooden tray for each of them, and although Sam's dad hardly ate anything any more, they still made up a plate of food for him, and then they'd sit around him and tell him about their days and about news from town. Family meals were the one thing that Rosie and Sam weren't allowed to miss – or be late for.

'We'll be back before you know it!' Rosie calls over.

A moment later, Rosie and Sam were peddling hard along the cliff path.

'Where are we going?' Sam called after her.

'You'll see . . .'

She was going so fast he could barely keep up with her.

They turned off the cliff path and onto a dirt track that led to a farm he knew well. Ever since he was little, his mum had taken him to visit the horses here.

'Why are we here?'

Rosie's cheeks were flushed pink and her eyes glassy from the effort of cycling. The wind had swept her hair into a tangle.

It was dusk now, only the smallest glimmer of light clung to the horizon.

'It's getting late, Rosie, we should head home.'

'This won't take a second,' Rosie said.

The farm looked more or less abandoned. A sold sign stood planted into the earth in front of the main house. It had been happening to lots of the farms in the area. Most of them were being converted into holiday cottages.

Rosie slipped her fingers into Sam's hand and guided him round to the stables. As they got close to one of the stable doors, she put a finger to her mouth.

'Shhh . . .' she said. 'We don't want to scare him.'

'Scare who?' Sam whispered.

Rosie pushed open the stable door. Lying in a pile of hay, a tangle of awkward limbs, was a small grey foal.

Rosie knelt down and stroked his side.

Sam looked around the stable. 'Where's his mother?'

'She didn't make it through the birth,' Rosie said. 'Ariel's on his own now.'

'Ariel?'

She grinned up at him. 'That's what I've named him.'

'You've named him?'

Rosie smiled. She put a hand under the foal's chin and lifted his head, then she took Sam's hand again.

'Ariel, I'd like you to meet Sam – Sam, I'd like you to meet Ariel . . .'

'What . . . ?'

'He's yours, Sam.'

'I don't understand.'

191

'The farmer's selling off all his horses. He wanted to find a good home for the foal – especially as he lost his mum.'

'You *bought* him?'

She nodded, her eyes dancing. 'I've been saving up tips from when I help Mum and Dad at the B&B. And pocket money and birthday money too. And the farmer gave me a special price when I said that Ariel would be living with us, at Flick's, and that we had lots of room for him to run around. That he'd be by the sea. And that we'd take good care of him – that you'd love him.'

Sam had dreamt of having a horse ever since he could remember. That was something Rosie knew about him.

'Does Mum know?'

Rosie nodded. 'Of course, we planned it together. She chipped in too.'

Sam inched forward and took the foal's head between his hands. 'Hello there, beautiful Ariel,' he said.

And then he leant his head against the foal's body. He felt the rise and fall of his ribcage and, somewhere deep inside his body, a new heart beating.

Rosie put her arms around Sam and, for a while, the three of them lay together in the warm hay, night falling around them.

Sam closed his eyes, feeling the warmth of the foal on one side and Rosie's body on the other. And then he lifted his body to sitting and took both of Rosie's hands and looked right into her eyes.

'I love you, Rosie.'

She smiled, sleepily. He eased a bit of straw out of her hair and then leant in and kissed her. He pressed her closer into his body. Then he slipped his hands under her T-shirt. His fingers fluttered across the slope of her stomach, her ribs and then the edge of her bra. Her breath sped up, warm against his neck. And then she found his mouth and kissed him hard.

He unhooked her bra and pulled it off with her T-shirt and lay her gently down into the hay. Then he looked at her, lying there just in her shorts, and he thought about how perfect she was. His perfect Rosie.

A moment later, he lay down on top of her and eased down her shorts and her underwear while she unbuckled the belt of his jeans. And then they fell into each other, into that warm, dark place that he never wanted to come back from.

By the time Sam felt the foal nudging him, it was midnight. He jumped up and pulled on his jeans.

'Rosie! Rosie!'

She stirred but didn't wake.

'Wake up, Rosie — we have to get home.'

She rubbed her eyes and blinked up at him.

'We missed supper. We've been away for hours. Mum will be frantic.'

And Sam was meant to be with his dad. He was always worst at night, it was why Sam sat beside him, every day, from when they finished supper until dawn.

They stumbled out of the stable, grabbed their bikes and cycled in silence through the dark night. The sea crashed against the cliffs below them. A thousand stars shone overhead.

It's the peonies Sam noticed first: they were scattered along the path that lead to the front door. His mum's gardening gloves sat on the front step, her canvas shoes kicked off. The front door itself was swung open.

He didn't wait for Rosie.

'Mum?' he called out as he ran through the house.

His voice echoed against the stone walls of the cottage.

'Mum? Dad?'

He ran up the stairs. None of the lights were on. And there was no light under his dad's door either – and his dad always kept the light on at night.

Sam's whole body was shaking now. He pushed open the door and as his eyes adjusted to the dark, he saw his mum standing by the window, looking out along the cliffs at the sea.

Before he even turned to his dad's bed, he knew that he was gone.

'Can I come and help you make the big horse for Ascot?' Jonah asks.

'It's the middle of the night, Jonah.'

'But you're going to the garage, aren't you?'

Sam shakes his head. 'I'm planning to go right back to bed, I'm exhausted.'

'No, you're not. You're going to work on the horse.' He pauses. 'Like you do every night.'

'I do, do I?'

Jonah nods.

'OK,' Sam says. 'But not for long. We're going to go swimming again, remember? We need you rested for that.'

Sam thought they should persevere with the swimming, so he's been taking Jonah swimming every Sunday. Sometimes Rosie comes with them but Jonah is always so desperate to go into the deep end and to practise holding his breath and to go on the slide and in the wave pool, that she gets left behind. So mostly, now, she stays home.

As Jonah pulls on his pyjama bottoms, he leans back into his bed and a shell rolls off the side onto the floor.

He snatches it up off the ground and shoves it under his pillow.

Sam begins to tuck the duvet in around Jonah's body.

'Do you think you can hear people, even if they're not there – I mean, even if they're not in the same place as you?' Jonah asks.

'I'm not sure . . .' Sam rubs his temples. 'I think we feel things and see things in our imaginations. People we want to see or people who used to be in our lives. It can feel very real.'

He hears his dad whispering beside him at the workbench: *Keep going until it's smooth as water,* he'd say, watching Sam polishing a piece of wood.

'Why do you ask, Jonah?'

'I was just wondering.'

'Right, half an hour, tops,' Sam says, going over to the door.

Jonah jumps up and follows him to the studio.


Sam switches on the garage light and watches Jonah walking across the concrete floor.

He kneels down next to a long piece of driftwood. 'Who gave you this bit?'

'My mum. She found it on the beach outside her house.'

'Your mum who lives by the sea?'

'Yes.' He pauses. 'She's your grandma now. Grandma Flick.'

'What's she like?'

'Bonkers!'

Jonah frowns.

'Good bonkers. She doesn't care much what people think of her – which is a good thing. And she's been really brave, living on her own, without my dad. Especially after Rosie and I moved away.'

'What does she do?'

'Do? Oh, lots of things. She loves to grow things in her garden. And she likes to find pieces of wood like this too.' He pauses. 'She can't wait to meet you.'

Jonah strokes the long curve of wood. 'Which part of the horse will you use this for?'

'The neck. It's the most beautiful part of the horse, or I think so, anyway. It's what makes a horse look elegant and proud and strong.'

Jonah stands. 'Could you teach me? To make a horse of my own – just a little one?'

Sam's heart swells. 'Of course.'

Sam goes over to his workbench and picks up a small piece of driftwood that he's been keeping for a while.

'Here,' he says, holding it out to Jonah.

Jonah comes over. 'Really?'

'Really.'

Jonah takes the bit of wood. Sam hands him a piece of sand-paper too.

'The wood looks smooth already – that's the work of the sea – but you need to make it smoother still. Think of a horse flying through the wind, the lines of his body, how clean they are.'

Jonah nods, holding the bit of driftwood and the piece of sandpaper.

'I don't know how.'

'Here.'

Sam comes to stand behind him. He takes Jonah's hand with the sandpaper and takes his other with the piece of wood. Then he brings his hands together and guides the sanding.

'You need to get into a rhythm.'

Jonah smiles as the wood begins to shine. Sam takes away his hands and lets Jonah sand on his own.

'Why don't we make this your special project,' Sam says. 'You can come and work on it whenever you want.'

But Jonah doesn't hear; he's too absorbed in sanding the small piece of driftwood in his hands.

## Sam

Later that night, Sam shoves the last of the bed sheets into the washing machine, slams shut the door and turns round.

'What are you doing?' Rosie's voice behind him.

She stands in the doorway dressed in her midwife uniform, her curls standing at crazy angles from her head.

'Did I wake you up?' Sam asks.

'I couldn't sleep. Too many thoughts going round in my head.'

Sam nods. 'I know.'

'Why are you doing the washing at three in the morning?' Rosie asks.

Sam sets the dial and hits the start button.

'I was working on the Ascot horse and it just wasn't going where I wanted it to. So I thought I'd do something domestic to get my mind off it,' Sam says, which is at least a bit true.

The washing machine chugs between them.

She leans over and looks through the door of the washing machine.

'Are those Jonah's sheets in there?'

'Yeah, I thought they could do with a change.'

'Didn't you change them a few days ago?'

Sam smiles and shrugs. 'Just getting into this domestic, stay-at-home-dad thing.'

Rosie comes up to him and takes both his hands.

'You're an amazing dad,' she says.

He looks down at Rosie's bare feet.

Only Sam isn't an amazing dad, is he? He's not even a good dad. A good dad would have told Rosie about Jonah's night sweats. A good dad would have found a way to help Jonah sleep and feel better.

On Monday, he'll make an appointment with Dr Barron, the local GP; get Jonah checked out, just for some peace of mind. And then, once Dr Barron says that everything's fine, he'll tell Rosie that there's nothing for them to worry about, that Jonah's still adjusting.

Rosie takes Sam's hands and looks up at him.

'We're doing OK, aren't we?' she asks.

He kisses the top of her head. 'Better than OK.'

Rosie leans her head against his chest. 'I love you, Sam.'

He feels the warmth of her body pressing against his. Her small breasts, the gentle hill of her stomach. He kisses her forehead and then the bridge of her nose and then her mouth. 'Why don't we go back to bed . . .' he whispers through her lips.

Rosie slips her hands under his T-shirt and strokes her fingers up and down his back. She'd done that every time since that first night when they made love in the stable in Criccieth. The night his dad died. They were fifteen. Too young, probably, but at the time, it had felt like the most natural thing in the world.

'Yes, let's go back to bed . . .' she says, her voice light and playful.

In the early days, before they started trying for a child, sex had been good.

They knew what each other needed, how to make their bodies fall into sync. There were nights when Sam felt so close to Rosie that it didn't seem possible that they would wake up and go about their days separately.

Which had made it all even more incomprehensible: surely if their bodies were so physically compatible, they should be able to have a child.

Sam takes Rosie's hand and guides her upstairs.

## Jonah

On Sunday night, Jonah lies in bed, unable to sleep. Hop jumps up and nestles in beside him. He's the most persistent creature Jonah's ever met.

'You can lie there, but I'm not going to stroke you,' Jonah says.

Hop chirrups and squeezes his body in closer.

There's a sharp *thwack* on the window.

Hop jumps off the bed and arches his back. His tail is puffed up like a feather duster.

Then there's another *thwack*.

Jonah climbs over Hop, goes to the window and throws open the curtain.

He looks down into the small garden and, on the swing that Rosie got for Jonah, sits the girl from school: Alice.

The street lamp next to the cottage makes her hair and her skin glow.

And she's wearing pyjamas.

Alice looks up, grins at Jonah, points to the window and mouths: 'Open up!'

Jonah yanks open the window. 'What are you doing here?'

Before he has the chance to finish his question, Alice is climbing up the side of the house, her small feet gripping onto bits of brick that poke out of the wall.

She's like Ariel, he thinks. How he can take any shape. Climb anywhere.

A second later, she's at the window, staring right into Jonah's face.

'Thought you were awake,' she says, beaming.

'You thought I was awake?'

'I've been keeping an eye on you, Jonah.'

She really is weird. No wonder the kids at school keep their distance.

Alice tumbles in through the window and rolls onto the carpet and then springs up onto her feet – just like Hop does.

Jonah stands frozen to the spot, staring at Alice. He hasn't got a clue what to say to this weird girl who's just broken into his room. He looks out of the window at the bit of wall she's just climbed up.

'You could have fallen . . .' he says.

'From that height?' She shakes her head. 'That was easy. I'm a climber.'

'A climber?'

'I go to a club outside school. It's how I get my exercise.'

Alice isn't allowed to do games lessons at school. It's linked to her allergies and her asthma, though Jonah has heard the girls in their class whispering that she's faking it just because she wants to get out of having to do PE.

'Oh.'

'You should come. You'd like it.'

Jonah keeps looking out. 'You came to see me in the middle of the night, on your own?' Sam and Rosie would worry if Jonah walked down the road on his own in the middle of the day.

'Oh, Dad's having a cigarette on the bridge. The smoke makes me cough so I said I'd come and see you.'

Jonah looks out at the bridge that chops Bridgeford in half. It divides the expensive houses on the far side from the not-expensive houses on this side. He squints and sees a figure leaning over the side of the bridge.

'He usually has more than one so we've got a few minutes.'

'A few minutes to do what?'

'To get to know each other better.'

Jonah wonders whether he's fallen into one of those daydreams he has when he's sleepy at school.

He rubs his eyes but Alice is still there.

'Do you go for walks in the dark with your dad often?' Jonah asks.

She nods. 'I get itchy. It's the bed sheets – I'm allergic to most kinds of fabric and most kinds of washing powder. Some nights it's OK, other nights I just can't lie still.'

Jonah wonders whether she gets sweaty too, like he does.

'So why aren't you sleeping? You always look tired at school.'

'Do you always ask this many questions?'

'Always. Dad says that if you're curious you'll never be bored. And if you never get bored, you'll always be happy.'

If someone punches you for being annoying, you might not be that happy, thinks Jonah.

'So, what's your reason for being up this late?' Alice says again, like not sleeping gives them a special kind of bond. She's obviously not going to let it drop.

'I get dreams that wake me up. And I get too hot.' He pauses and touches the red scarf wound round his neck. He wears it, even over his pyjamas. 'I get hot even when I'm cold.'

He doesn't know why he's telling her all this. Maybe if he gives her a few answers she'll find someone else to be curious about and leave him alone.

'I get too hot too, from the itching.'

'And your dad doesn't mind you climbing up the side of people's houses?'

'Oh no, he's used to my climbing. Plus, I've told him all about you.'

'You have?'

'Yeah. He thinks it's cool that we're friends.' She flicks her pale fringe out of her eyes and smiles.

Friends? He doesn't have anything against Alice, but he knows that being her friend is not going to help him with the other children at school. Everyone already thinks he's weird because he's adopted by Rosie and Sam and because he can't read or write. And because he doesn't come from Bridgeford. The last thing he needs is to be associated with the one person in the class who's seen as even weirder than he is.

She walks around the room picking things up and inspecting them.

'What's this?' she asks, holding up a card Trudi gave him with all her details on it so that he could get in touch with her whenever he needed to.

'It's from my social worker.'

'Wow, that's cool.'

'Not really.'

She traces the words with her fingers. 'Trudi Babalola. That's her *real* name?'

'Yes.'

'Do you call her when you're sad?'

'It's not really like that.'

Alice turns the card over and then puts it down and goes over to his bedside table, where she picks up the shell and puts it to her ear. 'Wow.'

Jonah lurches forward and snatches it way. 'Don't touch that.'

She puts her hands up like he's trying to shoot her and says: 'Sorry.'

'What are you doing here?' Jonah asks.

'Like I said, I saw you were up.'

'How?'

Alice goes over to the window and points at a house across the tracks. 'I live over there and you live here . . .'

'You live in *that* house?'

'Yeah.' She comes back and sits on the edge of his bed.

Jonah sits beside her and Hop comes over and plops into her lap.

'Cool cat!' she says, burying her head in his fur.

She keeps hugging him and then she lets out a massive sneeze and Hop leaps out of her arms and tries to get onto Jonah's lap. For once, Jonah doesn't push him away. If he were a cat, he'd be terrified of Alice too.

Alice sneezes a third time and then lets out a big laugh, much bigger than is right for her small body. 'I totally love cats, but I'm allergic.' She sneezes again.

Jonah looks at Alice's arm. She's pulled her sleeves up so he can see more of the rash this time – it creeps right up to the crook of her elbow, where it goes from pink to an angry red. There are scratch marks too.

'And your cat is awesome,' Alice says. 'I've never seen a three-legged cat before.'

'It's not a party trick,' Jonah says, feeling oddly defensive of the cat that, only a few moments ago, he was shooing out of his room.

'I know it's not a party trick,' says Alice. 'I meant it's cool how he doesn't let having three legs get in his way. How he just gets on with being a cat. *That's* cool.'

Alice still hasn't explained why she's standing, uninvited, in the middle of his bedroom. Not really.

'How did you know I lived here?' Jonah asks.

'I saw you through the window.' Alice reaches inside the bag slung over her shoulder and takes out one of those small tablet computers Jonah's seen some of the kids have at school. 'And I looked you up.'

Jonah doesn't understand much about computers. When they have lessons at school he tries really hard not to draw attention to the fact that he hardly knows how to switch them on, let alone look anything up.

'Your dad's famous,' Alice says.

'My dad?'

'Sam Keep.'

'He's not—'

'Not what?'

'Never mind. How is he famous?'

'He's an artist, right? He's got a website.'

She flicks her fingers across the screen. It shines a blue light across her face, making her look even more like an alien. Then she taps some words into it and shows it to him. There's a picture of Sam surrounded by his sculptures. There's one of him and Rosie too, standing arm in arm in front of the garage studio.

'He's won awards and stuff. Though not for a while – maybe he's going through a dry patch,' Alice says.

'He's not going through a dry patch. He's working hard on a proper life-sized horse for a really important bid.'

Jonah's not going to let anyone criticise Sam. Sam's horses are the most amazing sculptures he's ever seen.

'It's OK. Dad's an artist and he went through a dry patch too, when he and Mum got divorced, so I get it.'

All the grown-ups in England seem to be divorced. He once heard Mister Sir telling Mama that he was divorced.

'Why don't you live with your mama?'

'Oh, she wouldn't be able to look after me. She's a journalist so she's always zooming around the world. Dad says that the one good thing I've got from Mum is her curiosity. She has to be curious for her job.'

Jonah feels a thud in his chest. He wonders what he got from Mama.

'So you don't see her?'

'Not much. But she takes me on holiday sometimes, to the places she has to go for work that aren't too dangerous. That's fun.'

'Do you miss her?' Jonah asks.

'All the time. But Dad's cool. He's better at looking after me.'

Alice looks down at her arms and starts scratching at the pinky red streaks that go from her wrists to her elbows.

'You OK?' Jonah asks.

'Oh, it's just your cat. I take pills, I'll be fine.' She tilts her head to one side. 'You said you had dreams that made you wake up. What do you dream about?'

'Nothing.'

There's an awkward silence, which Jonah hopes will encourage her to leave.

'Anyway,' Alice says, looking back at her computer, 'I won't be long, I just wanted to come round and show you something.' She flicks her fingers across the screen and holds it up.

Jonah looks at a series of letters that he recognises as the alphabet. There's a frozen video of a cartoon woman with orange hair talking to cartoon children.

'It's the phonetic alphabet. Look – you press here . . .' Alice pushes her finger on the letter and the orange haired woman comes alive and makes a weird 'aaaa' sound. 'Dad made it for me when I was little, to help me learn to read.'

'Your dad *made* it?'

'He designs games. Not ones like this – he just did this for me, for fun. He makes save-the-world type games.'

'Save the world . . . ?'

'You know how most computer games are about shooting people and stuff?'

Jonah's never played a computer game in his life but he nods and says: 'Yeah.'

'Well, Dad says that that's totally warped so he's making these really cool games where you save people without killing other people.' She flicks her fringe out of her eyes again. 'Anyway, I thought you could use this game to help with your reading.'

Jonah feels himself blushing from his toes all the way up to his woolly black hair.

Miss Gater's been helping him with his reading, and Sam has too, even though he's not very good at it. Jonah doesn't need some silly computer game.

'I can read just fine.'

'No, you can't,' Alice says. 'And if you don't work at it now, it'll just get harder.'

Jonah gulps. 'I'd like you to leave now.'

'I just want to help. We don't have to tell anyone. And

anyway, not being able to read is nothing to be ashamed of. Dad says it's not unusual, that 13.7% of people in the world can't read. Plus, it's not hard. I basically taught myself.' She pauses. 'You don't need to feel bad about it. I bet there are loads of things I can't do that you can do.' She hands over the screen. 'I can help you learn on my iPad. We can meet up after school and stuff.'

Jonah stares at the computer screen and part of him wants to throw it out of the window and to tell Alice to go after it, but another part of him is excited. Rosie and Sam don't seem to make much money from Sam's sculptures or Rosie's delivering-babies work, they only have one computer downstairs and Sam keeps thumping it and complaining that it's crashed. It will be nice to use a proper computer sometimes.

'Can you really find anything using a computer?' Jonah asks.

Alice nods so excitedly that her fringe falls back into her eyes. 'Anything.' And then she grins. 'Dad says I could get most of my education from the internet, that teachers are a waste of government money – which is why he refuses to send me to private school – but he says that I should go to school anyway because it's good for my socialisation and because I've missed out already because of all my hospital stays because of my allergies.' She pauses and takes a breath.

Jonah wonders whether she has an off switch, like her computer. But she keeps going.

'Was there something in particular you wanted to look up, maybe I could help you?'

'Nothing, I was just asking,' says Jonah.

For a second Jonah feels a bit sorry for Alice.

*Every single person you meet on this earth is a child of God and every child of God deserves to be loved*, Mama had told Jonah more times than he could count. Which always made him think that God had some pretty weird children. But he knows what she meant: that you should be kind to people, even if you didn't feel like it; even if liking them makes your life more difficult.

Alice looks down at the computer and brushes her fingers across the screen. 'You get points for all the answers you get right, like a game. So you'll know how you're doing. You'll see, you'll be reading *The Tempest* in no time.' She grins even more widely.

She must have seen the book when he brought it into school that first time.

'Maybe we can meet every now and then,' Alice goes on.

Jonah looks at the watch on Alice's wrist and although he can't read the time and so can't work out how late it is, he knows he'll get in trouble with Rosie and Sam if they find Alice in his bedroom when he's meant to be asleep.

'I do not mean to be rude, but I think you should go home now,' Jonah says.

'Why do you speak like that sometimes?' Alice asks.

'Like what?'

'Like you come from a hundred years ago.'

He doesn't understand what she means.

'It's OK,' Alice says. 'I like it.' She pauses. 'Maybe you *were* born a hundred years ago.' Her eyes go wide. 'Maybe you're a time traveller, Jonah Keep! Now that would be really cool.'

She's so excited she's making Jonah's head hurt.

There's a whistling from outside. Hop's ears shoot up.

'And that'll be Dad,' Alice says. 'Time to go home.' She goes back to the window.

'Thank you for offering to help me with your computer ...' Jonah says.

'No probs,' Alice says and climbs back out onto the window ledge. She turns round one last time. 'Maybe you can teach me a bit more about what your life was like before you came to England. I don't know much about Africa . . .'

He thinks about how nice it would be to talk to someone about Kenya and Lamu and the sea. And Mama. But he's made a promise.

'Maybe,' he says.

'See you at school then, Jonah Keep.'

In that moment, Jonah realises that Alice probably needs a friend as much as he needs to learn how to read.

Before he has the chance to answer, she's disappeared through the window and a few moments later, Jonah watches her walk across the railway bridge, hand in hand with her dad.

## Sam

'I don't need to see the doctor, thank you very much,' Jonah says.

'It won't take long, Jonah.'

Sam stares at Jonah's bare feet. The doctor will probably take one look at him and draw the conclusion that of course a child who goes around with bare feet in England (even if it's meant to be summer), will get ill.

'Maybe we can stop and get some breakfast on the way home,' Sam suggests.

'That is very kind but I'm not very hungry.'

Rosie's driving herself crazy trying to find things that Jonah will eat. She's convinced that her cooking's to blame, but from what Sam can see, Jonah just isn't interested in food.

The door to the surgery opens and Alice Anderson skips in with her dad. They both have the same light hair and transparent skin.

'Hi, Jonah!' she squeals.

As Alice comes towards him, Jonah looks at the floor.

'Are you ill too?' Alice asks Jonah, like they've both been given a gold star.

Sam has her down perfectly: front row, hand up, straight as an arrow, regardless of whether there's a question or not. A girl who has no doubt warmed to Jonah because he tries hard and doesn't get into trouble. She makes Sam think of a little Rosie. She makes him think of the little girl he'd imagined they'd have one day.

Alice and her dad sit on the row of chairs under the window. She takes out a book with a gold sticker on it. When Sam saw the class reader that Mrs Boon gave Jonah, he was brought right back to his own struggles with reading at school. He remembers being given those stupid books too, the ones without proper stories. Even the pictures were rubbish.

He looks at Mr Anderson, who, from what people say, has basically raised Alice all by himself. The divorce was very public because Mrs Anderson is a famous journalist and he's a famous software designer. Sam swallows hard. He can't begin to imagine how he'd cope without Rosie.

Anyway, maybe Sam can pick up some tips from Mr Anderson. He's obviously doing a good job.

'Come on,' Sam says to Jonah.

Reluctantly, Jonah puts his backpack on his shoulder and walks over with Sam.

'Hi, I'm Sam, this is my son, Jonah,' Sam says. The words ring outside his head. When biological fathers call themselves Dad for the first time, do they feel like frauds too? He goes on. 'I think you know my wife, Rosie?'

Mr Anderson smiles. 'Yes, of course.'

'Alice and Jonah must be in the same class.'

'Yes – Alice has talked a great deal about Jonah.'

'Oh . . . ' Jonah hasn't mentioned any friends from school yet. Sam looks back to Jonah and clears his throat. 'So has Jonah . . . '

Jonah shoots him a look.

Sam catches his eye, giving him a *What was I meant to say?* look back.

Mr Anderson sweeps Alice's fringe out of her eyes.

'She's had another asthma attack,' he says. 'We might need to change the dosage on her inhaler.'

'I'm sorry . . . '

'It's all right. Alice has so many allergic reactions that we treat this place like an extension of home.'

'I'm going to be a doctor when I grow up so coming here is like work experience,' Alice says, swinging her legs and smiling.

Definitely a little Rosie. Or how Rosie used to be when they were young. Completely sure of what she wanted from the world. And that the world would give it to her – because it was a good place. She was always a few steps ahead of everyone else – and she spent most of her time yanking Sam's arm to make sure he was keeping up with her.

Nothing got in Rosie's way. Not her parents ignoring her. Not Sam's dad dying – and he was as much a dad to her as he was to Sam. Even in those first few years of their marriage, when they realised that having a child wouldn't come easily to them, she stayed hopeful. But even someone like Rosie can be stretched too far.

He doesn't know when Rosie handed him the baton – when she asked him to step out in front and be the one in charge of keeping their hope alive. All he knows is that it's his job now and he's not sure he can do it – not for someone with hopes as big as Rosie's.

Mr Anderson looks over to Jonah. 'How about Jonah, everything OK?'

'Oh, just a sore throat, probably a virus or something. I'm sure it's nothing but we thought it was best to get it checked out.'

'Definitely best. If I hadn't been insistent that the doctors pursue Alice's allergies, goodness knows what state she'd be in. You really have to push to get anything done.' He holds up his palm to an invisible door. 'Don't hold anything back when you speak to Dr Barron.'

'Thanks for the tip,' Sam says.

'Jonah Keep.' The receptionist calls out.

Hearing Jonah's name hooked up to his gives Sam a jolt of unexpected joy. He's really theirs.

'Dr Barron is ready for you . . . ' The receptionist adds.

'Come on,' Sam says.

Jonah rushes ahead of him, keener, it seems, to see the doctor than to stay here with his new friend.

When they get to the corridor, Sam asks, 'So you like Alice, Jonah?'

Jonah shrugs.

'What?' Sam asks.

'She's a bit strange,' Jonah says.

'Strange how?'

'She's kind of there all the time.'

Sam laughs. 'That's not necessarily a bad thing.' He thinks of Rosie again. 'You know that Rosie was my best friend when we were your age?'

Jonah's eyes widen. 'Really?'

'We grew up in the same town.'

'Wow.' Jonah pauses. 'I mean that's amazing.'

Sam's been noticing new words creeping into Jonah's vocabulary. How, over the days and weeks, his formality has been dissolving. *Kind of. Wow Cool.* The rhetorical, inflective *Really?* Trudi said that the first time she met Jonah, he sounded like he'd swallowed a 1950s English phrase book.

'Yeah, it's wow,' Sam says, smiling.

'So you know about Alice's allergies?' Sam asks Jonah.

'Alice's dad is always collecting her from school and taking her home or to the doctor or bringing in special food.' Jonah says. 'She's allergic to everything. Which is why Rosie isn't allowed to put any nuts in my packed lunch. Mrs Boon told all the parents. Because if Alice even breathes in the smell of a nut, she could die.'

When biological parents conceive a child, they don't expect their child to be sick or to have behaviour troubles or attachment issues. Whereas, as adopters, Rosie and Sam had got the message, loud and clear: their child would come to them damaged, and it was their job to make him whole again.

Maybe Rosie and Sam are at an advantage – they've been to all the lectures and training courses, they've read all the books. They're prepared. And maybe it's worse when your own child doesn't turn out like you expected.

'That must be hard for Alice – and her dad,' Sam says.

As they get closer to Dr Barron's door, Sam notices Jonah dragging his feet.

'There's nothing to be worried about, it'll be over before you know it.'

Jonah doesn't move from the doorway.

'Come on, Jonah,' Sam says and points to the chair.

Very slowly, Jonah sits down.

The first thing Dr Barron does is make Jonah stand on the scales.

'Well, you could eat a few more cream cakes, that's for sure,' Dr Barron says.

'He's not that interested in food,' Sam says.

Dr Barron's bushy eyebrows shoot up. 'A growing lad, not interested in food?'

Sam really hopes that Dr Barron has read the background notes they filled out when they registered Jonah at the surgery.

'Come and sit up here,' Dr Barron says, pointing to the doctor's bench. 'And take your T-shirt off for me.'

Jonah doesn't move.

'It won't take long, Jonah,' Sam says.

Jonah scrambles onto the couch and Dr Barron holds his cold stethoscope to Jonah's chest and back, makes him breathe in and out really loud and cough. Then he picks up a torch and a tongue compressor and says:

'Open wide.'

Jonah keeps his mouth clamped shut.

Sam goes over and takes Jonah's hand. 'It's OK, Dr Barron will help us to make your throat better.'

Jonah stares at the doctor, his brow furrowed.

'He's been finding it hard to swallow,' Sam says.

'Come on, open up,' Dr Barron says.

Very slowly, Jonah opens his mouth.

'Wider – Ahhh!' Dr Barron says.

Sam looks into Jonah's pink mouth, lit up by the torch.

Dr Barron goes very still. 'Could you open a little wider for me, Jonah?' His voice has gone slow and quiet.

Jonah stretches his mouth further. His eyes water and a couple of tears run down his cheeks.

Sam's chest contracts. 'OK, buddy?'

Jonah nods.

Dr Barron sits back down. He turns to his computer and makes some notes.

'Those tonsils are quite enlarged. Looks like a virus,' Dr Barron says, staring at his screen.

Sam breathes out.

'Any other symptoms?' Dr Barron asks, still typing.

Sam hesitates. And then he blurts it out. 'He sweats at night.'

Dr Barron moves away from his computer and looks at Sam. 'Often?'

Sam nods.

'Several times a week?' Dr Barron asks.

'Most nights.'

Jonah's head is hung so low it disappears into his shoulders.

'It's common for children to overheat at night . . . but if you like, I could get you referred.'

'Referred?' Sam asks.

'To paediatrics.'

'You mean at the hospital?'

'Yes. Just for a more thorough look.'

Sam's head spins. 'I thought you said it was just a virus?'

'It probably is. Just thought you'd want some peace of mind, Jonah being new to the family.' Dr Barron looks at Sam over his glasses. 'Rosie knows all the paeds consultants at Bridgeford Hospital, she could bring him in whenever she has a spare moment.'

Sam's stomach churns. If Rosie finds out that Jonah has a hospital appointment – if she finds out that he took Jonah to Dr Barron without telling her – she's going to lose it.

'Why don't we hold off on the appointment,' Sam says. 'See if it clears up.'

Sam helps Jonah put his school shirt and jumper back on.

'Well, talk it over with Rosie when you get home and give me a call,' Dr Barron says.

'Sure,' Sam says, easing Jonah into his coat. 'Will do.' He ushers Jonah out of Dr Barron's room as fast as he can.


Jonah doesn't say a word as they walk down the corridor.

As they go past reception, Alice's dad calls over: 'Everything OK?'

'All fine,' Sam says and speeds up.

He feels inadequate in front of this single dad who's been dealing, effortlessly it seems, with his little girl's illness.

For a while, Sam and Jonah walk down the High Street without saying a word.

Then Sam says, 'You'll tell me, won't you Jonah? If you feel any worse?'

Jonah nods.

'You don't have to be brave.'

Jonah goes quiet.

'I'm here to look after you.'

Jonah nods.

Sam takes a breath. 'Sure I can't tempt you with any breakfast?'

Jonah shakes his head.

'To school then?'

Jonah gives Sam a small smile, his eyes still watery from the throat inspection.

# Trudi

It's the first time they've met since the aborted trial. Trudi's been leaving messages on his mobile for months. Finally, he agreed to meet her for a coffee.

Peter jiggles his leg under the table so hard that Trudi's coffee spills over the rim.

'We need to get more information,' Trudi says.

Peter raises his eyebrows. 'We?'

Trudi feels her cheeks burn up. 'Look, I'm sorry about having barged into your office ...' She pauses. 'For shouting at you like it was your fault ... and for getting everything wet.'

'I had to have that chair re-upholstered.'

'Really?'

He shakes his head and smiles. 'No, of course not. I was more worried that you'd catch pneumonia or something, heading back into the rain like that.'

Trudi had caught a cold, but she hadn't allowed herself to take any time off work. She was determined to make something good come out of this whole mess Jonah had found himself in; she'd worked day and night to try and find him a family.

'Look, I'm really sorry, Trudi, but my boss is closing the case.'

Trudi's head snaps up. 'He's *what*?'

'It's been six months. Now that the Robin Morse case is closed, there really aren't any more leads for us to follow.'

'But we don't know anything yet.'

'Isn't Jonah settled in his new home, with his adopted parents?'

'Yes. But that's not the point. We need to tie up loose ends before the adoption hearing in October.'

Letting an adoption go through without the consent of the child's biological parents is risky. And it's Trudi's job to eliminate risk from her adoption cases. She prides herself on the success rate of the children she's placed. And she's not going to let anything go wrong for Jonah. He's been through enough. And she likes the Keeps. Of course she sees their weaknesses too: Rosie's desperation to have a child fizzed from every nerve ending in her body, matched in intensity by Sam's desperation to make Rosie happy. A dynamic Trudi has seen many times before and one that she knows to be wary of. Both adopters in the couple need to want the child equally; otherwise cracks appear when they hit difficulties. But Rosie and Sam are kind and thoughtful and open, and, above all, willing to reshape their whole lives for a child. They will give Jonah the love he needs and that's enough for Trudi. She's going to do everything she can to make sure this adoption doesn't fall through.

'As far as my boss is concerned, there aren't any loose ends. Robin Morse is serving his sentence.'

'What about finding his mum?'

'We've tried following as many leads as we can. Robin Morse didn't give us anything to go on – he was protecting her, obviously.' He pauses. 'There are more pressing cases.'

'Wow, my faith in the police force has just been totally restored.'

Peter blinks at her. 'We don't have the resources, Trudi.'

'You mean that finding a child's mother isn't a priority?'

'I didn't think that social workers were meant to be sentimental,' Peter says.

Trudi feels stung. 'I'm not being sentimental.' She takes a

218

breath to ease the anger swelling in her chest. 'If Jonah's mum –
or dad for that matter – suddenly shows up and asks to have
Jonah back, the Keeps will lose everything.'

'Won't that exact same thing happen if we chase them down?'

He's right, of course. It's a risk. But Trudi's got enough ammunition to prove neglect and to make a good case that Jonah should
stay in the care of Rosie and Sam Keep. And letting things go
wasn't her style.

'If we find them, we can be on the front foot,' she says.

Peter takes a sip of his black coffee and shakes his head.
'There's nothing I can do.'

Trudi pauses, weighing up whether her reading of DI Peter
Taylor's been wrong. That he's just like all the others: ready to
bow to the demands of his superiors the minute things get hard.

'We could keep looking,' Trudi says.

He raises his eyebrows. '*We?*'

'Off the books.'

He leans back in his chair and lets out a long breath. 'Like I
have hours of free time to carry on an investigation – and that's if
I'm stupid enough to risk my job by going against orders.'

'Robin Morse is allowed visitors, right?'

Peter shakes his head. 'No, Trudi, don't even go there.'

'I have to talk to him.'

'Didn't you hear what I just said? The case is closed. And
there's no reason why you should be granted visiting rights.'

'You could arrange it.'

'Excuse me?'

'Just one meeting. Press him a bit; see if we get some more
information. I reckon he's our key.'

'He could file a complaint. Claim harassment. He made it clear
that he didn't want any more contact to Jonah . . .'

'If what he said at the plea bargain's true, that he was set up, that he took Jonah here out of the goodness of his own heart, it means that he must care for him at least a bit. And the way Jonah talks about him . . . it sounds like they were close.' She tries to hold Peter's gaze. She can sense him softening. 'Under the radar . . . no one needs to know . . .'

'I could lose my job, Trudi. So could you.'

'Jonah's what matters here.'

Peter sits back. 'I guess you don't have anything to lose.'

'Sorry?'

'I can't afford to lose my job.' He looks at her and his eyes soften for the first time since he's sat down. 'I've got kids and a wife to support, Trudi.'

Trudi feels winded. 'Kids? I . . . I didn't know . . .'

She'd assumed Peter was a bachelor. No wedding ring. Long hours at the office. Ill-fitting suits. Terrible eating habits.

'If I don't pay my maintenance cheques, I'm the one who'll be standing in the dock.'

Trudi stares at him. 'You're divorced?'

He nods. 'I'm celebrating my one-year divorce next week.'

'I'm sorry.'

'Don't be.'

'I mean, I'm sorry I've put you in this position.' She reaches for her bag under the table and hooks it over her shoulder. 'I'll go now.' She stands up.

Peter holds out his palms.

'Look, I'll see what I can do. But don't get your hopes up.'

She sits back down and smiles. 'Really?'

He nods.

'Thank you!'

'One meeting and that's it.'

'One meeting,' she echoes. Then she leans over the table and grabs his hands and says: 'You're awesome.'

He blushes. 'I think you're just about the only person on the planet who's ever called me that.'

She reaches over and kisses his cheek. 'Well, you are.'


## Jonah


Alice and Jonah sit on the Year 1 swings. It's the 21st of July, the last day of term, and all the kids are bursting to go home.

This is where Alice spends her breaktimes and lunchtimes and going-home-times – mainly to avoid getting picked on by Billy and his friends. And because she likes the climbing frame.

After two weeks of ignoring her invitations to join her, Jonah caved in. Now he comes here without her even asking. And she's been coming over to the cottage too, to play the reading game on her computer.

They've worked out a code: she flashes twice with her torch and he switches his bedroom light on and off twice and that means that it's OK to come over.

Mrs Boon let them out early for hometime because she said it was criminal that they should be cooped up inside on such a lovely day. And because it's the last day of term so there's no more work to do.

Jonah thinks it's because she got tired of having to tell Billy to be quiet.

'Are you going to be around?' Alice says. 'This summer, I mean?'

'We're going to Sam's mum's house for a few days. It's in Wales.'

'That sounds cool.'

'Maybe.'

'Well, I'm here all summer. Dad's working on a new computer game.'

Alice's dad works all the time. She says he even works in holidays and over Christmas.

'So, when you get back, we'll hang out?' Alice asks.

'Sure.'

'I reckon that with the game and with the sessions you're having with Miss Gater, we can get you reading by September.'

'Really?'

Alice smiles. 'Really.'

For a while, they sit in silence, squinting at the sunshine.

Jonah kicks off his shoes and socks and lets his toes trail on the warm tarmac. He looks over at Alice. Her hair is so light in the sun, that she looks like she comes from another world.

He yawns. He's been getting more and more tired. Some days, it's so bad that he can hardly keep his eyes open in lessons.

Alice stops swinging and bites into an apple. She eats apples all day long. They seem to be the only thing she's not allergic to. She puts so much in her mouth that her cheeks puff out, making her look like a monkey.

She gulps it down and says:

'So it must be cool, living with Rosie and Sam.'

Jonah shrugs. 'Sam's OK. We go swimming. And he lets me help out in his workshop.'

Whenever Jonah's not in his bedroom or in the bath or at school, Jonah stays in the garage with Sam. Sam's been helping him work on the small driftwood horse Jonah started that night when he couldn't sleep. The other day, Sam called him a natural.

Up until now the only thing he's felt a natural at is holding his breath underwater.

'I'd love to have a mum like Rosie,' Alice says.

Rosie might be an improvement on Alice's mum, but Alice hasn't met Mama. If she had, she'd understand.

'You know, I wouldn't be here if weren't for Rosie,' Alice says.

Jonah blinks. 'Really?'

'Yep. She helped Mum give birth to me. I was breach, which means I was the wrong way round or something – which Dad says is just like me.' Alice gives Jonah a goofy smile. 'I'd basically stopped breathing. Yeah, Rosie's like the best midwife in the county. Dad says she's a local hero.'

Jonah's never given much thought to what Rosie does when she's not in the house burning their dinner. And he definitely hasn't ever thought of her as a hero.

'So what happened to your real parents?' Alice asked.

Jonah freezes.

Alice has asked a million questions in the last few weeks: he should have been prepared for her to come to this one eventually.

'Did they die or did they give you up for adoption?'

He swallows hard. His eyes water.

'I don't know,' Jonah says.

'You don't know what?'

'My parents.'

Alice's eyes pop out.

'What do you mean, you don't know your parents? Who did you live with before you moved in with Rosie and Sam?'

'With a foster carer.'

'And before that?'

'I don't know.'

'Well, where did you live then?'

223

He doesn't answer.

Alice hops off the swing. 'Did you have concussion or something?'

'No.' He says. He pauses. 'What's concussion?'

'It means you banged your head and some of your brain cells got knocked about, so you've forgotten stuff.'

He shakes his head. 'No, I didn't have concussion.'

She stands right in front of him, looking at him with her sharp blue eyes, like she can see right through to his bones.

'Best friends are meant to tell each other everything,' Alice says.

Jonah's cheeks burn up. He looks down at his bare feet. He's never really had a friend before, not a proper one, let alone a *best* friend.

He looks back up at her: 'You won't tell?'

'Who am I meant to tell?'

'I'm from Lamu.'

'Where's that?'

'It's an island in Kenya.'

'An African island? Wow, that's awesome.'

'You think so?'

'Definitely. You must find Bridgeford totally dull.'

Jonah smiles. 'A bit.'

'And your parents?'

'I don't know my dad.'

'What about your mum?'

He pauses. He'd promised Mama never to tell anyone about her. But he reckons she meant grown-ups and policemen. She wouldn't mind him speaking to Alice, would she? And Alice is right – it's not like she's going to tell anyone. She lives alone with her papa and she basically has no friends.

'Mama still lives on Lamu Island.'

A big space opens up in Jonah's chest and, for the first time since he left Mama, he feels he can breathe right to the top of his lungs.

'And why aren't you living with her now?'

'She wanted me to come to England to learn to read.'

Alice's pale eyebrows shoot up. 'That's it?'

'What do you mean, that's it?'

'Your mum sent you to a whole other continent just because she wants you to learn to read?'

Jonah swallows again. 'And to be a gentleman.'

Alice puts her hand over her mouth.

'Don't laugh.'

'I'm sorry, I'm sorry, you're just so old fashioned.' She gives him a nudge. 'I think you're a gentleman already.'

Jonah blushes.

'You're sure that's the only reason she sent you away? It all sounds a bit weird to me.'

Alice is so clever that she'll probably work it out, even if he doesn't tell her. But he can't break a promise that's not even his to break. Mama was speaking to Mister Sir. She didn't want Jonah to know.

'Do you love her?' Alice asks.

'Of course.'

'And miss her?'

'Yes. But I'm going back – one day. She promised.'

And Mama had promised. No matter what he had or hadn't heard that night in the hotel room with Mister Sir, he'd promised her that Jonah would come home.

Alice eats the last bit of apple core – she's the only person he knows who eats the whole thing, even the pips – and says: 'Well, I hope it's not too soon. Having you around is cool, Jonah Keep.'

He blushes even more.

She laughs and tugs at his scarf. 'Aren't you really hot in that?'

Jonah pushes away her hand. 'I'm fine.'

'You're an odd one,' Alice says.

Jonah shrugs. '*I'm* odd?'

A football arcs through the air, narrowly misses Alice's head and thumps into the Year 1 playground.

A moment later, Billy and his friends are heading towards them.

'Great . . .' Jonah mumbles.

'I'll handle it,' says Alice.

Which is what she always says. Only when Alice tries to handle things, they backfire. Worse than backfire: they explode right in her face.

'Leave it, Alice . . .' Jonah starts.

But she's already jumped off the swing and is running after the ball. She stoops down to pick it up and then throws it over to Billy.

'Didn't think girls could throw,' Billy says.

'That's funny, Billy, I didn't think you could *think*,' Alice shoots back. 'And as it happens, I'm as good with a football as you or any of your mates.'

Jonah hangs his head and looks down at his shoes and socks lying on the playground. This isn't going to end well.

'You reckon, eh?' Billy asks.

'I don't reckon,' Alice says, her hands on her hips. 'I know.'

When Alice gets an idea into her head, it takes a tornado to stop her. In fact, Jonah suspects that she'd give a tornado a run for its money.

'OK then, here's a bet,' says Billy.

This definitely isn't going to end well.

'Join our game and score a goal in the next ten minutes and we'll let you be part of the team,' Billy says.

'I don't want to be part of your silly team,' Alice says.

Phew.

'If I join a team, it'll be a proper team. One that has real training sessions. So you'd better come up with a better offer.'

Billy rummages around in his coat pocket and pulls out a bar of Cadbury's Dairy Milk.

'That's more like it,' Alice says, her face lighting up.

Jonah can't keep track of the things that Alice is allergic to, but he's pretty sure she's not meant to eat chocolate.

Jonah gets off the swing and walks towards her. 'I don't think this is a good idea,' he whispers.

'It's a *great* idea, Jonah.'

'How about your boyfriend? Would he care to join us?' Billy asks.

Jonah wants to melt into the tarmac.

'Yeah, Jonah's a beast,' Alice says.

A *what*?

Billy laughs. His mates shuffle and whisper behind him.

Sometimes, Jonah played football on the beach with Mister Sir; he even gave him an Arsenal shirt. Jonah had thought that maybe, when they lived together in England, Mister Sir might take him to a match. But Jonah's never played football properly, not in a team. And he's been too tired to do much running lately.

'Come on, put your shoes on, Jonah,' Alice says.

'Yeah, put your shoes on, we're not in Bongo Bongo Land!'

*Bongo Bongo land?*

'Shut up, Billy.' Alice says. 'Jonah comes from Lamu Island, which is one of the most beautiful places in the whole world. I bet you've never even left Bridgeford.'

Half of Jonah feels cross that she just blurted out to the whole of Bridgeford Primary that he's from Lamu, when it was meant to be a secret. But a bigger part of him feels kind of good that she's said something nice about where he's from. And that she's shut Billy up in the process.

A second later Alice and Jonah are standing in the middle of the playground. They've been put on the team that doesn't have Billy or his friends in it. A group made up of the less popular boys who usually get ignored by Billy and his gang, except when they need a team to play football against – and to beat.

Billy and his mates are good. Their footwork is fast and the minute the ball gets anywhere near Alice, they shove her out of the way and get the ball back. Jonah can hear Alice wheezing, but her feet won't stop moving and her eyes are wide and sparkling and her cheeks are pink and he knows that she's not going to give up without a fight.

Jonah's legs feel like they're stuck in concrete. He forces himself forward and, at last, he gets the ball off one of Billy's friends and shoots it to Alice.

Alice gives him a mile-wide grin and dribbles the ball for a bit. Then she positions herself in front of the goal and shoots.

Everything goes into slow motion. Billy and his mates freeze and stare at the ball as it shoots through the air. Alice stares too: she juts her chin forward as if it'll help nudge the ball closer to the goal. The goalie looks like he's in a trance too. He probably didn't expect the ball to come anywhere near him.

Behind them, some of the parents have started to arrive at the school gates.

But no one in the playground cares about that. All the kids are gathered around the game and are looking at what's going to happen to the ball.

It starts to fall from the sky and Jonah can see how, if the goalie doesn't move now, it'll plop neatly into the goal. Jonah's heart beats faster and he actually gets excited for the first time since Billy and Alice made their stupid bet.

And then there's a clink. The ball bounces off the edge of the goal and falls to the ground. It rolls to the side and stops at Mrs Boon's feet.

'Time to go home,' Mrs Boon says, slotting the ball under her arm.

Billy and his gang puff their chests and walk towards Alice.

'Told you that girls can't play football.' Billy gives Alice a slap on the back, which makes it look like he's being friendly, but he does it so hard that Alice staggers forward and coughs. Then she starts wheezing again, harder than before. She gets out her inhaler and sucks on it hard.

'Here, consolation prize,' Billy says and shoves the chocolate bar at her and then smiles at Mrs Boon as if to say: *look how kind and generous I'm being – even though she's lost the bet, I'm still giving her my chocolate.*

Mrs Boon smiles. 'That's a nice gesture, Billy.'

Jonah didn't think she'd be sucked in so easily. But then Mrs Boon's always hoping that Billy will turn good.

'But I'm afraid Alice isn't allowed that.' Mrs Boon holds out her hand for the chocolate.

Before Mrs Boon has the chance to take it away, Alice hands the chocolate bar to Jonah. 'I'm giving my prize to Jonah.'

'OK, Alice. That's kind,' says Mrs Boon.

And then everyone starts picking up their bags and filing towards the gates because the parents are turning up. He can see Rosie craning her neck, looking for him.

Jonah puts his arm around Alice's shoulder. 'You did really well.'

She shakes him off. 'No, I didn't.'

'You did. The ball missed the goal by a few millimetres. It was probably the wind or something.' Not that there's any wind, but it was close.

'I didn't win,' Alice says.

She grabs the chocolate bar and tears open the purple wrapper and shoves chocolate in her mouth.

'Are you sure you're allowed to eat that?' Jonah asks.

But she's not listening. It's like she wants to prove something to Billy by eating it – not that he's even watching.

'Alice? You heard what Mrs Boon said.'

'I'll be fine,' Alice says, taking another bite.

Although Jonah can see, in a second, that it's not right.

Alice's skin has gone from pink to bright red: all over her face and neck and chest. Her forearms are red too, a raw-red, like she's been stung by a jellyfish. He can tell she's struggling to swallow from the way she's gasping at the air. Alice bends over and crosses her arms over her stomach.

'Alice – are you OK?'

The chocolate wrapper drops out of her hands.

'Mrs Boon!' Jonah yells at the top of his lungs. 'Mrs Boon!'

A moment later, Alice is lying in the middle of the playground with millions of children around her. She's been sick and it's got all caught up in her hair. She's lying with her eyes closed and she's not moving. And she's stopped wheezing, which makes Jonah worry that she might have stopped breathing altogether.

He hasn't got a clue what to do. What he does know is that if someone doesn't help her, right now, it'll be too late.

He screws shut his eyes and does the only thing he can think

230

of: he rubs the magician's coin in his pocket. *Please, please make Alice better . . .*

But Alice still isn't waking up.

And then it hits him again: that there is nothing he can do to help.

A second later, Rosie's pushing him out of the way. She kneels next to Alice, grabs a plastic pen thing from her bag, lifts it in the air and shoves it into Alice's thigh.

Alice's body shudders.

Jonah gasps and looks away.

And then Alice opens her eyes. She looks right at Jonah and then she closes her eyes again, like she is too tired to keep her eyelids open.

Mrs Boon runs towards them, her bracelets jangling, her long skirt swishing around her ankles.

Jonah looks at Alice lying against Rosie's chest. Her eyes are closed and her skin is paler than ever. Jonah wants to yell at her. To tell her she's an idiot. That she shouldn't have agreed to the stupid football match. That she should never have bitten into that chocolate when she knows she's allergic to just about every ingredient written on the packet. But then he gets it. Alice wanted to feel normal. More than that, she wanted to feel part of a team – even if it's a crappy team. Because sometimes it gets lonely having to hang about on the edges of things, even if you're really good at reading and even if you have lots of money and even if you have the best dad in the world. Even if you have a best friend.

Then he looks at Rosie, stroking Alice's hair, even though it's all tangled with sick and he realises that all the magic coins in the world wouldn't have helped Alice – that she needed Rosie. Rosie saved her life. And from what Alice said, it's not the first time.

For a second Jonah doesn't see Rosie's messy hair or her scuffed shoes and he doesn't think about how she's always trying to make him eat things and how she wants him to call her Mum. He just sees her, looking after Alice in a way that no one else could. And he realises that maybe he does like her – just a little bit.

## Jonah

'I'm so, so glad you're all here.' Grandma Flick's voice floats to Jonah from the front of the car. 'I thought you'd never make it . . .'

They've been travelling for what feels like days. Hours and hours and hours on the train all the way from Bridgeford to London and then up all of England to Wales.

Rosie and Sam have gone on and on about how amazing Wales is but so far it just seems greyer and colder than England.

They're in a rusty Land Rover belonging to Grandma Flick, Sam's mum. They're dragging an empty horse trailer with them too: the trailer rattles and squeaks every time they hit a bump or pothole. Grandma Flick says it's bolted on so hard she couldn't get it off. Jonah can't wait to meet Sam's old horse, the one he got when his papa died.

Jonah's head drops and his eyelids close. The conversation around him rises and falls like waves.

Sam's sitting in the front next to Grandma Flick with Hop's basket on his knee. Rosie is in the back, next to Jonah.

'I've been so excited to meet little Jonah . . .' Flick says.

Jonah blinks open his eyes. Grandma Flick turns to give him

a big smile. She has a neat silver bob that swishes around her jaw when she moves her head.

The car swerves across the road. Hop yowls.

Sam grabs the steering wheel. 'Keep your eyes on the road, Mum.'

Grandma Flick gives Jonah a wink. 'Your dad forgets that I was driving long before he was born.'

Sam and Rosie go quiet.

Jonah doesn't correct her. Not yet.

Grandma Flick pushes her foot on the accelerator and the car leaps forward.

Rosie leans over Jonah and yanks at his seatbelt to make sure it's on properly.

Jonah shivers and pulls his scarf tighter around his neck. He rubs his eyes and looks out through the window to try and stay awake. It's dark. Really dark. Over the cliffs, the black sea shifts under the night sky. He wonders how it would feel to swim in that sea, whether it would be so cold that his whole body would freeze up.

'We're going to have such a jolly weekend . . .' Grandma Flick says.

He listens to the grown-ups voices weaving in and out of each other and thinks of the last time he went on a really long journey – one that took him half way across the world.

It's the night before he's due to leave for England and Jonah's sitting in the corridor of the hotel waiting for Mama and Mister Sir to finish their chat.

He turns round and presses his ear to the door.

'Don't you think we should tell him about Aunt Igwe ... ?' Mister Sir asks Mama.

Jonah's never heard of an Aunt Igwe before.

'I'm tired ...' Mama says. 'Let me sleep ...' Her voice is so quiet, Jonah can barely make it out.

'I just think it will be a bit of a shock ... it's not what he's expecting ...' Mister Sir says.

'We've been through this already,' Mama says.

Jonah pushes his ear harder against the door. He imagines Mister Sir standing there in his socks and boxer shorts, his white belly bulging over his waistband.

The conversation goes quiet, which makes Jonah worried that maybe they heard him leaning against the door.

He waits for another few minutes and then knocks on the door. No one answers.

He knocks again and then the door flies open. Mister Sir looms over Jonah.

'I thought you were going for a walk?' Mister Sir says.

Jonah darts under Mister Sir's arm and goes over to Mama's bed.

'Can I get in and sleep with you?'

Mama had set up some sheets and a pillow on the sofa, which is where Jonah is meant to sleep, but he doesn't want to sleep alone, not tonight.

Mama stirs in her bed and groans. 'I need to get some rest, Jonah ...' Her voice gets lost in the sound of honking from the traffic outside. Jonah wonders whether there are as many traffic jams in England as there are in Nairobi.

'Please, Mama?' He strokes her arm.

'Not tonight, Jonah. I'm tired, and you always kick in your sleep ...'

Jonah doesn't understand why Mama is so tired. She slept most of the afternoon while Mister Sir took Jonah out to buy clothes.

Mister Sir stubs his cigarette out on the windowsill and slams shut the window.

'Why don't I tuck you in,' Mister Sir says. 'I'll read to you.'

That was the best thing about Mister Sir: he read stories to him and to Mama – the actual words on the page.

'Thank you …' Mama says. She turns to the wall and sinks her head back into her pillow. Jonah can tell from her breathing that she has gone straight to sleep.

Mister Sir switches off the light and takes Jonah to the sofa. Then he kneels beside him and picks up the book he brought over for Jonah and Mama.

'Where did we get to, Jonah?'

'Miranda has seen Ferdinand for the first time and she loves him so much that she thinks he's not a real human being.'

Mister Sir smiles. 'You know the story well.'

'Thank you, Mister Sir,' Jonah says, pleased by the praise. Then he sits up.

Mister Sir starts reading from the beginning of the scene, and then he gets to Jonah's favourite bit, where Miranda is really surprised:

'What is't? A spirit? / Lord, how it looks about! Believe me, sir, / It carries a brave form. But 'tis a spirit.'

'May I ask a question?' Jonah asks.

Mister Sir smiles and ruffles Jonah's hair, only it's so short after this afternoon's haircut, that it doesn't ruffle at all.

'Of course.'

Jonah makes his voice go into a whisper so that Mama doesn't hear.

'Will Mama be OK? When I'm not here, I mean?'

235

Mister Sir puts the book down.

'Of course she will.' He pauses. 'You know, Jonah, it will do her good, to be able to look after herself for a bit.'

Jonah knows that it makes Mama tired, looking after him. That's why he doesn't mind so much about going to England. If it makes Mama stronger and better, then it will be a good thing.

'Why do you think Mama is so tired?'

'She's been working very hard.'

'But she sleeps *all* the time.'

Mister Sir is quiet for a very long time and then he says: 'Let's concentrate on getting you to England, Jonah. That's what your mama wants.'

Jonah wants to ask Mister Sir who Aunt Igwe is but Mama says that Jonah has to ration his questions because they can get tiresome and he wants to ask about Mama being tired more than he does about someone he's never met before, so he keeps his question to himself for the moment. Maybe Aunt Igwe is a surprise.

'You ready to sleep now?' Mister Sir asks.

Jonah nods, yawns, turns onto his tummy and buries his head in his pillow.

Mister Sir strokes Jonah's head and then goes to stand by the open window and takes out his packet of cigarettes. As Jonah goes to sleep, he watches Mister Sir smoking one cigarette after another, like he always does before he goes back to England.

In the middle of the night, he wakes up and notices that Mister Sir has gone to lie beside Mama. And a bit later, when he wakes up again, Jonah's sure that he can hear someone crying and that someone isn't Mama.

'Jonah ... Jonah ... We're here.'

Someone's shaking his shoulders. He blinks and looks out of the car window at a small, white house. Beyond the house, up on a hill, he sees the outline of a castle and he wonders if that's where Mister Sir lives. But despite Jonah's excitement, his limbs and eyes feel heavy and he can't help drifting off again.

'Maybe we should just take him straight to bed?'

'But he's hardly eaten a thing ... and he's sweated through his clothes, he needs a bath ...'

Rosie and Sam's voices blend into each other. And behind their voices, Jonah's sure he can hear the kicking of hooves and huffing and snorting.

Jonah's barely awake as Sam carries him into the house. It's only when they get to the bathroom that he wakes up properly.

Rosie starts to ease him out of his clothes when he remembers about the marks on his throat. He shakes himself awake and says, 'I can do this on my own.'

He hears a small sigh escaping Rosie's lips but she still tries to smile.

'Okay.' Then she notices Hop at her feet. 'I think he'd like to come in, though.'

Jonah stares at him pawing at the bathroom door.

'He's just trying to be your friend, you know,' Rosie says.

Jonah doesn't understand why they had to take a cat on holiday with them. Maybe Grandma Flick will agree that he's meant to sleep outside. But he knows that letting Hop in will make Rosie happy, so he opens the door for him.

As Jonah sinks into the steaming water, Hop puts his paws over the edge of the bathtub and looks at Jonah with his funny eyes.

Closing his eyes, Jonah sinks under the water and remembers

how it felt to look up at the sunlit surface of the sea when he went for swims with Mama. For a second, he hears her voice in his head: *Oh Jonah, my little fish . . .*

'Can I come in now?' Rosie asks.

She must have been waiting outside the door the whole time he was in the bath. He wraps the towel around himself, grabs the scarf on the floor and winds it around his neck.

'Jonah, are you sure you're not hungry?' Rosie asks as he comes out.

He looks at Rosie's pink face and frizzy hair.

'No, thank you,' he says.

'You just want to sleep?'

He nods. And then coughs. His chest and his throat feel raw.

'I hope you're not coming down with something,' Rosie says, putting her palm on his brow. He moves away from her.

'I'm fine.'

Jonah thinks about the trip to the doctors. Sam told him to let him know if his throat got worse and if he sweated again at night and if he found it hard to sleep. But he's worried that if he tells him then he'll make him go back to Bridgeford and he wants to see the sea and the horse.

Jonah swallows hard. It hurts so much.

Rosie takes Jonah up to a small room, helps him into his pyjamas and tucks him into bed. Sam comes in and they both kiss his head and say 'night, night' before walking to the door.

Sam switches off the light and turns round to look at Jonah.

'You're going to love the beach, J. We'll go for a long walk tomorrow morning. And you've got someone very special to meet too.'

Jonah watches Sam take Rosie's hand.

238

'Can I ask you something?' Jonah says, before they leave.

They turn round.

'Yes, my darling?' Rosie says.

'Is the castle Mister Sir's castle?'

Even though the room is dark, Jonah sees Rosie and Sam look at each other.

'What castle, J?' Sam asks.

'The castle I saw out of the window of the car.'

'Oh ...' Rosie says. 'Criccieth Castle? No, I'm afraid not, Jonah.'

Sam and Rosie stand so still and silent Jonah worries they're angry with him for having asked the question.

'When he comes out of prison, will he go back to living in his castle – wherever that castle is?'

Rosie comes to sit on the edge of Jonah's bed. Sam joins her.

'We don't know, I'm afraid, Jonah.'

'But DI Peter Taylor knows, doesn't he?' Jonah asks.

'Yes, he probably does,' Sam says.

Jonah remembers what Trudi told him about Mister Sir never really wanting him in the first place and that he should forget about him now and concentrate on his new life, but Jonah can't help thinking that if he's never going to see Mister Sir again, then he's never going to see Mama again either. Mister Sir was the one who was meant to bring him home one day.

The throbbing in his throat is so hard now that he feels like it's going to tear open. He's always thought that being in England would be temporary but sitting here, in Wales, with Rosie and Sam and Hop, he realises that he's probably going to have to live here for ever. That there's no way of going home.

Rosie and Sam don't say anything for a really long time. Then, in a quiet voice, Rosie says.

'Let's go and tuck you in.'

She pulls the sheets up around Jonah and then strokes his back like Mama used to when Jonah couldn't sleep. His eyes fill up with tears.

'It's going to be OK, Jonah . . . ' Sam says.

Jonah hears something padding into the room and then a warm bundle nestles onto the duvet against his side. He's too tired to move Hop now.

Jonah screws shut his eyes and listens to the sea being pulled in by the moon.


## Trudi


Trudi doesn't understand why this tall, skinny, balding detective sets a hive of butterflies fluttering in her stomach. Especially one as blood-boilingly frustrating as DI Peter Taylor. She's always imagined herself falling for a strong, dark, seductive type.

But then DI Peter Taylor's fantasies probably haven't involved a short, overweight, goofy-smiled Ugandan girl either.

Still, those butterflies in her stomach are going manic.

'So you think he'll tell us about her?' Trudi asks.

Peter tips two sugars into the coffee he got from the machine in the waiting area of the prison visitors block.

'We'll see,' he says.

Blood-boilingly frustrating, Trudi thinks again.

They've been meeting at Linda's, the café at the end of Trudi's road, once a week, for the last month. Not because there's been anything new to say about the case (sneaking Trudi in to see Robin Morse turned out to be easier than she'd thought), but not having anything specific to say didn't seem to stop Peter accepting her invitations.

He'd come in on a lunch break or for an early breakfast and order his black coffee and sit in front of her and listen to her complaining about Blessing and the laundrette and the red tape that she tripped over every day as she tried to bring families and children together, and she'd listen to his investigations. Sometimes he talked a bit about his girls too.

'Well, he's been in here for close to five months now. He's had time to think. I reckon he'll give us something,' Trudi says.

She's determined to find out who Jonah's mother is –and why she sent her seven-year-old son halfway around the world without a safety net at the other end.

Trudi has to find out for Jonah – and for Rosie and Sam. Because much as she's tried to reassure Rosie that Jonah was hers now, and that in four months it would all be legal, she can't brush away Rosie's concerns. Or her own. Jonah's biological mother might be difficult to trace, but, from the slight evidence they had from Robin Morse, she was alive. These days, an eight-hour flight away was nothing; if she'd managed to get Jonah over here, it wasn't crazy to think she might get on the plane herself one day. And she hadn't signed a single piece of paper to say that she was happy for Jonah to be adopted.

Jonah has a family and the chance of a future. Trudi wants to make sure it stays that way.

'Are we always kept waiting like this?' Trudi asks, looking around the grey, breeze-block walls. Wormwood Scrubs. Not in a million years had she anticipating visiting a prisoner here.

The bell above the door rings out.

They both look up.

'That's us,' says Peter.

He gets up and holds out his hand towards the door to the visiting room. There are rows of tables and chairs nailed to the floor. The visitors take a seat and, a few minutes later, the prisoners come in.

A tall, stocky man, a red beard and pale freckled skin scans the room.

His eyes fall on Trudi and Peter.

Peter stands up and holds out his hand. 'Thank you for agreeing to see us.'

'I didn't.'

Robin Morse sits down without taking Peter's hand.

And it's true. Peter has enough police clearance to get into any prison he wanted. He'd concocted some excuse about having to talk to Robin Morse and the prison authorities had bought it. And they hadn't questioned him bringing Trudi along either.

'I don't have much time,' Robin Morse says.

*Like you've got more important things to do*, Trudi thinks. She bites her tongue.

'We won't be long,' Peter says.

Robin Morse hasn't looked at Trudi once. He probably feels it, she thinks, that if it were up to her, he'd be locked up for life.

'I don't think there's anything I can help you with,' Robin Morse says.

Trudi ignores this and leans forward.

'What was the nature of your relationship to Jonah's mum?'

Robin holds his hands up. 'I don't think that's any of your business.'

'I'm Jonah's social worker.'

'I know who you are.'

'I need some information. To help him.' She pauses. 'You must still care about him.'

Peter shoots her a *slow-down* look but Robin's already talking.

'Jonah's mother and I were good friends,' Robin says. He takes a sip of coffee. 'More than friends. We've known each other for about five years.'

'You were one of her clients?' Trudi says.

He doesn't answer.

'And she asked you to take Jonah to England?'

Peter shoots her another look but Trudi ignores him. She wants to get as much information out of him as she can.

'Grace wanted him to have an education.'

Grace. It's the first time he's mentioned her name. That will help with the investigation.

From the startled look in Robin Morse's eyes, he's probably realised that he's given something away too.

'And you said you would provide that for him?' Trudi asks. 'A home? An education?'

Robin Morse's thick, red eyebrows shoot up. 'No – definitely not.'

'You *didn't* say you'd look after him?' Trudi asks.

Robin shakes his head. 'I said I'd organise the papers and take him to England for her. That's it. I went through all this with the lawyers.'

'And you were happy with that?' Trudi asks.

'Excuse me?'

'You were happy to take a seven-year-old thousands of miles from home and then dump him on social services?'

'Trudi . . .' Peter says.

'I've had enough of this.' Robin Morse gets up to go.

'I'm sorry.' Trudi stretches out her hand towards him. 'Please stay, just a bit longer.' She pauses. 'We need you to help us understand. Please, for Jonah.'

Very slowly, Robin Morse sits down.

'What was the plan?' Trudi asks, working hard to keep her voice calm and level. 'Help us make sense of it.'

'I was meant to hand Jonah over to his aunt.'

Of course, that's what he'd said to the judge too. Only Peter had traced every Igwe in the UK and had drawn a big fat blank.

'So Grace lied?'

Robin Morse pauses. Then he says. 'Something went wrong with the plan.'

He doesn't believe that, thinks Trudi. He's protecting her. He knows she lied. He told the judge that he was set up – it was a crucial part of his plea bargain.

'And so you decided to leave?'

'I have a family. A career. I fulfilled my part of the deal.'

'You abandoned a child.'

Another long pause. Trudi leaps in.

'Is there any other reason Grace might have sent Jonah to England? Anything that struck you as strange or suspicious about the situation?'

He hesitates.

'Anything at all?' Trudi prompts.

'Grace needed a rest.'

'A rest?'

'She was getting tired a lot. It was hard, looking after Jonah on her own. She works long hours.'

'You're telling me she abandoned her son because she felt *tired*?'

Peter shoots her another look but she ignores him.

'Does she love him?' Trudi asks.

'Trudi . . . ' Peter says.

'She's his mother, of course she loves him,' Robin snaps back.

A long silence.

'Like I said, I don't have anything else to give you besides what I told the judge.'

Only he does have more. Ten years as a social worker has given Trudi a sixth sense for when people are holding things back. And there's a shedload Robin Morse isn't saying.

Robin Morse stands up to go.

'Did you love her?' Trudi asks, her voice steady now.

Robin freezes.

'You did, didn't you? Otherwise Jonah wouldn't go on about you all the time.' She pauses. 'You were part of his life, Robin.'

He's gripping the back of the chair so tight that his knuckles are white as bone.

'You were like a father to him.'

From the corner of her eye, Trudi can see Peter jiggling his leg with impatience. She's gone too far. But then Peter knows her well enough to have anticipated that.

Trudi leans over and puts her hand over Robin's.

'We need you to help us find her.'

Very slowly, he sits back down.


## Rosie


Rosie stands looking out of Jonah's bedroom window. It's the room she had when she lived here with Flick, Alwyn and Sam.

Flick is walking along the beach with her straw hat and her faded dungarees, waving her walking stick at the waves. Ariel trots alongside her, carrying Sam and Jonah on his back. One of Sam's arms is wrapped tight around Jonah's body and the other holds the reins, though the old horse is so gentle that he'd never allow them to fall off.

Jonah's grin is wider than Rosie's ever seen it.

After a while, Sam lets Jonah down from the horse and he bounces ahead of them, running into the waves and kicking at them with his bare feet. The sea spray rises around him and then he runs back up onto the shore, waving his arms, his mouth a big O, no doubt surprised by how cold the sea is.

How many times has Rosie imagined their child on this beach? On that horse? Not a boy, necessarily, and not from Africa, but none of that matters: Jonah is their child now. In a few months, he'll be theirs for good.

When she woke up this morning, there was a lightness in her chest. At last, Jonah was warming to her. Yesterday, he'd let her bathe him and dry him and tuck him into bed.

Yes, everything is going to be better from now on. And no matter what it takes, she's going to be a good mother to him.

Rosie picks Jonah's pyjamas up off the floor. They're a little damp so she places them over the heater.

The door nudges open and Hop comes in. He looks at Rosie for a moment, his head tilted to one side, and then he leaps forward and starts playing with the laces of Jonah's brown shoes, which are poking out of his backpack.

Rosie smiles to herself as she thinks about how Jonah goes through the world in bare feet. She picks up one of his shoes and turns it around in her hands.

Hop keeps pawing at the laces of the other shoe.

'I suppose you go around in bare feet, don't you, Hop? But then yours are padded with fur, Jonah's always get so cold . . .'

And then she stops talking. The inside sole of the shoe she's holding is off centre, the back lipping up into the lining of the heel. She places her palm in the cavity of the shoe and tries to straighten it. But then she feels a sharp corner poking up by the foot arch.

Rosie sits on the bed and places the shoe on her lap. Hop comes up beside her and nudges her hand.

'Not now, Hop,' she says, brushing him away.

She rips out the sole.

And there it is, what she's been waiting for from the moment she read Jonah's file.

Right away, Rosie knows it's her. First, because there's no one else Jonah would have hidden a photo of. But more than that. Rosie knows it's her because it's like she's seen her already a thousand times in her imagination.

The woman in the photograph wears a lemon halter-neck dress, as bright as the sun. Her smile is as wide as Jonah's. Her lips full and red. Large brown eyes dance to her smile. Dark, glossy curls fall over her bare shoulders. Beads sweep down to the neckline of her dress. Bracelets shine on her thin wrists. The thread of a silver anklet. Beautiful, long nails to match her red lips. Legs that, for a small woman, seem to go on forever. And yellow heels to match her dress.

And in that moment Rosie gets it: if this is the template Jonah has for a mother, no wonder he keeps her at arm's length.

More than anything, besides her beauty and her elegance and her femininity, Rosie is struck by this young woman's *aliveness*: she's here, in Rosie's hands, looking up at her, smiling – ready, at any moment, to take Jonah away from them.

What should she do? Challenge Jonah for lying to them about not having a mother? Keep the photo and show it to Trudi so she can pass it on to the police? Or pretend that she never found it?

She looks out of the window again. They're coming back up the beach towards the house, Flick guiding Ariel, Jonah sitting on Sam's shoulders, his head flung back, laughing. Sam swings Jonah back to the ground and kisses his forehead.

It was thinking of Sam as a father, imagining him, just like this, that had made Rosie say yes when he asked her to marry him. It was the day of her eighteenth birthday and they were standing on the cliffs a little further on from Criccieth. Sam had so much love to give, she thought – enough to fill the biggest family in the world. They'd kissed and held onto each other and looked out to the vast sea and, in that moment, everything had seemed possible.

Rosie pulls her phone out the pocket of her jeans and takes a picture of the photograph. Then, before putting the photograph back under the insole of Jonah's shoe, she looks at his mother's face one more time.

*You gave him up . . .* She whispers. *You chose to let him go . . . He's my son now . . .*

And then she feels sick at her own words. How can Jonah be Rosie's son if his mother is still alive? If she hasn't even agreed for him to be adopted?

Rosie stands up, pushing Hop off her lap. She brushes Hop's fur off her jeans and then straightens her back. Threading her fingers through her hair, she tries to flatten the curls, smooths her lips together and sucks in her stomach.

*The prettiest girl to walk the earth . . .* Sam had said that day on the cliffs. And look at her now: a piece of flotsam washed up on the shore.

Rosie takes a breath. Focus on the future, she tells herself. On the 7th of October, a judge will stand in front of them and make Jonah legally theirs. And then, the rest of their lives can begin.

She promises herself that nothing's going to get in the way of that. Not even his mother.

## Jonah

'This is the spot,' Grandma Flick lifts her stick and points to a patch of earth behind the house.

Jonah looks at Grandma Flick with her dungarees and her long cardigan and the walking stick Sam made for her out of a piece of driftwood. If Prospero were an old woman rather than an old man, Jonah's sure that he's here, right now, standing in front of him, in the body of Grandma Flick. He suspects that Grandma Flick has magic powers too. Plus, she has a horse called Ariel and everyone knows that Ariel helps Prospero carry out his magic.

Grandma Flick puts down her stick, picks up a spade and pushes her foot into its metal side. Jonah watches it sink into the earth. In Kenya, the earth is packed so hard and dry that digging a hole takes days.

Hop scoots up behind them and looks into the hole as if he's spotted a mouse down there. When he finds it empty he goes and sits in a patch of sunlight.

Jonah wipes his brow. He's been flushing hot and cold all day. And he can't stop coughing, like there's something stuck in his chest.

'May I ask a question, Grandma Flick?' Jonah asks.

'Of course.'

'Why are you planting the sunflowers here?' Jonah looks at a worm squirming away from Grandma Flick's shovel.

'It needs to be warm and bright.' She looks up past the brim of her straw hat and squints at the sun. 'At least six to eight hours of sun a day.'

She digs another hole.

'May I help you?' Jonah asks.

Grandma Flick looks at him and blinks. 'Of course – here.' She hands him the shovel.

Jonah places his bare foot on the edge of the shovel and pushes his whole weight into it.

'Ow!' cries Jonah.

'Shoes are good for some things, aren't they, Jonah?' Grandma Flick smiles and raises one of her feet to show him her big, dusty, rubber soled trainers. 'Why don't you help me put the seeds in once we've got the hole to the right size?'

Jonah hands her back the shovel and rubs the sole of his foot. 'OK.'

'In the meantime, you can loosen the soil with this.' She gives him a hand rake. 'Pass it through the soil at the bottom of each hole so that the seeds can breathe and spread their roots.'

'What do sunflowers look like?' Jonah asks, raking at the soil.

'They're like big, yellow smiling faces – and their stems are tall and green. Just looking at them makes me happy.' She smiles at him. 'I should have planted them earlier in the year but I think we've made it just in the nick of time. You'll have to come back later in the summer to have a look.'

Jonah looks over to the small packet of seeds. He can't imagine how big yellow faces and long green stems could grow from something so little.

For a while Jonah and Grandma Flick work alongside each other in silence. The warm sun beats down on their backs and the sound of the sea crashes against the shore below them. Jonah's body relaxes and he forgets about feeling hot and cold and about his throat hurting whenever he swallows.

'Might I be allowed to live here?' Jonah asks. 'Instead of in London?'

If what Rosie and Sam said about Mister Sir is right, then there's no point in staying in London any more. And Jonah likes it better here.

'Oh, you'd get bored of it in a second, Jonah. Living with Rosie and Sam is much more fun than living in the middle of nowhere with little old me.'

'But you're not bored of living here.'

'No, I'm not.'

'Well, I don't think I'd ever get bored of it either.'

The sun filters through Grandma Flick's hat and makes shadows on her face.

Hop comes and lies closer to them.

'Do you miss Sam's papa?' Jonah asks and then he blushes and realises that that's exactly the kind of question Alice would ask.

Grandma Flick brushes some earth off her dungarees.

'I miss him every day.'

'Every day?' Jonah asks. 'Really?'

'If you love someone, that's the way it goes.'

'Does he speak to you, sometimes?'

She holds Jonah's gaze. 'Yes, yes he does.'

'How?'

'Oh, in all kinds of ways. He talks to me through the wind when it rattles the windows of the house. He talks to me through Ariel, when we ride along the beach. He talks to me through these sunflowers – he loved flowers.' Her gaze shifts to the horizon. 'And he talks to me through the sea ...'

Jonah gulps. 'The sea?'

'Yes.' She turns to face him again. 'Haven't you noticed, how the sea whispers?'

Jonah looks out at the sea. He'd always thought about how he and Mama spoke *under* the water, in that still, quiet place where no one else could interrupt them. And they didn't even use any words, they just looked at each other and knew what the other was saying. He'd never thought that maybe Mama's voice would come to him *over* the sea. And in other things too, like the wind. And maybe even the rain.

'Close your eyes, Jonah.' She brushes her fingertips over his eyelids. 'Now listen.'

Jonah strains his ears. For a while, all he can hear are the noises around the house. Hop scratching at the earth. A tractor in the next field. A plane droning overhead. But then, when those sounds settle, he hears it: a rushing ... a whispering ... and he's not sure what it's saying but it makes his heart swell and he knows the words must be good ones. And that it must be Mama, at last.

His eyes fly open. He smiles at Grandma Flick.

'You see?' Grandma Flick says.

Jonah nods.

'What does Sam's papa tell you?'

'Well, one of the things he's been telling me lately is how much he would have liked to meet you.'

'Really?'

'Definitely.' She takes Jonah's hand. 'He says he's happy for Rosie too. He loved Rosie very much.'

Jonah pulls his hand away. He doesn't see how Rosie comes into this.

'Why would he be happy for Rosie?'

'Because he always said that she was made to be a mother.'
Grandma Flick goes quiet for a while and then she says: 'You
know that Rosie's wanted you her whole life?'

Jonah puts down his small rake. 'She's wanted *me* her whole
life?' He doesn't understand. How can someone want someone
for their whole life who they've only met a few weeks ago?

Grandma Flick nods.

'When Rosie was a little girl and her parents were too busy to
play with her, she would come over here to spend time with us.
It was an odd thing – she was such a tomboy, so you wouldn't
have expected her to be interested in babies, but she was determined to be a midwife – and to have lots of babies of her own
one day. She talked about how she'd love them and look after
them—'

'That doesn't mean she wanted *me*.'

'Oh, she didn't know it would be you, Jonah, not exactly, but
she knew that she wanted to be a mother and you've made it
possible for her to do that.'

Grandma Flick stares right at Jonah and doesn't let him look
away. Then she goes on: 'And I hold to the belief that our children
are planned for us way before the beginning of time.' She leans
over and kisses Jonah's forehead. 'Every child has a mother that's
meant for him. And that goes for being adopted too.'

Jonah can't imagine a time that was *before the beginning* but
he knows that if there was one, it was Mama he was planned for.
Mama and no one else.

'Rosie isn't my mother.' He says it very quietly hoping that
maybe it will make it sound less rude. But he wants Grandma
Flick to understand.

Grandma Flick takes the rake out of Jonah's hand, puts down

253

her shovel and sits beside him. Then she takes off her hat and puts it on one of her knees.

'Tell me then, Jonah, who's your mother?'

'I don't have a mama.' His voice sounds like it's coming from far, far away, as far as the bit where the sea joins the sky.

For a long time, Grandma Flick doesn't answer. Then she asks, 'Is that what you called her?'

Jonah looks at Grandma Flick's eyes: they're as bright and deep and blue as the sea. 'What do you mean?'

'Did you call her *Mama*, back in Kenya?'

Jonah knows that he promised Mama not to tell anyone. And he knows that it's wrong to break promises. But he's already told Alice. And he feels he can trust Grandma Flick too because she doesn't really count as a grown-up.

Very slowly, he nods. 'Yes, I called her Mama.' He takes a quick breath. 'You won't tell Rosie and Sam, will you?'

'That's for you to do, Jonah,' Grandma Flick says. She takes his hand. 'But you know, you can tell Rosie and Sam your secrets. They're good, good people. The best people I know.'

Grandma Flick doesn't understand that it's not about good people and bad people. It's about how Jonah has to make sure that no one ever finds Mama.

He coughs and touches his throat with his hand.

'Is it sore?' Grandma Flick asks.

He shakes his head. But then, when he catches her eye again, he nods.

'Here ... ' She opens a flask, pours out some tea into a plastic cup. 'Thyme and rosemary with a bit of honey and turmeric. My special potion has the power to cure anything.'

Jonah takes a sip and lets the warm liquid slip down his throat. For a second, the raw feeling in his throat fades. He takes another sip.

'Good?' Grandma Flick asks.

He nods. Maybe Grandma Flick is a magician. Maybe she is Prospero.

'So, tell me about your mama … what's she like?'

Jonah hesitates, just for a beat, and then it tumbles out of him.

'She's pretty and always wears dresses and she's funny and she can dance and sing and everyone looks at her when she walks by and she swims in the sea at night, she's the best swimmer …' Swimming is one of the things Jonah remembers most about Mama.

Mama flips over and floats on her back, her arms spread wide. The dark water ripples around her.

Swimming at night was one of Jonah and Mama's favourite things to do.

'When you get to England, you mustn't tell anyone about me,' she says.

'Not tell them about you?' When Jonah gets to England, he wants to tell *everyone* about Mama. She's the one they'll want to hear about; she's the one everyone always wants to hear about.

'No. You mustn't tell them my name or where I live or anything else.'

'But—'

'It's for the best,' Mama says.

Mama always says *it's for the best* whenever she doesn't want to give Jonah a proper answer.

'Why is it for the best?'

Jonah treads water and watches Mama floating. She's staring up at the sky, her eyes lost in the stars and the moon. Sometimes, even when Mama is so close to Jonah that he can touch her – sometimes, even when she's hugging him so tight there's no space left between them – she still feels as far as that moon.

And then she comes back to him and it's like they're so close they're one person.

'If you tell them about me they'll come and find me and then you'll have to come back,' Mama says.

Considering that Jonah wasn't yet sure that he wanted to go to England, coming back didn't sound so bad.

'Why would they make me come back?' Jonah asks.

'Because people do not like little children not to be with their mamas.'

'I think they're right,' Jonah whispers.

'And they'll be very angry with me.'

'Who will be angry?'

'The police.'

Jonah freezes. Mama hates the police. The police make everything worse. And he never, ever wants them to get angry with Mama.

'Would it not be easier for me to stay here, then?' Jonah asks.

Mama flips back over and treads water, like Jonah.

'Jonah, we've talked about this ...' Her brown eyes go dark and shiny, which is always a warning to Jonah that she's going to get cross if he doesn't agree with her.

Mama paddles towards Jonah. The moon splinters in the water. Mama kisses Jonah's cheek. 'Come on, let's swim back.'

When they're standing on the cool, white sand, drying themselves off, with the moon and the stars looking down on them, Jonah asks again.

'Mama ... why can't you come with me, to England? The police wouldn't be angry if we went together, would they?'

Mama sighs. 'You know how you're going to England in a plane, Jonah?'

He nods. Ever since Mama told Jonah that he would be leaving, he'd been looking up at the planes: the small white birds with wings that didn't flap. And he'd tried to imagine himself up there too. Only the sky looked very far away.

'Well, seats on planes are expensive, even seats for a little boy like you. I've been working very hard to buy your ticket. We can't afford for me to come, Jonah.'

Mama rubs her long, dark hair with her towel. It will take her hours to make it all straight and glossy again.

'Maybe Mister Sir could pay for the seat,' Jonah says.

Mama frowns. 'No, Jonah. Mister Sir is doing more than enough to help us already. He's taking you to England – and he's going to look after you on the way there.' She pauses. 'It's not good to be in someone's debt. I can't ask him to do any more.'

Mama gives Jonah a hug and rubs his back.

'And what would I do all day long, my little Jonah, while you are at school learning to read and to become a gentleman? You'll be so busy that you won't have any time left for me.' Mama gives him a sad smile that makes her look even more beautiful. 'You'll forget I am even there. And then I'll feel all lost and lonely.'

Jonah puts his arms around Mama and hugs her tight. He would never be too busy to spend time with Mama. And he would never, ever forget her.

'I'll come home one day, though, won't I, Mama?'

Mama goes quiet for a long, long time and then she says: 'Yes, one day you'll come home, Jonah. I promise.'

'A woman after my own heart,' Grandma Flick says. 'The night swimming rather than the dresses and the dancing.'

'You swim in the dark too?'

Grandma Flick nods. 'Sometimes in August, when the sea's had the whole summer to warm up and when the tourists are beginning to trickle back to their homes in England, I go down late at night for a dip.'

Jonah smiles as he pictures wrinkly Grandma Flick running into the water.

When they've finished planting the sunflowers, Grandma Flick and Jonah sit in the sun and drink some more tea and eat some digestive biscuits. He nibbles a bit of the biscuit but then his tummy feels sore so, when Grandma Flick isn't looking, he crumbles it up over the dark earth.

Jonah notices a driftwood starfish leaning up against the wall of the house. He picks it up and turns it round in his hands.

'Did Sam make this?'

Grandma Flick nods. 'When he was ten.'

'Wow.' Jonah is not that far away from ten and he cannot imagine ever making anything that amazing. 'Did he collect bits of wood from the beach when he was very little, too?'

She nods. 'Even as a toddler, he'd pick up sticks and insist on bringing them home. Then, when he was old enough, his dad taught him to shape the wood into small sculptures: starfish and shells and jellyfish and tangles of seaweed. Then Sam would bring them back to the shore and wait for the water to take them back.'

'Could we go and find a piece of driftwood for Sam now?' Jonah asks.

He wants to give Sam something to say thank you for bringing him to the sea and to Ariel and to Grandma Flick.

Hop rolls over in the warm patch and stretches his limbs. He lifts his head and walks over to them like he wants to come on the walk too.

Grandma Flick nods. Her silver bob swishes along her jaw line. She's beautiful too, thinks Jonah. Not a Mama kind of beautiful but beautiful all the same.

'That sounds like a lovely idea, Jonah.' She screws the cap back onto the thermos. 'Let's go.'

## Sam

Sam lies in bed turning over the piece of driftwood that Jonah gave him. Jonah and Flick rushed in just before supper, Jonah holding it in front of him like a trophy: 'I found a good one, I found a good one . . . ' he squealed. 'It's for your Ascot horse.'

And it was a good one: a beautiful curve, a deep silver, smoothed by the sea.

Sam closes his eyes and makes himself a promise: he's going to get things right with Jonah; he's going to love him and keep him safe and make him happy – in a way that Jonah's father never did. And he's going to love Rosie too and keep her safe and make her happy. Taking care of them is the most important job in the world.

He checks his phone again. Still no message from Rosie.

It's dark. Jonah's already in bed. He's heard him coughing a few times but he thinks he's asleep. For now, at least.

They waited for Rosie to come back for supper but then she called to say she'd be home late and that they should go ahead without her. Which was wasn't like her. Sam couldn't remember a time when she hadn't sat next to Jonah, watching him pushing his food around.

Rosie had taken the car at lunchtime, saying she wanted to get some ingredients in town for a special, final breakfast before they headed home early tomorrow. She was determined to get the recipes right this time. But a bit of food shopping shouldn't have taken the whole afternoon. And now it was nearly 8pm and still she wasn't here.

He knows he shouldn't worry, that Rosie's been so much better than those low times when they were trying for a baby. But worrying about her has become a habit he slots back into whenever she disappears on him.

Two years ago, December. He'd been waiting for her to come home for hours. He'd called her mobile over and over. And then he'd called the local clinic, where she saw her patients. 'She left hours ago,' the receptionist told Sam. 'Yes, she seemed fine . . .'

She was probably doing some last-minute Christmas shopping, Sam had thought.

Only Rosie was never late. And if she was – or if she changed her plans – she called. It was the scary thing about living with someone as organised and thoughtful as Rosie: any deviation sent the fear of God into him.

He jumped into the car and circled Bridgeford for hours. The park. The second-hand bookshop. The café on the high street Rosie liked, even though it meant having to squeeze in between the pushchairs and breastfeeding mums.

Then he scanned through the contacts on his phone, thinking

about any friends she might have called. Only, Sam and Rosie had lost touch with most of their friends. Mainly because, these past few years, dinner dates had been swapped for play dates. And because their friends found it awkward, no doubt, having to avoid the topic which dominated their lives: children.

Exhausted from looking, he'd driven home. When he reached the front door of the cottage, it started snowing.

As he pushed the key into the front door, Hop darted out and that made Sam turn round and look down at the station. That's when he saw her, sitting on the bench of Platform 1. She didn't even seem to have noticed that it had started snowing. Small, icy snowflakes fell around her, landing like feathers on her curly hair, on her coat, her cheeks.

With Hop leading the way, he came and sat beside her and took her hand. She was frozen through.

For the next hour, Rosie refused to talk. So he just sat there, holding her hand.

Despite the cold, Hop sat nestled between them.

Two trains came and went.

And then she started to cry. Huge, gulping sobs and then big, hot tears poured out of her eyes and onto her cheeks and fell into her lap. So many tears that he remembers thinking she must have been storing an ocean inside her.

When her tears stopped for a moment, a few words came out. Slowly. Disjointed. With big pauses. Followed by more tears.

Rosie had developed a special bond with one of her patients: a sixteen-year-old girl. She'd had taken time outside her schedule to visit her. She'd sat next to the girl as she told her boyfriend about the pregnancy. And then her parents. Rosie had eased the fear out of her and made her believe that even though she still felt like a child herself, she could be a good mother.

And then that morning, an hour before she was due to meet Rosie, the girl took herself to an abortion clinic. She was twenty-four weeks pregnant.

And on that same day, on Rosie's lunch break, her period started again. They were on their second course of IVF.

Sam considers borrowing a car from one of the neighbours, or getting the bus into Porthmadog. He pictures Rosie sitting at the train station, staring down the tracks. And then he shakes off the thought. Things are good, aren't they? This was the happiest he'd seen her since Jonah moved in with them.

He picks up his phone and texts:

*Missing you . . . Come home . . . Drive safely . . . x*

An hour later, Sam wakes to Rosie kissing him. He blinks and looks up at her.

'Rosie?'

Her hair's been pulled straight; it falls in strange feathers around her face. She's done something to her eyebrows too: they're thinner, and the skin around them is red and puffy. And she's got lipstick on, a deep plum that makes her look pale as a ghost. He doesn't think he's ever seen Rosie wear lipstick, except perhaps at their wedding, and even then she'd smudged it off within a few hours.

'Like it?' Rosie asks.

He nods and smiles but all he can think is, *where's my Rosie?* The freckled, windswept, messy-haired Rosie with warm, soft lips that taste of salt?

Rosie climbs off the bed and arranges some bags by the wardrobe.

Sam sits up. 'You went clothes shopping?' He can't think of the last time she bought herself an item of clothing.

'Oh, just a few bits and pieces.'

'I thought you were going to the supermarket?'

'I did. Flick helped me tidy the things away in the kitchen.'

He wonders what his mum thinks of Rosie's new look. She'd always praised Sam for not falling for those heavily made-up, short-skirted, dyed-hair girls from their school in Porthmadog.

'We're going to have a feast, tomorrow,' Rosie says.

Which makes Sam's heart sink a little. Put too much food in front of Jonah and he freezes.

'I've had such a busy afternoon,' Rosie says, tucking a strand of hair behind her ear. He sees her catching her reflection in the dark bedroom window.

'Is everything OK, my love?' Sam asks.

'What do you mean?'

'You seem . . . a bit . . . .' He sighs. 'I don't know, you're just late home, that's all.'

*You look like someone else's wife*, is what he wants to say.

'Oh, I just lost track of time.'

Rosie doesn't lose track of time.

'How's Jonah's cough?' Rosie asks.

'Still there. It would have been nice to give him a few more days here, to clear away all those winter bugs.' Sam turns the piece of driftwood between his fingers. 'I think Jonah would like to stay here, too.'

'Wouldn't we all,' Rosie says.

Sam catches her hand. 'Could we think about it?'

'Think about what, Sam?'

'Moving back here?'

They'd had this conversation a million times. It wasn't that

263

Rosie didn't love Criccieth as much as he did, it's just that it had bittersweet memories for her. Her parents' old B&B standing derelict on the outskirts of town. The fact that, somehow, the dreams she and Sam had here as they were falling in love – the big family, his success as an artist – hadn't materialised. It was like she didn't trust the place.

'You can be a midwife anywhere—'

'You have to be near the London galleries, you know that.'

'I've been near the London galleries for twenty years now, Rosie, and what good has it done me? At least here I might get some inspiration again.'

Rosie kicks off her shoes. 'It's been a long day, Sam, let's not talk about this now.' She rubs her feet. He notices that her toenails are neatly shaped and painted. 'So how did Jonah do at dinner?'

'Fine … good …'

'Details?'

'He tried a boiled egg,' Sam says. 'I think he had a corner of toast.'

Rosie's shoulders slump. 'You *think*?'

'I wasn't really concentrating. Mum gave him bits to try. He looked happy.'

Jonah hadn't eaten any more than usual, but then he hadn't eaten any worse than usual either. Jonah just didn't eat. But he hadn't starved on them yet, had he? He was doing OK. One day they'd just have to accept that Julie had got it wrong and that Jonah wasn't interested in food.

Rosie slips out of her jeans and pulls her jumper over her head. 'I checked in on him just now,' Rosie says. 'He was sleeping …'

'That's good.'

Sam wonders how long it will take before Rosie picks up on

the fact that his night sweats are a regular thing. And that he hardly sleeps.

'He was holding the driftwood horse you've been making together.' Rosie goes on.

Sam nods. He'd noticed it too, how Jonah had started carrying it around with him everywhere. And how he holds it through the night.

She sits on the edge of the bed in her faded bra and knickers and despite the changes, he feels like he's got a bit of the old Rosie back.

'Come here,' Sam says, holding out his hand to her.

'Wait ... I've got something ...' Rosie dashes over to the pile of bags by the wardrobe.

Rosie pulls out a frilly lace nightie. He'd only ever seen her in pyjamas: thick, floral multipacks from M&S. *My cosy PJs* she calls them, the ones she climbs into after a long day at work.

She holds the nightie up to Sam.

'Isn't that a bit cold?' he asks. There are more holes than fabric.

She turns away from him for a moment, unclasps her bra, steps out of her knickers and pulls the nightie over her head.

'The idea, Sam, is that *you* warm me up,' she throws over her shoulder.

Then she does a twirl for him and comes over to the bed. She takes the piece of driftwood out of his fingers, places it on the bedside table and switches off the light.

Then she slips in beside him under the covers.

He feels her fingers stroking his chest, his stomach, then moving further down.

Sam lies back and closes his eyes. She hasn't been this relaxed and happy in years.

Reaching out for her, he pulls her close. He doesn't care about her strange new hairstyle or her lipstick or her eyebrows or the strange nightie she's wearing. She's his Rosie, his beautiful Rosie.

'I love you . . .' he says. 'So, so much . . .'

He hears the sea pulling at the shore. The moon spills in through the open curtains.

And they fall into each other.

'Sam . . .' A small voice comes through the dark.

He feels Rosie's body freeze. They untangle and sit up.

'Jonah?' Sam asks, squinting across the dark room.

Jonah has never come to their bedroom before, not here, not back in London.

Rosie jumps out of bed.

'Can you come and tuck me in?' Jonah asks.

'Of course,' Rosie says, reaching for Sam's jumper hanging off the back of a chair.

Jonah stands back. 'I would like Sam to come.'

Rosie stands in the middle of the room, her baggy jumper over her new nightie, her hairstyle messed up from being in bed. Her arms hang limply by their sides.

Hop slips in behind Jonah and slinks over to Rosie. He rubs his body against her bare legs.

'Of course . . .' Sam says, fumbling for his boxers under the sheets. He puts on some old socks, swings his legs out of bed and walks over to Rosie and kisses her cheek.

'I won't be long,' he whispers.


Sam follows Jonah back to his room. They sit on his bed and Jonah stares into his hands. Hop slips in through the open door, jumps on the bed and snuggles in beside him.

'Do you want to tell me what's wrong?'

266

'Promise you won't make me go back to London?'

'I don't see why I should do that,' says Sam, though he's beginning to worry.

Jonah grabs his throat. 'It's sore . . .'

'It's probably your cough, J.'

'Really sore. And it hurts here.'

He points to his sternum. 'And I couldn't breathe.'

Sam's heart starts to bang against his chest. He knows that he shouldn't have ignored Jonah's symptoms, but he really thought he'd feel better here.

'You couldn't breathe?'

Sam tries to remind himself that children exaggerate, that they say things that sound fantastical just to make themselves understood. Only Jonah's not like other children. He has to drag information out of him.

'My throat was closing up,' Jonah says. 'It felt like it was filling up with the sea.'

'Is it better now?'

Jonah gulps and nods his head.

'Maybe you've caught a cold,' Sam says, taking Jonah in his arms and swaying him from side to side. 'All that walking in bare feet in the freezing water.'

Jonah looks OK now, doesn't he? He looks fine. But Sam thinks back to Dr Barron's reaction when he looked down Jonah's throat. Maybe he should have spoken to Rosie about booking an appointment with a paediatrician.

'Why don't we go down to the kitchen to get you some hot lemon and honey. That's what Grandma Flick always made for me when I was little.'

Jonah nods and then holds out his hand.

Sam feels relieved that Rosie isn't here: just about now, she'd be going into panic mode. And then he feels guilty. She's Jonah's mum: she has a right to know when he's not well.

Sam takes Jonah's hand. 'You're going to be right as rain, Jonah – you know that?' And then he swings him up onto his shoulders and thunders down the downstairs, Jonah swaying and laughing above him.

## Jonah

Jonah gets up off the straw and gives Ariel a kiss on his long, grey nose. Hop weaves between Ariel's feet.

'I wish I could stay with you.' Jonah leans his head against Ariel's.

Hop weaves between Ariel's legs and chirrups, as though he's waiting for Jonah to say the same thing to him, too.

Jonah bends down and gives him a stroke. He wishes Alice could see him. Maybe she'd be allergic to Ariel just like she's allergic to Hop, but he knows she'd love this horse.

Although it was raining when he woke up, Jonah got up early and ran out of the house and came to see Ariel. He wants to spend as much time as possible with Ariel before going home.

'Jonah!' Grandma Flick calls out through the front door. 'Jonah!'

For some reason, Grandma Flick always seems to know where Jonah is. Maybe she is Prospero in disguise and maybe she does have magic powers.

'Coming!' Jonah calls back.

Jonah struggles with the lock to the small stable next to the house. The metal loop is rusty and the padlock won't fit. He pushes it harder and it gets stuck halfway. It will do, he thinks.

A few minutes later, Jonah sits at the kitchen table, his eyes blurry. After Sam left, Jonah didn't go back to sleep for hours: he was scared that his throat might close altogether, that he would stop breathing and never wake up. And then he felt this really hard lump on the side of his neck that he hadn't noticed before. You have to press it really hard to know it's there but it feels like it stands out a mile.

Jonah swallows hard. Even though it's really hot in the kitchen, he's wearing his woolly red scarf. His forehead is sweaty and he wishes he could take off the scarf, but he doesn't want anyone to see the lump, especially Rosie.

'You've outdone yourself, Rosie,' Grandma Flick says, sitting down at the table next to Jonah.

'Smells delicious,' Sam says, sitting next to Grandma Flick.

Jonah's stomach churns. All the smells are crashing against each other: frying bacon and sausages and eggs and the doughy pancakes, piled up in a tower in front of him, and butter melting on toast and bitter coffee spluttering out of Grandma Flick's old coffee machine. Even the oranges that Rosie has been pushing through Grandma Flick's juicer smell wrong.

Hop's standing next to Rosie by the stove, thumping his tail and looking up at the frying pans. Jonah hopes that Hop will eat all the food so that he doesn't have to.

Jonah coughs and sneezes. His eyes and nose stream.

'Here,' Grandma Flick pulls a hankie out from her sleeve.

Jonah blows his nose. His whole head feels like it's been stuffed with clumps of Hop's fur.

'I hope you haven't caught a summer cold,' Rosie says.

Jonah looks Rosie up and down. She's wearing a green dress he's never seen before: it's so bright that it making Jonah's headache worse.

Mama hates green.

Rosie's lips look strange too, like Mimi has drawn them on with her red felt tip. And her hair looks like it's been flattened by the same rain that flattened all of Grandma Flick's flowers overnight.

Hop scrambles up onto Jonah's lap and starts purring. For once, he doesn't push him away.

'Can I go back to my room with Hop?' Jonah asks.

The kitchen goes quiet. Hop stops purring. Grandma Flick and Sam look at each other. And then at Rosie, who's got her back to them at the stove. Then Rosie spins round, picks up a plate full of food and puts it down in front of Jonah.

'Eat up, Jonah.'

Rosie's cheeks are flushed red and the straight bits of her hair have gone frizzy around her hairline and one of her eyes is smudged.

'I'm not very hungry, thank you.'

Everything goes quiet again.

'We've got a long journey ahead of us, you need to keep your strength up,' Rosie says.

Jonah shakes his head.

'I'm asking you to eat,' Rosie says.

'Love . . . ' Sam says to her.

Jonah has learnt that, depending on the situation, *Love* can mean many things. Often, like now, it means: *please stop talking*.

'I'm very tired,' Jonah says, hoping that this will work.

Grandma Flick leans over. 'Rosie's gone to a lot of trouble to make our final breakfast together special. Maybe you could just have a little bite . . .'

Jonah frowns. He thought Grandma Flick was on his side.

'I can't . . .' He pushes Hop off his lap and stands up to go, but his hand catches a tumbler of orange juice and it crashes to the tiles. Hop jumps out of the way. The glass splinters and the lumpy yellow juice spreads everywhere.

'What a great idea,' Rosie says, staring at the broken glass.

Everyone looks up at her. There's something different in Rosie's eyes. It's the first time that he thinks that Mama and Rosie look a bit the same. Because, when she's angry at Jonah, Mama's eyes go dark and shiny too.

'I should have thought of it before!' She booms.

'Darling . . .' Sam says.

But Rosie doesn't notice anything that's going on around her any more. She just throws her hands up and says, 'Silly me, all this time I've been trying to feed my family and I didn't realise that the *floor* was hungry.' She looks around the kitchen table and picks up the plate of pancakes.

Grandma Flick stands up and tries to take the plate. 'Rosie, dear, why don't you have a rest . . . ?'

Only Rosie yanks the plate away from her and then drops it onto the floor. The plate cracks and the pancakes slide around in the orange juice. And then other things start crashing onto the floor.

Every time something smashes, Jonah jumps. He stares at Rosie throwing things around the kitchen.

Hop paws at a sausage that rolled under the table.

'Is this what you want, Jonah?' Rosie goes on. 'For the floor to eat all your food?'

'I ... I don't know ...' Jonah stutters and walks backwards towards the door. He's shivering now, and sweating.

'Come on, Rosie,' Sam says. 'You're scaring him.'

But Rosie keeps going. Her hands flap in all directions. There's flour in her hair and her skin is pink and shiny and her eyes aren't dark any more, they're pale and watery.

'Is that what your mother did, back in Kenya? Throw food at the floor?'

Jonah looks straight at Grandma Flick.

'You *told* her about Mama?'

Rosie holds onto the table like she's going to fall down.

Grandma Flick's face folds into a frown. 'Of course not, Jonah ...'

'Told me about what?' Rosie asks, her voice low. 'What haven't you said?' Tears are dropping down her cheeks now.

'You promised,' Jonah says to Grandma Flick. And then he runs out of the kitchen, through the hall, out through the front door and down the beach to the sea.

## Jonah

By the time Jonah's at the water, his T-shirt and jeans are drenched. The rain's falling hard and the wind has picked up. The dark sky and the dark sea look like they're growling at each other, and the waves are really high.

Jonah thinks he hears a neighing behind him and a kicking of hooves, but it must just be the wind.

Jonah doesn't care that he has clothes on and he doesn't care that he's cold and that it's raining and that his ears are ringing and that his head is pounding and that his throat is closing up again: he wants to be under the water, he wants to feel in his heart that Mama is speaking to him, even if he can't hear it with his ears.

He wades in.

His red scarf floats around him, slapping against his skin. The shock of the cold water against his stomach makes him stop for a second, but then he pushes forward harder and harder until his feet let go of the sea floor and he's floating free. He lets a big wave wash over him and when it's gone, he swims into another wave and another and another.

And then something pulls at his clothes and it's so strong, he thinks it must be another wave. He closes his eyes and lets his body fall through the dark water.

## Sam

'He's got pneumonia ...' Rosie shakes her head. 'And I didn't pick up on it.'

Sam looks at Jonah asleep in the hospital bed, his small body lost in the tangle of white sheets.

'You couldn't have known, Rosie ...'

'I'm a nurse, Sam. Picking up on medical symptoms is what I'm trained to do.'

For a long time, he doesn't say anything, because he knows that when he does, Rosie will pull away from him further than she has already. But he doesn't have a choice. She'll find out somehow, and that will be even worse.

'It's my fault,' he says.

'Don't be stupid,' she says, batting away his words with a flick of her hand.

'It is.'

He's been a big, lumbering, inexcusable idiot for keeping it from her. He convinced himself that keeping quiet was the right thing to do: because he loves her and didn't want to worry her; because Jonah was beginning to settle in with them and he didn't want to upset things; because it was probably nothing – Jonah was meant to get better. But Sam knows now that if only he'd said something, he could have prevented Jonah from getting worse. That this is his fault.

Sam takes a breath: 'I took him to the surgery.'

Rosie's eyes go dark. 'You did what?'

'He's been complaining about a sore throat ... and I noticed that he'd sweated through his pyjamas a few times ... so I took him to see Dr Barron.'

'*Dr Barron*?' Rosie's voice is shrill now.

'We just went for a check-up—'

'Will you stop saying *we*, Sam? This is you. You've been keeping something from me and now my little boy's sick ... .' She stops and catches her breath. Her eyes are wild.

'I was going to tell you, if his symptoms persisted. But he's been a bit better.'

'His *symptoms*? Christ, Sam.'

'You know he hasn't been eating—'

Rosie's face is red. 'What else haven't you been telling me?'

She's never looked at me with that much anger in her eyes, thinks Sam.

'Dr Barron said we should get him checked out.' He pauses. 'At the hospital.'

'God, Sam – and you didn't think it was worth telling me this?'

'I didn't want to upset you.'

'*Upset* me? I'm his mother! I'm meant to be upset by the things that happen to my child.'

'I know . . . I know . . .'

Rosie gets up and paces up and down the room. Sam sits on his chair, his head bowed. He's not cut out to be a dad. Maybe he's not even cut out to be a husband.

When Rosie sits down again, he touches her arm and says, 'You heard what the doctor said, Rosie – that with a bit of rest, some fluids and antibiotics, he'll be OK. We just have to be patient. And we'll be home soon.'

But she doesn't look at him.

Ever since Jonah's been in hospital, Rosie hasn't heard a word that Sam's said. Every time he draws close, she pulls away. Even before he told her about Dr Barron, she blamed him.

Sam knows that she'd hate him even more if she could hear his thoughts but he can't help them crashing into his head: if they hadn't adopted Jonah, if they'd been happy to be just the two of them, to accept that they couldn't have children – that maybe they were never meant to have children – they wouldn't be in this mess.

'We've failed him.' She bends over Jonah's bed, leans her head against his arm and closes her eyes.

It was Ariel who pulled Jonah out of the sea. Jonah must have left the stable door open but still, none of them understood how the old horse worked out that Jonah was on the beach or how he managed to get to Jonah before they did – or what made him wade into the sea and grab at Jonah's clothes with his muzzle. But the point was that if Ariel hadn't shown up when he did, Jonah might well have drowned.

By the time Sam, Rosie and Flick got to Jonah, he was coughing and spluttering on the shore. Sam thought that, at times like this, he'd be able to go into superhero mode – wasn't that what people said happened to parents when their child was in danger? That somehow you got pushed into doing the right thing – rescuing, giving first aid, saving ... That it was a natural instinct. Well, that hadn't happened to Sam. He just stood there on the beach, frozen, staring at Jonah.

Eventually, he'd carried him back to the house. At least that. He remembers thinking how light he was, his small body pressed into his chest. They nearly lost him, Sam kept thinking. They nearly lost their little boy.

He watched Rosie bathe him and wrap him up in warm towels. Even when he was in bed with a hot water bottle, his teeth wouldn't stop chattering. And then he started really burning up. Rosie went into nurse mode. She gave him Calpol and pressed wet flannels to his brow. Whenever Sam asked what he could do or tried to step in with a glass of water or a new flannel, she acted like he wasn't there. He knew that she had to be like this, that it was her nurse mode, that she was probably the same when she delivered babies: focused, locked in that zone in which nothing existed but her and her patient. And it was childish to think it, especially when Jonah was so sick, but he felt left out.

Sam's mum drove them straight over to the local GP. Jonah had a chest infection, the GP said, and called an ambulance to take him to the hospital.

Rosie went in the back of the ambulance with Jonah. She didn't let go of his hand for a second.

Sam and his mum followed in the Land Rover. As they drove along the cliff road, his mum pulled into a layby for a moment. She switched off the engine and leant over and pulled Sam into her arms.

He started sobbing uncontrollably and, for a while, they sat there, in the dark car, the sea crashing below them, and he remembered how they'd held each other like this on the night his dad died.

'It's going to be OK, Sammy,' she said after a while. 'He's going to be OK now.'

But when she pulled away, she was crying too.

That was two days ago. Jonah's been in hospital ever since.

A doctor comes in.

'Mr and Mrs Keep, can I have a word?'

Rosie raises her head and blinks.

'Where's the doctor who's been dealing with Jonah?'

'I'm the consultant paediatrician.' The doctor stretches his arm down the corridor. 'Maybe we could go to the family room.'

'I want to stay with Jonah,' Rosie says. She's been saying that over and over in the last forty-eight hours, as if keeping her eyes on him every second will make sure he's OK.

'He'll be asleep for a while,' the paediatrician says. 'And I'll ask the nurses to keep an eye on him. We won't be long.'

Rosie leans over to kiss Jonah's cheek, stands up and, without looking at Sam, follows the doctor out of the side room.


The doctor crosses his knees, leans forward and holds out his palms.

'So, we ran some extra blood tests ...' He pauses and looks from Rosie to Sam. 'I'd like to talk to you about those now.'

Sam's chest tightens. He stares down at the grey tea in the polystyrene cup a nurse brought in.

Rosie looks away from the consultant too. He watches her scan the wallpaper: the elephants and the giraffes and the monkeys; he knows that she's thinking of the adoption activity day, of the little girl she fell in love with, of Jonah who she didn't meet, of them all dressed up, waiting for their new lives to begin.

'Some anomalies have shown up,' the consultant goes on.

Rosie's gaze shifts back to the consultant.

'Anomalies?'

The doctor nods. His Adam's apple slides up and down his throat.

'Jonah's glands were so swollen we thought there might be an additional infection, glandular fever perhaps, a virus of some kind. But the swelling seems to be coming from another source.'

'What do you mean, another source?' Rosie asks.

The doctor points to his throat. 'Jonah has an unusual growth on the side of his neck. A swollen lymph node.'

Sam's stomach churns. His difficulty swallowing. The way his small fingers kept brushing his neck. Dr Barron's raised eyebrows when he looked into Jonah's throat. If only he'd gone to see a consultant back in Bridgeford, maybe they could have caught whatever it is with a round of antibiotics, some bed rest.

Sam clears his throat. 'He's been complaining about how it hurts when he swallows ... We took him to our local doctor ...'

Rosie spins round to look at Sam. '*We* took him?'

Sam's shoulders drop. 'I took him.'

The consultant raises his palms. 'The point is, we need to investigate further. You don't live here, do you?'

'We're from London.'

'Well, I suggest that, once Jonah is strong enough, you go home. I'll call Jonah's GP so that he makes a referral as quickly

278

as possible. Jonah will need a CT scan and a biopsy of the swollen lymph gland.'

Rosie stares at the doctor, shell-shocked. 'A biopsy?'

'It's routine when we see a lump like this. A small incision to test whether the lump is malignant.'

'I'm a nurse,' Rosie says. 'I know what a biopsy means.'

The doctor uncrosses his legs and sits up straight in his chair.

'I'm sorry, I didn't realise, Mrs Keep.'

'So I need to hear it straight,' Rosie says.

'He said it was routine, love . . . ' Sam says.

Rosie spins round. 'If you don't want to hear it, you can go.'

'Go . . . ? What do you mean?'

He looks at the dark shadows under her eyes, at her curls, all knotted up from days of sleeping on chairs next to Jonah.

Rosie turns back to the consultant. 'You think he has cancer?'

'No, we're not there yet, the lump may well be benign.'

Sam stands up and folds his arms and shakes his head. 'We were told it was common . . . that children get these symptoms when they're adjusting to a new family . . . Even Dr Barron said it was probably nothing to worry about . . . '

'But you went to see him because you were worried?' The consultant looks at Sam.

Sam realises how stupid he was not to see that consultant. Jonah didn't sleep or eat, he was always cold, he was losing weight, he sweated through his pyjamas. It was obvious that there was something wrong with Jonah. Something seriously wrong.

'I'm sorry . . . I should have . . . I didn't . . . ' Sam's voice breaks. He looks away from Rosie and the consultant at the small window at the end of the room.

The doctor leans towards Sam and Rosie, his eyebrows knitted together. 'Sam?'

Sam looks back at him.

'I know all this is a lot to take in, but we need to stay calm. And to take this one step at a time. We don't know anything for sure yet.'

Rosie looks up at him, her eyes swimming. 'I'm not going to slow down.' She blinks and pools of water gather in the crease of her eyes. 'I know how this works ...'

And then the three of them sit in silence and all Sam wants to do is to put his arms around Rosie and hold her tight and tell her that they're going to get through this together. Because he can't do this without her.

She looks at him for a moment and then shakes her head and gets up.

'I'm going to Jonah,' she says and walks out through the door.

AUGUST

# Jonah

Jonah lies in bed. His head hurts and every bit of his body feels like it's been stretched out of shape. He's sick of having to go to hospital all the time and he's sick of the tests, but Rosie says he has to have them to make sure his pneumonia doesn't come back.

Rosie and Sam have been rowing all the time. But not in a shouty way, like when Mama argues with Mister Sir, which is like a big storm that crashes through the night and then, the next morning, the sea and the sky is calm and blue and still again. When Sam and Rosie argue their voices go low and sad and there are big pauses between their words and it always ends in the same way: Rosie curls up in bed under her duvet and Sam goes to the garage to work on his horse.

They always argue about the same thing: Jonah. And how it's Sam's fault that he got pneumonia, which isn't really fair because Sam took him to the doctor.

Anyway, Jonah doesn't understand why they need to be so cross at each other. Soon he'll be better and they can forget all about the pneumonia.

He closes his eyes and tries to sleep but just then there's a thwack on his window.

Alice.

Although he's achy and tired he jumps out of bed and opens the window.

She's standing in the garden in the same kind of faded blue dungarees that Grandma Flick wears. Grandma Flick would love

Alice. And looking at her standing there, he realises how much he missed her when he was in Wales.

Her dad is by the garden gate.

'Hello, Mr Anderson,' Jonah calls down.

Mr Anderson waves back. 'I'll go for a walk.' He lights a cigarette and disappears down the garden path.

For a moment Alice and Jonah smile at each other and Jonah can feel the tips of his ears burning.

'I'll come down,' Jonah says to Alice and closes the window.

He ties his scarf round his neck and then runs down the stairs and through the front door. Hop is standing on the doorstep. He gives him a small stroke on the top of his head and then goes round to the garden and sits on the swing next to Alice.

'You haven't been signalling.' Alice kicks at a bit of earth. He notices that she's not wearing any shoes. 'And you've been back for days.'

'I'm sorry.'

'I've been totally bored without you.'

'I thought you never got bored?'

She blushes. Then she lifts her head and stares at him. 'Your face is all puffy. And your eyes are red.'

'That's why I haven't been able to come and see you. I've had pneumonia. Well, I've still got it, but I'm taking medicine to make me better.'

'Pn-eu-monia,' Alice says slowly. 'That's to do with your lungs, isn't it?'

Sometimes, Jonah wonders whether there's any medical condition that Alice hasn't read about.

Jonah nods. 'It's like a bad cold. It got into my chest.'

'Does it hurt?'

'Kind of. I had to go to hospital.'

'To hospital? In Wales?' Alice's eyes go wide. 'It must have been really bad then?'

'Yes – and here as well, in London. And now I'm having all these stupid tests.'

'Wow. That must have been cool. Can I come next time?'

Sometimes Alice forgets that medical things aren't cool for the people having them. When she's a doctor one day she'll have to be a bit more sensitive, Jonah thinks.

'Maybe, I'll ask Rosie and Sam.' Though they're so cross at the moment that they'll probably say no.

Alice tilts her head to one side. 'You must have missed your mum. I mean, when you were feeling really poorly.'

Jonah feels a thud in his chest.

She goes on. 'Even though I love Dad more and live with him and everything, I always miss my mum when I'm sick.'

Jonah looks over to the bridge. He can see the glow of Mr Anderson's cigarette. He wonders whether, if he'd had a mama and a papa, he would have loved one of them more than the other.

Jonah closes his eyes and feels the warm August air brushing against his bare arms.

'Perhaps you could call her or something,' Alice says.

He opens his eyes and shakes his head. 'It's not that easy.'

'I could help you write a letter?'

'I don't have an address.'

And Mama can't read, not when there aren't pictures, but he doesn't want to tell Alice that in case she has a bad thought about Mama.

'Your mum lives on Lamu Island, right? Maybe we can just put that on the envelope. It would probably get to her.'

The missing-Alice-feelings Jonah had a few moments ago in his room are beginning to fade fast.

'It's just a thought. Take it or leave it,' Alice says. Then she looks up at the frame of the swing. 'I've been meaning to ask for ages — why did Rosie buy a baby swing along with the proper swing?'

He shrugs. 'She probably had it already.'

Alice shakes her head. 'No, she didn't. I watched the van drop the swings off a few weeks before you moved in.'

He's starting to feel really tired again. His head is foggy and his eyes are sore.

'I'd better go back up to my room,' he says.

She touches his arm. 'Can I come round again tomorrow?'

Jonah smiles. 'Of course.'

Alice jumps down off the swing. Jonah looks at her bare feet; they're covered in grey soot.

'Why don't you have any shoes on?' he asks her.

'I wanted to feel what it was like to be you.' She kisses his cheek and skips off down the path towards her dad.


## Sam


Sam stands in the kitchen, staring at his mobile phone.

Above him, he hears the floorboards creak. They've spent the whole day at the hospital, doing more tests, followed by a talk with a consultant while one of the nurses took Jonah for an ice cream in the cafeteria.

Jonah still thinks that all he's got is pneumonia. Which was Rosie's decision, like everything else is right now.

Rosie's taken him upstairs for a sleep.

Sam dials his mum's number. The phone rings out for ages. He imagines the shrill ring of his mum's old dial-phone bouncing off the walls of the house he grew up in.

Sam's tried to call her every day since they got back from Wales but she never answers. She doesn't have a mobile phone, so he has to rely on her hearing the landline. Only she's not likely to hear the landline, not from the garden, where he guesses she's spending all her time now.

In those last few days in Wales, Sam watched her bring home crateloads of plants from the garden centre, followed by mad planting sessions – rows and rows of vegetables that would never get eaten. It was like stepping back into a time warp. As he watched his mum retreat to the garden, he half-expected to come in and find his father lying in the spare room, a drip attached to his arm, his frail body fading into the white sheets.

His mum didn't need to wait for test results or conversations with consultants. She knew that Jonah was sick. Really sick.

The phone keeps ringing and Sam's about to end the call when he hears a click on the line.

'Mum?'

A silence, and then her breath comes in, heavy from having rushed back into the house.

'Mum?'

There's a pause.

'So, what did the doctors say?'

'We don't have a full picture yet. But it's serious.'

'I know that Sam. Just give me the facts.'

'He's got Burkitt's Lymphoma, a form of childhood cancer.'

There's an even longer pause. He hears her drop into the chair in the hall next to the phone.

'Mum?'

'I heard you.'

'They've got to do another biopsy and some more tests, to see how advanced it is.'

She doesn't answer.

He feels his hands shaking. 'I ... I don't know what to do, Mum.'

Another silence.

She clears her throat.

'You're going to show up, Sammy.'

'What do you mean?'

But he doesn't need to ask. She knows him too well. She knows that when things go wrong, he retreats to the garage, hoping that the work will swallow him whole, like she does in her garden.

'Jonah needs you. And so does Rosie,' she says.

He feels a thickness in his throat. He swallows hard.

'About Rosie ...' Sam starts. 'I'm worried.'

'She'll be fine. As long as you're there for Jonah.'

'But I want to be there for *her*. I want to make sure *we're* OK ... I can't bear the thought of losing her ...'

'You can't do that, Sam.' She pauses.

'Do what?'

'You can't carve up your family into separate little parcels. You, Rosie and Jonah are a family now. You've got to work through this together.'

She's right. They're a family now. But it's more than that. Jonah's become the join between them, which means that if anything goes wrong with him, it will tear them apart. And he can't let that happen.

'I don't think I can do this, Mum.'

'You can. And you will. That girl's been there for you since you were nine years old. This is your chance to show up for her.'

'I've been there for her, too ...' he starts, but his voice trails off. He knows his mum's right about this too. Rosie's always been the strong one.

After a long while, Sam says:

'Maybe we're not the right people to look after him.'

'For goodness sake, Sammy, Jonah's your son.'

'Is he?' The words come out of nowhere. He can't believe he's actually said them out loud.

'What on earth do you mean?'

'We've known Jonah, what – three months? Not even that?'

He feels like he's letting Jonah down at the time he most needs him, but he can't help it. If he has to choose between Rosie and Jonah, he'll choose Rosie, every time. She's his life.

'Jonah's not even legally ours, Mum. And there are so many loose ends ...'

'Stop right there.'

'I'm just saying it like it is. I can't talk to Rosie about this – I need you to understand.'

'Jonah *is* your son.' She says it slowly and deliberately and in a way that he knows he's not allowed to counter.

His dad had always taught him to tell the truth. *Especially to people you love. Because those are the ones you'll be most tempted to lie to. Because it's easier. But lying's a poison; it always ends up killing what you love.*

Sam had once prided himself on the fact that he'd lived up to his dad's words. Rosie boasted to her friends that Sam was the most honest guy she knew – *sometimes, he's too honest for his own good*, she'd laugh.

But that truthfulness had slipped over the last few months. Since Jonah? Since before Jonah? He wasn't sure. But he'd changed, he knew that much.

Maybe his dad had been wrong. Maybe you lie to the people you love because they're the ones you want to protect. And that's a good thing. Isn't that why Rosie doesn't want to tell Jonah about his cancer? Because she understands that once you let the truth loose, you have no control over it any more, over the damage it will do.

'Do you want me to come down?' his mum says. 'To help out a bit?' Her voice is softer.

She's never been to Bridgeford, not once. He doesn't imagine she's ever been this far south.

'You'd be miserable here, Mum. And there's not much to do. Not yet. We've got a lot of waiting to do before we work out a treatment plan. More tests . . . .'

'How's Jonah taking all this?'

He hesitates. As much as she loves Rosie, his mum wouldn't like that they're keeping this from him.

'He's still not sleeping at night. Or eating. And the tumour is putting a lot of pressure on his throat . . . But he's being brave.'

There's a long silence.

'Tell Jonah that I love him.'

'Yes, of course.'

'And that his sunflower is growing.'

Sam's eyes well up. 'Sure.'

'And promise me something, Sammy?'

He feels his heart sink. 'Sure.'

'Promise me that you'll keep showing up? Every second of every day until this whole thing is over.'

'Over?'

Sam gets a sick feeling in the pit of his stomach.

'All this is going to take a long time, Mum. We don't know whether Jonah's going to respond to the treatments . . . '

'I don't care how long it takes, Sammy. I need you to promise me that you'll be there.'

But how can he promise when every part of him wants to take Rosie and run a million miles away from this situation they've landed themselves in?

'I'll try,' he says.

'You'll do better than try, Sammy. You'll do it.'

He hears Jonah's door click closed upstairs and Rosie's footsteps on the stairs.

'Sammy – I need you to say it.'

Sam takes a breath. 'I'll do it, Mum – I'll do it.'

She hangs up and, a moment before Rosie comes into the kitchen, he stands there, his eyes closed, his mum's voice ringing in his ears, and he knows that he's done it again. He's let the truth slip away from him.

*I'm sorry, Dad,* he whispers.

## Trudi

Trudi sits in her car, looking up at Sam and Rosie's cottage. Their three-legged cat paws at the front door, trying to escape the drizzle. The windows of Trudi's old Peugeot steam up and for a moment she think that maybe she'll just stay here, the rest of the world at a safe distance. And maybe, after a while, she'll drive away. She'll go back home and dodge her mum's questions about Peter and close her bedroom door and call her boss and say that maybe someone else could work with the Keeps.

Because she doesn't know if she could face this.

Rosie hadn't wanted to go into specifics over the phone, but the word cancer was enough.

As she listened to Rosie, Trudi thought of the little boy she picked up at Heathrow airport at Christmas, at how much he's been through already, and she understood, then and there, that she had to find Jonah's mother. And no longer just because she wants the adoption to go through.

Any mother, even a mother who's abandoned her child, has the right to know if her son is sick. *Grace* has to know about Jonah. Even if that means that Rosie and Sam will lose him.

The cat turns from the front door and seems to notice Trudi. His mouth stretches open and though she can't hear the sound, she knows that he's meowing right at her. *Come on,* he's saying.

Trudi grabs her handbag and steps out of the car.

Rosie stands on the doorstep in her nurse's uniform. There are dark shadows under her eyes and her skin looks grey. She's pulled back her curly hair with a brown rubber band.

Trudi puts her arm around Rosie's shoulders. Rosie closes her eyes and her body relaxes at the human contact.

Then she steps away from her and takes a breath. 'Let's go in.'

Hop follows them to the kitchen, weaving between their legs.

Trudi steps over a pile of clothes spilling out of the open washing machine. The sink is heaped up with bowls and whisks and wooden spoons. The counters are cluttered with bags of fruit and vegetables. A cookery book titled *Healing Foods* lies on the side.

Rosie follows Trudi's gaze and blushes.

'The consultant said that a healthy diet can help. That we need to keep his immune system strong. I'm learning to make some things.'

'I'm sure you're doing everything you can.' Trudi looks around. 'Where's Sam?'

'He's taken Jonah swimming. We thought it was best to keep going as normal – as far as possible, you know.'

'How much have you told Jonah?'

'He knows he's poorly.'

'That's it?'

'That's all he needs to know for now.'

Trudi sucks in her breath. If there's one thing she's learnt about these situations it's that children need to be told the truth. Or as much of the truth as they can cope with, which is usually more than parents realise.

'I thought I'd be talking to both you and Sam,' Trudi says. 'Maybe I should come back another time.'

Sam was the one who calmed Rosie down, who gave Trudi cues that helped her to understand how Rosie might respond to her words. This conversation was going to be even harder than she thought.

Rosie shakes her head. 'We agreed it would be best for me to chat to you first.'

'OK . . .' Trudi says.

As she sits down at the kitchen table, Trudi looks round at the dirty coffee mugs and breakfast plates. Rosie puts a cup of tea in front of her and then slumps on a chair.

Hop jumps onto her lap and buries his head against her stomach.

'I'm sorry to make you have to go through all this again, Rosie, but I need some details about Jonah's condition.'

Rosie nods.

'You said over the phone that it was cancer . . .' The word sticks in her throat.

Rosie nods again. She strokes Hop, not looking up.

'A form of childhood cancer?' Trudi prompts.

'We're waiting for him to have another biopsy.' Rosie sucks in her breath. 'A more invasive one. It will tell us what stage the cancer has reached and how treatable it is.'

'So you're still in the dark?'

'We know from the initial tests that Jonah has Burkitt's Lymphoma. An African variant. He has a lymphatic tumour attached to one of the bones in his jaw.' There's a distance in Rosie's words, like she's speaking about one of her patients rather than the little boy she's come to love.

Trudi shakes her head. 'We did a thorough health check when he arrived ...'

'It wouldn't have shown up. He might not even have had it yet. Once Burkitt's takes root, it develops fast. And his symptoms only started showing when he came to us.' Rosie pauses and looks up at the ceiling in the way people do when they want to keep the tears from spilling out of their eyes. She sniffs and looks back at Trudi, her eyes rimmed red. 'Even I didn't spot all of them. I guess that makes me a pretty rubbish mother, doesn't it?'

'No, it doesn't, Rosie. You've done everything you can for Jonah.' Trudi takes a sip of tea. 'Did Sam notice anything? He's been around more ...'

'He decided not to worry me.'

Trudi picks up the strain in Rosie's voice.

Rosie stops stroking Hop and folds her hands on the table. 'The consultant says that Jonah must have had chronic malaria when he was very little. But I guess we never got his medical history.'

*We really have to find Grace*, thinks Trudi. Robin Morse told them that before he brought Jonah to England, Grace and Jonah lived on the North Coast. He refused to be any clearer than that, as if giving them half the information they needed was less of a betrayal.

'And malaria is connected to this type of cancer?'

'Chronic malaria is believed to reduce resistance to EBV, which allows the cancer to take hold.'

Trudi's head is spinning. 'EBV?'

'Epstein-Barr Virus.'

Rosie's words hang between them.

Trudi has spent her career working with children who've had to cope with all kinds of difficulties, trying to find them homes, helping adopters to cope with whatever problems the children brought with them. But nothing has come close to this.

'What can they do to help him?' Trudi asks.

'More biopsies. More scans and blood tests. And then his first round of chemo, in a couple of weeks.'

Trudi reaches forward and takes Rosie's hands. 'I'm so, so sorry.'

Rosie's hands are limp and clammy.

'I need to know whether you've found Jonah's mum,' Rosie says, her voice hard now. 'Because she needs to know.'

So Rosie's drawn the same conclusion as Trudi. Trudi's surprised. She'd thought Rosie would want to keep this as far away from Jonah's mother as possible.

'Let's take a step at a time,' Trudi says.

'We don't have time for steps, Trudi.'

Trudi feels another jolt. She hasn't yet let herself think that Jonah might not make it.

'What does Sam think?'

'That doesn't matter.'

'It does, Rosie. I've told you, right from the start, that we need a joint approach.'

'I invited you to come here this morning so we could talk – the two of us. I need you to tell me whether you've found her. Whether you're even looking for her.'

Trudi has never seen Rosie like this before. The Rosie she knew was always anxious to get things right, would do anything to make Trudi think well of her. But it's gone past that now.

'There's a lot we need to talk about, Rosie. We need to focus on you and Sam and Jonah. You're our priority. The post-adoption support team is going to help too—'

Rosie pushes Hop off her lap, stands up and goes to the kitchen sink. She looks out through the window at the rain.

'Do you know her name?' Rosie asks.

'Her name?'

'Jonah's mother.'

Trudi stands up and goes over to Rosie. She has to give her something.

'Grace. Her name's Grace.'

Rosie's shoulders drop.

'Grace . . .' she says, as though she's trying out the name.

Trudi knows what Rosie's thinking: that a name makes her real. It's how she'd felt too in that meeting with Robin Morse.

Rosie takes out her phone, swipes through a few screens and puts it down on the table in front of Trudi.

A woman in a lemon dress, a smile as wide as the Atlantic, looks up at Trudi. She picks up the phone and looks closer. As thin as Jonah, tiny bones at her wrists and ankles. Her collarbone pushes up sharply against her skin.

Trudi's breath catches in her throat. With a photo, a concrete image of Grace, Peter will be able to deepen his search. This changes everything.

'How did you get this?'

'Jonah.'

'He showed it to you?'

Rosie pauses.

'No, I found it. He keeps the photograph hidden in his shoe.'

'Have you spoken to him about it?'

'No. He doesn't want us to know he has a mother, and I can't tell him that I've been looking through his things.'

Trudi still doesn't understand why Jonah refuses to acknowledge his mum. He must be protecting her from something.

'Can you email this to me?' Trudi asks.

'So you *are* looking for her?'

Trudi nods, very slowly. 'Not officially.'

'What does that mean?'

'My boss doesn't know. Neither does DI Taylor's.'

'So I guess we're both keeping secrets then?' Rosie says.

'I guess so.'

Only Trudi wasn't keeping secrets from her husband and her little boy.

Rosie goes over to the washing machine and finishes stuffing in bed sheets and a pair of small pyjamas into the drum.

'Children who suffer from Burkitt's Lymphoma sweat at night ...' Rosie explains, pouring washing liquid into the drawer. Then she adds fabric conditioner and slams shut the door. 'And then are the other things. Loss of appetite. Difficulty swallowing if the swelling pushes on the throat. Tiredness.' She pauses. 'I didn't need Sam to tell me, it was staring me right in the face.'

Hop jumps onto the washing machine and settles on a bunch of old towels.

'This isn't your fault, Rosie.'

Rosie lets out a cold laugh. 'That's what Sam says.'

'And he's right.'

Rosie spins round. 'You know who *is* right?' She folds her arms across her chest. 'Whoever it is up there who decided that we shouldn't be parents.' She pauses. 'We should have got the message, shouldn't we Trudi? We should have just accepted that we're not cut out to be parents. That we're a liability . . .'

'You've been through so, so much, Rosie.'

'That's no excuse though, is it? For failing to look after my child.'

'Let's sit down.' Trudi stretches her arm out to the chairs at the kitchen table. 'There's something I need to talk to you about.' She pauses. 'I was hoping to talk to you with Sam but as he's not here . . .'

Rosie doesn't answer so Trudi puts her arm around her and guides her back to the chair. Rosie follows numbly, as though she has no strength to do anything else. She slumps back into her chair.

'You don't have to go through with this,' Trudi says.

The spinning and chugging of the washing machine fills the kitchen. Hop jumps off and bolts out of the door like he's seen a ghost.

'Before the making of the Adoption Order, adoptees can hand a child back,' Trudi goes on.

The machine gets louder, wheezing and thumping now.

Rosie doesn't say a word.

'It's called an adoption breakdown . . . or an adoption disruption.'

Trudi hates these words. And she hates having to say them now. But it's her job to let them know that they're free to walk away. 'Taking on Jonah in this condition will put a huge strain on your lives.'

Trudi looks at Rosie's eyes, wide and glassy. 'Rosie?'

'Jonah *is* our life now.'

'There's your marriage to think of, Rosie . . .'

Rosie looks up. 'You don't think we can cope, is that it?'

'Of course I think you can cope. I just want you to know you have a choice. And from what you've told me, things are going to get much harder with Jonah. His treatment. The uncertainty of the treatment's outcome . . .'

'Do you think I don't know that?'

'I'm sorry. This is coming out wrong.' Trudi holds out her hands. 'I just want you to know that there are options. Jonah could go back to Julie's. Or we could find him another family.'

'Or he can go back to his mum, right? His real mum.'

'That wouldn't happen unless we were sure that he'd receive the treatment he needed.'

'There are hospitals in Kenya, aren't there?'

'Yes.' Trudi pushes away her cup of tea, stands up and comes over to Rosie. She touches Rosie's arm. 'We're on the same side, Rosie.'

The front door slams shut.

A voice echoes through the flat. 'Jonah – come back and take your coat off, you're dripping everywhere . . .'

Rosie and Trudi both look up. Jonah's standing in the doorway of the kitchen, Hop in his arms. He's staring right at them.

## Jonah

Jonah runs upstairs to his bedroom. He grabs all the books and boxes and clothes and piles them up against the door. Then he goes to his backpack, pulls out the white shell and curls up on his bed.

Hop jumps up and snuggles into Jonah's lap and for once, Jonah doesn't push him away.

Jonah closes his eyes and holds the shell to his ears.

*I know you might be tired or that maybe you're cross that I got ill, but please say something now ...*

But he can't hear a thing. Not even the usual whooshing of the sea.

A knock on the door.

'Jonah? Can we come in?' Rosie's voice.

The door handle rattles and the door pushes against all the things Jonah's piled up on the floor.

'Go away!' Jonah calls out.

'Jonah, please let us in, we want to explain ...' Sam's voice this time.

'No!' Jonah shouts back.

Jonah asked Sam why he had to spend all those days in hospital when they were in Wales and why they had to go to the hospital again when they got back to Bridgeford and why he had to have all those scans and injections and why Rosie was walking around with a sad face all the time. And all Sam had said was that Jonah was a bit poorly and that they were going to make him better.

*You'll be right as rain,* Sam had said. But that was a stupid expression. There was nothing right about rain, especially the rain in England: it was cold and dirty and never stopped. And it was a lie too. What Rosie and Trudi said just now didn't sound like *a bit poorly.* They said he was really sick, so sick he might have to go and live with a different family. Or go home to Mama. Which means that they must be looking for Mama.

Jonah presses himself up closer to the wall. Hop snuggles into the crook between his thighs and his tummy, looks at Jonah with his funny eyes and then looks over to the door.

'I'm not letting them in . . . ' Jonah says to Hop.

But then the door flies open. Jonah's books and clothes skid across the floor.

Trudi stands over him.

'You're not allowed to come in here,' Jonah says. 'Rosie said that this is my private space. That no one will ever come in here if I don't want them to.'

But that was probably a lie, along with all the other lies the grown-ups have told him.

Trudi closes the door behind her and comes to sit on the edge of Jonah's bed.

'Do you remember the chat we had the first time we met, Jonah?' she asks.

Jonah closes his eyes and holds his shell to his ear and pretends she's not there.

A warm hand rests on his arm.

'Jonah, do you remember how I said you could trust me?'

His eyes fly open. 'But I can't trust you, can I? You put me with Julie and Mimi and I liked them and then you made me come here and now I've got a best friend here . . . and I've got used to being with Rosie and Sam – and you want to take me away and put me somewhere else. And you said I would like England and that things would be OK. But things are not OK at all.' He takes a breath. 'And you've never listened to me about Mister Sir.'

'I know that things are hard right now. And I know that we haven't always got things right. But you can trust me, Jonah. It's my job to make sure you're OK. It's Sam and Rosie's job too. But we can't do that if you won't talk to us.'

'You're the one who doesn't talk to me. No one tells me anything.'

'Why don't we make a deal, then? I'll answer all the questions you have, right here, right now, and then you answer some of mine.'

Jonah sits up. 'I can ask you anything?'

Trudi nods. 'Anything.'

'What did you mean, downstairs, when you were talking to Rosie. About me being sick?'

Trudi looks at her hands. Lots of lines criss-cross her palms and she's staring at them so hard it is like she's hoping that maybe they will give her an answer.

After a while, she looks up at him and says:

'You're not very well, Jonah. Not well at all. And it's going to take a lot of work to make you better.'

'Am I going to die?'

Mama had taken him to funerals at her church. He understood about people dying. And he understood that children died too. Mama said that you have to be happy when people die because they're going back to be with the Lord and that that's the best place in the world to be.

But Jonah's not sure he wants to go to another world, not yet.

'We don't know, Jonah. What we do know is that we have the very best doctors working to make you better.'

'So when am I leaving?'

Jonah follow's Trudi's gaze as she stares out of the window. The rain is falling hard now, big fat drops are throwing themselves at the glass, making the outside world wobbly.

He thought it was meant to be the summer but if was a real summer, it shouldn't be raining.

Nothing about England is right.

She looks back at him. 'Do you want to stay here?'

He shrugs. He doesn't know where he wants to be any more.

Hop goes and sits on Trudi's lap. She strokes him on his tummy and he purrs really loud.

'Now it's my turn,' Trudi says. 'I need to ask you a few questions and, this time, you need to tell me everything you know.'

Jonah nods.

'Promise?'

Jonah nods again.

'I want you to tell me about Grace.'

The tight, raw feeling in Jonah's throat gets worse. He swallows hard. His eyes water.

'Your mama,' Trudi goes on.

Jonah doesn't answer.

'She would want to know about you being ill.'

Jonah looks at the shell lying on his pillow.

'I don't have a mama.'

'Come on, Jonah.' Trudi's voice is loud now, like Mrs Boon when she's giving you her last warning. 'We know about your mama. We know that she's called Grace. We know that, until you left Kenya, you were living with her ...'

Jonah looks up at Trudi. Mama said that if he was really careful not to say anything, no one would ever know about her or about their lives together. That Mama would be his secret. But she'd been wrong about that, too.

'How did you find out?'

'That doesn't matter right now.'

'You said I can ask any questions and that you'd answer them.'

Trudi doesn't say anything.

'It was Grandma Flick, wasn't it?'

303

'Grandma Flick?' Trudi shakes her head. 'No ... It was DI Peter Taylor, the policeman.'

'He wouldn't have found Mama.'

'Why do you say that?'

'Mama knows how to hide from the police.'

'She does?'

Jonah nods but then gets a sick feeling in his tummy. He's said too much.

'So who told you?' Jonah asks.

And then he gets it. Besides Grandma Flick, there's only one other person he's told about Mama. And then he remembers the first time Alice came up to his room and how she said how cool Trudi's name was. And how, just the other day, she went on about how he should find a way to tell Mama that he was poorly. Alice must have looked Trudi up on her computer and found her phone number or something and told her everything.

He wouldn't forgive her for this. Not ever.

'What will you do?' Jonah asks.

'What do you mean?'

'When you find Mama?'

'I don't know, Jonah ... '

'She doesn't want me to come home.'

Trudi looks him right in the eye. 'Why not, Jonah?'

'She says she'll get in trouble with the police.' He gulps. 'But maybe you or DI Taylor could explain what happened. That she just wanted me to learn to read and to be a gentleman and that she needed a rest ... '

'Oh, Jonah ... '

'She won't get in trouble, will she?' He needs to know for sure.

Trudi doesn't answer, which tells Jonah all he needs to know.

Mama was right. He should never have told anyone about her. Not Alice. Not Grandma Flick. He shouldn't even have admitted anything to Trudi just now.

And that's when he realises that there's only one thing left for him to do.

He straightens his back and puts on a smile, like the smiles English people give each other even when they're not smiling inside.

'I want to stay with Rosie and Sam.' Jonah is proud of how clear and sure he has made his voice sound. 'If that is OK with you.'

Trudi nods. 'I'll see what I can do.' Then she takes his hands. 'Whatever happens, Jonah, I promise that we'll do everything in our power to make you better.'

'I know,' Jonah says.

'But you're going to have to help us, Jonah. You're going to have to tell us a bit more about your mama and what things were like back in Kenya.'

Jonah hears a creak on the floorboards outside his room. He blinks and makes his English smile bigger. 'I'll be happy to help,' he says.

Trudi tilts her head to one side and stares at him for a moment and then says, 'Good.' She looks back to the door. 'Now, I think that Rosie and Sam would like to see you. Would you be OK with that?'

Jonah nods, his smile still held in place. 'That would be very nice, thank you.'

# Sam

Sam and Rosie have been lying in bed for hours, neither of them saying a word.

All Sam can think about is the hospital: the beeps and drips and the shuffling of the nurses' shoes. A picture of the future, lit by stark strip lights: hospital visits; check-ups; waiting for test results; holding their breath for a doctor to make some great pronouncement which will determine the rest of their lives.

If Jonah is as sick as the consultants are suggesting, they're going to end up at square one again: without a child. Worse than that, they're going to *lose* a child. And whatever his mum told him about needing to show up, to be there for Rosie, to understand that Jonah's part of them now, he doesn't know if he can face it all again, not after what happened with his dad.

Sam sits up and turns on the bedside lamp. He crosses his arms over his chest and lets out a long breath.

Rosie shifts under the covers and mumbles. 'What is it?'

'We have to be realistic about all this, Rosie.'

She sits up, presses her back against the headboard and rubs her eyes. 'What do you mean?'

'You heard what the consultant said . . .'

'We can't give up on him, Sam.'

'That's not fair, Rosie.'

'It is fair. You're expecting things to go wrong, you're . . .'

His jaw tightens. 'I'm what?'

'I don't know. You're jinxing it or something.'

'*Jinxing* it? Seriously?'

'All I'm saying is that thinking the worst doesn't help.'

He shakes his head. 'I'm tired of all this, Rosie.'

She turns away from him and swings her bare legs over the side of the bed. A beat of silence and then, in a low whisper, she says, '*Tired*? Of what, exactly?'

He stares at the carpet. 'Of what this is doing to us.'

'Don't speak about Jonah like he's a problem. He's our son.'

He turns to face her. 'I know, my love. I know.'

Sam remembers nights like this one, during rounds of IVF, during the adoption process. He'd tried to talk to her then too, to warn her that it was all too much, that her *at any cost* attitude to having a child might just be too great. That there were other possibilities.

Didn't they have so much going for them as a couple? They were best friends. More than best friends – they were family. They laughed together, they understood each other, they'd shared their childhood together – they'd been a family since they were nine years old. How many couples went that far back?

*Couldn't we be happy, just the two of us?* he'd thought.

Only he'd kept those thoughts to himself. She would have seen it as giving up on their dream. So he'd convinced himself that he wanted a child as much as she did. And they'd pressed on. And he'd grown fond of Jonah, of course he had. More than fond. But now here they are, a few months into their adoption, and yet another hurdle's been thrown in their path.

Can't Rosie accept that they maybe they're not meant to be parents? And couldn't she understand that, if they're going to survive as a couple, they have to focus on what's left of their marriage?

Sam takes a breath.

'His cancer has gone undiagnosed, Rosie. That's what the

consultant said. It means the disease has been tap-dancing its way through his lymphatic system for months . . . whatever happens, it's not going to be OK.'

'I know what the consultant said.'

'So we have to talk about it.'

'All we have to talk about is how we're going to get him better.'

Sam gets out of bed. He paces the room. 'I can't do this any more, Rosie.'

Rosie walks up to him and looks at him, straight on. Her eyes swim with tears. 'What choice do we have?'

He knows that he should take her in his arms, that he should tell her that she's right, that they'll find a way to beat the cancer, whatever stage it's reached. But this time he can't find the words or the strength to go along with her.

'It's dishonest, Rosie. Not to square up to it, to look this thing in the eye and call it out for what it is – a cruel, ugly, disease that could destroy Jonah's life.' He pauses. 'That could destroy *our* lives.'

Rosie crumples to the floor. He looks at the curve of her spine pushing up against her T-shirt, at her bare legs in his boxer shorts, her shins pressing onto the carpet.

He kneels beside her and places his hand on the small of her back.

'You said you talked to Trudi?' he asks.

She nods but doesn't look up.

'So what did she say?'

Rosie doesn't move. He draws her into his body and strokes her hair.

'She must have experience in this, right?'

Rosie sniffs and wipes the back of her hand over her eyes. 'No one has experience in this, Sam.'

'But there have to be procedures. I mean, for when unexpected things like this happen . . .'

Rosie's body goes stiff in his arms.

'Rosie?'

'She said we had to wait for the results.'

'That's all?'

Rosie nods.

'Maybe we should have a meeting, see her together?'

She still doesn't move, though he can hear her heart beating harder through her ribcage.

'There's nothing to talk about,' Rosie says. 'We just have to be here for Jonah. That's it.'

Rosie pulls herself out of his arms, stands up, goes back to the bed, switches off the bedside lamp, slips under the covers and turns her back to him.

## Jonah

Jonah lies back on his bed, fully dressed, and waits. Soon, Rosie will be fast asleep and Sam will go to the garage. And then it will be safe for him to leave.

He touches the lump on his neck. In a few days, he's meant to have an operation, which will help the doctors work out how sick he really is. But Jonah doesn't want any more tests or operations.

He lies back and closes his eyes.

A pebble hits the window.

He screws shut his eyes harder.

Another pebble.

He clenches his fists by his sides. He's not going to open the window for her, not in a million years. She went behind his back. Friends don't do that. Especially best friends.

Jonah takes a deep breath. Soon, none of this will matter any more.

'Jonah!' Alice's voice comes into his room, muffled by the thin pane of glass.

Hop jumps off the bed and jumps up onto the windowsill.

'Hop! Tell Jonah I'm here!' Alice yells.

Jonah can feel her staring through the window.

'Jonah! It's me!'

Hop meows.

The window rattles as she bangs on it with her fist.

But Jonah doesn't move, not until he can hear her climbing back down the side of the house. Then he gets up and goes to the window and watches Alice walking across the bridge with her father, her hair a white halo under the streetlights.

## Trudi

Trudi checks her phone in case there's a message from Peter – he's been working hard on locating Grace. But there's nothing.

The door opens and Sam walks into Linda's Café. When she first met him, she remembers thinking that he was one of those men who'd always look like a boy: wide-eyed and clumsy and full of energy.

Now he walks with a stoop in his shoulders and his eyes are fixed on the floor.

As he walks over to the counter and places his order with Linda, Trudi looks for Rosie, but she doesn't seem to be there.

'Sam!' she calls over and waves him over to the table by the window.

He spots her and gives her a tired smile. There are bags under his eyes.

'Thanks for meeting me,' Sam says, sitting down.

'Where's Rosie?'

Sam scratches his head. 'Rosie? Oh, she's looking after Jonah.'

Trudi doesn't like talking to Rosie and Sam separately: now, more than ever, they need a joint approach. But she understands that they need to take turns to look after Jonah, that they're run off their feet with all the tests and hospital visits.

'Of course.' Trudi stirs a sugar into her latte. 'How's Jonah doing?'

Sam threads his fingers through his hair. She notices some grey streaks by his temples.

'Better than we are,' Sam says.

'What do you mean?'

'Oh, nothing really. Just that he's been quite upbeat these past few days.'

'Even after what happened the other day?'

'Yeah. It's weird. Maybe he feels relieved, to know . . .'

That doesn't sound like a child's reasoning, thinks Trudi. But never mind, at least Jonah seems to be coping.

'And you – and Rosie. How are you guys bearing up?'

Linda comes over and puts an espresso in front of Sam. He swallows the coffee in one gulp and wipes his mouth with a napkin.

311

'Sam – how are things with you and Rosie?'

Sam puts down the napkin and clears his throat.

'What are our options?'

'Your options?'

'You must have come across something like this before. Things going wrong before an adoption becomes legal. A child getting sick or something.'

'Oh … Yes.' She takes a sip of coffee, grateful for the sweet, warm milk. 'Didn't Rosie talk it through with you?'

'Rosie?' Sam hesitates. 'Sure, she talked to me.' He scratches his head again. 'I just wanted to go through the details with you.'

There's something off in Sam's tone.

'Well, there's not much more I can add. You need to take your time, to really discuss it, and to reach a decision, together.'

Sam looks out of the window at the rushing cars and then, slowly, he turns to face her. 'We have discussed it. We'd like you to look into the possibility of Jonah finding a new home.'


## Jonah


Jonah waits until everything goes quiet. Until Hop, lying beside him on the bed, has sunk into sleep. Until the only sound that breaks through the night is the chug, chugging of trains pulling in and out of the station.

He lifts his legs over the side of the bed. Hop stretches and sits up on the duvet. He looks at Jonah, his brown eye and his blue eye shining in the dark room.

'It's OK, Hop, you can go back to sleep.'

But Hop comes over and sits on Jonah's lap.

Jonah pushes him gently onto the floor.

Hop's eyes follow Jonah as he walks around the room, deciding what he's going to pack and what he is going to leave. If he doesn't take too much, Rosie and Sam won't suspect that he's gone and that will buy Jonah some time.

He packs his copy of *The Tempest*, his magic coin and the driftwood horse that he's been making with Sam. With everything that's happened, they haven't had time to finish it, but Jonah doesn't mind. Maybe he can work out how to do the last bits himself.

He leaves behind the shell; he won't need that where he's going. He hesitates for a moment over Mama's red bible but then leaves that behind too.

Then he opens the wardrobe and puts on the clothes Mister Sir bought him in Nairobi. He slips the photograph of Mama out of his shoes, puts it in his backpack, and pushes the shoes under the bed. He never liked those silly shoes.

A few minutes later, he's tiptoeing along the landing. Hop follows him and when they get to Sam and Rosie's door, Hop leaps onto the bed and nestles in next to Rosie, who's lying there alone, a big white space beside her.

Having Jonah here has made them cross with each other, and sad: it will be better when he's gone.

As Jonah steps back out into the hall, Hop sits up on the bed, his ears stiff, his eyes shining in the dark room.

'Night night, Hop,' Jonah whispers.

And then he goes to the kitchen and looks at all the fruit and vegetables lying on the counter. Rosie's been cutting up bits of mango and melon into tiny pieces, soft sweet fruit that's meant

313

to slide down his throat without hurting. *Eat what you can, Jonah*, she keeps telling him. She doesn't get cross any more when he says he's not hungry.

Jonah realises that Mama never cooked for him. They either went out with her Mister Sirs or they ate fruit and bread back in the hut. He never thought he'd miss Rosie's cooking but as he looks around the kitchen and thinks of all the dishes she's tried to make for him these past few months, his breath catches in his throat.

*Night night, Rosie . . .* he says, looking to the stairs.

*Night night, Sam . . .* he whispers towards the garage door.

*Night night, cottage . . .*

Then he goes to the front door and steps out onto the porch.

He looks back one last time at the cottage and then steps out into the dark night.


## Jonah


For hours, Jonah sits on the train platform. He knows that the trains going into Paddington leave from platform 2 and that's where he needs to go. The slats of the bench push against his thighs and a cool breeze cuts through the warm night.

*Even in summer, England's cold*, thinks Jonah.

A twittering of birds pierces the night. The moon is white like his breath was when he first arrived, back in December. And all the stars have disappeared. It'll be morning soon. And then Rosie will wake up for her shift and look out of the kitchen window and she might see him – and if she does, she'll come tearing down to the station and drag him back to the cottage.

And a little part of Jonah wishes that would happen. But he brushes away the thought. He doesn't have a choice: he has to go.

He looks down the tracks again. *Please come soon, train* . . .

And then he looks up past the bridge to Alice's house. There's a small light on in her window. He breathes in and his heart pushes up against his ribcage.

When he heard Trudi and Rosie talking about Mama in the kitchen, the first thing Jonah wanted to do was to tell Alice about it. He thought that Alice could help him work out a plan to warn Mama that they were coming for her. And then he found out that she'd betrayed him. That she was the one who'd gone to see Trudi behind his back and told her about Mama and where she was living.

Alice is the first proper friend Jonah's ever had and now he's lost her too.

As he looks back down at the tracks, he spots something moving along the gravel. A white body, a crooked tail, shiny eyes – one blue, one brown. And a nicked ear.

Jonah dashes to the edge of the platform.

'What are you doing down there, you silly cat!'

Hop wobbles and then sits down in the middle of the tracks.

'What are you *doing*?'

Jonah looks up and down the tracks. Somewhere, out along the dark tracks, the horn of a train echoes through the night.

His stomach folds in on itself.

He looks at the big black sign that Rosie read out to him when they took the train to Paddington. Thanks to Alice, he can read it for himself now: £1,000 PENALTY FOR CROSSING THE TRACKS.

But policemen probably made that rule, and policemen, like

Mama says, aren't to be trusted. Look at DI Taylor – he made Mister Sir go to prison.

He jumps down. Hop moves further along the tracks.

'Hop – you're being an idiot!'

In the distance, the headlights of the oncoming train beam down the tracks.

Jonah runs towards Hop.

The chugging of the train fills his head.

The horn blares louder now, and closer.

Hop still doesn't move.

Jonah lurches forward, scoops Hop up into his arms and holds him tight as he meows.

'Silly, silly Hop.'

Jonah runs to the side of the tracks and, still holding Hop and with one arm, he lifts himself back up onto the platform.

A train grinds its gears and pulls into the station.

Jonah collapses on the platform floor.

One or two passengers step out. He can hear them whispering as they walk past him. But he can't move. He just needs to sit here for a while, with Hop.

After a few minutes, Jonah puts Hop down.

'I have to go now. You'd better go back up to the cottage.'

'Which is where you should be, isn't it?' A voice from behind him.

Jonah jumps. And then spins round.

An old woman with a silver bob, wearing dungarees and big dusty shoes, stands in front of him, smiling. In her arms, she's holding a flower, its head as big and bright as the sun.

# Trudi

Trudi clomps down the back stairs of the laundrette.

'Trudi Babalola – where are you off to without kissing your auntie goodbye?' Blessing's voice rings across the laundrette and into the stairwell.

Trudi's beginning to wonder whether she'll ever join the ranks of grown-ups: people with husbands and families and dogs and a garden and a bathroom she doesn't have to share with her aunt and a proper car that doesn't break down.

The only place Trudi feels like an adult is at work, but then the minute she comes back home, it's like time folds in on itself and she's ten again.

She walks into the laundrette.

'You're wearing a skirt.' Blessing claps her hands. 'You haven't worn a skirt in years.'

'All my jeans are in the wash.' A stupid lie: they live over a laundrette, it's not like there's a queue for the washing machine.

Blessing holds up her hands. 'You look nice, is all I'm saying.'

'Thanks.'

'It's so exciting that you're going on a date.'

Trudi rolls her eyes. 'It's a meeting – for work.'

'At this time?' Blessing taps her watch theatrically.

'You know my job doesn't follow office hours.'

And Peter's hours are even crazier than Trudi's. Thank goodness Linda's Café stays open late.

'I hope he has honourable intentions,' Blessing says.

'Who?'

'That policeman.'

'I'm not meeting Peter.'

There's something about lying to a religious person that's always made Trudi feel nervous. Maybe she should call her boss on the way to the café to discuss Jonah's case – that would count as a meeting, wouldn't it?

Blessing puts her hands on her hips and smiles so widely Trudi's worried her face might stretch out of shape. '*Peter*?'

Trudi sighs. 'DI Taylor.'

*Just get yourself out of the door,* Trudi thinks.

'Well, I think DI Taylor will like it.'

'Like what?'

'Your new skirt.'

Trudi's beginning to lose the will to live.

'It's not new.' She lies. Again.

Before Blessing has the chance to continue her commentary, Trudi's standing on the pavement outside the laundrette. She sucks in her stomach to ease the pinch from the skirt's waistband and pines for her old pair of jeans.

Trudi looks through the window of Linda's Café and sees, straight away, that he's not there. Every time she sets out to meet him, she gets the same fear: that he's chosen to end what he calls their *working relationship*.

As Trudi walks in, Linda signals for her to come over to the counter. She leans over and hands Trudi a Post-It.

'He left this for you.'

Trudi takes the Post-It. There's a coffee stain in the corner and it's lost its stickiness. She squints at Peter's scrawled words.

'It says he'll be late. A job came up,' Linda grins. 'DI Prince Charming was very insistent that you should get the message.'

Trudi looks up from the note. 'Prince *what*?'

'Maybe he'll come back with a glass slipper,' Linda says.

'Seriously?' Trudi shakes her head.

'He said you forgot your shoes in his office once.'

Trudi realises she never asked for her heels back. Not that she wants them. Stupid shoes.

'If that's not an overture, I don't know what is,' Linda goes on.

'An overture? Isn't that something to do with opera?'

Linda shakes her head and smiles. 'You're a hopeless case, Trudi.'

Linda and Blessing should get together and start a dating agency. Maybe then they'd turn their attention from Trudi to some other poor soul who actually needs their help.

'Anyway, we're meeting to discuss work.'

'Of course you are.'

'For goodness sake, Linda, just get me a coffee.'

As Linda moves to the espresso machine she calls over her shoulder, 'I'll have you know that many a happy relationship has flourished in my café.'

'What, amongst the Formica tables and chipped mugs?'

Linda spins round. 'Hey!'

'I'm kidding, Linda. It's eighties chic.'

She smiles. 'Eighties chic, I like that.'

If ever Trudi won the lottery, she'd give a big chunk of her money to Linda to create her dream café: shelves of books and a corner with beanbags and toys for kids and china mugs and hanging baskets of roses to put outside the front door.

Linda deserves that: she does more for the community than all the local services put together.

Trudi looks back at the Post-It. 'What time did he leave this?'

'About an hour ago.'

'Thanks, Linda,' Trudi says.

'I've reserved your table.'

Looking over at the table by the window where she and Peter always sit, Trudi notices a paper napkin with *reserved* scribbled across it in Linda's curly writing.

Trudi sits at the table by the window for two hours, her nerves ever more jittery from all the coffee refills. She plays Mikado with the cocktail sticks. She empties packets of sweetener and makes a snow mountain. She flips through a tabloid.

Then she checks her watch, clears up the mess, swigs back the last bit of coffee, and gets up to go.

As she puts on her coat, she hears sirens and then blue lights flash into the window. Which is hardly unusual in London, except that the flashing lights don't stop and suddenly there's a loud honking and a minute later she makes out Peter's tall, skinny figure getting out of the driver's seat of a police car.

Peter sees her through the window and waves.

He parks his car on the double yellow lines right in front of the café and rushes in.

Linda grins at him from the counter. 'You'd better have a good excuse,' she calls over to him.

Peter ignores her and runs over to the table.

'I didn't think that was legal,' Trudi says.

'What?'

'To use the lights and sirens when there isn't an emergency.'

'There was an emergency.'

'There was?'

Peter nods. 'I stood you up.'

'Stood me up? So this was meant to be a date?' The words slip out.

Peter's cheeks flush pink.

'I was called out to an immigration case at Heathrow. A family with illegal papers. Drugs. The works.'

Sometimes Trudi forgets that, just like for her, Jonah is only one of many cases that Peter and his team deal with every day. And Jonah's case isn't even officially on his books any more.

'I have to be back at Heathrow in half an hour, but I wanted to make sure you knew I hadn't abandoned you.'

'Very chivalrous.'

*Chivalrous? As in, knight in shining armour chivalrous?* Linda's talk of glass slippers must have got to her. Trudi wishes she could gaffer-tape shut her mouth.

'Anyway, I'm sorry,' he says.

The sharp edge of his Adam's apple slides up and down his throat. She notices a shaving nick on his neck.

'You're here now,' Trudi says gently.

'You must be hungry,' he says. 'I'm starving.' He beckons Linda over. 'Two portions of cheesy chips.'

'At your service,' Linda says, giving him a salute.

Trudi tries not to be offended by the fact that Peter didn't ask her what she wanted, that he assumed she was a chips girl rather than a salad girl. But of course he's right. She could murder a plate of cheesy chips.

Trudi doesn't trust herself to say anything in case it comes out sounding embarrassing or just plain stupid, so they sit in silence for a bit. She takes out her phone and notices a missed call and a text, both from Rosie.

*We're going in for the biopsy tomorrow. Then we wait for the news. x.*

'All OK?' Peter asks.

Before she has the chance to answer, the chips arrive. Peter dives in. He swallows hard, wiping his lips between mouthfuls.

'So I have some information,' he says.

Trudi puts down the chip she's holding. Her heart thumps. 'Go on.'

'We've found Grace.'

Trudi looks out through the window. At the far end of the street, a couple walk along the pavement, swinging a toddler between their arms; they lift him high up into air and he throws back his head, laughing. She thinks about Jonah and Rosie and Sam and how, no matter how bad their situation is right now, they're a family. And how she doesn't understand what's made them decide not to keep Jonah.

Peter goes on.

'Once Robin Morse told us that Grace worked along the Lamu coast, I got in touch with some contacts at the airport in Manda. The local taxi boat driver took her back to the island on the 26th of December.'

'And you've located her?'

'We can't be a hundred per cent sure, but there have been some sightings that match the images from the CCTV footage we got from Jomo Kenyatta airport. And the photo you sent through to me.'

Trudi keeps watching the family. They're heading into an Italian restaurant across the road.

'Christ, Trudi, are you even listening?'

She looks back at him. 'I'm sorry.'

'I thought you'd be happy. Getting this information hasn't been easy, you know.'

And he's right. She's the one who's been pushing for them to locate Grace. Because her gut tells her that it's the right thing to do: that they have to let her know what's going on with Jonah. But now that they've actually found her, she feels numb.

'Thank you, Peter. I know this took a lot of work.' She pauses. 'It's just that things have got complicated.'

Peter sits back. 'Now that we've got a lead, my boss says we can re-open the case.'

Trudi's head snaps up. 'He's re-opened the case?'

'Good news, eh? I'm flying out to Kenya in two days' time.'

'You're going out there?'

Peter nods.

All this is going too fast.

'I'm coming,' Trudi says.

He laughs. 'It's not a holiday, Trudi.'

She feels stung. 'I know it's not a bloody holiday. I need to speak to Grace.'

'We have to take one step at a time.'

How many times had she used those words – with foster parents, with adopters, with children? She understands now how bloody infuriating they are.

'We don't have the time for steps.' Trudi takes a breath. 'Jonah's ill.'

'Ill?'

She breathes in sharply. 'Cancer.'

Peter's eyes go wide. 'God . . .'

She knows that she's not meant to disclose sensitive case details but then she and Peter have been off script for so long now that those rules don't apply.

'He's starting chemo in a few weeks.'

Peter shakes his head. 'It's just wrong. Kids shouldn't get sick like that.'

'So you see, Peter, it's urgent. I have to talk to Grace.'

He reaches out to touch her hand but then pulls his fingers back and folds his arms across his chest.

'I'm sorry, Trudi, but, no matter how much I'd like to, I still can't take you with me.'

She leans forward and locks into his gaze. 'You don't understand. I have to find Grace. She might be Jonah's only hope of a family.' She feels her eyes well up.

'What do you mean? Jonah's got Sam and Rosie, doesn't he?'

'Things are so messed up. I don't know what Sam and Rosie are going to do but it looks like they've got cold feet – that Jonah getting sick is all too much for them . . .'

'That doesn't sound like them.'

No, it doesn't. But there it is. Sam made it more than clear that they wanted Trudi to look into other options for Jonah.

'I thought you didn't want him to move back to Kenya.' He pauses. 'You said that she gave him up . . .'

'I don't want him to go back. I don't want him to leave Rosie and Sam. And I don't want him to have cancer. But I don't get to decide, do I?' She presses her palms against her eyes, wishing that the whole world would stop, just for a second.

Peter pulls her hands away and holds them in his. 'I know this is hard, Trudi.'

She doesn't answer.

'Maybe all this will work out for the best. You heard what Robin Morse said: Grace sent Jonah to England because she cares about him. It's a big sacrifice, letting go of your kid like that.' He squeezes her hands tight. 'We'll work it out.'

She looks up, blinking. 'So you'll let me come with you?'

He leans back and lets out a long breath. 'I can't.'

Trudi folds her arms across her chest and looks out of the window at the passing cars.

'Look, maybe it's best we don't bring up Jonah's illness with

Grace, not straight away,' Peter says. 'I'll go out there, deal with the legalities. Tell her that Jonah is happy with his new family ...' He searches for her gaze and then fixes his eyes on hers. 'Once I've got a lay of the land, we can think about how to proceed with Grace and Jonah. I'll handle it sensitively, I promise.'

Very slowly, Trudi nods. But it doesn't feel right. She has to see Grace for herself, to work out what kind of woman she is – and whether she'll give Jonah the love and the care that he needs.

Linda comes over and clears away the chips. 'Coffee?'

Trudi's had so many coffees, she won't sleep for the next week, but she nods. 'Sure, why not.'

They watch Linda walk away. Then Peter looks down at Trudi's skirt.

'You look nice.'

'My jeans are in the wash.'

Right there. She's ten years old again. And lying.

'Well, I like it. The skirt, I mean. It suits you.'

'Thanks.' She looks up at him. 'Much as you'd like to ... ?'

He catches her eye. 'Sorry?'

'You said: "Much as I'd like to, I can't take you with me" ...'

And then she regrets it. Because it's just a saying, right? It doesn't mean anything.

He takes her hand, without hesitating this time.

'If you're asking me whether I'd like to fly with you to one of the most beautiful parts of the world, the answer is yes.' He pauses. 'There's nothing on this earth I'd like more.'

# Jonah

Jonah feels like he's floating in a warm, dark sea.

He doesn't know if Mama's talking to him or if he's remembering her voice from the times when they used to swim together, but he can hear her, now, in his head, and that's good enough.

It's been coming to him every day for the last week, ever since Grandma Flick found him about to get on the train.

*What are you doing here, Jonah?* It's Mama's strict voice, the one she uses when Jonah's walked off too far and she has to come looking for him.

*The doctors are going to make me better, Mama,* he says.

A big, dark silence.

Maybe he's scared her off.

Maybe he should have told her that he was somewhere else.

They're under the water now, looking at each other, small bubbles rising from their mouths and their noses.

*Can you read yet, Jonah?*

*Nearly, Mama.*

He wants to explain that he hasn't had the chance. That the school Julie sent him to didn't let them take books home and that Mrs Boon doesn't have enough control over the class for them to learn anything and that it's been the holidays and that now that he's sick, he might not be able to go back, or not properly, anyway. And then he thinks about Alice and the reading game her dad made and how she's been helping him. And then he gets a sick feeling in his stomach because Alice betrayed him and no matter how much he misses her, he's never going to talk to her again.

*And are you a gentleman yet? A True English Gentleman?*

*I don't know, Mama . . .*

A True English Gentleman would have kept her secret, wouldn't he?

*Mama, there's something I have to tell you . . .*

He needs to warn her that they're looking for her.

*I'm sorry, Mama . . .*

His voice echoes through the water. She's drifting away from him.

His blood moves slowly through his veins, his heart a dull thump in his ears.

*I'm scared,* he wants to tell Mama. He wants her to come back, to hold him and to say it's going to be OK. But he doesn't deserve that, not after what he's done.

The side of his neck feels like it's on fire.

*The general anaesthetic will make you sleep so deeply that you won't remember a thing,* the surgeon promised him.

But he doesn't know about the pictures in Jonah's head. How he sees everything.

He slips further down in the water. He's running out of breath. He's drowning, drowning in his own skin, his blood . . .

White lights glare overhead.

He blinks. Red fireworks flash behind his eyelids.

His limbs feel like they've been bolted to the ground.

His eyes burn.

'Jonah . . . Jonah . . .'

*I'm sorry, Mama. I'm sorry I let you down.*

Someone is stroking his head now.

*Mama, is that you?*

He blinks open his eyes.

Rosie's face comes into focus.

'You're back with us.' Rosie smiles and kisses his forehead.

# Rosie

Rosie watches Sam sitting on the plastic chair in the family room. He's leaning forward, forearms on his knees, head hung low. He brushes sandpaper over the piece of driftwood Jonah gave him in Wales; scraping away as if he might find an answer in a knot or twist of the wood.

She knows what Sam's thinking: maybe if he shapes that piece of wood just right, things will work out for Jonah. She's been clinging to signs too. Anything to give her hope that he'll make it. Or better: that the consultants have got it wrong; that the blood tests got mixed up; that the biopsy will reveal that the lump is benign after all. Or maybe the consultant will call them in with a smile on her face and announce that the cancer hasn't spread, that with a bit of treatment, he'll be just fine.

These thoughts are crashing into each other so hard, that Rosie's head feels like it's going to explode.

At least Flick is staying with them now. She knows Sam better than anyone. And Rosie's beginning to feel that maybe she understands Jonah better than any of them too. Goodness knows where Jonah would be right now if she hadn't shown up when she did.

Rosie looks up at the clock that has the face of a giraffe; the numbers swim in front of her eyes. They've spent so many days in this room that she's lost track of time.

More tests than Rosie could ever have imagined. Blood tests, scans to check his brain, his lungs, his heart. At night, when she tries to sleep, the initials flash behind her eyes: CT, MRI, PET, EC, MUGA …

After the scans came the bone marrow test and the lumbar puncture. And the twenty-four-hour urine collection to assess whether his kidneys are working.

'We don't want to leave any stone unturned,' the consultant said. A young woman called Ms Bridges. Too young, Rosie thinks, whenever she looks at Ms Bridges' smooth skin and her blonde hair, to understand what it means to be a mother.

'We have to give Jonah the best chance possible to fight this cancer. And to do that we have to know exactly what we're dealing with,' Ms Bridges went on.

And so their little boy has had just about every bit of his small body poked and prodded. No wonder he wanted to run away.

The operation Jonah is having now is an excision biopsy of the lymph node on his neck. The swelling on his face has tripled in size over the last week; it's as if the Burkitt's diagnosis has given Jonah's body permission to let rip.

He's only been in surgery for an hour but it feels like he's been away from her for a lifetime. Rosie hates being shut up in this room. She should be sitting next to him in the operating theatre, holding his hand.

And after this operation, once all the test results have come through, they're due to sit in front of the consultant, and she'll give them a mark out of four, a roman numeral, as if they've just sat an exam.

Ms Bridges has been through it with them before:

*I* means the cancer is localised to a specific site with only a small group of lymph nodes affected.

*IV* means that the Lymphoma is in the bone marrow or in the central nervous system.

Rosie isn't prepared to let her mind get even close to the implications of a stage IV cancer.

All she's focusing on now is getting through the tests and then starting the first round of chemo.

There's a knock on the door. Trudi walks in, balancing two cups of coffee.

'I swiped two mugs from the nurses' station. Thought you could do with a break from polystyrene.' Her smile takes over her face.

Rosie's glad that Trudi's here. Trudi understands they can't give up on Jonah, no matter what happens.

She puts the mugs down on the coffee table between Rosie and Sam, pulls up a chair and sits down in front of them.

'So, how are you both bearing up?'

'We'll be better when Jonah's off the operating table.' Rosie says. 'And once we have his results through.'

'Of course.' Trudi gets her diary out of her handbag. 'I just wanted to come and offer some moral support. And to put a date in the diary to talk about the best way forward.'

Sam stops sandpapering his piece of wood, but he still doesn't look up.

Rosie crosses her arms. 'Like I said, we need to wait for the results. There's nothing to discuss until then.'

Trudi looks over at Sam again.

'I thought we could maybe go through some options. We need to think about Jonah's future.'

Rosie gets a scrunched-up tissue out of her pocket, blows her nose and wipes her eyes. Her head pounds. Not enough sleep. Too much coffee. And too much waiting.

She wants to take Jonah home. And she doesn't care if he doesn't eat a mouthful of her food or if he refuses to wear his shoes or if he spends an hour in the bath or whether he asks for Sam to read him his bedtime story, instead of her.

She just wants to go back to how things were before they went to Wales. When there was still the chance that, with time and effort and love, they could build the family they'd dreamt of.

'I've spoken to Julie,' Trudi says.

Rosie looks up. 'Why were you speaking to Julie?'

Sam drops his piece of wood. He bends over, picks it up and shoves it in his pocket along with the sandpaper.

'She's being very positive,' Trudi goes on. 'But we need to consider all of Jonah's options.'

'I don't understand,' Rosie says.

'I thought you'd discussed this,' Trudi says, looking from Rosie to Sam.

'Discussed what?' Rosie's hands are shaking. 'For goodness sake, will someone explain to me what's going on?'

'That you feel it would be better not to go through with the adoption.'

Rosie tries to speak but she doesn't have the breath to get the words out. Nothing feels solid any more.

Sam comes and stands beside her. She turns away from him and looks at the row of daisies painted along the bottom of the wall.

'That wasn't exactly what I said,' Sam says to Trudi.

His voice feels like it's coming from the end of a long tunnel, and suddenly Rosie realises that it's Sam who doesn't feel solid any more. The one constant in her life.

'You were quite clear, Sam,' Trudi says. 'You said that you and Rosie had to consider your marriage . . .'

Rosie spins round and takes a breath. 'The two of you met? Without me?'

'Sam said you didn't want to leave Jonah's side . . . that he was speaking for both of you,' Trudi says.

331

'So, while Jonah's been going through all these tests, you were out talking to Trudi behind my back?'

'It's not like that.'

'It sounds *exactly* like that.'

Trudi's eyes dart between Rosie and Sam. His cheeks flush.

Rosie feels her jaw tighten. Sam knows that this isn't the deal: that you don't go and see the social worker to talk about your son's future – without your wife.

Of course it's been stressful, and they haven't been talking much lately, but they were on the same page, weren't they? They both wanted Jonah. They'd keep him, no matter what.

'Why didn't you talk to me, Sam?' Rosie asks.

'You didn't want to discuss it.'

Rosie drops onto a chair. She hangs her head and stares at a coffee stain on the carpet. How many families had sat here, drinking crap coffee and waiting for bad news? How many couples had fallen apart in this very room?

In a calm, quiet voice, she says: 'We're keeping him, Sam.'

Sam doesn't respond.

Trudi holds out her hands. 'It sounds like you've got a lot to talk about. But before you do, there's something else we need to discuss.'

At that moment, Ms Bridges walks into the family room, wearing scrubs; a green mask hangs loose at her neck.

She smiles. 'Jonah's safely out of theatre. He's still very sleepy but he's back on the ward. You can go and see him now.'

Rosie leaps out of her chair. Nothing matters now except Jonah. She wants to see him, this second.

Sam stands up too.

'I want to go alone, Sam,' Rosie says.

'Sorry?'

'I need to see him on my own.'

Sam looks wounded. But he's gone behind her back. He's told Trudi that he doesn't want to keep Jonah. He doesn't get to rush to Jonah's bedside.

Trudi steps forward. 'Look, why don't we sit down, just for a moment. I need to talk something through with you.'

Rosie shakes her head. 'I need to see Jonah.'

'It won't take long.'

Ms Bridges exchanges a glance with Trudi and then looks at Rosie.

'Jonah will still be very drowsy. A few more minutes won't make a difference.'

'OK,' Rosie says. 'But make it quick.'

Ms Bridges disappears down the corridor and Sam and Rosie come back to sit on the chairs in the family room. Sam reaches for her hand but she shifts away. Trudi clears her throat.

'Before we think about Jonah's future, we have to deal with some news that's come in, news that opens up a whole new scenario.'

Rosie's stomach churns. She doesn't want to hear any of this. All she wants is to be with Jonah.

'You've found her.' Sam's voice is cool and steady.

Did they talk about this too, behind her back? What else has he kept from her?

Trudi nods. 'Yes, we have.'

Rosie's chest contracts. She can't breathe.

'I received confirmation yesterday,' Trudi says.

The room spins. The painted clouds and flowers and rainbows crash into each other.

'What are you talking about?' Rosie asks. 'Who did you find?'

Sam comes over and puts his hand on the small of Rosie's back. 'They've found Jonah's mother. They've found Grace.'

# Sam

Two days later, Sam and Rosie follow Ms Bridges into a side room off the ward.

Sam looks at the hospital bed, stripped bare. A folded out bed beside it, the same kind that Rosie's been sleeping on whenever Jonah's had to stay over. He wonders who the last child was who lay in that bed. And the parent who lay beside him. And where they all are now.

'Thank you for coming in,' Ms Bridges says, pulling up a couple of chairs. 'Take a seat.'

Rosie and Sam sit down, stiffly. She hasn't talked to him since their conversation with Trudi. Since they found out that they weren't on the same page any more. And that DI Taylor had located Grace.

They've been called in to hear how sick Jonah really is. Sam doesn't think he can take much more, but he has to be strong for Rosie. To make up for the mess he's made of things.

He reaches for her hand but she snatches it away.

Ms Bridges leans against the edge of the bed, her clipboard flat against her knees.

'How's Jonah doing?'

'He's got cancer,' Rosie snaps back.

Ms Bridges nods. 'I just meant, after the biopsy.'

'He's with his grandmother,' Sam says. 'She's making a fuss of him.'

In just over a week, their garden has had a makeover. She's been doing it with Jonah.

Ms Bridges smiles at him. 'Good, good.'

He wonders whether she can see the cracks between him and Rosie.

'How far has it spread?' Rosie asks, her eyes fixed on the young consultant's face.

'Before I go any further, I want you to be reassured that, comparatively speaking, the statistics for Burkitt's are good—'

'70% survival rate. We know,' Rosie says.

'That's right ...'

'But that number changes depending on what stage the cancer's reached,' Rosie goes on. 'Doesn't it?'

'Yes ... But there are many factors to take into account—'

'So what stage is Jonah?'

'Give her a chance, love,' Sam says.

Rosie glares at him. 'If you don't want to hear how Jonah is, you don't have to be here.'

Ms Bridges shifts from foot to foot.

Sam shakes his head. 'Of course I want to stay.'

He knows Rosie's punishing him for what he's done. That she wants him to feel that he doesn't have a say in Jonah's life any more.

He'd tried to explain to her why he'd gone to see Trudi on his own. That he was scared. Scared of losing Jonah like he'd lost his father. Scared that he might lose Rosie too: that, over the years, so many holes had been shot into the foundations of their marriage, that he was worried it wouldn't stand up to another crisis. But she'd refused to listen. Spent all her time tidying the house and shopping and fussing over Jonah – and on the phone to Trudi.

And he realises now that Rosie was right – that his mum was right when she called him that day: it was stupid of him to go behind her back. All he's done is to push her further away.

Rosie looks back at Ms Bridges as though Sam's not even in the room.

'Like I said,' Ms Bridges goes on. 'We have every reason to hope that the treatment Jonah receives will make a significant difference.'

'Just tell us, please.'

Ms Bridges takes a breath.

Sam feels sorry for her. She's so young. Maybe she's just qualified. Maybe they're the first parents she's had to deal with on her own.

'Stage IV,' Ms Bridge says.

Sam bows his head and presses the heels of his hands into his eyes.

'So we start treatment—' Rosie says.

Ms Bridges holds out a hand. 'There's something else . . .'

'Something *else*?' Rosie's voice is frayed.

'We've come across a complication.'

Rosie's eyes go wide. 'A complication to Stage IV cancer?'

Ms Bridges nods. 'We think we've got to the origins of the Lymphoma.'

'Malaria,' Rosie says. 'He had malaria as a child. He told us that. You spotted it in the first round of tests.'

Sweat gathers along Sam's hairline. He can feel it. That, in a second from now, Ms Bridges is going to say something that will make this situation a whole lot worse.

Ms Bridges takes a breath.

'Jonah is HIV positive.'

Sam looks up, startled: 'He has AIDS? That's what you're saying?'

'No, he doesn't have AIDS, not yet. But he does have the HIV virus, so we'll need to watch him carefully, especially with his immune system being as weak as it is.'

Rosie walks to the window and looks out at the bright August day. He can feel her heart sinking.

Sam turns to Ms Bridges and asks, 'How long has he had the virus?'

'We can't be sure, but it's likely he's had it from birth. It's quite possible for babies who are born with HIV not to show any symptoms until they're much older. And a child with undiagnosed HIV is at a much higher risk of developing Burkitt's Lymphoma.'

Rosie turns round. 'He got HIV from his mum?'

'Most likely, yes,' Ms Bridges says.

'And why haven't you picked this up until now?' Sam asks.

Ms Bridges' cheeks flush pink. She looks down at her clipboard and then slowly starts speaking.

'The HIV symptoms – fevers, night sweats, enlarged glands, poor eating – are nearly identical to those experienced by a patient with Burkitt's Lymphoma.'

Sam looks over to Rosie, expecting her to wade in, but she's staring out of the window again. It's like she's shut down.

'But the blood tests?' Sam asks. 'Shouldn't those have shown something up?'

Ms Bridges puts down her clipboard on the bed and looks at Sam. 'It's the same deal as with the symptoms. Abnormal full blood count, including lymphocytes, could easily be due to Burkitt's—'

'So what made you spot it?'

'I saw a pattern. Low lymphocytes on full blood counts. And the African origin of the cancer. I thought it would make sense to test him for HIV.'

'You didn't think to tell us this before?'

'It's not common practice.'

'To do what, tell us the truth?' Sam asks.

He feels like a hypocrite, lecturing this young doctor about truth when he hasn't been honest with Rosie.

He looks over to Rosie. Her eyes are far away.

'It's not common practice to speculate,' Ms Bridges says. 'I wanted to be sure.'

Sam sits back. He feels empty. 'So what happens now?'

'It's complicated. HIV may be accelerated by Burkitt's and by the chemo he'll need to have to have, which will weaken his immune system.'

Sam buries his head in his hands. Christ.

'We'll need to do blood tests, every few months, to monitor the HIV status. Before the chemo starts, we'll give him antiretroviral tablets which will help fight HIV.' She pauses. 'But it won't eradicate it.'

'So you're saying that the treatment for his cancer will make his HIV worse?' Sam asks.

'Possibly. Yes. We'll have to monitor his weight loss. And watch carefully for infections.'

How can this much crap happen in the body of one small boy, Sam thinks?

He hears voices behind the door.

Footsteps.

Outside the window, the beeping of a lorry, reversing.

The ticking of the clock on the far wall.

Rosie's breathing, carrying the weight of what they've just heard.

He sits up. 'So when does the chemo start?'

'Ideally, in the next few days.'

Rosie comes back from the window and stands over Sam and Ms Bridges.

'We need a week,' she says.

Sam stares at her. She wants to *delay* Jonah's treatment?

Ms Bridges stands up. 'It's advisable to start treatment as soon as possible.'

'We need your permission to take Jonah out of the country.'

'Out of the country?' Ms Bridges asks.

'Rosie?' Sam says.

'Just a week. I'll look after him. I'll make sure he takes his antiretroviral tablets. And I'll make contact with local clinics, in case he needs more support.'

'What local clinics?' Sam asks. 'What are you talking about, Rosie?'

For the first time in days she turns and looks him right in the eye. 'The clinics in Lamu. Kenya.'

## Sam

Flick takes the washing basket out of Sam's arms and puts it down on the floor. Then she goes over to Rosie, who's drying the dishes, and eases the tea towel out of her fingers.

'Will you two just go and speak to him?'

Sam feels like he's nine years old again and that he and Rosie are being told off for kicking a football into the window of his dad's workshop.

'Jonah knows that you went to see the consultant to get the test results. And he'll have noticed you both walking around the house moping for the past twenty-four hours.' She puts her hands on her hips and looks slowly from Rosie to Sam, back to Sam. 'He's not stupid.'

Sam tries to catch Rosie's gaze but she looks away to the window that leads out to the garden.

'I'll do the clearing up,' his mum says. 'For goodness sake, that's why I'm here.'

Sam goes over to Rosie. 'Mum's right.'

She nods, slowly, but still doesn't look at him.

'Do you know where Jonah is?' Sam asks his mum.

'Where do you think he is?' She smiles. 'He won't stop working on that horse of his.'

The garage. Of course.

As Rosie and Sam get to the door of the garage, Sam turns to face Rosie and says: 'I'll tell him.'

He has to show her that even if they disagree on the adoption, he still cares about Jonah and he wants to help her get through this.

Rosie frowns. 'You sure?'

Her eyes are full of doubt. She never used to look at him like that.

'Yes. I want to do it.'

She gives a small shrug, which tells him that she's going along with it, but it doesn't mean she thinks it's a good idea. Or that he won't muck it up.

Sam pushes open the door.

And then he stops and stares into the dim room.

Jonah's sitting at Sam's place on the bench, the glow of the orange work lamp haloing his head and casting long shadows of his hands against the garage wall. He's working at a knot in the wood of the small driftwood horse he started in his first week with them.

Looking at Jonah, sitting there, filling a space that he's lived in alone for so many years, Sam's heart shifts. He suddenly can't imagine this room, his workshop, without Jonah in it.

'Sam?' Rosie whispers behind him. She nudges him gently and they both walk into the garage.

Jonah looks up at them and smiles. 'He's starting to look like Ariel – don't you think?' He holds up the small horse for their inspection.

Sam's heart doesn't shift this time: it breaks.

'Yes,' Sam says, 'it does, it really does.'

'Are you going to work on your horse?' Jonah asks, looking round at the Ascot horse, standing at the far end of the garage.

Sam hasn't touched the horse since they came back from the meeting with Ms Bridges. Everything seems so trivial next to Jonah's diagnosis.

He pulls up a stool for Rosie to sit on and then sits next to Jonah on the workbench.

'We need to talk to you about something, J.'

Jonah puts down his horse and his bit of sandpaper. Sam looks at the small horse lying on its side and remembers the hundreds and hundreds of small horses he made while his father was dying.

Jonah looks from Sam to Rosie. 'Am I going to die?'

'Oh, Jonah . . . ' Rosie stands up, goes over and presses his head against her.

Sam watches Rosie rocking Jonah back and forth and he realises that it's not just his workshop that wouldn't make sense any more without Jonah here. It's Rosie too. Jonah's part of her. He's part of them both.

Jonah pulls away and looks at Sam. 'Am I?'

Sam edges along the bench and puts his arms around both Rosie and Jonah. Rosie moves away and goes to sit back down on her chair.

341

He realises that she's not close to forgiving him, and that it will take more than these words, than this day, to convince her that she can trust him.

Sam takes Jonah's small hands in his.

'You're very sick, Jonah. You know that you've got cancer, which means that the cells in your body have stopped working like they're meant to.'

'They're attacking my body? That's why I got the lump on my throat?' Jonah says.

'Yes, that's right. And it's what made you tired – and, I know it doesn't make sense, but it's what's stopped you from sleeping too. It's what's made you sweat at night. It's what's made it hard for you to eat. It's why you got pneumonia.'

'You've told me all that stuff already.'

Sam nods. 'I know.'

'So what did the doctor say? Will I get medicine to make me better? Will I be able to go back to school properly?'

'Medicine will help,' Sam says. 'But it's going to take time. And some of the medicine won't be very nice. It'll sometimes make you feel much worse before it makes you better.'

'But I *will* get better, won't I?"

Rosie sucks in her breath.

'Yes. Yes, you will get better,' Sam says.

He thinks back to the adoption activity day and how he thought that when the magician made promises to the children about those coins, he set them up for disappointment. Is that what he's doing now?

Rosie lifts her head and stares at Sam. He can't read whether he's said the right thing or whether he's just gone and blown it.

'Whatever happens, we're going to do everything we can to help you get better.' He pauses and looks at Rosie. 'Aren't we, love?'

She nods but avoids his gaze. Her eyes are fixed on Jonah.

'There's something else we need to talk to you about, Jonah,' she says. 'We're taking you to Kenya.'

She's telling him now? And Sam's still not sure that taking him all that way, when he's so sick, is a good idea.

Jonah's eyes go wide. 'To Kenya?'

Rosie nods. She comes over and kneels in front of him. 'To see your mama. She needs to know that you're poorly.'

Jonah shakes his head. His eyes fill with tears. 'She can't know . . .'

Rosie puts her hand on his back. 'It's OK, Jonah.'

He shakes her off. 'It's not OK. She won't like it.'

'Won't like what?' Sam asks.

'She wants me to be well. To be able to read. To be a True English Gentleman.' He gulps between the words.

Rosie stands up and turns away from them both. She brushes the pads of her thumbs under each eye.

'I'll go and help Grandma Flick,' she says and, before he has the chance to stop her, she's gone and closed the garage door behind her.

Jonah's kicking at a bit of sandpaper on the floor.

Sam looks around the room. Then he notices something on the Ascot horse. One of the two bits of driftwood that he's been struggling to bring together on a join have been sanded down and eased into place.

He walks over to the horse and strokes the smooth join. 'Did you do this, Jonah?'

Jonah looks up and nods.

Sam feels his heart lift. 'All by yourself?'

Jonah nods again.

'You've got to meet your deadline,' Jonah says. 'For the Ascot bid.'

Then his shoulders drop again and he stares at the dusty garage floor.

Sam comes over and sits back next to Jonah.

'It's going to be OK, Jonah. Your Mama loves you. She'll want to see you . . .'

Jonah keeps staring at the floor and then, in a low, quiet voice, he says:

'Will you leave me there?'

'Leave you where . . . ?'

'In Kenya.' Jonah blinks. 'Are you giving me back?'

Sam can't believe what he's hearing. All this time he's been sure that Jonah would jump at the chance of getting away from them. Especially if it meant going back home to the sea he loves so much and to his mama.

Sam lifts Jonah's chin until he's staring right into his big, brown eyes.

'Look at me, Jonah.'

Jonah tries to shift his head away but Sam redirects his head until their eyes meet.

'Rosie and I are going to be here for you. For as long as you want us to be.' He pauses. 'We love you.' And after another pause, much longer this time, he says. 'I love you, Jonah.'

## Jonah

Jonah sits on the swing in the garden next to the cottage. He kicks at the dry grass. It's been hot all week: proper blue skies, no clouds.

Grandma Flick kneels on the paving stones, planting herbs

344

in orange pots. Hop sits beside her, stretched out and sunning himself.

Jonah looks across the railway bridge to Alice's house. The curtains to her bedroom are drawn. She hasn't flashed her torch for over a week now.

Grandma Flick puts down her watering can and follows his gaze. 'Is that where your friend lives?'

'She's not my friend.'

'Why's that, then?'

Jonah shrugs. 'She can't be trusted.'

Grandma Flick sucks in her breath. 'That's a big accusation.'

Jonah shrugs again. 'Well, she can't.'

Grandma Flicks comes over and starts to push him gently on the swing. She makes him think so much of Alice that his heart hurts.

'Learning to forgive our friends is one of life's most important lessons,' Grandma Flick says.

'I don't want to forgive her.' As he swings up into the sky, Jonah stares at Alice's window.

'Well, why don't you explain it to me and I'll see if I can offer a fresh pair of eyes on the situation.'

'I don't need fresh eyes.' He pauses. 'And anyway, it doesn't matter any more.' He catches the ground with his feet to stop the swing and jumps off.

Tomorrow, they're flying out to Kenya. They're going to find Mama. He should feel happy but instead he feels sick. Sick at the thought of how she'll react. How cross she'll be that he's told people about her, how she'll get in trouble for sending him away. How she didn't want him to come back, not yet. And how she won't want to hear about him being ill.

'If it doesn't matter any more, there's no harm in telling me about it,' Grandma Flick says.

345

Jonah loves Grandma Flick but she can be annoying.

'She told Trudi about Mama.'

'Come again?'

'I told her about Mama and that she lived on Lamu and then she decided that Trudi should know and so she went to speak to her behind my back.' Jonah kicks at the earth.

Grandma Flick grabs his hand to make him stop kicking.

Hop stands up, stretches and comes to stand next to Grandma Flick, like he's taking sides.

'She did no such thing,' Grandma Flick says.

'You don't even know Alice.'

'I know that Trudi found out about your mama from that man.'

'What man?'

'The man who brought you over.'

'Mister Sir?' Jonah shakes his head. 'He wouldn't. Not in a million years. Mama told him all her secrets and he knew that he shouldn't tell anyone.' He pauses. 'Mister Sir loves Mama.'

Grandma Flick bends down, lifts Hop into her arms and strokes him gently.

'Well, he wasn't meant to walk out on you either, was he?' she says gently.

Jonah's stomach clenches up.

'He promised to look after you, didn't he? And he didn't keep that promise.'

She's right. Of course she's right.

Jonah looks up. 'So you don't think it was Alice?'

'I know it wasn't Alice.'

Jonah runs inside.

'Jonah!' Grandma Flick calls after him but he keeps running. He runs through the kitchen, past the garage door behind which Sam has been hiding for days. He runs up the stairs, past Rosie and Sam's bedroom, where Rosie's packing for their trip. He runs into his bedroom, winds his scarf around his neck and then grabs the shell Mama gave him and stuffs it into his backpack. Then he runs back out of the cottage and across the railway bridge.

'I'm afraid she's not feeling very well,' Mr Anderson says.

'I have to talk to her.'

'Her eczema has flared up really badly. She's not up to visitors.'

'She'll want to see me.'

Eventually, Mr Anderson lets Jonah in.

Jonah's never been in their house before. It's always been Alice who's come over. And now he knows why. It's like another world. The high ceilings, the big staircase, the thick, soft carpet, the paintings hung on the wall with little lights above them. It's the kind of house he imagined Mister Sir living in.

'Her bedroom's the one right at the top,' Mr Anderson says.

'I know.'

Jonah runs up the big staircase and then stops outside her door and knocks gently.

No one answers.

'Alice . . . it's me . . .'

Still no answer.

Very gently, he opens the door.

He was right, the curtains are drawn. The air is grainy and smells of sleep. A fan clicks on the ceiling. In a corner of the room, on a big double bed, Alice lies under a white sheet, sleeping. Her arms are exposed and he can see how red and angry the eczema is – it covers every bit of her skin. Her neck is red too, and her cheeks.

He sits on the side of her bed.

'Alice . . . ?'

She blinks open her eyes.

'Jonah?'

'I'm sorry, Alice.'

She sits up and rubs her eyes. 'What are you doing here?'

'I've been an idiot.' He pauses. 'I thought you'd told, about Mama.'

She shakes her heard. Her eyes are glassy. 'I'd never share a secret you told me.'

'I know . . . I know that now. I'm sorry.'

'Is that why you've been ignoring me?'

He nods. 'I'm sorry.' He doesn't know what else to say. He touches a red bit on her arm. 'What made it flare up like this?'

She looks down at her arms. 'It's nothing.'

'It doesn't look like nothing.'

She lifts her head and catches his eye and then she starts crying, properly now. 'It's nothing compared to you.' She gulps. 'I thought you had pneumonia . . . but Dad said you're really sick.' She gulps again. 'He said you've got cancer.'

Jonah nods.

'I've got this other thing now too. They only just found it.'

'What other thing?'

'It's called HIV. It's what made me get cancer.'

Alice's eyes go wobbly again.

'Are you going to die?'

'No.'

'But how do you know?'

'I know.'

'Will you tell me? If you are?'

'I said, I'm not going to die.'

He holds out the shell he's been carrying and places it on her lap.

'Your shell?'

'I'm sorry I snapped at you.'

'When?'

'The first time you came to my room, when you wanted to listen to it.'

Alice laughs. 'Oh, I was being nosy and annoying.'

'You were being curious. Curious is good.'

She wipes her eyes with the back of her hand and smiles.

'So why are you giving me your shell?'

'So we can talk.' He pauses. 'When I'm away.'

She sits up straight. 'You're going away?'

'Tomorrow. To Kenya.'

Alice's eyes go wide. 'To see your mum?'

He nods.

'You must be so happy.'

He shakes his head. 'She'll be angry. She didn't want me to come back. Not yet.'

'But you're poorly. Really poorly.'

'She won't like that either.'

'You can't help being ill, Jonah.'

He doesn't answer.

'You'll miss your birthday ... I mean, you won't be here to celebrate it.'

With everything that's gone on these past few weeks, Jonah's hardly thought about his birthday. The last thing he could have imagined was that he would be back with Mama on the day he turned eight.

Alice swings her legs out of bed and goes over to her desk which is pressed up to the window that he's looked at a hundred times.

She pulls out her iPad. 'I was going to wrap it,' she says. 'Before we fell out.' She hands it to him.

'You're giving me your computer?'

'Dad gets new ones for his work all the time. And anyway, I want you to practise while you're away.' She hands him the iPad. 'Then you can show off how good your reading is when you get back.'

Jonah's heart feels like one of those massive rocks that sit under the sea: so big and heavy that they don't move for hundreds of years. Alice doesn't realise that he might never come back.

He takes the iPad. 'Thanks.'

She comes back to sit on the bed and cradles the shell in her hands. 'So how does this work?'

'Mama gave it to me to take to England, so I could hear the sea.' He pauses. 'So I could hear her.'

Alice holds the shell to her ear. 'I guess there isn't much reception out there, so we might not be able to FaceTime.'

Jonah stares at her blankly.

'I just meant that the shell will come in handy. And anyway, it's much nicer than using computers.'

She closes her eyes for a really long time. Her face softens and she looks like she's floated off to some faraway place.

Alice opens her eyes, smiles and looks at Jonah. 'I'll listen to this every minute you're gone.'

'People might think you're a bit weird, going around with a shell glued to your ear.'

'I don't care.'

Alice throws her arms around Jonah and holds him tight and, for a second, he remembers what it was like to be held by Mama.

# Sam

Jonah sinks his body deep into the airplane seat and presses his head into Rosie's shoulder. Sam watches her stroke Jonah's head, forcing herself to keep her own eyes open.

'You should get some rest,' he whispers.

She shakes her head. 'I'm fine.'

They still haven't talked, not properly. Not about the fact that he went behind her back with Trudi. Not about the row they had in front of Ms Bridges about taking Jonah to Kenya. Not about that afternoon in the garage with Jonah. He knows that she's still angry with him. Maybe part of her wishes he weren't even sitting here on the plane with them.

But he knows they have to do this together: that they both have to be here for Jonah.

Rosie draws Jonah closer to her and closes her eyes.

A few months ago, Sam would have been thrilled to see his little boy and the woman he loves, close like this. A family at last. Why is it that, the moment life gives you what you want, it takes something else away while you're not watching?

The last few days have been a whirlwind of packing and paperwork and hospital visits and reassuring Jonah that going to Kenya to see his mum was OK.

Sam's worried about the impact the trip will have on Jonah's health. He knows from watching his father die, that cancer patients have to be kept stable. Any upheaval drains them of energy and compromises the effectiveness of their treatment. And Jonah has HIV too: his body can't cope with any more strain.

As a nurse, Rosie must know that. And still she's obsessed with flying Jonah halfway across the world on a wild goose chase after a woman who gave up her son.

But there's no going back now. In a few hours, they'll be landing in Jomo Kenyatta airport and then on to Manda and after that Lamu. And then they'll have to face whatever life throws at them.

Sam looks behind him between the gap in the seats to where Trudi is sleeping. She asked for holiday leave and used her own money for the ticket. She and Rosie organised the trip together, mostly without consulting him. And whenever he's pressed Trudi for details about Grace, she's been cagey, said there might be complications on the other end, that it could take a while to locate her.

His mum paid for their flights. 'There's no point in sitting on money at my age,' she'd said. She'd do anything for Sam and Rosie – and now Jonah, too, the grandson she's fallen in love with.

Rosie opens her eyes. She eases the red scarf from around Jonah's neck, sweeps her fingers across the swollen gland and pulls him in closer.

Shortly before they land, Sam plucks up the courage to talk to Rosie.

'You sure you're OK about meeting Grace?'

Rosie gives him a firm nod.

Ever since Jonah's diagnosis, a fierce determination has taken hold of her. It frightens him, how absolute she is that they can fight this. And that this trip isn't going to end in disaster.

'You know what Trudi said. We might not find her. She might have moved on.'

'If she was in the Lamu area three days ago, she can't have got far. We'll find her.'

'And then ...'

'We'll tell her about Jonah.'

'And what if she wants to keep him?'

'Then she gets to keep him.'

This was something else he couldn't understand. After so many years of fighting to have a child, after months battling to get Jonah to accept her, Rosie was willing to just hand him back?

And the horrible irony of it is that Rosie's reached this new conclusion just as Sam's come round to wanting to keep Jonah.

'She's his mother,' Rosie says. 'She deserves to know that he's ill. And she gets to decide what happens to him.'

'She abandoned him.'

'We don't know that.'

'We know that, at the age of seven, he found himself alone in one of the biggest airports in the world.'

In the early days of Jonah's adoption, they'd agreed on this: that no true mother could do that to her child.

'We'll get to hear her story,' Rosie says. 'That will help Jonah.'

These days, every conversation feels like an argument.

For a second, he imagines what the flight home would be like without Jonah. Whether there would be anything left of them as a couple.

'You need to hold onto each other,' his mum said last night. 'The three of you.'

'As long as we do this together,' he says to Rosie.

But she doesn't hear him. Jonah stirs and, already, her attention is on him, the rest of the world forgotten.

# Trudi

Trudi is the last to step off the taxi boat from Manda to Lamu. She breathes in the place. Miles of white, empty beach. The sky big and low and fiercely blue. She's never seen anything so beautiful. She closes her eyes and tilts her head to the sun.

When she opens her eyes again, she looks over to Rosie and Sam, standing next to her on the shore. They stand stiffly, holding their bags, a chasm between them.

Jonah sits down in the sand and takes off his shoes and socks. Then he runs into the sea, kicking up the water until it sprays around him like a thousand stars.

Jonah looks up, smiles at Trudi and waves. For a moment, she forgets that he's ill and thinks, instead, of the little boy for whom this bit of the world is home. His own magical island. And her resolve begins to weaken.

There was one thing she'd been certain of when helping Rosie to organise this trip: that Jonah would fly back to England with them. But watching him now, she wonders whether she's got it all wrong.

She pulls her mobile phone out of her bag, takes a breath to steady her nerves and sends Peter a text.

*I'm here. x*

Trudi stares at her phone, hoping to receive an immediate answer, but there's no response.

She's been warned that reception on Lamu isn't good. Maybe he hasn't got the message.

She looks over to the small group of huts on the tip of the

peninsula. Peter mentioned he was staying at a place called Kizingo; he said it was near the spot where he'd found Grace. Trudi looked it up on the internet and booked two huts, asking for the owner's discretion – she didn't want Peter to know that they were coming.

'How romantic,' Blessing had said, when she explained.

She doesn't think that there's anything romantic about this situation. They're doing this for Jonah.

And she doesn't know how resistant Peter will be to her coming here. If there is anything between them, her showing up like this could well put an end to it. But Trudi has to do this. Because it's what Rosie wants. But more than that: because, in her gut, she knows that, if anything good is going to come out of this horrible situation, Jonah's mothers have to meet.

Trudi's phone rings. She puts down her bag and answers.

'What the hell, Trudi?' Peter's voice rings out and despite the anger in his tone she feels her chest lift.

Rosie and Sam look at her. She turns away and cups her hand over her the phone. She hasn't told them yet that they're not meant to be here either.

'We had to come,' she whispers.

'We?'

Trudi's throat tightens. She swallows. 'The Keeps. And Jonah.' She pauses. 'And me.'

There's a long silence.

'Where are you?' Peter asks. His voice crackles. The reception's bad.

'At Kizingo.'

Another silence.

'I'll be there in half an hour.'

'I'm sorry …' Trudi says, but he's already hung up.

# Jonah

They stand outside Mama's hut. The blue sky that stretched over them on the boat to Lamu has gone grey: a wilder, more beautiful grey than in England. He's always liked the out of season time, how, in the space of a few minutes, the face of the island can change from a smile to a frown.

Jonah hears Trudi whisper to DI Peter Taylor, 'You're sure it's here?'

He nods. 'It's here.'

DI Peter Taylor turns to look at Rosie and Sam.

'I'll go in first, to prepare her.'

'I'll come too,' Trudi says.

The policeman puts his hand up. 'Not yet.'

DI Peter has been snapping at Trudi the whole way over by boat.

Trudi ignores him and follows him in anyway.

In about two seconds, they're back, looking wide-eyed and pale.

Jonah could have told them that Mama wouldn't be here. He's always known when she was out for a walk or a drink or a dance with one of her Mister Sirs; when she was asleep and when she was awake; when she wanted him to be there and when she wanted him to stay away.

And when she'd packed up the hut ready for them to move on.

He looks through the open flap of the hut: apart from two bare mattresses on the floor, his and Mama's, it's empty.

DI Peter shakes his head. 'She was here . . .'

Rosie turns to Jonah. 'Do you remember this place?'

Jonah nods. The sound of the birds singing on the makuti roof. The feeling that you were sleeping under the stars. The rise and fall of the sea. Mama singing him to sleep.

'And do you think she's still living here?' Rosie asks.

Jonah shakes his head.

If Mama were here, all her dresses and shoes and hats and jewellery would be here too. And she would have the books that the Mister Sirs gave her. And there would be flowers in jars, and shells decorating the walls. And it would smell of her perfume.

'If you spoke to her here a few days ago, she can't have gone far,' Trudi says.

DI Peter clenches his jaw, like it's Trudi's fault that Mama left.

'Why don't we go back to Kizingo?' Sam says. 'Unpack, freshen up ...'

'No.' Rosie holds out her palms like she's blocking him. 'We came here to look for Grace. If she's on the move, we can't waste any time.'

DI Peter gets out his mobile phone. 'Let me make a few calls.'

Jonah's heart thumps. The only times Mama and him left the hut and went to live somewhere else was when the police came looking for them. Maybe, when DI Peter spoke to her the other day, she got scared and ran away. Or maybe there are other police who found her, the police who walk around with guns. Who don't like Mama's job. Who will be angry with her for sending Jonah to England.

And then he thinks about the one person who'll know.

Jonah comes and stands in the middle of the grown-ups.

'I know who can help us find Mama.'

Rosie's face lights up. 'You do?'

He nods.

And then, without saying any more, he takes DI Peter and his social worker and his adoptive parents back to the boat and guides them to Shela, to the small white house where Mama always went when she needed a rest.

Miss Mary sits outside on a chair, her watery grey eyes far away.

When she sees Jonah, she leans over, picks up her cane and pushes herself up to standing. She's got much older and creakier since Jonah last saw her.

'Jonah!' she says, like she's been expecting him. She takes his head in her hands and kisses his cheeks and then, like she always used to when he and Mama had been away for a while, she flutters her hands over his face. 'You've become quite the young man.' Then she brushes her hands down his shoulders and his arms and finally puts her palms on his chest and closes her eyes. 'Have you been keeping warm?'

Jonah feels a tingling in his skin, like he always did when Miss Mary put her hands on him.

He steps away from her and tightens the scarf around his neck. 'I am very well, thank you Miss Mary.'

He knows how strange he looks, wearing his scarf here in Kenya where everyone goes around in T-shirts, but he doesn't want Miss Mary to see the plaster on his neck. If she finds out that he's ill, she'll tell Mama and Jonah's still not sure he wants Mama to know.

But Jonah can feel Miss Mary staring at his scarf and he remembers what Mama always used to say: *Miss Mary can feel everything through her fingers.* And the other thing she said too, after he got malaria: *Jonah has a weakness in him . . .*

'Do you know where Mama is?' he asks her.

Miss Mary nods and looks over to the door of her house. She lives in the bottom bit and rents out the top floor to tourists.

'She's inside.'

Jonah lets out a big sigh of relief. If Mama's here, it means she's not scared about the police.

'Your mama's very tired,' Miss Mary says.

'She's *still* tired?'

There are two reasons why Mama shouldn't be tired: first, because she was meant to have had a rest while Jonah was away – and he's been away for eight months now – and second, Miss Mary always makes Mama feel better. That's her job.

'She will be glad to see you. Just be gentle.'

Jonah is not so sure that Mama will be happy to see him. Besides not being able to read and not being a gentleman and being sick, he's broken his promise about never, ever telling anyone about her. She'll never forgive him for that.

At least he's kept the biggest secret – what he heard that night in the hotel room when she was talking to Mister Sir. The real reason why she sent him to England.

He turns round to Rosie, Sam, DI Peter and Trudi.

'Can I go in on my own?'

The grown-ups look at each other and he's sure that DI Peter is going to say no, but Rosie kneels down in front of him and takes Jonah's hands and says:

'Of course you can. We'll be right here if you need us.'

Sam steps forward. 'You sure you're OK to do this on your own, Jonah?'

For a second, Jonah wants to say: *No, I'm not sure, I want you to come with me.* He's got used to Rosie and Sam being next to him when things are hard.

But he knows he has to do this on his own.

'I'll be fine, thank you.'

Before he loses his nerve, he pushes open the door to Miss Mary's house.

Mama is asleep on Miss Mary's sofa, a thin white sheet covers her body. Everything about her seems to have shrunk; she's so small and thin, she makes him think a bit of Alice. He wishes Alice were with him now.

He can see all the bones in Mama's cheeks and around her eyes and along her neck. Her hair has got thin and ragged-looking. There are purple-black smudges under her eyes and she's not wearing any make-up. Under the sheet, she's wearing an old grey T-shirt and she's tied an old kikoy around her hips. And when he gets close, he doesn't smell her perfume: instead, a sour, closed-in odour rises from her breath.

She told Mister Sir that Miss Mary would make her better.

Jonah puts down his backpack, kneels beside the sofa and strokes her thin arm resting on the sheet.

'Mama . . .' he whispers.

Her eyelids flicker open and she smiles. She looks up at him, her eyes glazed, like she's still dreaming. And then she sits up, suddenly.

'Jonah?'

'It's OK, Mama . . .'

She rubs her eyes and looks at him again.

'What are you doing here, Jonah?' She blinks, as though, at any moment, she expects her vision to adjust and Jonah to disappear.

He takes both her hands. 'I've just come for a visit.' He leans over and kisses her cheek; her skin feels clammy. 'I've got so many stories to tell you about England, Mama. It's not like in the books . . . not a bit . . . but it's OK, once you get used to it . . .'

Mama smiles, but she looks tired and he thinks about what Miss Mary said about not wearing her out. She touches his cheek with the back of her hand and he thinks he sees her looking at his neck.

'Are you all right, my little fish?'

Jonah remembers what Rosie said, that it was up to him to tell her that he was poorly. His fingers flutter to his scarf. He feels the edge of the plaster covering the lump.

'Yes,' he says. 'I live in a little house by a train station. The trains shake the house, and it rains a lot, but it's fun watching people come and go. I have my own room. And there's a cat called Hop – Sam says he's a Buddhist ... And Sam takes me swimming and there's a girl called Alice who's got short hair and allergies and can read really fast ...'

Jonah's words tumble over each: he wants to tell Mama everything about his new life. And saying all these things makes him realise how much he misses England. And that he wants her to come back with him and see for herself. Maybe they could live together in a small house near Rosie and Sam. Maybe the doctors who've been looking after him can make her better too.

And then he feels guilty about talking about England so much when Mama has been here on her own.

'That all sounds wonderful, Jonah.' She looks at him with her big brown eyes, bigger than ever now that her face is so thin.

He waits for her to ask why he's come back so soon but it's like she was expecting him.

'The people I'm living with want to meet you.' He gulps. 'I tried really hard not to let them know about you – so you wouldn't get in trouble – but they found you without me telling them ... I'm sorry, Mama.'

Mama sits up straighter. Her collarbone juts out of her skin.

'The people you're staying with found me?'

'Yes, Rosie and Sam – but they didn't really do it themselves, DI Peter did. You've met DI Peter? He found you at our old hut?'

Mama nods. 'Yes, I've met Peter.'

'Trudi says he's a good policeman, Mama, and that he won't get you in trouble.'

She doesn't answer.

Jonah pauses. 'Mister Sir didn't want me to live with him. He left me at the airport.' Jonah waits for Mama to say something about being shocked and disappointed and angry but she keeps quiet. 'He broke his promise to us, Mama.' He pauses. 'Or that's what Trudi says.'

Mama looks down at the floor.

'Mama?'

'I know,' she says.

'You know what?'

She hangs her head and doesn't answer.

A hollow feeling settles in Jonah's chest. She knew that Mister Sir was going to walk away from him. She knew that Jonah was never meant to live with Mister Sir.

Jonah stands up and moves away from the sofa. Without looking at her, he says:

'There never was an Aunt Igwe to pick me up, was there?'

For a while after Trudi explained to him about Mister Sir not wanting him to live with his family in his castle, Jonah had thought that maybe Mama *had* wanted him to stay with people she knew in England. That maybe there was an Aunt Igwe. That maybe that Mama hadn't told him because it was all meant to be a surprise.

Only Mama never lies to him. Or that's what he's always thought. And now it turns out that every single story she's told him about his trip to England was made up. More made up than the plays of William Shakespeare.

Mama looks out through the small window of Miss Mary's lounge.

'Mister Sir told me that people in England look after children, no matter where they're from. That it's a good place.' She pauses. 'And I knew that you'd find people who would love you.'

Jonah drops Mama's hand. So she sent him off on his own, without anyone to go to?

'How did you know?'

'England is a good place. The Mister Sirs . . . '

'England is not full of Mister Sirs, Mama.'

He wonders whether he should tell her about Mister Sir being in prison but she looks so tired that he thinks he'll save that for another day.

'I still knew you would be all right, Jonah,' Mama says. 'Otherwise I wouldn't have sent you there.'

'So you tricked Mister Sir?' He clenches his fists at his side.

All Jonah wants right now is to run out of Miss Mary's house and keep going – far, far away from Mama and Rosie and Sam and Trudi and DI Peter Taylor.

'You tricked me, too,' Jonah says.

'Oh, my darling . . . ' Mama coughs and although it's really hot she starts shivering.

Although Jonah's angry with her for breaking his trust, the only thing he can think about is how cold she looks and how he should give her his scarf. But then she'd ask about the bandage on his neck and he doesn't want to explain about that, not now.

'I did what I could . . . ' Mama starts again but the coughing takes over, a big, heaving, rattly cough that goes right through her chest.

Jonah wonders what Mister Sir would think if he could see Mama. Whether he would still find her beautiful. Whether he would still want to come on holiday to spend time with her. And whether he'd forgive her for telling him lies about Aunt Igwe.

Mama's forehead is sweating and her teeth are chattering. She pulls the sheet up around her.

'Are you very sick, Mama?'

She starts coughing again, for a good minute, and then it takes her a long time to catch her breath.

Eventually, she says, 'Oh, you don't need to worry about me, Jonah.' She smiles. 'I'll be right as rain.'

It was one of the phrases they'd learnt together before he left. It's something Sam says too.

'Rain is not very right – not English rain, anyway.'

Mama leans back and closes her eyes.

Jonah grabs her hand. 'The doctors in England are good, Mama. You could come back with us and you would get proper treatment.'

Mama looks straight at him. 'How do you know about doctors, Jonah?'

He feels his skin burning up. He can't tell Mama about the cancer in his body. Or the HIV. Not now that she is so ill herself.

'The woman who looks after me, Rosie, is a nurse. She delivers babies. She told me about the doctors.'

It's the first time in his life that Jonah has lied to Mama, but then she hadn't told him the whole truth either.

Mama shakes her head, her eyes still closed. 'I don't need any doctors. Miss Mary is looking after me. I'll be fine.'

Only Mama doesn't look a bit fine. And Mama's cold is so bad that he worries that all of Miss Mary's prayers and even her special healing hands won't be able to help her.

Jonah gulps. 'Mister Sir said you wouldn't be fine, not if you didn't go to the hospital. And you didn't listen to him either. I heard you that night . . .'

When the dawn sunlight filters through the shutters of the hotel room, Jonah hears Mama stirring. He opens his eyes and looks over at the bed. She's on her own so Mister Sir must have gone back to his room.

After a bit, Mama gets up and walks through the door that leads to Mister Sir's room. She closes the door behind her but it doesn't shut fully.

Mama has warned Jonah that it's rude to spy on people, but he can't help himself. He waits for a few more seconds, to make sure that Mama isn't coming back, and then goes over to the door and listens.

'I can't sleep,' Mama says to Mister Sir.

Although the room is still dark, Jonah watches Mama climbing into Mister Sir's bed.

Sleepily, Mister Sir puts his arms around Mama.

'I don't know if I'm doing the right thing,' Mama says.

Jonah can hear the tears in Mama's voice.

'He's my life.'

'You have to get yourself better,' Mister Sir says.

'I know . . .' Mama says.

Mister Sir sits up and leans against the headboard. He takes Mama's hands and looks right into her eyes.

'You need to go to hospital, Grace.'

A knot forms in Jonah's stomach. Why does Mama need to go to hospital?

'I'll be fine,' Mama says.

'You're not going to be fine. Your immune system is getting weaker by the day. Without proper treatment you don't have a hope in hell of beating this.' Mister Sir is talking loudly now and gripping Mama's hands so tight that Jonah's worried he's hurting her.

'If it's money . . . ' Mister Sir says, his voice calmer now.

'I'll go and stay with Mary for a bit.'

'Mary? Seriously? She isn't a doctor, not even close.'

Mama pulls her hands away from Mister Sir and says, 'I didn't come in here to argue . . . '

'I'm taking Jonah to England because we made a deal: because you said it would help you focus on getting better.'

Jonah doesn't understand. Mama said he was going to England to learn to read and to become A True English Gentleman. And yes, him being away was going to help Mama rest because she was tired from working so hard. But Mister Sir is making it sound like the only reason Jonah's going is because Mama is sick. Really sick.

'I'll get better in my own way,' Mama says.

'What – you think your God is going to save you over all the other people who've got this?' He gives her a cold laugh that Jonah doesn't like at all. 'You think he's going to save you over the people getting proper medical treatment? Even your God isn't that crazy.'

Jonah doesn't understand what Mama can have that Miss Mary can't help her get better. Maybe it's malaria, which he got when he was little. But then he got better from that, didn't he?

The knot in his stomach gets so tight he feels like he can't breathe.

Jonah puts his fingers on the door handle. Mama has to tell

him the truth now. And she has to let him stay and look after her.

He steps forward.

'Promise me,' Mama says to Mister Sir. 'Promise me you'll never tell Jonah.'

'Grace . . .'

'I want him to remember me how I am now.'

Mister Sir shakes his head. And then he starts crying. Big, gulping tears that Jonah could never have imagined coming out of Mister Sir's eyes.

Mama takes Mister Sir in his arms.

'Promise me, Robin. Promise me you won't tell him?'

Mister Sir is shaking and crying and, for a long time, he stays in Mama's arms, not saying a word.

And then, very quietly, he says: 'I promise.'

'So you've known all this time,' Mama says. Her eyes are sad, but there's something else in them too, like when she's proud of him for holding his breath underwater for a long time or for making up a good story from the pictures in their books.

Jonah nods.

Tears sting his eyes. He sniffs them back.

'What's wrong with you, Mama?'

'I have something called HIV.'

Jonah bites his lip. That's what Rosie said he has too. That's what made him get the cancer. Which means that mama might have the cancer too. His head spins so fast that his eyes go blurry. Maybe he gave it to Mama. Maybe it's all his fault.

'I'm going to stay,' Jonah says.

Mama sits up again. 'Stay where?'

'With you.'

'No, Jonah ...'

'I'm going to help you get better.' He puts his hands on his knees and clenches his fists.

Mama leans forward, uncurls his hand and kisses his palm.

'The only thing you have to do, my Jonah, is to look after yourself.' She holds his hand to her cheek. 'Promise me that you'll do that?'

Promise? What good are promises? No one keeps them. Even Jonah has broken the promises he made to Mama.

They look at each other and for a long time, neither of them says anything. Then Mama puts his hand down and shifts her gaze to Jonah's backpack.

'Do you have our book in there?'

'Of course.'

'So you've learnt to read?'

'A bit.' He pauses. He's already lied to Mama once today, he doesn't want to do it again. 'It's been harder to learn to read in England than I thought it would be. But I've been trying really hard. I have a friend, Alice, she's been helping me.' He lifts his backpack onto his knees and pulls out the iPad. 'She gave me this. It's a computer. Her dad designed a game to help with reading. Alice is really cool ...'

And then he stops. When he thinks about never seeing Alice again, he gets an empty feeling in his chest.

'Well, why don't you read to me a little – as much as you can – and then I'll have a rest and we'll talk some more later.'

He wants to tell her that Rosie and Sam really want to see her, and that Trudi will want to speak to her too. And he needs to tell her about the adoption and that she has to explain to them that he's not meant to be in England for ever, that he's coming back here, and that even if he has come to like Rosie and Sam and Hop and Grandma Flick, he doesn't need a new family because he's got Mama.

But she looks so tired, he's worried she won't be able to take it all in.

So instead, he puts away Alice's computer and takes out his copy of *The Tempest*. Then he lies next to her on the sofa, like they used to.

He props the book up on his chest and starts reading from the bit right at the end, where Prospero decides to stop being a magician and to leave the island. They never got to the end and he wants Mama to know what happened

He puts his forefinger finger under the words, like Alice taught him. And he can feel her, right here beside him, guiding his hand.

Jonah reads the bit about Ariel at the end of the play:

*My A-r-iel, chick,*

*That ... is ... thy ... ch-arge: then to the el-e-ments ...*

*B ... be free, and fare thou well!*

'Fare thou well ...' Mama mouths, her eyes closed. 'Such beautiful words ... fare thou well ...'

Jonah keeps going for a few lines and then notices that Mama's asleep. He puts the book down next to her, so that she can look at it when she wakes up. She must have missed not having it all this time. And, no matter what she said, he's going to stay with her, so there's no point him carrying it around any more. And then he takes out the coin the magician gave him and places it in the palm of her hand; she needs more magic than he does right now.

Before he gets up to go, he takes out one more thing from his bag: the small wooden driftwood horse that he's been making with Sam. Jonah places it on top of the book. Maybe his reading isn't very good but he wants her to see that he's learnt some things. Sometimes, Mama would take him by boat to Manda and they would watch the wild horses running along the beach. She'll love the sculpture.

He puts his backpack on his shoulders and before he walks back out through the front door of Miss Mary's house he whispers:

'I'm home, Mama. Home to stay.'

## Rosie

Rosie stares up at the clouds gathering in the sky. While Jonah's been talking to his mum, she and Sam have stood awkwardly in front of Miss Mary, watching her suck her teeth and rock back and forth on her bench.

Trudi and Peter went for a drink in town: Peter said to call them once they'd had the time they needed with Grace and then he'll come and ask her some questions.

After a long while, Miss Mary leans towards them and says: 'Jonah should not be here.'

'We thought it was important for him to see his mother,' Sam says.

Miss Mary shakes her head. 'His mother doesn't want to see him.'

'Well, maybe this time, she doesn't get to choose what Jonah does or doesn't do.' Rosie blurts out. 'Maybe this time—'

Sam puts his hand on the small of her back. 'It's OK, my love.'

She closes her eyes, feeling the familiar comfort of his touch.

Miss Mary turns her head to face Rosie. Her pale eyes seem to look right through her.

'You will see ...' Miss Mary says. Then she stands up slowly. 'Please excuse me, I have to go and check on one of my patients.'

Rosie and Sam shoot each other a glance. A *patient*? Miss Mary is as old as the hills, her eyesight is failing and she can barely walk. How does she have a patient?

Miss Mary hesitates a moment. 'You could come with me. My patient is pregnant.'

Rosie doesn't remember telling Miss Mary that she was a midwife. Rosie wonders whether it was Miss Mary who helped Grace bring Jonah into the world. Whether she saw him, all scrunched up and new on the first day of his life.

'I think I'll wait here for Jonah, if that's OK,' Rosie says.

Miss Mary shrugs. 'Just do not let Jonah tire her out. And make sure you do not upset her.'

'Upset *her*?' Rosie can feel her jaw dropping.

Sam presses her arm and says, 'Why don't we sit down for a bit, Rosie? Take a load off while we wait for Jonah?'

Rosie is too tired to argue. They sit down on the steps leading up to the front door and watch Miss Mary shuffling up the cobbled road that leads into the centre of Shela.

Rosie leans her head into Sam's shoulder. She doesn't know whether it's out of tiredness or familiarity, but at this moment, his shoulder is the only thing that feels right. She doesn't have the energy to keep up the distance between them or to begin to think what will happen to them if Jonah doesn't fly back with them in four days' time.

She looks out at the sea. The clouds are shifting fast now. Shadows dance on the surface of the water. It feels like a miracle to be here.

371

They spent their honeymoon in North Wales, a little further up the coast from Flick's house. It rained all week but they hadn't minded. They'd never have allowed themselves to dream of coming to a place as far away and exotic as Kenya. And now, having bitten a huge chunk out of Flick's savings, here they are, standing on an island that feels like it's on the very tip of the world. The most beautiful place they'll ever see. And all Rosie can think is that she wants to be back home, in their small cottage, with Jonah.

Rosie hears the door click open behind her. She stands up and sees Jonah standing at the top of the steps, blinking into the sun.

'Jonah – everything OK?'

Jonah walks down a few steps.

'Miss Mary was right. Mama's very tired.'

Rosie is growing impatient with all this talk about Grace and her tiredness. Jonah has cancer for goodness sake, and HIV – and he's a child. However tired Grace is, it doesn't come close to what he's been through these last few weeks.

Rosie goes and puts her arm around his shoulders; he leans in and lets her hug him.

She holds onto Jonah for a long time and then she says: 'It must have been hard to see her after such a long time.'

Jonah steps back from Rosie's arms. 'She knew about Mister Sir. She knew he never wanted me to live with him.'

Rosie looks up at Sam and they hold each other's gaze for a moment. Her eyes fill with tears. She blinks, takes a breath and pulls Jonah's hands into hers. 'I'm so sorry, Jonah.'

Sam joins them on the top step and folds them both into his arms.

A sob escapes from Jonah's lips. Rosie feels his small body heaving against her chest.

'I know it's really hard to understand this,' Sam whispers, still holding onto them both. 'But everything your Mama did was because she loved you.'

Rosie's body stiffens. She's not sure she'll ever be able to believe that. Nothing could make her give up a child.

Jonah sniffs. Then he stands back and rubs his eyes. Rosie strokes his cheek. Then she looks towards the front door, which Jonah left ajar.

'Jonah, would you mind if I went and spoke to your mama?'

Jonah looks at her for a beat. 'She's sleeping . . .'

'I'll go in and wait for her to wake up, then.'

'What are you going to tell her?'

'I just want to get to know her a bit.' She pauses. 'I know how much she means to you.'

Jonah goes very quiet. After a while, he says:

'I think I should be there when you speak to her.'

'It's all right, Jonah.' A quiet voice from behind them.

A woman stands in the doorway, her hair thin and brittle, the nails on her bare feet ragged, a few smudges of nail varnish left in the corners. She has dark shadows under her eyes and her skin is yellow. She couldn't look more different than the woman Rosie saw in Jonah's photo.

'I would also like to talk to you,' Grace says to Rosie. 'Alone.'

Sam puts his arm around Jonah. 'Why don't we go back to Kizingo, get our trunks and towels and go for a swim? You've been talking about swimming in the sea ever since we left England.'

Jonah looks from his mama to Rosie and back to his mama. And then, in a quiet voice, he says, 'OK. But only if I can come back later.'

'That sounds like a deal,' Sam says.

Jonah nods slowly but, as he walks down the beach with Sam, he keeps turning round to look at his mama.

Rosie watches Sam helping Jonah back into the boat.

'I'm glad he has a papa,' Grace says.

Rosie turns to face her. 'You are?'

Grace nods and holds her thin arm towards the door. 'Why don't you come in?'

They walk into a room, which seems to serve as a kitchen, living-room and bedroom. A fan clicks overhead. Rosie looks at the sofa with its deep indentation, scrunched-up sheets and pile of pillows. Only a tiny shaft of light comes through the closed curtains.

Sitting on the side of the sofa is Jonah's copy of *The Tempest*, the coin the magician gave the children at the adoption activity day and Jonah's small driftwood horse.

Rosie's heart contracts. Does the fact that Jonah left these things behind mean that he's said goodbye to Grace? Or does it mean that he wants to stay, that he's put them here because this is his new home?

'You live here?' Rosie asks.

'For now, yes.' Grace goes to the kitchen and takes a glass tumbler from the counter. 'Can I offer you something to drink?'

'I'm fine.'

Grace comes back to sit on the edge of the sofa, her breathing heavy. Rosie looks at her tiny frame, lost in the fabric of her clothes. And then she notices a red mark on Grace's calf. And another one, a little higher up.

Although she hadn't articulated it to herself, not fully, Rosie realises that she's been expecting this.

Over the last few weeks Rosie has trawled the internet for

374

research on Burkitt's Lymphoma and its correlation to HIV. How the virus has been sleeping in Jonah's body since before he was born and how now, just as Jonah found his home with them, it woke up and triggered the cancer. And that treating both is like cracking the world's most difficult sum.

'How long have you got?' Rosie asks.

Grace lifts her head and smiles and, for a moment, Rosie sees the ghost of the beautiful woman she once was.

Grace pauses and then looks out through the slit in the curtains and says: 'Oh, when The Lord decides it's time.'

'You've been sick for a while, then?'

Grace nods.

Rosie takes a breath. 'And that's why you sent Jonah to England?'

Grace looks straight at Rosie and nods again.

Rosie's legs feel like they're going to buckle. She grabs a chair, places it next to the sofa and sits down next to Grace.

What would she have done, had she been in Grace's shoes? Would she have had the courage to let go of her child?

'Are you receiving treatment?' Rosie asks.

Five years ago, Rosie helped a woman with AIDS carry her baby full term. Relatively speaking, the epidemic in the UK is small, but Rosie has come across a few cases. Her patient died a few days after her baby was born; the baby girl was taken away by social services.

Rosie still thinks of that little girl sometimes, of whether the virus has been sleeping in her body too, and whether it's woken up. She's thought about how much she wanted to take her home on the day she was born. And how maybe her wish came true when Jonah came to them.

'Miss Mary looks after me,' Grace says. 'Jesus works through her.'

Rosie feels a stab of annoyance. In her work, Rosie has comes across people with this kind of belief system: a commitment to some divine power, which they think will cure them. So they refuse medical treatment. More often than not, they die.

'There are hospitals in Nairobi,' Rosie says. 'And we could find some local treatment clinics too . . . I believe there's one on Lamu.'

The right medication could ease her pain, make her comfortable, maybe even give her a few more weeks. Perhaps she and Sam could raise a bit of money – maybe it went further here.

'Will you take care of him?' Grace asks.

The two women lock eyes.

'He needs someone like you.' Grace pauses. 'A good mother.'

Ever since Rosie read Jonah's case file, she's dreamt of these words: a blessing from Jonah's mother, the possibility of his being fully theirs. But now that Rosie's here, sitting in front of Grace, she feels that old anger swelling in her chest.

No matter how big the sacrifice or how good the motivation, Grace sent Jonah to England without a soul waiting for him on the other side. And Grace doesn't know the first thing about Rosie – she's handing her child over to a stranger.

'I've been praying so hard for Jonah,' Grace goes on. 'I knew he would find the right home.'

Rosie bites her tongue. *Anything could have happened to Jonah*, she wants to say. *The fact that he's ended up with Sam and me is nothing short of a miracle.*

'Tell me, is he happy? Is he doing well?'

So Jonah hasn't told her that he's ill.

'Jonah's doing fine.'

'At school?'

'In general.'

'That's good.'

Rosie can't breathe in this small room with its clicking fan and its white walls and the woman who failed Jonah. She shouldn't be here. There's nothing for them to say to each other.

She gets up off the chair and walks towards the door.

'I know you'll make him better,' Grace calls after her.

Rosie turns round. 'Sorry?'

How stupid to think that either she or Jonah could have kept it from Grace: you don't have to be a mother to see that Jonah is ill.

Grace holds Rosie's gaze.

'What do you know?' Rosie asks.

'When he was little, Jonah had malaria. He was very sick.'

In that moment, Rosie gets it. Keeping Jonah's illness from Grace isn't even at issue here.

'You sent him away because you thought he'd get ill, didn't you?'

Grace places her palms, one over the other, on her chest. 'After the malaria, Miss Mary said that Jonah had a weakness in his body, that she could feel it.'

You don't need a spiritual healer to tell you about the consequences of childhood malaria. Rosie clenches her fists. By not getting Jonah the care he needed, Grace created an opportunity for the cancer to take root. For the HIV she'd passed to him to wake up.

Grace did all this to him.

But there's one thing that doesn't make sense.

'So, if Miss Mary can cure anyone, if she's treating you – why didn't you keep Jonah with you? And why don't you keep him with you now?'

Grace wipes a sheen of sweat off her brow.

'I know it is difficult for you to understand about the way we do things here,' Grace says. 'About how Miss Mary works. That her work goes deeper than curing people.'

'*Deeper* than curing? How does that work?'

'You don't understand our world, Rosie. And you think I don't understand your world either. And maybe I don't. But I know enough. I've learnt over the years. And I understand that Jonah needs to be with you.'

Rosie walks slowly back to the sofa, sits down beside Grace.

Grace leans back and looks out of the small window with a view of the sea.

'Jonah will teach you,' Grace says. 'He will bring our worlds together.'

The anger seeps out of Rosie. She takes Grace's hand.

'Jonah has Burkitt's Lymphoma.' She pauses. 'It's cancer.'

Grace closes her eyes for a moment and then says:

'It is connected to the malaria?' She pauses. 'And the HIV?'

Rosie looks at this young frail woman. A moment ago, she wanted to shout at her for making Jonah ill. Now she wants to protect her from the worst truth in the world: that she's hurt her child.

'Yes,' Rosie says quietly.

A tear drops from each of Grace's eyes onto the bed sheets. Her mouth falls slack. She shakes her head.

'You didn't think you'd passed it on?' Rosie asks.

'I prayed I hadn't.'

Grace closes her eyes and sways back and forth, a tormented expression on her face. Something inside her has broken.

'We're doing everything we can to help him,' Rosie goes on. 'We're getting him the very best medical help.'

Grace looks at Rosie and for the first time, there's a bit of light in her eyes.

'So he will get better?'

'We can't know for sure. The treatment is complicated. But we're going to give it our best shot.'

Grace leans forward. 'But *you* know, though, don't you? You know like a mother knows? That he will be well again?'

Rosie feels her own eyes welling up. 'I'm not a mother. I've never been a mother – I'll never *be* a mother ...'

Grace reaches out and takes her hand. 'Yes, you are. And with you, Jonah will get better.'

And if he doesn't? Rosie thinks. Will that confirm what she's always feared, that she should never have been allowed to have a child?

'You love him,' Grace says.

Rosie nods. 'Of course I love him.' She chokes on her words. 'More than anything.'

Grace touches Rosie's cheek and wipes away a tear.

'Then that is enough.'

She tries to lifts her legs onto the sofa but doesn't have the strength. Rosie cradles Grace's calves in her arms and helps her up.

Grace lies back on the pillows.

'I'm sorry, I get tired so easily.' Grace closes her eyes. 'I need to sleep now.'

'Yes, of course.'

Rosie stands up but she doesn't want to go. There are too many half-started sentences. There are too many questions she still has to ask.

'Maybe I can come back later – introduce you to Sam, my husband?'

Grace nods slowly but she doesn't open her eyes or speak.

'And Jonah – we can bring Jonah back. We can extend our stay. Give you as long as you need with him ...'

'Will you read to me?' Grace asks, her voice so quiet that Rosie can barely make it out.

'Read?'

Still not opening her eyes, Grace lifts the book lying beside her.

'Jonah's book?' Rosie asks.

Grace nods.

Rosie opens it where Jonah left his bookmark. It's the final scene, where Prospero is giving up his magic.

She takes a breath and starts reading from Prospero's last speech, the one she remembers most vividly from school: a magician hanging up his cloak for the last time:

*Now my charms are all o'erthrown,*

*And what strength I have's mine own,*

*Which is most faint . . .*

Rosie stops reading. Grace's breathing has grown slow and deep. And then it disappears altogether.

## Sam

'This beats Bridgeford Pool, eh?' Sam flips onto his back and looks up at the sky.

Thick grey clouds glide fast across the sun. They're so bright, they shine like silver. Even the clouds out here are beautiful.

Jonah stands in the water beside Sam. He's been quiet ever since they left his mum, and he keeps looking down the coast towards Shela.

*This is it,* thinks Sam. *This is my chance to be a dad, the kind of dad Jonah's never had.* Situations like these only come around once in a lifetime, the big tests, the ones that children remember for ever.

Sam turns onto his front and plants his feet back on the bottom of the sea.

'You OK?' he asks Jonah.

Jonah nods.

Sam looks out across the wide expanse of sea. 'This how you remember it?'

Jonah nods again but his eyes are still fixed on Shela.

'It must have been hard, seeing your mum.'

Sam can't get the image of Grace out of his head: the ghost of a woman, more bones than flesh. Goodness knows what's going through Jonah's head right now.

Jonah brushes the surface of the water with his fingertips. The sun catches the ripples.

'You're being so brave,' Sam says. 'Rosie and I are very proud of you, you know?'

*Rosie and I.* A united front. That's what they have to be for Jonah over the next few days. And this is a test for them, too. For Sam. A chance for him to make up for all the ways he's let her down in the last few months.

Jonah looks up at him, his brow furrowed. 'Are there good doctors in Kenya?'

'Doctors?'

'Like the ones in England?'

'I'm sure there are, yes.'

'And hospitals?'

'Probably. In Nairobi, certainly.'

Jonah frowns. 'Not here?'

'On Lamu?'

Jonah nods.

'I don't know, Jonah. We could ask Peter to look into it.'

Sam's throat goes tight. They've only been on Lamu a few hours and already Jonah's decided that he wants to stay here.

*We have to go along with whatever Jonah decides*, Rosie has said, over and over; he knew she was trying to convince herself as much as anyone. *He's had enough imposed on him. We're going to have to respect his wishes.*

But Sam isn't so sure. In a few days Jonah will be eight years old – still a child. And, regardless of what Sam said to Trudi a week back, about how maybe Jonah would do better with another family, he realises now that he can't let go of the little boy he's come to call his son.

Jonah's diagnosis. Their journey here. Seeing Grace. And now Jonah's hinting that he doesn't want to leave – it's all coming clear for Sam. He wants Jonah to come home with them. For as long as they're allowed to have him, he wants Jonah to be theirs.

'Could we ask Peter, then?' Jonah asks.

'Sure.'

Jonah disappears under the water. When he surfaces, he says, 'Could we swim out to the rock?'

Sam follows Jonah's gaze out to sea. He's heard about this rock before, the one Jonah and his mum used to swim to, far out beyond where the tourists paddled. The water's choppy today so Sam can only make out the tip jutting out of the water.

'It's quite far, Jonah.'

He's worried that Jonah won't have the strength to swim for so long any more, especially now that he's sick.

'It's an easy swim,' Jonah says, already taking off. 'Race you there!'

'I'm not sure . . . ' Sam calls after him.

Jonah keeps swimming so Sam paddles after him. It only takes a few strokes for him to feel out of breath.

'Jonah! Not so fast!'

But Jonah's gliding through the water, hardly seeming to make an effort at all.

It's as if Jonah wants to prove that his old life still exists.

Sam struggles to keep up with him.

When they get to the rock, Jonah scrambles up. Sam follows, cutting his foot on a cluster of sharp barnacles. He wheezes as he catches his breath. As he looks at the shore in the distance, he worries that he won't have the strength to swim all the way back. He scans the horizon, wondering whether they can hitch a lift on one of the taxi boats that brought them over from the airport.

'Cool view, isn't it?' Jonah says.

And he's right. On one side of them, the horizon stretches out to what feels like the end of the world: sky and water meet in a curved line, smooth and beautiful. And on the other side, the coastline lies wide open, the Kizingo huts as small as shells on the white sand.

Jonah looks down at the trail of blood on Sam's foot. 'The salt water will disinfect your cut.'

'I'm not used to all this adventure.' Sam smiles. 'Did you used to come out here often?'

'Mama and I swam here most days. Sometimes I came out on my own, though when I did that, I didn't tell her. She'd get worried.'

Sam thinks about how, under different circumstances, they could have shared stories with Grace about their little boy.

'Your mama's right. It's a long way out.'

'Oh, it's not really that far.'

'Well, you're a strong swimmer, that's for sure. Maybe, when we get home, we could sign you up for some swim team trials at the Bridgeford pool – I've noticed how you like to watch them train . . .'

Sam wants to keep their life back in England alive for Jonah, to remind him of the things he'll miss if he doesn't come home with them.

A long silence hangs between them. After a while, Jonah says: 'Mama needs me.'

Sam wishes he could have heard the conversation Jonah had with Grace. More specifically what she said to him and whether she put pressure on him to stay and take care of her. The very thought of it sends of jolt of anger through his body.

When's Grace going to start thinking about what's good for Jonah?

'Your mum's a grown-up, Jonah. It's not your job to look after her.'

He scrunches up his brow again. 'I've always looked after Mama.'

This is the closest Jonah has come to mentioning his old life, here in Kenya, with Grace.

'Mama got tired,' he goes on. 'I had to make sure she slept and had food.'

'That's a big responsibility.'

Jonah shrugs. 'Mama looked after me, too.'

'Well, right now, all you should worry about is getting yourself well again.'

'I feel better here,' Jonah says.

And he does look better. His skin is filled with light. His eyes shine. His whole body seems to have given out a big sigh of relief. But Sam knows that this is just an illusion. That the cancer is still there, and that it will continue to spread if he doesn't get treatment.

'You need to have some special treatments to make sure you're better, Jonah. I know you feel better but you're still sick, very sick.'

'Mama's more sick. Much more sick.'

When Sam saw the state Grace was in, this was what he'd feared, but he hadn't wanted to take his thoughts any further.

'What did your mama tell you?'

Jonah is quiet for a long time. So long that Sam's worried he's probed too far and that Jonah's retreated back into his shell.

'She didn't tell me,' Jonah says. 'But I know. And I'm going to find doctors to look after her, like the doctors have been looking after me back home.'

*Back home.* He'd just used those words about England. Sam feels a fillip of hope.

'But I have to persuade her first.'

'Persuade her?'

'She doesn't believe in doctors. She only believes in God. And Miss Mary's hands.'

'I see.'

'But I can persuade her. And when she gets medicine and feels better, she'll understand. I'll help her to understand.'

'This is all a lot for you to take in, Jonah. How about, when we get back to our hut, we have a chat with Rosie and make a plan for how we can help your mum before we go back—?'

'No.'

The clouds thicken above them. A raindrop lands on Sam's arm.

'You don't want us to help?' Sam asks.

'I'm not going back to England.'

Sam's stomach churns. 'Oh, Jonah . . .'

He has to find a way to change Jonah's mind. To make him see that it will be better for everyone if he comes back to England.

Jonah stands up and puts his hands over his arms, ready to dive back in.

'I'm going to swim for a bit,' Jonah says.

'Swim where?' Sam's only just got his breath back from swimming out here.

'Under the water.'

Sam looks down into the deep blue of the sea around the rock. So deep it's almost black.

'I don't think that's a good idea . . .'

'It's OK, I'm a dolphin.'

'You are?'

Jonah nods and grins. 'It's what Mister Sir called me. He said I must have been a dolphin in a past life.' He pauses. 'He said that, if I learnt to hold my breath for a really long time, maybe I'll be a dolphin in my next life, too.'

Sam's breath catches in his throat.

'Well, dolphin or not, you haven't swum this far in ages, Jonah. Why don't you stay up here with me?'

But before he has time to stop him, Jonah's body slides down into the dark water.


## Jonah


The world under the sea feels more familiar to Jonah than anything on land. He used to swim out here with Mama. She would sit on the rock, the sun warming her skin, and then she'd dive in and join him and they'd practise holding their breaths. And they'd talk to each other, whispering their secrets as small bubbles of oxygen escaped from their lips.

Mama had promised Jonah that, when he was in England, she would still come out to their rock and that, when she did, he'd know it in his heart. But from what she looked like today, Jonah can't imagine Mama paddling on the shore, let alone coming all the way out here.

All those times, when he was back in England, he'd imagined her under the water, talking to him, when she probably hadn't even left her bed. No wonder he'd stopped hearing her voice.

Jonah flips onto his back and looks up at the light filtering through the surface of the water – bright, even on a grey day like today.

Jonah isn't trained like he used to be, so he knows that he won't manage more than two or three minutes. That's why he needs to go deep quickly if he wants to enjoy the world down here before having to come up again.

And so Jonah dives deeper. The temperature drops. Goosebumps rise on his skin. His limbs and head go numb. And the weight of the last eight months floats away from his body and up through the water – far, far away from him.

Down here, he isn't sick any more. And neither is Mama.

He kicks his feet, throws his arms in arcs by his side and goes deeper.

*Mama* . . . Jonah calls out in his head. *Mama, it's me, Jonah* . . .

He strains to hear. Blood rushes in his ears. His head feels like it's floating. And he's finding it hard to keep his eyes open.

*Mama* . . .

And then he sees her. Not the whole of her, just bits at a time. First her arms, gliding through the water.

Then her legs, her feet woven together by seaweed like a mermaid's tail.

And then her hair, long and thick and black, trailing behind her in the water.

*Mama* . . .

He goes deeper. Swims faster. Tries to catch hold of her. He wants to see her face. Hear her voice.

*Mama . . .*

His head feels even lighter, light and empty as a balloon.

*Mama . . .*

He reaches for her hand, but then she slips away from him. For a second, she disappears into one of the caves and then she shoots up again.

*Look at me, Mama . . .*

At last he catches up with her. For a moment, she turns to face him. And she doesn't look like the Mama he saw today but like the Mama he remembers. The Mama who laughed and sang and danced. The Mama with a big smile and big brown eyes, and smooth skin. The Mama with the yellow dress, like on the photo.

*I love you, Mama.*

He reaches out and catches her hand and for a moment, he feels her fingers in his.

And then she dissolves.

Bubbles shoot up around him.

And she's gone.

## Jonah

A moment later, thick arms clamp around Jonah's waist. He's yanked back up to the surface. His head shoots out of the water. He coughs and splutters and gasps at the air.

It's raining hard. The sky is as dark as night. Waves rise around them. Jonah blinks away the water from his eyes and looks at the face in front of him.

Sam pulls him towards his torso and holds him tight.

'Thank God . . . ' Sam keeps saying as he breathes and coughs. 'Thank God, Jonah . . . '

When they get back to the shore, Rosie, DI Peter and Trudi are standing on the beach. The rain has stopped and the grey clouds have thinned. Blades of sunlight fall onto the sand.

When she sees him, Rosie runs into the water, not stopping to take off her clothes or shoes. She waves her arms. Her face is red and blotchy and her hair is a jumble of frizz and curls.

'Where have you been?' she yells at them.

Sam lets Jonah climb off his back. He insisted on carrying Jonah, even though Jonah told him he was fine, that he had just done what he always did when he came to the rock. That, in fact, going under the water made him feel better than he's felt for a long, long time. But Sam hadn't listened.

Sam is breathing hard and his skin has pink and white blotches on it.

Rosie grabs hold of Jonah's hand and then Sam's and pulls them towards the shore.

'What happened?' Rosie asks.

Sam lets go of her hand, wipes the water from his eyes, looks at Jonah and smiles.

'Oh, we just got a bit carried away, didn't we, J?'

He brushes his hand over Jonah's head.

Jonah nods. Sam made him promise not to say how far they'd swum or how long Jonah had stayed under the water.

'I'm officially old . . . ' Sam says, between breaths.

Further up on the beach, Trudi and DI Peter are craning their necks, as though they want to hear what everyone's saying. They must have come back to Kizingo with Rosie.

Rosie lifts Jonah out of the water and although he's much too big for her to carry and although it makes her clothes all wet, she holds him to her really tight.

'Everything OK, love?' Sam asks.

Rosie squeezes Jonah tighter.

'Rosie?'

Rosie puts Jonah down. 'You had a good swim, then?' she asks Jonah, her eyes watery.

'Yes,' Jonah says. 'Did you talk to Mama?'

Rosie nods. And then the watery bits in her eyes plop down her cheeks.

'Rosie?' Sam's brow scrunches up.

Rosie folds her arms over her chest, looks down at the water and says, 'We need to talk, Sam.'

Sam's face falls.

A knot forms in Jonah's tummy. He's heard grown-ups use the words, 'we need to talk,' enough times to know that it means something's wrong. Maybe Rosie's cross that Sam took Jonah out for such a long swim when he's meant to be sick. He thinks about telling her that it was his idea but just then Trudi walks up to them, her sandals in her hands, her skirt hitched up.

'Why don't we get you showered and dressed, Jonah,' she says. 'And then Peter and I will take you for an ice-cream. Peter said he found a place a bit further up the beach.'

Jonah wants to stay with Rosie and Sam and to ask Rosie more about her conversation with Mama, but he can tell that they want to talk alone, just like when Mama had private conversations with Mister Sir.

As Jonah walks back up the beach with DI Peter and Trudi, he looks over his shoulder.

Sam and Rosie are sitting in the sand, their heads bent low. They haven't sat that close for ages. And Rosie hasn't put her head on Sam's shoulder like that for weeks and weeks. And she hasn't let Sam take her hand to kiss it like that for ages either.

It makes him glad but it also makes the knot in his stomach tighten: something's definitely not right.

In the old lady's house, in Shela, four men lift the body of a young mother onto their shoulders. She's as light as the summer breeze. As they take her out onto the street, they nod to the old woman, sitting with her back to the wall of her house.

Further on along the coast, a child sits on the sand, the sea washing over his feet. He watches the water rise and fall and wonders what it would be like to be pulled far, far out to sea.

A little way from him sit a man and a woman who've promised that they'll never leave him. But that's what his mama said too.

On the next wave, a shell washes up beside him, like the one he brought to England. He holds the shell to his ear and closes his eyes and tears drop down his cheeks and into the sea.

On the beach, a little further up from the child, a policeman and a social worker sit next to each other, their elbows touching. They look at the boy and then out to the horizon. Their work has prepared them for this world; they are familiar with the rhythms of loss. But today, in this moment, they have no words.

In another part of the world, a little girl stands at her bedroom window. Red thistles blossom along her arms and she uses every bit of her strength not to scratch them.

She watches the trains pull in and out of the station, hoping that, one day, her best friend will step out onto the platform and look up her with his brown eyes and wave.

Then the little girl lifts the shell to her ear.

*Come home . . .* she whispers.

Back in the small town of Shela, the old lady picks up her cane, walks into her house, sits at her kitchen table and writes a note. When she's finished, she folds up the paper and takes it down to the shore. She hands it to the man waiting in the boat.

*Here, take this* . . . she tells him. *Now go. As fast as you can.*

# Trudi

Trudi and Rosie stand at the back of the church.

'You'll be home soon. And then we can focus on the adoption.'
Trudi presses Rosie's hands in hers.

They watch Sam and Jonah walking down the aisle and settling on the front row with Miss Mary.

'I'd better join them,' Rosie says.

'Of course.'

Rosie looks up at Trudi, her eyes tired.

'Thank you, Trudi. For everything.'

Trudi smiles. 'I'd do it all over again. You, Sam and Jonah are meant to be together.'

'You think it's going to work out?' Rosie asks.

'Yes, it's going to work out.'

But as Trudi watches Rosie walking down the aisle, her eyes fixed on the coffin by the altar, Trudi isn't sure she believes her own words. Jonah's going to have so much to contend with in the coming months: mourning his mum, undergoing treatment, getting used to the fact that England is his home now, for good. But at least they know where they stand now. No more surprises. No more tearing across the world, chasing a ghost.

Trudi hangs back. She doesn't feel it's right to be at the front with Grace's family.

Peter comes into the church and stands beside her.

'You doing OK?' Peter asks.

They haven't had it out yet, about her coming to Lamu against his wishes. She hopes he understands, now, why she had to come.

'I'll be fine.'

He slips his hand into hers. A ball of warmth bursts in her stomach.

'It'll be good to get home,' he says.

She nods and, without thinking, leans her head against his shoulder. He puts his arm around her and kisses the top of her head.

Trudi looks round the empty church. She imagines it wasn't the kind of funeral Grace had hoped for. If Kenyan funerals were anything like those Trudi had attended as a little girl, in Uganda, mourners should be spilling out of the doors; the altar should be crowded with sacrificed animals – to appease the spirits in the afterlife, to show respect to the soul of the departed. And the funeral should last for days, even weeks.

Blessing and Albert had all but ruined themselves paying for Trudi's parents' funeral.

But from what Miss Mary said, Grace had alienated her family a long time ago: by moving away, by refusing to speak their native tongue, through the job she did – and she'd committed the worst crime of all: she'd given away her only child.

And then came the shame of her illness.

So here Grace was, with nothing but a handful of mourners to see her into the afterlife.

Trudi believes in respecting the dead, which is why she'd pooled her cash together with Peter's to make Rosie and Sam's contributions stretch a little further, enough for the basics: a rented casket, a priest, a small choir, a bit of food afterwards.

But none of that matters much to Trudi. She's concerned with the living.

She looks over at the Keeps. Jonah sits between them, his head held high. When they told him about Grace, he nodded, like he knew it was coming. One of these days, it'll all sink in, of course, that the woman he's loved his whole life is no longer there. Rosie and Sam will have to be ready for that. But Grace is confident that Jonah will get through it. He's the strongest little boy she's ever met.

'I'm going to make damn sure they're OK,' she says to Peter. 'That they get to stay together. That Jonah gets the treatment he needs.'

She expects him to warn her to be careful of the promises she makes, that she can't fix the world. But instead, he kisses her head again and whispers, 'I know you are.'

He takes a strand of her hair and smooths it between his fingers. 'I like it like this.'

'Like this?'

'Free.'

'Free?' She laughs. 'A mess, you mean.'

After weeks of neglect, her plaits are in such a state that she's just taken them out. She feels like she's carrying a bush on her head.

'Well, I like it,' he says again.

And then she remembers that first comment he made about her hair, that night, sitting in Blessing's flat. *I like the natural look . . .*

Trudi wonders what will happen when she and Peter go home to England. Whether their lives will continue to grow towards each other or whether, once they get back to their grey skies and their jobs, without the investigation to bring them together, they'll stop seeing each other.

She blinks away the thought and leans her head deeper into his chest.

The priest walks out of a small room to the left of the altar and comes to stand in front of the coffin.

'Let us pray . . .' he says to the tiny congregation.

Everyone bows their heads.

'We give thanks for the life of our sister, Grace . . .'

Trudi hears heavy footsteps outside the church.

A moment later, a man strides in, a goat slung across his shoulders and, behind him, a trail of men and women and children, all brightly dressed, also carrying sacrificed animals. They sing and dance and mutter prayers as they walk down the aisle.

There's a warrior in traditional dress waving a spear, probably from a Luo community, on the west coast, right on the other side of the country.

Trudi's pulse races so hard now that she feels like she's going to pass out.

Who told them?

The man leading the procession places the goat on the altar and turns round to look at the congregation, which has now swelled.

'Forgive the interruption.' The man's voice is loud and strong.

Miss Mary stands up, her hand trembling at her throat.

Rosie and Sam hold Jonah tight.

'What the hell is going on?' whispers Peter.

'Maybe someone told her family – maybe they've decided to honour her after all,' Trudi says. 'Let's go and sit with Jonah.'

Peter nods and they walk to the front. They slip into the pew behind Rosie and Sam. Trudi puts her hand on Rosie's shoulder.

Rosie turns round; she's biting her lip.

'Who are they?' she asks.

'Probably family,' Trudi says. 'Try not to worry. This is how people celebrate the dead.'

Trudi looks back to the man standing at the altar and her breath catches in her throat.

She turns to Miss Mary.

'Do you know who he is?' she whispers, nudging her head towards the man at the front.

Miss Mary bows her head.

Trudi looks at him again. His eyes are fixed on Jonah. And then it hits her: she knows exactly who he is. And from how he's looking at Jonah, she knows why he's here too.

## Jonah

Later that night, as he sits on the beach, Jonah watches the flames from the bonfire flicker over Odikinyi's face.

He's tried to picture his papa's face a million times, but all he ever saw was one of the Mister Sirs. They're the only papas he's ever known. This man with his huge smile, his big brown eyes and his tall, thin body, couldn't look any more different from the Mister Sirs Mama spent her time with. Or any more different from Sam, either.

Jonah rubs his eyes. He's beginning to wonder whether this day will ever end.

Last night, he couldn't sleep: he kept thinking about Mama and whether she was in heaven yet and whether she was better there and whether she would still remember him and speak to him.

And then, just as his eyelids were dropping, Rosie came to wake him up for the funeral. And after Odikinyi turned up with everyone, they'd spent the day eating and talking and eating some more until everyone was full and exhausted.

When all the people from Mama's village left and Miss Mary went back to her house in Shela, Jonah, Rosie, Sam, Trudi, DI Peter and Odikinyi took the boat back to Kizingo.

Everyone except Jonah and Odikinyi are sitting at the bar. Rosie keeps looking over at them. Ever since the funeral, she's been biting her lip and scrunching up her brow and looking like she did when he had all those tests at the hospital.

'So, you really didn't know about me?' Jonah asks his papa.

'I'm afraid not, Jonah.'

'But why didn't Mama tell you?'

Odikinyi looks into the bonfire. 'She didn't want to bring me shame.'

Jonah feels a dull thud in his chest.

'Shame? Because of me?'

He looks at Jonah, his eyes a liquid brown.

'It was not about you, Jonah. Your mama and I grew up Catholics. Which means that we should have been married before we had you.'

'But why?'

Odikinyi gives Jonah a smile; for a second, Jonah feels like he's looking in a mirror. Until today, he'd always thought he looked like Mama, but that was only half of him.

'It doesn't make sense to me now either,' Odikinyi says. 'But back then, your mama and I believed what we'd been taught by our priests and by the Bible teachings we read every day. What God thought mattered to your mama, very much.'

'I know,' Jonah says.

But Mama thought God could make her better, and he let her die.

Odikinyi looks up at the dark sky. Jonah looks up too, at the thousands of stars, and wonders whether Mama really is up there

399

and whether she is happy – and whether maybe she can see him.

'Did you live with Mama in Kisumu?'

She talked about it sometimes, a little place by the sea.

'Yes. I still live there now.'

'Is it far?'

'Yes, it's on the other side of Kenya. I travelled all night to be here on time for your mama's funeral.'

'Why did Mama live so far away from her home?'

Odikinyi looks into the flames and doesn't answer for a long time. Then he looks at Jonah and says, 'I think she came here *because* it was far away from her home. From people who might look down on her for having a baby without being married.' He pauses. 'And because she thought that I wouldn't be able to find her here.'

Jonah's jaw tightens. 'Did you try to look?'

'Of course. But if someone doesn't want to be found . . .'

Jonah thinks about how upset Rosie and Sam were the first time they went to Bridgeford Pool and they couldn't find him. And how upset Grandma Flick was when she found him at the station when he was about to run away.

If he went missing, they'd keep looking for ever.

Maybe Odikinyi did not love Mama enough to find her.

'DI Peter found Mama all the way from England.'

'Ah, but DI Peter is a policeman.'

'But he was in *England*. You were *here*.'

Odikinyi holds out his palms. 'Look, Jonah, you know your mama. How stubborn she could be. How when she made her mind up about something, nothing could change it. She did all she could to disappear. She even changed her name . . .'

'Her name? You mean Mama is not called Grace?'

Jonah has run out of space in his head for new information.

400

Odikinyi smiles again. 'Grace suits her. It's the name she chose. But it wasn't the name her family gave her. She had a Luo name, like me.'

'A Luo name?'

'Yes. A beautiful name: Atieno.'

'Atieno . . .' Jonah says, feeling the *A* on the roof of his mouth and the *t* on his tongue and the *o* between his lips.

'Atieno means *one born at night* . . . my name means *one born in the morning*. We used to joke that it's what made us get on so well – and fight like cat and dog too.' He laughs. 'We're as different as night and day.'

Jonah thinks about how Rosie and Sam are really different too and how they love each other. And he thinks about Peter and Trudi. And he thinks about Alice and how she couldn't be more different from him, and then he feels sad that he wasn't able to tell Mama more about her.

'I searched for your mama for a very long time, Jonah. But you are right, I did stop looking.' He pauses. 'But that was for a reason.'

Jonah looks up at him and they hold each other's gaze.

'I have a family, Jonah. A wife and three children. They live with me back in Kisumu.'

A family?

'You would be the oldest, Jonah. A big brother to your sisters.'

'*Sisters?*'

'They are all girls. They are quite a handful, but you would like them.' He pauses. 'They need a big brother to look after them.'

He wonders what Alice would make of that: that he was not an only child, like her, after all. That he had sisters, even if they were only half-sisters. And then he realises what Odikinyi just said: he wants Jonah to come home with him.

Jonah's heart races. He doesn't want to think about that, not today when there's been so much to take in already.

'How did you find Mama – now, I mean?'

'A friend of hers got in touch with me.'

'A friend?'

Jonah realises that he doesn't know anything about the life that Mama had while he was away, about the people she saw and talked to and became friends with. Just like Mama will never meet Alice.

'Did Mama's friend tell you that she was sick?'

Odikinyi nods. 'It makes me very sad that I was not here to help her.'

He wonders whether someone told Odikinyi that Jonah is sick too. Jonah hopes not; maybe his papa won't like him when he finds out there is something wrong with him. But then, if Jonah does go and live with Odikinyi, he will have to see doctors to make him better, so his papa will have to know.

Jonah's head hurts from thinking of what lies ahead of him. Yesterday, he thought he would stay here on Lamu to look after Mama. And then she died and he thought he would go back to England with Rosie and Sam. And now it sounds like he's going to live in another place altogether, with a papa and a family he does not know.

'I'm learning to read,' Jonah says. He wants Odikinyi to know that he's not just any boy.

Odikinyi smiles. 'Your mama would have liked that.'

'She liked books when she lived in Kisumu?'

'Oh, your mama loved books from the day she was born. She said they were the key to life. The Bible, of course. But other stories too.'

Jonah smiles. 'We read stories together.' He pauses. 'Well, we told each other stories.'

It feels strange to be speaking to someone who knew Mama as well as he did. Maybe even better. Strange and nice.

He looks up at Odikinyi. 'Can you read?'

Odikinyi stares out across the dark sea. 'No. I left school very young, to work on my father's fishing boat.'

Jonah knows that it is not a good thought to have but he is not sure he wants a papa who cannot read. Even if Sam's slow and stumbly, at least he can share books with Jonah.

'I'll be eight tomorrow,' Jonah says.

'That's a very grown-up age to be.'

Jonah shrugs. 'Maybe.'

Odikinyi straightens his spine and looks right at Jonah.

'So grown-up that you will be able to make up your own mind.'

'Make up my mind about what?'

Odikinyi pauses.

'About whether you want to come home with me.'

Jonah swallows hard. He feels the old pain in his throat.

'It's *my* decision?'

'I think it should be, yes.'

Jonah thinks about all the times in his life that he's wished a grown-up would let him decide: how he wanted to stay with Mama rather than go to England; how he wanted Peter and Trudi to find Mister Sir so that he could live with him; how, yesterday, he wanted Mama to let him stay and look after her and not go home with Rosie and Sam. But now, deciding is the last thing he wants to do. He's too tired to make up his mind about anything, let alone something as big as this.

He looks back up at the stars: *what do you want me to do, Mama?*

'You can sleep on it, Jonah, there's no rush.'

'But the plane is leaving tomorrow ...' Jonah says. 'It's all booked.'

'Oh, I see.'

Jonah gets up and looks towards the Kizingo bar.

'I'd like to go and see Rosie and Sam for a bit.'

Odikinyi nods. 'They've been very good to you, haven't they?'

'Yes.'

'Do you love them?'

Jonah looks at Rosie and Sam, sitting next to Peter and Trudi. Sam is playing with a piece of driftwood.

'Yes, I love them.'

'And do you love your life back in England?'

Jonah thinks about England and Wales and he feels a big pang of sadness: for Hop, for Alice, for Grandma Flick and Ariel and the sunflowers growing in her garden and the sea, even if it's dark and cold, and for Sam's studio in the garage and all his driftwood horses; and for Mrs Boon, who tries so hard to teach them. He even feels a pang for the grey skies and the rain and the damp in the air and having to wear shoes; and the smelly public pool in Bridgeford; and all the hospital appointments.

His eyes sting.

'It's OK, Jonah. England has become your home.'

He nods and sniffs away the tears.

'Like I said, it's your decision. I won't force you to come with me.'

Jonah thinks about having a family, a proper family, people who look like him, and a papa who is actually his papa.

'I'll think about it,' Jonah says.

And then he turns and runs up the beach to Rosie and Sam.

# Sam

Sam watches Rosie and Jonah heading up the beach to their hut. Jonah slips his hand into Rosie's and it's like something comes loose in Sam's chest: they're so close to being a family and this man, a stranger, is about to take it all away from them.

Rosie turns back and looks at him for a moment and he knows exactly what she's communicating: *Fix it*.

And by fix it, she means, *make sure Jonah comes home with us tomorrow*.

Peter and Trudi stand in front of Sam and Odikinyi, stealing glances at each other and shuffling their feet in the sand.

'Why don't we go for a walk?' Peter says to Trudi.

Peter is as tall as Odikinyi: next to them both, Sam feels tiny.

'Good idea,' Trudi says. 'I want to enjoy Lamu before we head back to rainy England.' She leans into Peter and he puts his arm around her.

Sam has noticed how close Trudi and Peter have grown since they've been here. It makes him think of how things were between him and Rosie when they were young. Maybe, when they get back to England, they can find their way back to each other again.

It's cowardly, but he wishes Trudi could stay for a bit. She'd know what to say to Odikinyi; she'd get through to him about Jonah needing to come home with them. But then maybe that's not what she thinks, maybe now that she's met Odikinyi and seen how tall and strong he is, how he's got a wife and a family back in Kisumu, how he'd be more than able to look after Jonah, his biological son, she thinks he'd be better off staying.

But then Trudi steps forward and presses Sam's hand.

'See you later, Sam,' she says.

And in that moment, he knows, that she's on their side. That even if Odikinyi is Jonah's biological father, even if he is capable of looking after Jonah, she wants Jonah to be sitting next to them on the flight home tomorrow.

'Keep an eye out for the dolphins,' Odikinyi says.

'You can see dolphins at night?' Peter asks.

He nods. 'When they sleep, half their brain remains awake. If they lost consciousness, they wouldn't be able to breathe underwater. They swim more slowly than in the day, making sure to keep their blowholes exposed, and they surface every now and then for a breath. It's pretty magical.'

Odikinyi smiles and it breaks Sam's heart a bit, how much he looks like Jonah.

'I take tourists out at night sometimes, in my fishing boat. It's a little side-business I run.'

Sam remembers what Jonah told him on the day they arrived, out on the rock: that Mister Sir thought he was a dolphin in a past life, which accounts for him being able to hold his breath underwater for so long. Maybe that also accounted for why he never really sleeps.

'I'd love to see some sleeping-swimming dolphins,' Trudi says.

Odikinyi and Sam watch Peter and Trudi walk off down the beach.

The two men stand in silence for a while. Then Odikinyi says: 'It's been quite a day.'

'Yes.' Sam feels himself shrinking. And although he knows that he has to speak to him – that it's the job Rosie has given him – he hasn't got the first idea as to where to begin.

'Why don't we go for a drink?' Odikinyi nods at the Kizingo bar.

It's been a long time since Sam has had a drink at a bar, with another man, but he needs something to help him hold his nerve. 'Sure.'

As they sit on the bar stools and wait for their drinks to arrive, Sam leaps right in.

'So you want Jonah back?'

'*Back*?' Odikinyi raises his eyebrows. 'I never had him to start with. Atieno – Grace – didn't tell me I had a son.'

Sam tries to imagine what that would feel like if life had taken him away from Rosie. And if she'd borne his child without telling him.

'But you do want him, right? Now that you know about him?'

Odikinyi nods. 'Of course. He is my son.' He pauses. 'Wouldn't you want that too, Sam? To have back the son that you'd lost?'

Sam clenches his jaw. He knows that he can't be angry at Odikinyi for not being a father to a child he never knew about, but still, there's a bitter taste in his mouth as he thinks about this man sweeping into Jonah's life, claiming a son he hasn't had anything to do with for the first eight years of his life.

And he feels even angrier because, deep down, he knows that Odikinyi is right: if Sam were Jonah's biological father, if he had the luxury of being in that position, he'd want him back in a heartbeat.

Odikinyi orders the drinks, something called Konyagi, a drink distilled from sugar cane. They wait in silence until they arrive and as soon as they do, Sam empties his glass.

Odikinyi takes a sip and puts down his glass.

'The thing is, Sam, it is not my decision.'

A beat of hope echoes in his chest. So he's going to ask Trudi? Defer to the professional?

'I told Jonah that he should decide.'

'You did what?'

'He's old enough.'

'He's a child.'

'In Kenya, Jonah is considered a young man. I was running my father's business by the age of ten.'

Sam shakes his head. He doesn't know whether he should be happy that Odikinyi isn't claiming a right to Jonah, or whether he should be furious at him for having put Jonah in this position.

'Who told you about Grace's funeral?'

'Miss Mary. She sent a relative to Kisumu to find me.'

So Miss Mary betrayed her best friend.

'Grace wanted Jonah to be with us,' Sam says. 'It's what she told Rosie on the day she died. Miss Mary knows that.'

'Miss Mary is a traditional Kenyan. She understands that family comes first.'

Miss Mary understands *family*? What's that supposed to mean? That just because Sam and Rosie live in England, just because they haven't been able to have children of their own, they're not Jonah's biological parents, they *don't* get family? They've probably thought more about family than Odikinyi or Mary will ever understand.

'We are Jonah's family,' Sam says.

'I know this must be very difficult.' Odikinyi puts his hands over Sam's. 'Please don't see me as a threat.'

Sam's instinct is to pull his hand away. First, because in England a man would never dream of touching another man in this way, especially a stranger. And second, because Sam's meant to be angry at him. But the truth is that Sam feels strangely moved by this physical contact from Jonah's father. Odikinyi must be just as upset at the thought of losing Jonah as they are. But the thing is, he *is* a threat. A threat to them having the child they dreamt of.

408

'I just want the best for Jonah. We share that hope, don't we?' Odikinyi says.

Sam pulls his hand away. 'You don't have the first clue what's best for Jonah.'

Sam hears his words as though they're coming from outside him. He must have spoken loud because people from the bar are looking over at him.

He takes a breath. Rosie warned him not tell Odikinyi too much, that it could damage their chance of keeping Jonah. But it's the only thing Sam can think of right now. Because he knows, in his gut, that Jonah is going to choose his father. Kenya is home, more so than England will ever be.

'Jonah needs our help.' Sam's voice is calm and steady now.

'I know that you can offer him much more than I can – in some ways . . . ' Odikinyi takes another sip of his drink. 'He told me how he's learning to read, that he likes England . . . '

'It's not about that.'

Sam clenches his fists, willing courage into his body. He knows that what he's going to say next is a gamble: that it could make Odikinyi want to wash his hands of Jonah – or that it could fuel his determination to have him. But he has to take that risk. And he has to tell Odikinyi the truth.

'Jonah's very ill. He has cancer.' Sam pauses. 'And HIV.'

For a long time, Odikinyi sits still, looking through the gap between the makuti roof and the wall of the bar to the dark sea.

And then, very slowly, he takes some bank notes out of his pocket, places them on the counter, gets up, pushes his stool under the bar and walks out into the night.

# Trudi

They walk for hours along the beach. She wonders whether he's thinking the same thing: that if they keep walking, that if they get far enough, they'll get lost and forget where they came from and never have to go home.

Her phone buzzes. Another missed call from Blessing.

At first, Blessing didn't like the thought of Trudi shooting off to Africa on some wild goose chase, but when Trudi told her that Peter was already in Kenya, Blessing changed her mind and offered to help with the air fare. Trudi omitted the part about Peter not wanting her to come – and the part about him not knowing that she was coming.

If Trudi answers the phone now, Blessing will keep her talking for hours, and she doesn't have the energy for that. She switches off her phone and shoves it into the back pocket of her shorts.

She looks at Peter. His shoulders have lost their stoop, he walks taller, his spine straight, his eyes fixed ahead of him rather than on the ground. He hasn't shaved since they got here, which gives him a handsome, rugged look. He's rolled up the sleeves of his shirt and his trouser legs and he's wearing his shoes without socks.

'Shall we sit down for a bit? See if we can spot one of those dolphins?' he asks her.

Trudi nods and they sit on the sand, which is cool from the night air. She looks out at the sea and says:

'Do you think Jonah would be happy with Odikinyi?'

He hesitates. 'I think Jonah can adapt to anything.'

'That wasn't my question.'

'I know.'

'Kisumu is a long way away.'

'But it's still Kenya. He's lived here since he was born – it's still more his home than England.'

Trudi knows Peter is right, but she can't accept it. Jonah's meant to be with the Keeps.

'Did you find out anything about clinics?'

Trudi had asked Peter to do some research on treatment centres for Burkitt's Lymphoma. It's so widespread in the Kenyan, Tanzanian and Ugandan corridor, that she was certain there had to be some help around.

He nods slowly. 'There's a clinic in Kisumu.'

She looks up at him. 'There is?'

'That's not the answer you wanted, was it?'

She looks down at the sand. 'No, it's not.'

'You think he should go back with the Keeps?'

'I know it goes against everything I've been trained to think – about how a child will be happier with his biological family. But yes, I think he should go back with the Keeps. I think they'd give him the life he needs.' She thinks about her parents, how they dreamt of her being a doctor or a lawyer, of making something of her life. 'They'd give him the life that Grace wanted for him.'

For a while, Peter doesn't say anything, and then, with the tips of his fingers, he lifts her chin.

'I agree. But it's out of our hands now, Trudi.' He pauses. 'Out of *your* hands.'

'But—'

Before she has the chance to go on, he places his fingers on her lips.

'Shush. Let's not talk about work. Not tonight.'

411

She laughs through his fingers. 'Look who's talking.' And then she presses her lips into his fingers and kisses them.

Peter takes her hand and holds it up to the moon and looks at it. 'Every part of you is beautiful,' he says.

She shakes her head. Beautiful had always felt like too big and grand a word for her.

'It's true.' He pauses and looks her in the eye. 'You're beautiful.'

Her throat tightens so she can hardly breathe.

'Close your eyes,' he says.

She lets her eyelids drop. Her heart hammers so fast she thinks it's going to leap right out of her chest.

She listens to the night. To the water as it pulls into the shore. To music spilling out of one of the villas higher up the beach. To a splashing far out at sea: a rising and dipping and the distinct cry of a dolphin.

And then she feels his lips against hers, his breath warm, his movements gentle. He folds her hands into his as he kisses her, and she draws him in closer.

## Rosie

Rosie lies in bed watching dawn filtering in through the makuti roof. It's 5.30am. In an hour or so the sun will rise on their new life.

She barely slept last night. Whenever she closed her eyes, a film played behind her eyelids: Jonah swimming away from her, dipping in and out of the water, heading for the place where the sky meets the sea.

Sam came back late: alcohol on his breath, his eyes unfocused and his words slurred. He must have been talking to Odikinyi for hours. When she suggested they go outside to talk, so as not to disturb Jonah who was asleep on a fold-out bed in a corner of the hut, Sam mumbled that he was tired, that they'd deal with things in the morning.

'By morning, it will be too late,' she'd whispered. 'We'll be packing our things to go home. We have to have an answer now.'

But Sam had turned over and switched off the light and gone to sleep, leaving her to lie in the dark, her mind racing.

She walks over to Jonah. There's a glow in his skin. Sam's noticed it too: that he's seemed better since being here. Maybe the medication is beginning to kick in. Or maybe it's just that he feels at home here.

She knows it's a stupid thought, one that goes against everything Ms Bridges explained to them, a thought that she's shooed away a thousand times, but she can't help but feel that if Jonah hadn't come to them, he might not have got sick. That somehow, it's her fault.

Kneeling beside his bed, she strokes his cheek.

'Happy birthday, my treasure,' she whispers.

His eyelids flutter but he doesn't wake up.

This wasn't how she'd imagined Jonah's first birthday with them. They were meant to be back home: a picnic in the park, a cake, balloons, party hats, Hop playing with tissue paper and string. She'd have invited Alice and her dad. She'd have taught Jonah to blow out his eight candles, all in one go, and to make a wish.

Because she has to keep believing that, later today, he'll be on the plane home with them.

She's not ready to say goodbye. She won't ever be ready for that.

Rosie goes to the bathroom, puts on her swimming costume, wraps her towel around her and heads out down past the huts and down to the sea.

As she steps into the water, she thinks of Jonah, how he might have swum at this exact spot, how this beach and this sea and this sand were his home for much longer than the small railway cottage, and the park and the streets of Bridgeford. That it's not fair to take him away from here.

*I like going under the water because it's where Mama talks to me*, he said, last night, as she tucked him in.

It was the first time he'd spoken to her so openly about his mama.

As she floats in the sea, the cool water rippling around her, she thinks about the hours Jonah spent in the bathtub back home. How he'd grown to love the local pool. How he ran into the sea on that stormy day in Wales. *My little fish*, she'd called him once, and he'd burst into tears.

She understands, now. She understands it all. That it was his way of feeling close to his mama. That she must have used those same words.

If they do bring him home, she'll do everything she can to help him keep his memories of Grace alive.

*Do you think she'll talk to me again?* he'd asked her last night. *Now that she's gone, I mean?*

Rosie wasn't a religious person. And she didn't want to make Jonah false promises. But she believes this: that when people die, they live on in the people who love them. And so she'd said: *Yes. It might take a little while, but yes, yes she will.*

The sun, a ball of fire now, lifts out of the sea. For the first time, she doesn't feel scared of the water. She feels like she could swim all the way to the sun until it fills her with its light and warmth; with something that will help her survive the next twenty-four hours.

When she gets back to the shore, she sits for a while, looking out at the horizon.

Then something catches her eye at the far end of the beach. A boat swings onto the shore. A man, tall and dark, walks towards it, carrying a bag.

She stands up and holds her hand over her brow to block out the sun, to make sure that she's seeing right.

The driver of the boat holds out his hand and helps Odikinyi on board. A moment later, he pulls the cord of the engine. It splutters to life and the boat tears away.

Where's he going this early?

'Rosie!'

A voice from behind her. Deep and full and old.

She turns round. Miss Mary walks along the beach with her cane. She must have taken a boat from Shela early this morning.

Rosie looks back at Odikinyi's boat: it's heading towards Manda island.

'He left this for you,' Miss Mary says, pressing a letter into her hand. 'He came to see me late last night. He asked me to write it for him.'

Rosie tears open the envelope but then she sees a small figure walking down from the Kizingo huts. Jonah, his eyes fixed on his father's boat, a white speck disappearing into the dawn.

# 7TH OCTOBER

*Bridgeford*

# Jonah

Jonah sits on his bed, listening to the sounds of the cottage.

Rosie, Sam and Grandma Flick are having breakfast in the kitchen downstairs.

The doorbell has been going all morning – every time a new guest arrives. Peter and Trudi and Cathy, the social worker that helped Sam and Rosie get Jonah to start with.

They're all here for Jonah's special day.

Hop jumps up beside Jonah.

'You've got more fur than I do, these days.' Jonah strokes Hop's back and then passes his palm over his own bald head.

After the first course of chemo, bits of his hair came off on his pillow and in the bath. After a while, his head was patterned with bald patches and thin clumps. So Rosie took him to the barbers in Bridgeford, and when they stepped out onto the high street, she kissed the top of his bald head and said: 'You look dashing.'

He wasn't so sure about that but when Jonah bumped into Billy and his gang at the park, they didn't tease him or push him around. In fact, they looked a bit scared of *him*.

'It's because it makes you look cool and tough,' Alice said.

Though Jonah suspects they just felt sorry for him – or worse, that they were scared of coming too close in case he's contagious.

He reaches into his bedside drawer and takes out the letter he's read over and over since that last morning in Kenya, the morning he watched his papa shooting off across the water in his boat.

The handwriting is Miss Mary's but the words are Papa's.

*I know I said it was your choice, Jonah ... but I had to do the right thing ... they know how to look after you in England ... I couldn't forgive myself if something happened to you ... you can come back to visit whenever you want ... Rosie and Sam are good people ...*

Jonah folds the letter and puts it back in the drawer.

He shuts his eyes a moment and wonders where his papa is right now and what he's doing. Whether he's in his fishing boat. Whether he's taking tourists out to look at the dolphins. Whether he's thinking of him.

Jonah stands up. He feels lightheaded and dizzy and a bit nauseous, as he has been ever since he started the last round of treatment.

He goes to look at the long mirror on the back of his wardrobe. He woke up early this morning to put on his new suit. Sam bought it for him from the charity shop in town and Grandma Flick, who's been living with them since the summer, took out her sewing machine to make it fit properly. They bought him a new shirt and a new tie from Marks and Spencer's – and new shoes too, though he still prefers going around in bare feet. When it's not too cold, Rosie lets him do that now.

Mama stands behind him and catches his eye in the mirror.

*You look like a True English Gentleman, Jonah.*

He smiles back at her.

'Even with no hair?' He remembers how she cried when he had it cut short with Mister Sir in Nairobi.

*Even with no hair,* she says, smiling.

She's started talking to him again, and not just when he's underwater. It was Rosie who taught him that he had to listen for her in his heart, that that's a place from which she'd always speak to him.

Jonah goes to the window and looks out at a train stopping in the station. He thinks of the day he sat on the platform, wanting to run back to Mama in Kenya. He still thinks of running away sometimes, of how maybe it would be easier for everyone. How Grandma Flick could go back to Wales and to Ariel and Sam could focus more on his sculptures and Rosie could go back to delivering babies.

The other day, Trudi had talked to him about the court hearing. That it was his choice, whether he wanted to be legally adopted by Rosie and Sam. That he had the right to change his mind.

But he could tell that Trudi didn't want him to change his mind. And she's right. Whenever he thinks of a life without Rosie and Sam and Hop and Grandma Flick and Alice and the railway cottage, he gets an empty feeling. He's meant to be here now. It's what Mama would have wanted.

A face appears in front of him at the window.

Alice beams at him through the glass.

He opens the window and she tumbles in, clutching a brown paper package. As she falls onto the carpet, Jonah hears a loud tear and that's when he realises that she's wearing a dress. A yellow dress.

'Stupid, stupid thing,' Alice says, yanking up the skirt of her dress and inspecting the tear.

She's brushed her hair too. It's smooth and shiny and curls down over her back and shoulders. She's put something glossy and sticky on her lips and there's white sparkly powder on her cheeks and eyelids.

'Dad made me wear it. Said it was a special occasion.' She rolls her eyes.

Then she looks him up and down. 'You scrub up well, Jonah Keep.'

'I guess we both do.'

She scrunches up her nose and looks down at the torn, muddy hem of her dress. 'You think so?'

He takes her hand and they go and stand in front of the mirror and stare at their reflection for a bit.

'Definitely,' he says.

She pushes the package at him.

'Thanks,' he says and sits down on the edge of his bed and takes off the scraps of Sellotape holding down the corners.

Jonah takes the book out of the brown paper.

They've been reading lots of books together. Whenever Alice isn't at school, she comes with him for his chemo sessions at the hospital and sits next to him while he waits for the chemicals to finish coming through the drip and into his body, and they read together. He's getting really good.

'Thought it was time to move on,' Alice says, sitting down next to him. 'It's my favourite.'

He reads the cover: *Twelfth Night,* by William Shakespeare.

'It starts with a shipwreck too, but it's a bit more jolly. Dad says I'm like Viola, the main character – and that she's more plucky than Miranda from *The Tempest*. And that she likes wearing boy's clothes too. Though she gets really soppy about this duke, which I'm not so sure about . . .'

He opens the front page and reads Alice's neat handwriting:

*And remember: The rain it raineth every day . . .*

Jonah looks up and grins. 'You think I need reminding?'

'You'll get it when you reach the end of the play.'

Jonah reads the rest of the inscription:

*For your Adoption Day. Glad you got shipwrecked with us. Alice x.*

Jonah kisses Alice's cheek. 'Thanks,' he says.

'Thought we could read it together.' She smiles. 'Or you could read it to me for a change.'

Jonah nods and places the book on his pillow.

'Are you going to be OK?' Alice asks, her brow furrowed.

'Today?'

'No, not today.'

She hasn't asked him any more questions about his cancer, not since that first time back in August, when he told her that he was sick.

'I've got a seventy per cent chance.'

'I hate numbers.'

'It's a good number.'

She bites her lip, just like Rosie does.

'But it's not a guarantee, is it?'

He feels a lump in his throat. Not the swollen lump that they've been zapping with the chemo, but a lump that pushes up his throat whenever he thinks of Mama.

'No, no it's not. But Ms Bridges said the chemo's going well and that the tablets I took before the chemo helped too.' He cricks his neck to one side. 'And look, it's gone right down.'

Alice's cheeks are flushed and her eyes are shining.

'But the chemo will have made your immune system weak, that's what Dad said. That you could get pneumonia again because of the HIV. And that getting pneumonia a second time is even worse than the first time . . . ' The words tumble out of her.

'It's OK. I'm taking special tablets to help with that. Ms Bridges says that I'll have blood tests every week to see if they are working.'

'So they might not work?'

'I'm going to get better,' Jonah says. 'I promise.'

423

A tear drops down Alice's cheek.

'You promise?'

He nods. And then he thinks about all the promises people have made to him and how promises can sometimes end up hurting people.

'I promise that I'm going to do everything I can to get better.' He takes a breath. 'And I promise that you'll always be my best friend.'

'I'm your best friend?'

'For ever.' Jonah stands up and holds out his hand. 'Come on, let's go downstairs.'

They go out onto the landing, Hop following.

For a moment, Jonah looks down through the open kitchen door at all the people who are now his life.

There's Sam and Rosie and Grandma Flick and Trudi and Peter and Cathy and Alice's dad, who's just come in too. And then he spots Julie and Mimi. His heart lifts in his chest: Rosie and Sam didn't say they were coming. Mimi's already eating one of the cakes Rosie made. She looks up and sees Jonah and then starts kicking loose from Julie's arms.

'Jonah! Jonah!' She runs up the stairs and throws herself at his legs.

Jonah lifts her into his arms.

She scrunches up her nose and touches his head. 'Where's Jonah's hair?'

'It fell out,' Jonah says.

Mimi's eyes go wide. 'Fell out?'

'Don't worry, it'll grow back soon,' Jonah says.

As he holds Mimi in his arms, Jonah looks at everyone milling around smiling and laughing and chatting, drinking tea and coffee and eating cake under the *Happy Adoption Day* banners. Rosie said that he would have two birthdays from now on: his real birthday, in August, when they'd go to the seaside and think about Jonah's mum and how it was the day that she'd brought Jonah into the world; and his other birthday, in October, when he became their son.

He walks down the stairs with Mimi and Alice. Hop darts in front of them, purring excitedly at all the people in the kitchen.

'Jonah!' Rosie dashes out of the kitchen and calls out again: 'Jonah, it's time to go!'

Then she looks up and realises he's standing right there in front of her.

'Oh . . .' she says and smiles.

Jonah puts Mimi down and then kneels beside her and takes her hand. 'Do you remember Rosie?' he asks her.

She looks at Rosie with a furrowed brow.

'Jonah's new mummy?' Mimi says.

Jonah looks at Rosie and then, very slowly, he nods and says: 'Yes, Jonah's new mummy.'

Rosie's eyes film over and then she kneels down beside Jonah and squeezes Jonah so tight that he thinks she's going to squeeze all the breath out of him.

Mimi runs back to Julie and then Sam comes over to Jonah.

'I've got a surprise for you, buddy,' he says.

Sam takes Jonah's hand and guides him through the kitchen, past the banners and the balloons and the cakes and the cards, and to the door, which leads into the garage.

Jonah feels everyone following behind them.

Sam puts his hand on the door of the garage and smiles.

'Ready?'

He'd heard Sam working late last night. Sanding and welding and hammering. Jonah had wanted to go down to help him, but Rosie made him promise to get some rest before his big day.

Hop comes and stands beside them and meows at the closed door.

'Just a minute, Hop,' Sam says.

Sam turns to Jonah and puts his hands over his eyes. Jonah hears him turn the door handle and he hears Hop jumping and chirruping ahead of them.

His eyes still closed, Jonah steps forward.

He can feel it before he sees it. How tall and strong it is. The patterns of light and shade in the wood. Its smooth lines. Its head standing tall and proud.

Sam pulls his hand away. 'Look, Jonah.'

Jonah blinks.

It's beautiful. More beautiful than in his imagination.

Sam's opened the big garage door that leads to the drive, and the sun's streaming in. The bronze joins shine and the morning air weaves in through its driftwood limbs. The horse's front leg is raised, just a little, as though, at any moment, it's going to break into a run.

'You're going to win the bid, I just know it.'

Sam kisses the top of his head. 'If you like it, J, I've won already.' Sam looks up at the horse. 'And it's yours. Your adoption day present.'

Jonah goes up to the horse and leans his head against his neck and closes his eyes.

He thinks of how Mama sometimes took him by boat to Manda where they'd watch wild horses running along the shore. That's how he likes to think of her now, sitting on the back of a horse in her yellow dress, her head thrown back, her hair floating behind her, laughing as the horse gallops faster and faster along the shore, its hooves kicking up the water, the spray a shower of stars lit up by the sun.

# 25TH DECEMBER

## *Criccieth*

# Rosie

Jonah stands on the water's edge, clutching the glass bottle they chose in the gift shop in Criccieth. Hop plays at his feet, dashing towards the water and then running away from it when it comes too close to his paws.

The sea is dark and choppy, the wind bitter, but small streaks of light are filtering through the clouds.

'You think this is a good idea?' Rosie asks Sam.

They're standing a few yards behind him on the beach.

'It's what he wanted,' Sam says.

Ever since Rosie watched Odikinyi leaving on his boat on their last day in Kenya, she'd decided that Jonah should have more say in his life, that he'd had more than his share of grown-ups imposing where he should go and what he should do and who he should love. Of course he was still a child, but with a bit of courage, they could support him in making his own decisions, even if it was painful.

And so Rosie and Sam have worked hard, over the last few months, to make sure Jonah had a say in the decisions about his treatment, about going back to school, about whether he wanted their name. He'd said he wanted their name but that he wanted something to remember his mama by too. So now, when Mrs Boon calls the register, she asks for Jonah Atieno Keep. It has a certain ring to it.

So of course they'd talked this through with Jonah too.

The funeral had been such a blur, they'd all been in shock, so Rosie thought it was important for Jonah to have a chance to say goodbye to his mama in his own way. Trudi had said it was a good idea, that it would help him with his grief.

Jonah hadn't even hesitated: 'The sea outside Grandma Flick's house.'

They've decided to spend as much of their time up here as possible. Every weekend they're free, every holiday. Who knows, maybe one day they'll move here for good.

Jonah looks back at Sam and Rosie and Rosie knows that he wants them to be with him now. They gave him some space, knowing that he needed time with his thoughts about his mama.

He's been standing there, alone, looking at the sea, for what feels like an age and it's taken every ounce of self-control not to run over and wrap him in her arms.

Sam takes Rosie's hand and they walk over to Jonah.

'You think she'll like it?' Jonah asks, looking from Rosie to Sam.

Rosie puts her arm around him and kisses the top of his head. She doesn't know where Jonah finds the strength or the courage to face it all: losing his mother, the months of treatments and now this, saying goodbye.

'She'll love it.'

Sam hugs them both and, for a moment, as the waves crash against the shore and the wind whistles around them, Rosie loses herself in the warmth and breath of the two people she loves most in the world.

'And I'll be able to come back all the time? To see her?' Jonah asks.

'Of course.' Rosie whispers by his ear. 'Whenever you like.'

Jonah pulls away. 'I'm ready to do it now.'

'OK,' Rosie says.

They've been out here for ages. Every part of her feels frozen through. Jonah's been staring out at the sea, clutching that glass bottle, for what feels like ages. She wonders whether Grace has been speaking to him through the sea, like she used to. She still feels a small pinch, sometimes, at the thought that she'll never match up to Grace. But she knows that she's the lucky one, that she's the one who gets to care for Jonah, to love him every day.

Jonah pulls a piece of paper out of his coat pocket.

When they'd talked to Jonah about creating a small ceremony to say goodbye to his mama, he'd set it as his goal to write her a letter; he said Alice would help him.

He straightens the paper out against the wind and starts reading.

The words float over to where Sam and Rosie are standing.

*Mama . . .*

*I hear you in the wind and in the rain . . .*

*I hear you in the sun and in the stars . . .*

*I hear you in the sky and in the sea . . .*

*I hear you here, in my heart, with me . . .*

It's the first letter he's ever written.

For a while the three of them stand in silence, letting the words sink in. Rosie hopes with all her heart that Grace can see Jonah: her little boy, a reader and now a writer too. There is so much Rosie would like to share with Grace. So many things she knows Grace would be proud of.

Jonah puts the piece of paper into the bottle and pushes in the cork plug. Then he takes off his shoes and socks, rolls up the hem of his trousers and wades into the water, not flinching at the cold.

Very gently, he places the bottle on the waves. It bobs on the surface for a while and then a big wave soars up above it and pulls it under.

431

Rosie takes one of Flick's sunflowers out of the cloth bag on her shoulder and, one by one, tears the petals off the flower head and scatters them into the water.

In another one of their conversations, Jonah told her that yellow was his mother's favourite colour. The sunflower petals make Rosie think of the dress Grace wore in the photo she found when they were here last summer. A dress as bright as the sun.

Rosie looks out at the water and then she closes her eyes.

*Love him* ... Rosie hears Grace's words coming to her on the wind and the waves.

*As if I could do anything else* ... Rosie whispers back.

And in that moment, Rosie realises that it's true, what Cathy said to them all those years ago, when they first decided to adopt: that a child can have two mothers, that one doesn't cancel the other out. Because a child can never have too much love.

Rosie gives Jonah what's left of the sunflower. 'Why don't you scatter the last few petals yourself?'

Jonah nods. He places the petals in the palm of his hand and stretches his arm out to the sky, his eyes closed. His lips move, as though he's saying a prayer. And then, very slowly, he opens his fingers.

Rosie and Sam watch the petals rise from his fingertips. They catch the wind and settle over the water.

Jonah blinks and then looks up at the sky and a wide grin takes over his face.

'It's snowing,' he says.

Rosie and Sam look up too.

She'd felt it in the air. The bite that comes before that first snowfall. The brightening of the sky, even though it was sunset.

'Mama said there'd be snow when I came to England ...' he says.

He dances on the shore, spinning, trying to catch the small white flakes in his open palms, on his cheeks, his lips, on his tongue.

Sam puts his arm around Rosie and pulls her in close.

'Our miracle,' Sam says.

Rosie nods.

He's in remission. Which doesn't mean that the cancer has gone altogether or that it won't return. And the HIV virus hasn't yet been eradicated – in fact, it's been made worse by the chemo. But for now, for a little while longer at least, he's theirs. Which is more than they could ever have hoped for.

'Why don't we go inside to warm up,' Rosie calls over to Jonah.

'Once the snow has settled a bit, we can come back out and help you build your first snowman,' Sam adds. 'Maybe Alice will be here by then.'

That had been Jonah's idea too: to invite Alice and her dad to Grandma Flick's for Christmas.

'Cool!' Jonah jumps and tries to catch a snowflake and then skips ahead of them along the beach. Hop runs alongside him, trying hard to keep up.

Before they turn into the garden gate, Rosie stops and looks back at the sea, at the place where Jonah placed the bottle with his letter, where she scattered the petals.

'Thank you . . .' she whispers at the sea and at the swirling white of the sky. 'Thank you for giving us Jonah . . .'

In a small garden overlooking the sea, a little boy builds his first snowman. Sea and snow: it's what his mama promised him, the first time he came to England.

Next to the boy, a little girl with white blonde hair and transparent skin sticks a carrot in the middle of the snowman's face.

Then she steals the boy's woolly red scarf and winds it round the snowman's neck.

A little further along, a mother and a father watch their son dancing around the snowman, hand in hand with his best friend. The father puts his arm around the mother's shoulders and they both think about how this was where their story began – and how this, too, is a new beginning.

By the door to the house, a grandmother stands and smiles at the grandson she knew would come to them one day.

The little girl's father stands beside her.

'He seems well,' the girl's father says.

The grandmother nods. 'Yes.'

She can see through his skin to his flesh and blood, to the dark cells, that, for the moment, have gone to sleep.

Yes, he's theirs for now.

For a while, the three-legged cat dances with the children in the snow. Then, when he's tired of his paws being wet and cold, he goes down to the stall next to the house. He climbs in through an open window and drops down on the straw, where he falls asleep, pressed up against the warm body of the old grey horse.

Back in London, a social worker and a policeman sit at the kitchen table of a small flat above a laundrette. Also at the table, sit two children: a boy and a girl, long-limbed, freckles peppering their cheeks.

The social worker's hair is big and wild, because that's how he says he likes it. She smiles at the children and then she looks down at the speck of a diamond on her ring finger.

An older woman, who sits at the head of the table, takes the hands of the children, and the children take the hands of their father and the woman who will be their stepmother soon.

They bow their heads to say grace.

Across town, a man sits on the edge of his bed in his cell. Clean-shaven. No suit. No gold watch. He looks at his pinboard. At the photograph of his wife and children. And beside it, the photograph of a little boy and his mother: they're holding hands, the sun beating down on their faces, their feet in the sea.

He takes out a copy of *The Tempest*, an old, battered copy he's borrowed from the prison library, and starts reading.

Four thousand miles away, on the stretch of coast at Kisumu, a father takes his fishing boat out into the still, clear waters. He smiles at the white men and women with their hats and their sunglasses and their phones. And then he points, far out to sea. A dolphin rises from the water. The father looks to the horizon and thinks of the little boy who came into his life for the blink of an eye, before he let him go again.

And far out to sea, where the water is so deep it's black, a small glass bottle floats on the waves, carrying the words of a little boy to the place where the earth meets the sky.

# Acknowledgements

This has been my most research heavy book so far, and for me, research means talking to experts, who understand the issues I write about on both a cerebral and emotional level. Whilst any errors are entirely my own, I'd like to thank the following for their time, their openness and their patience.

Sally Beaumont, who works as an Adoption Activity Days Service Manager for CoramBAAF (the British Association of Adoption and Fostering.) Sally's willingness to let me attend an adoption activity day, and her subsequent answers to my many questions, was vital in helping me to understand the adoption scene in the UK and allowed me to craft one of the most crucial scenes to the novel.

Neil Bidston, the GP who invited me into his home (and inbox) and answered all my medical questions about the childhood cancer, Burkitt's Lymphoma. Neil has a gift for making complex medical issues beautifully clear. His patients are very lucky to have him.

Mark Milliken-Smith, one of our country's leading QCs, for sitting with me on the side of a cricket pitch at Wellington College and helping me understand the legal ramifications of bringing a child, illegally, into the country and then abandoning him.

Mary-Jo, who helped me fall in love with Lamu when I visited in 2009. Kizingo is a real place: a small patch of paradise.

Thank you also to the couples and adoptive children who have spoken to me about their personal experiences of infertility and adoption. Thank you to Rossana Novella for sparking the desire to write about this issue. And thank you, in particular, to my dear godmother, Anne Jaquet Holtz and her son (my godson) Adrien, who was adopted from Romania when he was 18 months old: you are a bright beacon of hope for everyone involved in the adoption process.

Thank you, of course, to my faithful and talented agent, Bryony Woods and to my brilliant editor, Manpreet, who always has such a clear vision for my novels. Thank you also to the whole team at Little, Brown who work tirelessly to put my stories into the hands of readers around the world.

Finally, thank you to my faithful friends and family who inspire me, put up with me and encourage me to keep writing, no matter what. Linda Gibson and Helen Dahlke, the dearest friends a writer could hope for. Richard Louis George for giving me a place to write and for being so kind. Charlie Penny, for looking after Tennessee as I wrote. Mama, my most constant reader. Hugh Macgregor, for quite simply being there every step of the way. Seb and Vi, my faithful cats – especially Vi who has now passed away but is still here in spirit. And my daughter, Tennessee Skye: writing this book has made me realise, more than ever, how lucky I am to have you.

# The Return of Norah Wells

**One family. Two mothers. Which one will they choose?
A moving family drama perfect for fans of Dorothy
Koomson, Harriet Evans and Lisa Jewell.**

One ordinary morning, Norah Wells walked out of her house
on Willoughby Street and never looked back. Six years later,
she returns to the home she left only to find another woman
in her place. Fay held Norah's family together after she
disappeared, she shares a bed with Norah's husband and
Norah's youngest daughter calls Fay 'Mummy'.

Now that Norah has returned, everyone has questions.
Where has she been? Why did she leave? And why is she back?
As each member of the family tries to find the answers they
need, they must also face up to the most pressing question of
all – what happens to The Mother Who Stayed when The
Mother Who Left comes back?

Powerful, emotional and perceptive, *The Return of Norah Wells*
is a novel about what it takes to hold a family together and
what you're willing to sacrifice for the ones you love.

Available now